Discover more at millsandboon.co.uk

A SNOWBOUND SCANDAL

JESSICA LEMMON

WILD WYOMING NIGHTS

JOANNE ROCK

MILLS & BOON

First Published in Great Britain 2018
by Mills & Boon, an imprint of HarperCollinsPublishers,
1 London Bridge Street, London, SE1 9GF

A Snowbound Scandal © 2018 Jessica Lemmon
Wild Wyoming Nights © 2018 Joanne Rock

ISBN: 978-0-263-93614-8

0818

MIX
Paper from
responsible sources
FSC™ C007454

www.fsc.org

This book is produced from independently certified FSC™
paper to ensure responsible forest management.

For more information visit: www.harpercollins.co.uk/green

Printed and bound in Spain
by CPI, Barcelona

A SNOWBOUND SCANDAL

JESSICA LEMMON

For John.
There's no one I'd rather be
snowed in with than you.

One

Mayor Chase Ferguson's best friend and head of his security team strolled into his office, sheet of paper in hand.

"Busy?" Emmett asked.

"Extremely," Chase answered, droll. He'd been staring at the same spot on the wall for going on twenty minutes trying to figure out how to answer the governor's email.

"I won't be long." Emmett wasn't smiling, but Chase could tell his best bud was amused. Emmett knew Chase better than anyone—better than his own family in some cases. With a flick of his fingers, Emmett dropped the sheet of paper on the desk.

Chase lifted the printed color photo. In it, a delicate, thin woman, mouth open in an angry shout was holding a poster board. On the poster was a photo of a bird dripping with black goo and the words painted around the image read OIL KILLS. An angry crowd in the background held similar signs, but it was the woman in clear focus that snared his attention.

Soft, dark curls blew over fine cheekbones and plump lips. Even now, years later, he didn't have to try to recall the feel of her elegant, slim body against his. Mimi Andrix was runway-model thin with small breasts and subtle curves. The years had been good to her, depending on how recently this photo was taken.

"When was it taken?" Chase asked.

"Three years ago, in Houston."

"How did you come across it?"

"One of your campaign staff alerted me. It was mailed to the office alongside a letter threatening to send it to Jamie Holland."

Chase's opponent. An all around 'not-so-nice guy with questionable ties to big, bad men in Texas, and involved in too many illegal activities to list.

"We're trying to find out where it's from, but so far no luck," Emmett said in the same flat, matter-of-fact tone.

Chase grunted. Ah, election season. He was on his second term and preferred to stay where he was for as long as his city allowed him. Not only was he one of Dallas's youngest mayors, but he was also one of the few politicians interested in the seat who was unbribable. As a son of the Fergusons and one-third owner of Ferguson Oil, Chase had plenty of money of his own. He didn't crave power or prestige. He craved justice. Staying in office meant crowding out potentially corrupt politicians. Jamie Holland, for example.

"I recognized her right away." Emmett tapped the edge of the photo. He'd been on the three-month-long trip where Chase had met Mimi. Emmett was one of the few people who knew what had transpired between them all those summers ago. All that had gone well before it'd gone sideways.

"She should know that she's a potential target for publicity." Mimi hated politics. She wouldn't appreciate being dragged into the mud during his upcoming campaign if and when news of their previous relationship saw the light of day.

"I tracked her down. She lives in Bigfork. You have a

trip scheduled for Montana soon, don't you? Why not tell her in person?" His friend smirked knowingly.

"Somehow I doubt she'd welcome me with open arms." The last time Chase had seen her, he'd put her on a plane leaving Dallas for Bigfork. Her face was red from a combination of anger and devastation—both of which he'd put into her expression. She'd hated him then and he doubted her feelings for him had warmed since.

"She works for a conservation society. Some environmental group. Her bio on the website mentioned 'saving the planet.'"

That drew a proud smile to Chase's mouth. Mimi's giving and loving heart had been so huge it'd encapsulated not only him, but the environmental causes she'd cared about so passionately. Not until she'd come with him to Dallas did she know the extent of Chase's involvement in *one of the biggest enemies to the environment*—her words. The oil industry was his family's industry.

But she didn't call it quits between them when she found out. Chase was surprised she'd seen around his inherited billions that had come from the very industry destroying the causes she'd championed, but she had. She'd tearfully told him she didn't hold it against him and that they'd work through it and that the only thing that mattered was how they felt for each other.

He'd been the one who'd ended it. It'd killed him to do it. Even though they never would've worked out, he'd cared about her and would've preferred ending their relationship on better terms.

"Do you ever wonder," Emmett said as he turned for the door, "if you two had married how that would've gone?"

"No." Chase never second-guessed decisions. The point of making one was that you didn't have to revisit it.

"Seeing that photo made me wonder if she'd have bent to your will and become a proper politician's wife, or if you would've caved to hers and been alongside her protesting the evils of big oil."

The bagel Chase had for breakfast turned to stone in his stomach. He didn't like thinking about what would've happened. What could've happened.

What a colossal waste of resources.

"The first one," he answered. Which was exactly why he hadn't continued a relationship with Mimi. She was too good at being who she was to be dragged into politics, having to explain herself or apologize for her past. Chase's desire to protect her had dominated his decision to put her on that airplane. Clean breaks were best, and he'd told her as much at the time.

Emmett shut the door behind him, leaving Chase in his office with thoughts he didn't care to have. He'd had plenty of brief relationships in the ten years since he and Mimi had ended theirs. He didn't know if it was the age they'd been at the time—him twenty-six to her twenty-three—or if it'd been the high of a summer fling, but she stood out in his mind to this day. The rare act of being wrapped in her arms for three months had felt more like three years.

Whatever it was, she'd left a mark. An indelible one.

Back then, he hadn't been as conservative as he was now. He'd been more like his father, Rider. With a rough edge. His mother, Eleanor, had taken it upon herself to sand those edges down on her boys. It'd worked on Chase, and while Zach fell into line with the company, his wild streak was still strong. Chase's had been buried long ago. Hell, it was probably on the bottom of Flathead Lake in Montana.

Once he'd become certain of his political interests, he'd gladly gone from rough to refined. If he hadn't gone the refined route, he imagined he'd have turned out like Emmett, who was best described as rough on the edges *and* in the middle. Emmett had started out in security—a perfect fit for his bulk and brawn—and it wasn't long before Chase had asked him to run his security detail.

Emmett was still in charge of security, but his duties now spanned anything that had to do with Chase's position as mayor. Loyalty was the one luxury you couldn't buy in the world of politics, so Chase considered himself lucky that a lifelong friend had his back.

He lifted the photo again and tried to imagine himself with Mimi today. It'd been ten years since he'd seen her— since he'd said goodbye. She'd accused him of being a coward. Of being too obtuse to see what she'd seen so clearly. She'd stood on the airfield before boarding the private plane and shouted over the whining engine that they loved each other and were the kind of couple who could last forever.

If you give us a chance.

He hadn't, though.

Chase pulled the lap drawer on his desk open and locked the photo inside. Despite Mimi's passionate argument, he'd known then that they couldn't know if they'd last forever after only a handful of months. No matter how good the sex had been or the way the minutes had folded over into hours and rolled into days and morphed into months.

The smile that found his face now wasn't one of regret, but of memory. The weeks and months before their bitter end had been filled with Mimi's laugh and her fingers ruffling his hair. He recalled the way she sighed in his ear, hot and quiet, when he made love to her. She'd dragged him to the lake on more than one occasion, torn off her clothes and his, and talked him into skinny-dipping in the full moon's light.

Hopefully no photos of those nights resurfaced next.

Yes, he had a lot of good memories from that summer. Like the time they had sneaked onto a massive property overlooking the lake. The house was disgustingly arrogant in its placement and had boasted shamelessly from its many windowed rooms.

Eight bedrooms. Six bathrooms. Fifteen thousand square feet.

He knew because he'd kept a close eye on the property over the years, waiting on the elusive owner to die or move out.

The owner had put the mansion up for sale three years ago, and Chase purchased it for a cool sixteen mil. It'd been completely remodeled by then. During his walk-through he'd been awestruck by the fact that the inside was more immaculate and braggadocian than the outside. Multiple fireplaces, a hot tub alongside an indoor heated pool surrounded by huge rocks and a wine cellar to name a few of the amenities.

With the purchase of the mansion he also became owner of a good slice of the Flathead Lake shoreline. Since he'd purchased the place he'd been there three—no, *four*— times. He tried to visit once a year, minimum. During those trips, thoughts of Mimi didn't cling to him like moss on a rock, but passed by like a leaf on the surface of a stream. He didn't linger on memory or the past. What was the point?

He stood from his desk to take in the city outside his office window. Dallas sat fat and happy, calm and cooling down for autumn. He was eighteen months out from reelection, and though reelection efforts were always in swing, they wouldn't be in *full* swing for a while.

His scheduled trip to Bigfork was likely his last chance to flee town, to untangle himself from the political spider web for a bit. If the worst happened—if Mimi became embroiled in political mudslinging, it'd be best if he were here in Dallas, not in her backyard.

He contemplated skipping the trip for all of two seconds. He could handle the press—good or bad. It's how he'd been elected. He wasn't shying away from the trip because of Mimi, nor was he going there for her.

The past was the past and the future was all that mattered.

Decision made.

Bigfork, here he came.

"Honestly, Stefanie." Eleanor Ferguson tsked her only daughter from across the dining room table.

Stefanie rolled her eyes. Her mother tended to bring out the child in her. Probably because she was treated like one whenever they gathered for holidays. Or a *pseudo*holiday like this one.

She slid a glance over at her brothers. Chase, in a suit and tie, fresh from working late, sat rigidly in his chair. He hoisted one regal eyebrow at her but otherwise stayed silent. Zach sat next to his wife, Penelope, but he was too preoccupied with his ten-month-old daughter to pay attention to his bickering mother and sister.

The other party at the table wasn't family at all. Emmett Keaton, Chase's head of security and best friend, sat at the head of the table opposite her father. He silently ate a few forked green beans and watched her, expressionless as per his usual.

God, he made her *crazy*.

He'd been breathing down her neck since that unfortunate run-in with one of Chase's sworn political enemies. Emmett had watched over her like a hawk since. She'd been so aware of his presence lately, she looked forward to any event that didn't include him. Yet here he was.

"This doesn't count as Thanksgiving," Stef dropped her napkin on her empty plate and her mother, who'd been insisting she take the serving spoon, dropped it back into the mashed potatoes with a sigh.

The chef-prepared meal—Mom didn't cook—was top-notch. Golden, buttery turkey, stuffing, French green beans, and a gravy boat brimming with brown gravy. There was only one problem.

"Thanksgiving isn't for another two weeks. This is just…" Stef shook her head. "Wrong."

Emmett grunted what might've been a laugh and she sliced him with a glare. He shoveled another bite into his mouth and chewed.

"Why is he here?" she asked the table collectively.

"Rider. Remind your daughter she is to have manners in this house." Elle looked over at her husband.

"Stef, sweetheart." Her dad smiled. "We're all making sacrifices. You think I want to be on a boat during my favorite holiday of the year?"

"It's a *cruise*," her mom corrected.

"Em's here because he can't turn down a free meal," Chase said conversationally.

Emmett grunted again. Stef guessed that was his way of agreeing with his friend.

Neanderthal.

"It doesn't seem right for everyone to leave during Thanksgiving." Sacrilegious, even, but she didn't want to be melodramatic. But honestly, did tradition mean nothing to anyone but her? Chase was vacationing at a lake in Montana by himself; Zach and Pen were traveling with their daughter Olivia to visit Pen's parents in Chicago, which was, *okay, fine*, excusable; and her parents were going to be floating in the Atlantic Ocean wearing bathing suits and drinking mai tais.

"I'll be here," Emmett offered.

"Lucky me." Stefanie mimicked his sarcastic smile and he went back to his food. She'd rather eat a microwaved frozen meal by herself than take him up on a shared turkey-day dinner.

"Stef, my parents would love to have you if you want to

come to Chicago with us." Pen lifted her fussing daughter from the high chair. Zach shot his wife a look that said they hadn't talked about this.

Her brother's wife was sweet and thoughtful and sharp and beautiful. If Zach hadn't pulled his head from his rear and married Pen, Stef would've seriously considered it. Penelope Ferguson had granted them all a beautiful niece-slash-granddaughter, and Pen's presence at parties made Stef's life a lot brighter. As much as she'd love to hang with Pen over the holidays, however, Stef would never dream of intruding on Pen's time with her family. This would be their first Thanksgiving with Olivia.

"I appreciate that," Stef smiled over at her sister-in-law. "But I'll be all right. I'll just…decorate for Christmas early."

"You mean late," Zach said. "You barely waited until Halloween last year before you adorned everything that crossed your path in red, green and gold."

Stef curled her lip at her brother. Zach smirked.

"If you change your mind, let us know." Pen excused herself from the table to take care of Olivia and Zach stood with her.

"Need help?"

"No, I have her." She kissed him and he smiled, adoration on his face.

So. Stinking. Sweet.

"I'm not inviting you to Montana." Chase scooped more mashed potatoes onto his plate. "So don't ask."

"I don't want to spend Thanksgiving with you, anyway," she teased.

He pointed at her with his fork when he said, "Good."

Her oldest brother had always looked out for her, had always been there for her. She could guarantee if she wanted to abscond to Montana with Chase, he wouldn't hesitate taking her along. But he deserved a break, too. There'd been so much fatigue in his eyes tonight. Must've been a hell of a week in the mayor's office.

"How are you spending the holiday, Emmett?" Elle asked.

"I'll be on call. Security never sleeps."

Stef eyed him over the rim of her water glass, trying to decide if that was true or not. She didn't know Emmett that well, only that he and Chase had been friends for years, and that Emmett was part of the backdrop of nearly every big event in recent history. She assumed that behind those hulking shoulders and permanent scowl of his, she'd find a loner who worked 24/7, and not much else. He didn't seem to have a life other than one involving the Ferguson family.

Not five minutes later, Penelope returned without Olivia, explaining her daughter had missed a nap and was too tired to deal with dinner.

"It's Zach's turn so I'm off the clock." She refilled her wineglass with dark red wine and gestured to Stef with the tipped bottle. "Join me?"

"Always." Stef allowed Pen to fill her glass, feeling a ping of loneliness. Stef was used to her family being around, to big parties and to-dos year-round. Save when Zach had lived in Chicago for a stint, they'd been together as a family most of the time. The business they held stakes in kept them in each other's orbit.

So, yeah, Stef wasn't used to being alone, but that didn't mean she couldn't be. This year she'd embrace Thanksgiving on her own and build that muscle.

It was time her family started seeing her as a twenty-nine-year-old anyway.

Two

Bundled in her knee-length pea coat, Miriam Andrix marched up the asphalt-covered parking lot, her head down to thwart the icy wind. She was born and raised in Montana, but every winter she experienced here made her a bit less tolerant of the cold. Which was ridiculous. She was only thirty-three, for Pete's sake. It wasn't as if she was her seventy-five-year-old grandmother who kept the thermostat set on eighty degrees at home.

She peeked up from her trudge so that she didn't mow over a shopper who'd just overspent on groceries, and then tucked her chin again and watched her laced boots move her forward. Her destination? Whole Foods Market in search of fixings for sweet potato pie, as assigned by her mother. This was the first year Miriam had been placed in charge of dessert. Typically, she made a side dish like potatoes au gratin or cranberry sauce.

Mom's rules were anything but simple when asking her four children to participate in the preparation of Thanksgiving dinner: no canned ingredients, organic if you can. She also provided the family recipe cards for the requested dish—tweaked by each generation to add an extra dash of cinnamon here or an additional crushed garlic clove there. And since Miriam was responsible for a dessert she wasn't comfortable making, she wasn't taking any chances on shopping at the corner market. She might well spend her entire paycheck in here, but at least she could guarantee that only the most beautiful sweet potatoes would go into her pie.

At the entrance of Whole Foods, the automated doors swished aside and the fragrant scent of mulled cider wafted out. She lifted her head and closed her eyes to inhale her most favorite scent—autumn—when a competing smell mingled with the cider.

Sandalwood. Pine. A touch of leather… And eerily familiar. As was the voice that crashed into her like a runaway shopping cart.

"Mimi?"

She snapped her head up and her gaze collided with a man taller than her by several inches, his devastatingly handsome face broken up by the frown on his forehead and additional lines at the corners of his gray-green eyes. His jaw sported a barely-there five o'clock shadow, and his hair was in the same disarray she remembered from ten years ago—the one crooked part of Chase Ferguson that couldn't be tamed.

"Chase. Hi." She blinked again at the man in front of her, having the half-crazed thought that she'd summoned him with her mind. A week ago she'd received a photo of herself in an envelope she'd had to sign for. Along with the photo was a letter from the mayor of Dallas's office—Chase's office—that was signed by a woman's hand. Miriam had read the two neatly typed paragraphs and tossed the letter into the trash. There was no action step for her, merely a "making you aware" note that she might be mentioned in Mayor Chase Ferguson's upcoming campaign and "may be called upon in the future" for her cooperation.

But throwing the letter into the wastebasket hadn't removed the memories of Chase from her head. For a solid week, she'd reflected on the summer they'd spent together, fumed anew at the senseless way he'd cast her aside and played out a few scenarios wherein she'd enjoy humiliating his mother—whom Miriam blamed in part for Chase breaking things off.

"I didn't expect to run into you while I was here," the man from her past was saying. It was the same deep, silken voice she remembered, but his Texas drawl was diminished, no doubt due to rigorous training from a speech coach.

"That's my line," she said with a flat smile, stepping aside to allow a woman pushing a stroller to go in ahead of her.

Chase palmed Miriam's arm and physically moved her to the side of the automated door, and if she was still twenty-three and over-the-moon crazy about him, she might have said that his hand was warm and brought back memories of the summer they spent with each other, most of those days wearing as little clothing as was legal. Sometimes less.

"Yes, I suppose that would be your line." His smile hitched at one corner and dropped like it'd never been there. He adjusted the paper grocery bag in the crook of his arm.

"What are you doing in Montana?" She had to ask. Because seriously—*what*?

"My annual break from the political hoopla."

Annual?

A brisk wind cut through her coat and she pulled her shoulders under her ears. "I received a letter mentioning said hoopla."

"Good. It's only fair for you to know. We suspect someone on my opponent's camp dug that photo up." He sounded so distant standing not a foot away from her. The same way the letter had sounded—probably because it'd been written by a member of his staff and not Chase himself. Too many years had passed for that to hurt, but part of her had felt the sting of loss that he hadn't bothered with a personal note.

"Where are you staying?"

"I have a place here."

"You do?" News to her.

"On Flathead Lake."

Another memory hit her—one of her cajoling him into skinn-dipping in that lake. On the shoreline on private property in the middle of a warm July night. The water had been cold despite the calendar's date, but Miriam had talked him into it. Watching Chase undress and dive in ahead of her had been one of the highlights of her summer. He had a great ass.

She studied his broad shoulders and tall form, feeling that same commanding presence now. The pull he had on her might have shrunk, but he sure hadn't. If anything, he'd grown both physically and figuratively. Hell, he was as big as Texas in a way—in charge of part of the gargantuan state with a billionaire fortune in his back pocket.

"Pinecone Drive," he said as if he'd been waiting to share that bit of intel.

"You don't mean…the house on the hill with all the windows?" She adjusted her purse strap on her shoulder as the doors swished open again. More cinnamon smells assaulted her and tempted her into the warmth, out of the brisk wind and away from the physical reminder of the summer fling that had gone from scorching hot to corpse cold in three months' time.

"One and the same. I bought it a few years back. I always liked the way it looked. I don't visit much, unfortunately."

"And now you're here with…your family?" *Wife? Kids?* she thought but didn't add.

"Alone. My parents are going on a cruise to Barbados and my brother Zach and his wife and their daughter are spending the holiday in Chicago."

"Zach's married." She smiled at the idea of Chase's younger brother married with a child. She'd only met him once, but had warm memories of the smiling blond guy with green eyes. Chase's younger sister had been fresh out of high school at the time but Miriam had met her too, in passing. "And Stefanie?"

"She's good. Single. It's good for her."

"Yeah. It's good for me, too," Miriam couldn't help saying.

"For me, as well."

They had a mini standoff, meeting each other's gazes for a few seconds. In that protracted moment, she could feel a whisper of the past roll over them. It spoke of what could've been if they'd stayed together instead of separated. What would've been if... So many ifs.

Miriam tore her gaze away from him and looked through the glass doors at the cornucopia of produce waiting to greet her. She'd be safe in there. Safe from her past snuggling up and threatening to suffocate her. Standing next to Chase made her want to simultaneously move closer and back away.

A defense mechanism, no doubt.

"I'd better get going. I have to buy ingredients for sweet potato pies for my family's Thanksgiving."

"My favorite."

"It is?"

"But I couldn't find it in the freezer section, so..." Chase reached into the grocery bag and pulled out a frozen cherry pie, then from behind it a frozen pizza.

"You can't be serious. Pizza for Thanksgiving dinner?"

"I have wine at the house, too. I can be fancy."

He was "fancy" incarnate. From his shiny shoes to the expensive suit hiding under a long, dark coat. A tie was cinched at his neck just so. He smelled of wealth and warmth. It was harder to imagine him eating a meal that came from a box than it was to picture him pouring wine from a bottle with a thousand-dollar price tag.

"If frozen pizza sounds too labor-intensive, I may go the route of grilled cheese," he said. "I have a loaf of sourdough and three types of cheddar in this bag." He offered a brief smile. She watched his frowning forehead relax and a hint of levity tickle his lips. The transformation kicked her in the stomach. In that brief half of a second Chase had looked years younger. *Ten years* younger to be precise. He'd reminded her of the boy she'd fallen in love with.

And oh, how she'd fallen. So hard that if she'd broken bones it'd have been less painful than the broken heart she'd suffered. He hadn't been there to catch her. He'd simply stepped out of the way.

"Well. Enjoy your bread and cheese, in whichever form you choose." She offered a curt nod, and without ending the conversation gracefully, turned away.

"Mimi, wait." A masculine hand shot out in front of her, his arm brushing hers as he offered a business card. His deep voice rumbled in her ear, "My personal cell number if you have any issues. Any at all."

She swallowed thickly before accepting the card. Then nodded, and, without looking back, dashed into the grocery. She skipped the temptation of a cider with whipped cream at the cafe, terrified that any delay might prompt Chase to follow her in and resume their stilted conversation.

A conversation that had no place in the current year. A conversation that could only end in an argument since she and Chase were on the opposite sides of many, many topics.

Not the least of which was the state of her heart when she'd boarded a plane that long-ago summer.

She stopped at the display of sweet potatoes, but there were only two knobby yams left. She clucked her tongue at her timing, which couldn't be worse. Both for sweet potato shopping and running into ex-boyfriends who should look a lot less tempting.

The simple black-and-white business card weighed

heavy in her hand but she couldn't part with it just yet. She shoved it into her purse and instead debated her next step. Either bribe the woman next to her into relinquishing a few of her sweet potatoes or buy the damn things in a can and hope to God her mother didn't notice.

Three

"Kristine Andrix. Saver of the day!" her youngest sister announced as she strode into Miriam's apartment the next evening. Kristine placed a handled paper sack on the counter and Miriam peeked inside, gawking at the gorgeous produce within.

"Oh, they're beautiful!"

"And organic. I bought them last week since I started eating sweet potatoes for breakfast."

"Breakfast?" Ever the health nut, Kris was always up to some culinary experiment or another. Last year she was vegan and brought her own Tofurkey to Thanksgiving dinner; this year she was vegetarian but only ate "whole foods."

"Yeah. You bake the potato ahead of time, then in the morning pull it out of the fridge, warm it and top it with peanut butter and cinnamon."

"That…actually sounds delicious." Miriam moved to the sink to scrub the spuds. "What time are you driving to mom's tomorrow?"

"I'm going tonight."

"Tonight?" So much for the wine she'd picked up. She was hoping they could share a glass while she regaled her sister with the tale of the Billionaire Mayor in Bigfork.

"Brendan and I were invited to stay the night." She waggled her eyebrows.

"In the same room?"

"Crazy, right? Dad never would've allowed it." Kris's mouth pulled into a sad smile. They all missed him so much. The holidays were the hardest. "I think Wendy helped lighten up the entire household."

"Yes, all it took was her bringing Rosalie home for Christmas."

"Mom prides herself in being progressive."

"I'm bummed, though. I was hoping we could polish off a bottle of wine like we used to…" Miriam decided not to add the words "before Brendan" to that statement. She wouldn't rob her sister of her happiness. She placed the washed potatoes on a pan and Kristine started stabbing them with a fork.

"Why not go tonight?" Kris lived in Bigfork, not too far from Miriam.

"I have work to do. A report that should've been done earlier this week."

"Seems unfair for you to work on the biggest drinking day of the year." Her sister quirked her lips.

"Well, I'm staying Thanksgiving night so that we can raid the stores at the crack of dawn on the biggest *shopping* day of the year."

"Too bad you're not still dating Gerard. Brendan would've had someone to talk to."

"Gerard wasn't a great talker." It'd been the reason they split. He hardly shared anything about his life, little or big. How his workday went, his plans for the weekend or the fact that he'd been seeing another woman at the same time he'd dated Miriam. His silence had been absolute on that front. "We have a horrible track record of having boyfriends at the same time, don't we?"

"The worst."

Kristine and Miriam were ten months apart. Their older siblings Ross and Wendy had a six-and four-year gap on Miriam, respectively. Given that the two youngest Andrix daughters had never *not* remembered the other being around, Kristine and Miriam felt more like twins. They shared the same wavy dark hair that curled on the ends, and had similar full-lipped pouts. Kristine was built more like Wendy, though, on the curvier side, whereas Miriam couldn't do enough leg exercises to thicken her spindles into anything resembling *curves*.

"Speaking of boyfriends…" Potatoes wrapped in foil, Miriam slid the tray into the oven. She set the timer and then leaned on the counter while Kristine poured herself a glass of water from the pitcher. "I ran into Chase Ferguson at Whole Foods."

Mouth agape, Kris blinked. "Come again?"

"I was walking in and he was walking out. He's on vacation. I guess he bought the estate on Pinecone Drive."

"The one with the indoor pool and the wine cellar and a million bedrooms?"

"Uh-huh. And fifteen thousand square feet overlooking Flathead Lake."

"Wow." Kris's eyes sought the ceiling in awe, then jerked back to Miriam. "You seem awfully calm about this."

"I've had a few hours to cope."

"You were so in love with him." Kris shook her head in a pitying fashion. "Like, *gone*."

"Yes, thank you for that reminder."

"What'd he look like?"

"Oh, you know. Tall, dark and handsome."

"Ouch." Her sister winced. "Who's he here with?"

"No one. Not a single soul."

"Really…because his wife and kids are in a Tuscan villa on holiday while he's here writing his memoirs?"

"There is no wife. There are no kids," Miriam said. "At

least I don't think there are any kids. We didn't get past him mentioning he was single."

"Sounds like you two had quite the conversation." Her sister deftly raised one eyebrow.

"We mostly stood shivering in the cold while trying to find the balance between polite and concise. His parents and siblings are going out of town over Thanksgiving weekend, so he came here to enjoy his rarely used mansion and eat frozen pizza instead." Miriam fingered the bent corner of the recipe card her mother had given her. "He said sweet potato pie was his favorite. I never knew that. Do you know why?"

"I'm assuming because in the short summer months you two spent boinking each other in the lake, you never broached the topic of pie preferences?"

"Fair point." Miriam smiled. "I was going to say it's because we ended before sweet potato pie season. It's been ages since I've thought about him… I mean *really* thought about him. It was a silly summer fling and I was swept up." Her gut pinged with warning at the lie. Miriam ignored that ping. She would rather make believe she never loved him than consider that she'd been right about them living happily ever after if he hadn't discarded her so callously. Half kidding, she added, "I could invite him to Mom's for dinner. Bury that axe for good."

"Do it."

She faced her sister's wide-eyed gaze. "What? Why? I was joking."

"Burying the axe for good would be cathartic. Once you're around each other again you'll both see that you are *not* the Miriam of ten years ago. You're the Miriam of today. It'd do Chase good to see what he's been missing."

"Thanks, Kris." Miriam was touched, but not sure she agreed. "He's not missing much. Other than a job I love, I have no husband, children or Nobel Peace Prize to wave in his face."

"None of that matters." Kristine swept Miriam's cell phone off the dining room table and offered it, but then frowned. "Unless… You probably don't have his private number. I didn't think about that."

"Actually, I do. He handed me his card."

"Bury the lead why don't you! Why'd he give you that?" Kris was grinning, her eyes twinkling. "For like, a holiday hookup?" She blinked, then screwed her eyes toward the ceiling. "That'd be a great book title."

Her sister the freelance editor never shut her brain off.

"It would be a great title *for a work of fiction*." Miriam snatched her phone away and shoved it into her back pocket. "Remember that protest I did years ago with a conservation group in Houston?"

"Big oil, right?"

Miriam nodded and explained the letter that'd arrived last week. "He didn't plan on seeing me while he was here, so I don't know what the offer of calling him if I need anything was about."

"Told you. Holiday hookup." Her sister shrugged. "You should invite him for no other reason than we can skewer him at the dinner table about being a dirty politician while you're the Snow White of Bigfork."

Miriam had to laugh at her sister's imagination.

"Plus, it'd be fun to watch Mom go from simmer to boiling over while she tries to make sense of a mayor at her table."

"It was a dumb idea. Forget I mentioned it." Miriam just hadn't liked the thought of him alone on a holiday. How ridiculous was that? She wasn't in charge of his well-being.

"Spoilsport."

Topic dead, they went back to chatting about everything but sexy mayors and summer flings.

Two hours later, the pies had finished baking and were cooling on the stovetop. Miriam had poured herself a glass of red after Kristine left, and camped out on the sofa, laptop and charts spread on the coffee table for work. But the website she'd pulled up had nothing to do with work. It was the City of Dallas website, particularly Chase's headshot. He looked merely handsome in that still frame. He'd been devastatingly gorgeous in person.

Chase's business card in hand, she rubbed her thumb over his phone number.

One glass of wine was all it took to weaken her resolve. That and the smell of sweet potato pie in the air.

"Damn him."

She swiped the screen of her phone, dialed the first eight digits of the phone number, then paused.

Why should she care if her ex-boyfriend ate alone on Thanksgiving? Shouldn't she embrace the idea of the jerk who broke her heart spending the holiday alone in a way-too-big-for-one mansion? Except she'd always been horrible at holding grudges, and even the blurry, faded memories of her broken heart couldn't keep her from completing the task.

She dialed the remaining digits and waited patiently while the phone rang once, twice and then a third time. When she was about to give up, a silken voice made love to her ear canal.

"Chase Ferguson."

"Chase. Hi. Um, hi. It's Miriam."

"Miriam?"

"Andrix," she said through clenched teeth. Was it that he'd had so many other women in his life over the last decade that he couldn't keep track of them? Or was it that he'd forgotten her already even though she'd bumped into him yesterday afternoon?

"I know. I think of you as Mimi."

That husky voice curled around her like a hug. He'd always called her Mimi, and to date had been the only person who had, save her best friend in the third grade. Her family either called her Miriam or Meems.

"Is everything all right?" If that was concern in his voice, she couldn't place it. His tone was even. His words measured.

"Everything is fine. I, um." She cleared her throat, took a fortifying sip of her wine and continued. "My mother lives about twenty minutes north of Bigfork. We make enough for Thanksgiving dinner to feed ten extra people. You're welcome to join us tomorrow night."

She pressed her lips together before she rattled off what would be served and how she'd baked two pies that were presumably his favorite. She wasn't begging him to show up, simply extending an invitation as an old acquaintance.

Silence greeted her from the other end of the phone.

"Chase?"

"No. Thank you."

She waited for an explanation. None came. Not even a lame excuse about having to work like she'd used tonight. Though she truly did have to work. She scowled at her laptop and his handsome mug before snapping the lid shut.

"Will there be anything else?" he asked. Tersely.

At his formal tone, ire slipped into her bloodstream as stealthily as a drug. Her back went ramrod straight; her eyebrows crashed down.

"No," she snapped. "That concludes my business with you."

"Very well."

She waited for goodbye but he didn't offer one. So she hung up on him.

"Jerk." She tossed the phone on the coffee table and rose to refill her glass. She'd called out of the kindness of her heart and he'd made her feel foolish and desperate.

Just like ten years ago.

"This is who he is, Miriam," she told herself as she poured more wine. "A man who owns a sixteen-million-dollar mansion he rarely visits. A man whose only interest is to increase his bank statement and buy up beautiful bits of land because he can."

She swallowed a mouthful of wine and considered that, as much disdain as she'd had for Chase's mother then and still, Eleanor Ferguson had been right.

Miriam and Chase were better off apart.

Four

Miriam hadn't been in her mother's kitchen for more than five minutes before she started airing her grievances about Chase and the phone call from last night.

Kristine was placing freshly baked rolls into a basket and her brother Ross snatched another one and dunked the end of it into the gravy.

"He's the mayor of what?" their older brother asked around a bite.

"Dallas, dummy," Kris replied. "And stop eating my rolls. I made three dozen and you've already snarfed three of them."

"Four." He argued. His mouth curling into a Grinchy smile.

Kristine sacrificed one more that she tossed at him, but Ross, former college football player that he was, caught it easily, struck a Heisman pose and absconded to the dining room.

"He doesn't act thirty-nine," Kris grumbled. "Anyway. Chase is a jerk and I'm sorry you had to deal with that."

"Yeah, well. I'm sorry I didn't say what I thought to say until *after* I hung up."

"Such as." Kristine motioned with a roll for Miriam to go on.

"I would've informed him that I wasn't one of his underlings and I deserved better treatment than a haughty *No. Thank you.*" She dipped her voice into a dopey tone that didn't sound like him, but made her feel better. "I'd have told him that I became a success without his billions and in a field where I wasn't causing global warming. My line of work is admirable."

"It is, sweetie."

"Thank you."

Miriam had completed her degree in agricultural sciences, going on to do compliance work behind a desk for a few years until she realized how wholly unsatisfying it was to push papers from one side of her desk to another. Five years ago, she'd found the Montana Conservation Society and stumbled into her calling. She'd started as program manager and was then promoted to director of student affairs. She mostly worked with teenagers. She taught them how to respect their environment and care for the world they all shared. She found it incredibly rewarding to watch those kids grow and change. Several of the students who came through MCS wouldn't so much as step on an ant if they could help it by the time she was through with them.

And yet Chase had dismissed her like she was a temp on his payroll.

"I should've gone over to his big, audacious house and told him what I think of his wasteful habits and egomaniacal behavior."

"Who, dear?" Her mother stepped into the kitchen and gestured to the basket of rolls. "Kristine, to the table with those, please. We're about to start."

"No one," Miriam answered. "Just… No one."

Kris shuffled into the dining room and Judy Andrix watched her go before narrowing her eyes and squaring her jaw. Since Miriam's father, Alan, had died five years ago of complications from heart surgery, her mom had taken it on herself to play both the role of mom and dad. It wasn't easy for any of them to lose him, but their mother had taken the brunt of that blow. Thirty-nine years of marriage was a lifetime.

"Miriam, would you grab those bottles of wine and take them to the table for me?"

"Sure thing." Relieved the conversation was over, she did as she was asked.

Halfway into dinner, however, her wine remained untouched and her food mostly uneaten.

"Meems, what's going on in your world?" Wendy's girlfriend, Rosalie, asked conversationally.

Miriam blinked out of her stupor and realized she'd been staring at her mashed potatoes, Chase on her mind. "Work. That's about it."

"How did the camp go this summer? I meant to ask but I was so busy."

Busy being a surgeon. It happened.

Miriam filled her in on the camp for eighth graders she'd cochaperoned. "You haven't lived until you've been in charge of thirty hormone-riddled teens in tents."

Wendy nudged Rosalie with her shoulder. "That's what I keep warning her about every time she brings up having children."

"Children are great," Ross's wife, Cecilia, said at the exact moment their five-year-old daughter Raven threw her butter-covered roll on the floor.

"Raven!" While Ross went about explaining to his daughter that the food belonged on her plate and not on the rug, Wendy and Rosalie answered questions from Kristine about having children. Surrogate, they agreed, but they weren't against adoption.

Mom interjected that she didn't care *how* any of them went about it so long as she was given another grandchild.

"Or two," she added with a pointed look at Kris and

Brendan, who wisely filled his mouth full of stuffing rather than comment. "Meems, have you been seeing anyone?"

And that's when the last strand on the rope of Miriam's dwindling patience snapped.

"I'm sorry." She stood abruptly from the table and the room silenced. Even Raven seemed to sense the importance of the moment and stopped her complaining. Every pair of eyes swiveled to Miriam. "I have to run an errand."

"What? Now?" Her mother's voice rose.

"I'll be back in an hour, tops. That leaves plenty of time for dessert. Feel free to start playing games without me." She could easily make the round trip to Bigfork and back before the traditional board game battle began. And she didn't mind at all ousting herself from a conversation involving families and children when there was a man very nearby who was going about his evening as if she didn't matter. Been there, done that. She didn't care to suffer a repeat of ten years ago.

Miriam rushed into the kitchen and rifled through her mother's cupboard for a plastic storage container. She sliced one of her pies and slid three large wedges into the container before snapping on the lid. She'd show him what he was missing all right.

She was pulling her coat over her shoulders when her mother appeared in the doorway of the kitchen. Judy eyed the pie in the container.

"Where on earth are you going in the middle of Thanksgiving dinner?" Her mother was a narrow, thin woman whose supermodel good looks couldn't be ignored, even if she was in her early sixties.

"I don't expect you to understand." Miriam gave her mother's arm a squeeze. "But there's someone I *have* to talk to or I won't be able to enjoy a single second of my holiday. I just… It's something I have to do."

"And a phone call won't cut it?" Judy leveled a knowing smile at her third child.

"No." Miriam wouldn't risk a repeat of that robotic blow-off from last night.

"It's snowing again."

It was, but... "I have four-wheel drive."

"I suppose if I stand here and try to talk you out of it, you'll go anyway, only a little later than you intended on account of my keeping you." Her mother folded her arms over her chest. She knew her daughter well.

"One hour. Tops." Miriam repeated, wrapping her hand around the doorknob.

"At least take the mayor a plate of food," her mother called before Miriam could escape. "You can't *only* show up with pie."

"How did you—?" Miriam leaned around her mother to glare beyond the doorway where Kristine sat in Dad's former seat at the table.

Kris blew a kiss and waggled her fingers in a wave.

Only a year old, the Ford F-150 was equipped to glide through snow like it was popped corn. But as she drove closer to Bigfork, the visibility dropped and it was more like trudging through wet sand. It wasn't "her" truck, per se, but had been provided graciously by MCS. She'd been begging for two years for a vehicle that could haul, tow and not give out if she had to drive up a mountain and rescue someone's lost dog. Sure, that had only happened *once*, but she'd had to hike most of it on foot since her compact car hadn't been equipped for the elements. It was practical for her to have a vehicle that could handle Montana's terrain.

Thanks to those elements, the twenty-minute drive to Bigfork was stretching to sixty. She'd encountered traffic and low visibility, and on top of that her gas gauge was dangerously close to E. At a top speed of twelve miles per hour, she was getting nowhere *slowly*. Because she'd underestimated the weatherman and overestimated her F-150, there was no way she'd make it back to her mother's house in this mess.

But Miriam still intended to make her way to Chase's. She wasn't giving up a scant few miles from his house. No way.

At a stoplight, she keyed in a quick text to Kris. I'm going to be celebrating at home alone tonight! Bigfork is buried. :(

Before the stoplight turned green, Miriam's phone rang.

"You have to come back!" Kris said in greeting.

"It's a mess out here." Windshield wipers swiped away the gathering snow and Miriam turned right toward Pinecone Drive and the mayor of Dallas.

"I thought that storm was supposed to miss us."

"Yeah, well, evidently Bigfork caught the edge of it. I'm in a winter wonderland."

"You're still on the road?" asked her downtrodden sister.

"I am, but I'm almost home. Tell everyone I'm sorry. I'll call later when I get settled." She forced a smile as she mentally kicked her own butt for leaving her mom's house. "Hey, maybe you can video chat me in later."

"Is that Miriam? Is she all right?" their mother called in the distance.

"She's fine!" Kris called back. Then to Miriam, "I'll let her know you're all right and home safe… That is where you're going, right? Home?"

"Of course."

"Meems."

"I have to go." Miriam hung up on Kris, who clearly could not be trusted with sensitive information, and resumed her drive to Chase's mansion. If Miriam didn't go to him like she'd vowed, the entire trip would be a waste.

Once she looked him in the eye and made sure he understood who she'd become, she could be on her way. Who was she? A woman who didn't take crap from anyone. A woman who'd found herself *and* her way in the decade that separated them. Her biggest worry was that she'd remained a still frame in his mind: standing next to a private plane, tears running down her face, begging him not to leave.

Or worse, the one who'd emailed and called him after she'd come home to Montana. She'd been so weak back then, but Chase had always maintained his strength.

"Clean break," he'd told her, and he'd meant it.

Meanwhile, she'd continued to declare her love for him and had reiterated her claim that they were meant to be. Never had she been so wrong before or since.

Chase's mother, Eleanor, had seen Miriam not as a lifelong mate for her son, but a preoccupation he couldn't afford. Miriam knew because the only phone call answered from Chase's cell phone happened to be answered by Eleanor herself.

On Thanksgiving.

Miriam blinked in shock. She'd completely forgotten that fact.

But yes, it'd been Thanksgiving. She remembered excusing herself from the room while her siblings and parents were unboxing a new board game. Then she'd shut herself in Kristine's bedroom and called Chase. She'd been thinking then about how she was the only one of them at the table not coupled off.

The more things changed...

She heard those words in her late father's voice, her heart squeezing as she remembered his big laugh and bigger presence. He'd been comforting, but notably frustrated while she nursed her broken heart that winter. He'd been exactly what a father should be.

She turned into the lakeside neighborhood where the

wealthiest residents of Bigfork lived, rolled by the snowy, pricey new builds with their lack of trees and yard space, and toward the older part of the neighborhood. The houses closer to the lake sat on high hills, were spread much farther apart and had exponentially higher price tags.

Ten minutes of slow-crawling her way toward Pinecone Drive, and she was navigating through dark trees and an abandoned road piled deep with snow.

This is a bad idea.

Not braving the storm—she was confident in her driving abilities and her trusty Ford to get her both in *and* out of this mess—but confronting Chase. That phone call from ten years ago replayed in her mind and her gloved hands gripped the steering wheel, her shoulders wilting.

Chase Ferguson's phone. Who is this?

The woman who'd answered had been older. An air of sophistication outlined every word she spoke. Miriam had recognized Eleanor's voice instantly, but she refused to let the woman bully her. Her future with Chase involved only them—or so she'd believed.

Listen, darling. I appreciate that you have an affinity for my son, however I can't allow this to continue. He has aspirations for a political seat. He has a future involving Ferguson Oil. Can you honestly tell me that you wouldn't be a hindrance to those goals? If you love him, truly, you'll support him by letting him live his life here in Dallas without you.

Miriam never found out if Chase had asked his mother to handle his dirty work for him, or if Eleanor had taken the call and kept her son in the dark. In the end, Miriam guessed it didn't matter.

She'd reached out. He'd stayed hidden.

Dumb. Dumb of her to come tonight.

At the base of the gargantuan property, she waited for the wipers to swipe the gathering snow from the windshield to assess the situation. The property was nestled in the trees, the clearing blocked by a gate with a keypad she'd have to drive up to. Her truck would make it, of that she was sure. And even if she wasn't, she wasn't risking using the last of her fuel to turn back. She could only hope that Chase had a few gallons of gasoline to fill her tank up so that she could drive home, or else…

No. She wasn't entertaining that thought.

She climbed the steep, snowy hill, her tires sliding enough that her heart hammered against her throat. Thankfully, the driveway evened out at the gate so she didn't slide backwards in the snow. She pressed a button on a callbox to request to be let in. A camera lens attached to the device stared at her from its unblinking mechanical eye. Miriam grabbed the container of sweet potato pie from the passenger seat.

While she waited, snow covered her windshield and drifted inside. *He might not be here*, she thought miserably. Or maybe he'd been caught in the storm while gathering supplies and was holed up in a hotel somewhere—

"Mimi." Chase's low timbre sailed out of the speaker, at once surprised and scolding.

"Hi." She waggled the container. "Pie delivery. I won't stay long." There was a significant pause, but no response. She swore she could feel his laser-like glare through the camera. A buzz sounded as the iron gates swung aside through the gathering snow.

The white stuff on the driveway was untouched by tires or boot prints. After debating leaving her truck running, she shut it off to save fuel and climbed out. The walkway to the front door had been shoveled at some point, but since then a few inches of snow had filled in the gaps.

She shuddered as icy wind sliced through her hair, the temperature colder coming off the frigid lake below. A porch light snapped on and Chase appeared outside wearing a sweater and jeans and sneakers that didn't appear weather resistant.

"Running shoes in this weather. Are you crazy?" She pulled three containers filled with his dinner and dessert from the passenger seat and then shut the door.

"You're calling me crazy? What the hell are you doing here?"

"I told you I won't be long." She shoved the pie container into his hand and his scowl deepened. Her teeth chattered, partially from nerves. This was the moment she'd been waiting for—to set Chase Ferguson straight. On her terms. She glanced around at the pale moonlit mounds of snow. Okay, not exactly her terms, but it was too late to back out now.

"Get inside," he commanded, his breath visible in the cold. Out of habit she locked her truck and it beeped briefly, letting her know. Chase glared over her shoulder at the sound, but she refused to let him scare her off from what she came here to say. She was going to set him straight, then turn this big bastard around and drive straight home.

Do not pass Go. Do not collect $200.

She'd really miss playing games with her family tonight. A dart of regret shocked her ribcage. And then a dart of something else when Chase cupped her elbow and started toward the house.

"Watch your step," his low voice rumbled as he gestured to the nearly invisible porch steps. "You'd better have a good reason for being here other than bringing me pie."

Oh, no worries, Mayor McCheese. I have one.

Five

Chase had known Miriam was headstrong, but driving through a snowstorm to bring him dinner was a touch more than headstrong. It was dangerous. Miriam being in danger wasn't acceptable—especially when he was the cause.

Inside, he shut the door behind them as she checked out the interior of the house. He looked with her, admiring the rich warm-colored woods and the tall, beamed ceilings. Every inch of this place had been polished to dustless perfection, and it should've been, given what he paid his housekeepers.

Logs were stacked in the fireplace, the matches sitting next to a newspaper pages he'd twisted for kindling. He'd left his task when the buzzer to the gate rang. He'd had groceries for the week delivered that morning and a cord of firewood had been delivered after that. The weatherman had predicted the storm with its massive amounts of snow to miss Bigfork, but Chase wasn't taking the risk. Luckily, he'd heeded the warnings and overprepared…which was less than he could say for his gorgeous houseguest.

"Would you mind directing me to the 'wing' where you keep your kitchen, Daddy Warbucks?" Mimi asked with a snide smile.

Nice to see her sharp wit was intact.

"What are you doing here?" It was the most obvious question and the answer she should have offered upon showing up unannounced at his doorstep.

"You said if I needed anything…" She craned her chin to look up at him since he'd already ascended the three steps leading to the kitchen. She was even more beautiful than he remembered. Her cheeks had lost some of their fullness allowing rose-colored cheekbones to angle across her model-like features. The thinness of her face made her lips appear even more plump—and far more kissable than they ought to.

He took the remaining containers from her and gestured to the entryway closet with his head. "Hang up your coat."

"I'm not staying that long. The storm is worsening and—"

"And you're going to wait it out here." Over his dead body she'd navigate through this blizzard tonight.

"No. I will not be doing that." Her eyebrows climbed her forehead. "But I will accept a gallon or two of gas for the short drive home from here. I don't want to get—"

"Coat, Mimi." He came down the stairs to hover over her, his nostrils flared. "Then walk past the living room, take a right and you'll see the kitchen."

"I'll follow you," she snapped, but slipped her coat off and draped it over her arm.

He could do without the attitude, but at least she'd met him halfway.

He settled the containers—one with the sweet potato pie she'd showed him at the gate and the other two overflowing with Thanksgiving dinner.

A long *would you get a load of this* whistle of appreciation came from behind him.

"Wow. Every inch of this place is more amazing than the last."

She turned a one-eighty as she inventoried the kitchen:

the wide island in the center, the floor-to-ceiling cabinets, six-burner gas stove, and a shiny, double-doored fridge. She tossed her coat over one of the stools at the island. Slim jeans accentuated her mile-long legs and a cranberry sweater with a scoop neck revealed creamy, pale skin. No cleavage—a fact she'd bemoaned plenty when they were together a decade ago. He couldn't have cared less. The sight of her in a string bikini, and the way the chilly lake water caused her nipples to point from behind the bright blue top, had been more than enough to pique his interest.

"Yeah, so turkey, stuffing, green beans. All the basics." She folded her fingers together while she talked. "Sweet potato pie is for dessert, though, I suppose you're grown-up and could spoil your dinner if you wanted. Did you eat?"

"What the hell are you doing here, Mimi?" he repeated.

At his tone, she narrowed eyes as brown as the forest floor. Deep mulch in color and blasting him with an accusation she hadn't spoken yet.

"I'm here—" she pointed at the ground, seeming to gather her courage "—to show you that I'm no longer the besotted twenty-three-year-old you left on an airfield in Dallas. You may be a billionaire oil tycoon politician with a mansion the size of your hometown, but I became someone, too."

"Is that so?" He came out from behind the island in the center of the kitchen and Mimi took a hesitant step back. He wouldn't allow her to make him out to be some billionaire asshole without an argument in his own defense. "Tell me, then, how you're the next incarnation of Mother Teresa."

She snapped her mouth shut then opened it to let out a little tut of surprise. "I didn't say I was Mother Teresa."

"No, but you implied I'm the devil incarnate, so I assumed…"

"You have no idea what I implied. You don't know me. You *knew* me."

"Likewise." He scanned her from chestnut hair to the toes of her knee-high boots. She dressed differently than she used to and not just because the season had changed. There was something more formal about her. Less playful than he remembered. "You grew up. I grew up. It happens."

"Unlike you, I don't sit around counting the zeroes in my bank account. I actually *help* people."

"So do I. Are you going to cut the crap and tell me why you're here?" It was the last time he was going to ask.

"I just did! You weren't listening on the phone, so I had to come here in person to—"

"Bullshit. You made a twenty-minute drive—"

"That took over an hour."

"—in this weather carting cold Thanksgiving dinner and my favorite pie. Don't tell me you came all this way to put me in my place."

Her pink tongue touched lips painted cranberry red to match her sweater. He knew too well that unlike the tart fruit, she tasted as sweet as honey.

"I thought you'd appreciate it."

"I do. But that doesn't explain why you're here."

She shrugged with one dark eyebrow and tightened plush lips he'd kissed more times than he could recall. He'd made every attempt to kiss the sunshine off her skin that summer. Back then he could've buried his nose in her coconut-scented hair and never come up for air.

Until reality had intruded.

"I tried to invite you to dinner at my family's house so you wouldn't have to eat alone," she huffed.

"So I'm the equivalent of a stray dog in need of a bone." He spread his arms to indicate the expansive room in which he was standing. "Do I look like I can't fend for myself?"

"You said no!" she practically shouted.

"As was my prerogative."

What was she up to? He kept his voice even, his tone

neutral. He'd been yelled at by a great number of people in his career, and it was his second nature to tamp down any emotions that didn't lead to an effective solution.

The line of her mouth softened. Her eyebrows lowered. Naked vulnerability bled into her expression.

Then he figured it out. It slapped him upside the head, jarring his brain.

I'm an idiot.

"I hurt your feelings," he stated. Could he have been more obtuse? "That's why you're here."

She made a *pfft* sound but he was right. He could tell by the way she shifted her weight onto one boot—almost squirming in his presence. Some things about Mimi had changed in the last ten years, but some things hadn't. She was the same stubborn, beautiful, hopeful woman he'd made love to back then, but with an even sturdier backbone and harder head. She brought him Thanksgiving dinner tonight not because he was a charity case but because—

"It bothered you to picture me eating alone," he told her.

"Why would I care about a pompous, overblown—"

"Admit it."

He heard a deep sucking sound as she pulled in a lungful of oxygen.

"Fine," she blew out on an exhale. "I was sitting in front of a dressed turkey thinking that if you *weren't* such a stubborn jackass, you would've been there enjoying the spoils of a home-cooked meal. Rare in your case, as I recall."

It was true. Eleanor Ferguson didn't cook. She catered.

"I took it upon myself to deliver both dinner and a message, planning to turn and drive straight back to my family's house knowing that you were both fed *and* informed." A crease appeared between her brows. "Only now I'll be heading to my apartment instead of back for dessert with my family."

He could see and feel the regret coming off her. The expression didn't erase the elegance of her features, and accentuated the firmer, straighter line of her backbone. She was a confusing whirlwind of attributes, but Chase saw through her air of confidence. She couldn't hide behind the one quality she'd never possessed: ambivalence.

Mimi had never been ambivalent or calloused to the needs of others. No matter how badly they'd treated her in the past.

"Tell me more about what you do," he said, turning to lift the lids of the containers.

"What I do?"

"Yes." Even cool, the food was an inviting array of holiday fragrances. Thyme and sage and butter.

"Um. Okay. I'm the director of student affairs for the Montana Conservation Society. I work mostly with teenagers, but I've also spearheaded a recent and very important recycling campaign with a local apartment complex."

He punched the buttons on the microwave—first removing a small plastic container of cranberry sauce thoughtfully included "on the side."

"One of many," Mimi added.

"You're as passionate as I remember." He pulled two forks from a drawer and laid them on the island.

"Is that a nice way of saying I'm misguided?"

"Not at all. The world needs more advocates like you."

Her mouth was frozen in a half gape, like she was shocked he'd paid her a compliment. "Thank you."

"You're welcome."

They stood on opposite sides of the island—what a metaphor for how they'd left things—in silence as the remainder of the seconds ticked down on the microwave before it beeped. He set the containers between him and Mimi, grabbed an open bottle of wine and two glasses and poured himself one.

She placed a finger on the neck of the bottle when he tipped it toward her glass. "I'm leaving."

"I can't let you do that." He poured the wine anyway and set the glass in front of her. She frowned. He offered her a fork. She shook her head.

"I ate already. This is for you."

Chase locked eyes with the woman who used to love him, with the woman he'd nearly loved more than his own common sense. "Thank you."

He dug in, scooping a bite of turkey, mashed potatoes and stuffing, dunking the fork into the cranberry sauce before closing his eyes and savoring the flavors of a slow-cooked, took-all-day-to-make meal. Before he meant to, he moaned his approval.

Without another glance in her direction, he unapologetically took another big bite.

Six

Watching Chase eat bordered on pornographic.

Or maybe Miriam didn't get out much. She rested her top teeth on her bottom lip and watched as he moaned around another bite. Her mouth watered, not for the food, but for *him*. Hearing those familiar moans reminded her of the time they'd spent together. Naked. No holds barred.

Not why you came here, she reminded herself sternly.

Yet here she stood, a woman who'd been literally naked before him, and was at this moment metaphorically naked before him. He'd figured out—before she'd admitted it to herself—that she'd come here not only to give him a piece of her mind but also to give herself the comfort of knowing he'd had a home-cooked meal on Thanksgiving.

With one masculine hand, he cradled the red wine, swirled the liquid in the glass and took a sip. She watched his throat work while he swallowed, her own going dry. It was an erotic scene to take in for a woman who was currently not having sex with anyone but herself.

She balled her fist as a flutter of desire took flight between her thighs. Now she wanted wine, dammit. And maybe to touch him. Just once.

He heartily ate another scoop of his food, then pushed her wine glass closer to her. An offer.

An offer she wouldn't accept.

Couldn't accept.

She wasn't unlike Little Red Riding Hood, having run to the wrong house for shelter. Only in this case, the Big Bad Wolf wasn't dining on Red's beloved grandmother but Miriam's family's home cooking.

An insistent niggling warned her that she could be next—and hadn't this particular "wolf" already consumed her heart?

"So, I'm going to go." She'd risk her gas tank running dry before she stayed another minute and found herself trapped with him.

When she grabbed her coat and stood, a warm hand grasped her much cooler one. Chase's fingers stroked hers before lightly squeezing, his eyes studying her for a long moment, his fork hovering over his unfinished dinner.

Finally, he said, "I'll see you out."

"That's not necessary."

He did as he pleased and stood, his hand on her lower back as he walked with her. Outside, the wind pushed against the front door, causing the wood to creak. She and Chase exchanged glances. Had she waited too long?

"For the record, I don't want you to leave."

What she'd have given to hear those words on that airfield ten years ago.

"I'll be all right."

"You can't know that." He frowned out of either concern or anger, she couldn't tell which. "How was the hill?"

She shrugged one shoulder and wouldn't look him in the eye. His sloped driveway had been slick, but she'd made it… Barely. She wasn't looking forward to going back down.

"Mimi—" His phone rang and he reached into his pocket. Whatever he'd been about to say to her hung in the air like the sexual tension that was once between them.

It wasn't here now, but *something* was. If she were being honest, she might describe it as sadness. Or hope. Funny how hard those two were to tell apart.

Chase's side of the conversation was filled with one-or two-word responses giving her no idea who he was talking to or what about. "I see. Thank you. Yes." Until the farewell. "You too, Emmett."

"Emmett?" She knew that name… She narrowed her eyes, her mind seeking the particular storage cabinet for that nugget of information while Chase pocketed his phone. A second later she located the memory. "Your friend, Emmett? The one who had several torrid affairs here in Bigfork while you…"

She trailed off. *While you just had the one with me.*

Chase hadn't been interested in multiple girls that summer. Remarkably, amidst a beach littered with tiny bikinis stuffed with big breasts and curvy hips, Miriam had caught his eye. With her plain brown hair and superslim physique, she hadn't expected the tall, dark-haired, muscular specimen playing flip cup with his friends to notice her.

She and her friend Mandie had stood on the sidelines watching as, round after round, his side of the table won each game. He and Emmett would high-five and Chase would smile, all white teeth and tanned skin… She'd fallen in love the moment his eyes clashed with hers, but she'd never dreamed she'd get any nearer to him than the other side of that patch of sand.

"Yes, one and the same." Chase interrupted the memory. The bright colorful summer vision receded into the neutrals of the mansion's interior. His careful smile was a ghost of what it had been and hers was now much harder to earn.

"I'm glad you're still friends." She'd long ago lost touch with Mandie, her work friend when she'd been waiting tables at the Crab Shucker that summer. She hadn't thought of Mandie in ages, but now Miriam wondered what became of her. Mandie had gone home with Emmett back then. Neither of them had any interest in a second night together, despite Mandie's raving that he was *the lay of the year*. She advised Miriam not to get *too caught up on that Texas boy*, meaning Chase, but Miriam had been completely caught up.

So, Eleanor Ferguson wasn't the only one right about their relationship. Maybe it really had been in Miriam's head—the love she'd been so sure she felt for him. Maybe it'd been mere appreciation. Infatuation…

"Stay." Chase's gray-green eyes were warm and inviting, his voice a time capsule back to not-so-innocent days. The request was siren-call sweet, but she'd not risk herself for it.

"No." She yanked open the front door, shocked when the howling wind shoved her back a few inches. Snow billowed in, swirling around her feet, and her now wet, cold fingers slipped from the knob.

Chase caught her, an arm looped around her back, and shoved the door closed with the flat of one palm. She hung there, suspended by the corded forearm at her back, clutching his shirt in one fist, and nearly drowned in his lake-colored eyes.

"I can stay for a while longer," she squeaked, the decision having been made for her.

His handsome face split into a brilliant smile and a laugh bobbed his throat. He released her and moved away, robbing her of his heat and attention. She hated how cold she felt with him gone. It was like a cloud had come out to mask the sun.

"Melodramatic much?" she mumbled to herself, hanging her coat in the entryway closet. Then she followed where he went. That, too, was a reaction she wasn't going to explore.

He stood in the center of the sunken living room and flipped on the television over the hearth. A local station was sharing the latest weather report from Bigfork. A wind-blown, red-faced woman confirmed Miriam's fears.

"Travel of any sort is not only dangerous but could be life-threatening!" Gale Schneider, broadcasting from what appeared to be the inside of a violently shaken snow globe, shouted over the wind. The hood of her downy coat was up, but the wind lashed, blowing the material like a flag on a pole. "Montana authorities warn that anyone watching should stay where they are unless they absolutely must travel!" she continued. "If you're in your vehicle, you may want to find the closest open service station or convenience store until the storm blows over. Back to you, Joan."

A little spike of fear stabbed her belly.

"Mother Nature and your local weather reporter agree with me," Chase told her. He pointed the remote and the television winked off. "You're staying. No sense in risking driving home to your empty apartment."

She hated that she agreed with him.

"Is there anything you need from your truck that might make your stay here more comfortable?" His voice was seductive and low, the offer sincere and chivalrous.

"My purse," she confirmed numbly. "And my overnight bag." She'd never taken it into her mother's house since her arms were full of pie and she'd been put to work the moment she crossed the kitchen's threshold.

"That's convenient." His eyebrows jumped and he walked past her. She warred with the urge to explain herself, but decided against it. She'd come in here with her defenses up and where had that landed her?

She regretted having been robbed of her grand exit. After declaring what a successful adult she'd become, she really, *really* wanted to watch Chase's mansion dwindle in the rearview mirror. It would have been poetic.

From the entryway closet where he was pulling on his coat, he said, "I'll need your keys."

"Sure you can handle the snow, Dallas?" she asked on her approach. "I can. I'm a born-and-bred Montanan."

"And I'm a born-and-bred Texan. I'm not afraid of a little snow." He popped the collar on his coat and held out his palm. She dropped her keyring into it.

Before he slipped out the door, he said, "Don't eat my pie."

After reassuring her entire family she was fine—*really, yes, really, I'm fine, stop asking*—Miriam pressed the end button on her cell and stared out the window at the white-washed landscape.

From her vantage point in the sunken living room, she couldn't see farther than the deck. She knew what was down there—the lake and a good portion of the shoreline that Chase owned along with this property. In another life, she'd been bikini clad on that beach, making out with the man she was snowed in with tonight.

Life had a twisted sense of humor.

Kristine's reaction had bordered on comical once she'd learned that Miriam was in Chase's mansion. She'd darted to another part of their mother's house and hissed into the phone, "Do not have sex with him!"

"Only if you swear to keep it a secret that I'm here," Miriam volleyed back.

Kris had humbly apologized for letting the mayor out of the bag, but she wasn't through yet. "Do *not* have sex with that disgustingly beautiful man, Meems. Remember, this is not a second chance. You're not trapped with him because fate said so, but because you're too stubborn not to drive into a snowstorm to deliver the man pie."

Miriam had lowered her voice—though there was no need, since Chase was in the kitchen, which was approximately the width of her entire apartment's floor plan—and assured her sister that it'd be a cold day in hell before that happened.

She was acutely aware it was a cold day indeed and further aware that this might be hell since she was stranded with the former object of her passion and affection.

Again with the melodrama?

She'd told herself repeatedly that she'd leave the moment the snow stopped, but she'd also been watching Gale on TV, and even on Mute, Miriam's plan was becoming the stuff of fiction.

"Do you at least have condoms?" Kris had asked.

At which point, Miriam said goodbye and ended the call. Why would she have condoms? She'd planned on attending a family weekend as a happy single, not getting naked with the mayor of Dallas.

That…shouldn't sound as inviting as it did.

The snow swirled outside the wide windows and her vision blurred at the edges. She really was stuck here.

"Last chance." A velvet voice smoothed over her shoulder.

She blinked the winter wonderland into focus and turned to find an offered plate with a single slice of sweet potato pie in the middle.

Chase held up a shiny, tined instrument. "I brought you a clean fork."

"Did you like it?" She inhaled, catching some of his sandalwood-and-spice smell in her nostrils.

"Exquisite."

What a Chase Ferguson word. He'd always had a formal edge alongside the rough-and-tumble. Then she'd met his parents and figured out why. He was practically royalty—not that they had royalty in the United States but she imagined billionaires as their *own* sort of royalty.

"If you liked it so much, why offer me your last piece?"

"The gentlemanly thing to do would've been to offer you the *first* piece, Mimi. Who the hell have you been dating for the last ten years?"

"You don't want to know," she said around a low chuckle.

For a split second—maybe even half a second—she understood why her sister warned her against falling into bed with him again. Damn, he was charming.

"Share it with you?" She accepted the fork, noticing his fork pressed into his other palm.

"I was hoping you'd say that." Just like that, they were coexisting in a moment of amicability.

"Let's sit." He took his seat in the middle of the plush walnut-colored leather sofa, forcing her to take the seat next to him. Her leg brushed his and warmth seeped through her jeans.

She ignored the nervous skip of her heart and ate a forkful of pie. "Not bad for my first time."

"You nailed it," he told her, taking a bite himself.

"Why are you here in Bigfork?"

He finished chewing before answering. And when he did, he leaned a hairbreadth closer to her.

"I suppose you're looking for a bigger answer than vacation."

She let her silence be her "Yes."

"It was already scheduled when your photo crossed my desk. If that article goes live and the press finds out I'm in the same city as you, it'll be a circus."

"But you didn't reschedule your trip."

He ate another bite of pie. "I don't make decisions based on what might happen."

Didn't she know that too well? He hadn't taken the chance on her based on "what might happen" either.

Her gaze snagged on her suitcase standing in the mouth of the hallway.

"I guess this situation would look bad."

"Not bad." He offered her the plate holding the last bite. "But definitely…conspicuous. I don't have anything to hide from the press. Do you?"

Seven

Short of sitting in a tree at Mountainway Park to keep it from being chopped down, or driving ten miles over the speed limit, or skinny-dipping with Chase in Flathead Lake, Miriam didn't make a habit of breaking the law. She imagined he would've disagreed with saving a tree that she'd later learned was infested with ash borer beetles, but he'd give her a pass when it came to the speeding. And she knew exactly how he'd felt about stripping naked and cannonballing into Flathead Lake off a private dock—firmly *against*. But once she'd goaded him properly, he'd stripped down and dived in, resurfacing in the moonlight wearing a huge smile a few seconds later.

They hadn't agreed on everything, and she'd argued her differing points of view fervently while they were together. He had nothing against the oil industry—later, she'd learned why—but they'd always agreed to disagree and then made out, their lips fusing and disqualifying their brains from further participation. Arguments made up a small part of their summer together. Mostly, they'd made love and stared into each other's eyes, hardly able to believe they'd found their other half...

Or at least *she'd* done that.

"You know, I will have some wine." She burst off the

sofa and moved to the kitchen. A scant glass of red would be enough to calm her, but wouldn't erase the recurring memories. Evidently nothing would keep them at bay. She splashed a few more inches into the glass he'd left on the kitchen island for her and swallowed a drink.

He joined her, placing the empty pie plate in the sink and palming his own balloon-shaped glass.

"What would you have been doing this evening if you weren't trapped here with me?"

"'Trapped' is an interesting way to phrase it." The next sip tasted better than the last. "My brother and two sisters and their significant others are most likely embroiled in a board-game battle. We save Monopoly for last since it's better to play when everyone's had more wine."

"Ah, Monopoly. Ender of relationships."

She couldn't picture Chase doing something as commonplace as playing board games. Unless it was backgammon. Chess, maybe. Whatever games stuffy rich people played.

She frowned at the unkind thought, but then gave herself a pass. She hadn't seen him in ten years, so it was wholly possible he *was* the Monopoly guy—minus the monocle—gobbling up property to expand his portfolio. Making under-the-table deals with dirty politicians to advance his own gain. Sweeping the Free Parking money and hiding his spoils under the board...

"So. What have you been up to since I saw you last?" She sat on one of the stools, resting an elbow on the surface of the island.

Rather than sit, he flattened both hands on the countertop and studied her before answering.

"I was a city council member for a while. Served on the board of public works. Even did a stint at Ferguson Oil as director of something-or-other." He hoisted one eyebrow. "Ruining the environment and all that."

"The oil business is no better for the planet than the cattle business, Chase. You know that."

"What would you have my family do, Miriam? Go into the vegan faux-meat business and start from scratch?"

She felt her cheeks redden in challenge. Determined not to slip into shallow arguments as they had in the past—there'd be no making up by making out tonight—she gestured to the wine bottle. "This is very good. A favorite of yours?"

"One of the favorites. I packed a dozen bottles from my wine cellar and brought them up."

"On your private jet?" She snorted.

"Yes. But I bought a car when I landed," he said, completely serious.

"A problem easily solved for you."

"You didn't used to resent my financial status," he shot back.

Her face was aflame. He was right. She hadn't had a problem with his financial status back then. Why would she have? He'd been hers. She was too busy building castles in the sky to judge him for being wealthy.

She hid her rosy cheeks behind the wide rim of her wineglass and took another sip, then spoke without looking at him. "I'm sorry. That was rude."

"Tell me more about what you do," he said, smoothly changing the subject. He stood from his lean on the island and reclaimed his wineglass, hip against the far counter instead.

"I work outside a lot. Mostly in the warmer months. Winter is spent planning the spring and summer camps for the kids and writing the itineraries. Though I also help out the wildlife preserve."

"Saving the world."

"What's wrong with saving the world?" she snapped.

"Nothing." His confused frown was sincere. "You

should try to save the world, or at least part of it. It's what I'm doing."

Choosing to say nothing seemed the best response. She pressed her lips together.

"I crowd them out," he continued explaining. "The bad guys. Someone who would take advantage of the city funds and allow his or her palm to be greased by those who want special treatment. If I'm in office, those guys aren't."

She'd never thought of it that way.

"Last year my sister Stefanie helped me organize a fund-raiser for adoptions for families who couldn't conceive." He tilted his head, a teasing spark in his eye. "Or can you also find something wrong with my supporting orphans, too?"

No, she really couldn't. And that was the problem. She couldn't vilify him, which meant liking him again. And liking him could lead to...

Nothing.

She would never allow her liking him to lead to anything more. The risk was too great.

"Look, we don't have to make peace with what happened between us, Mimi," he said, reading her mind, "but we do have to live together for an evening. Can we table the discussions revolving around the topics we argue about? Focus on the ones we agree upon?"

"Is there one?" She finished her wine and sent a longing look at the bottle, wrestling with the idea of sinking into the reprieve of a second glass.

"We agree on two topics so far. Pie. And wine." He tipped the bottle over her glass and poured. She admired his strong fingers and tanned skin. How could a man's hand be sexy?

Because it's attached to the rest of him.

Right. Good point.

"I'm going to start a fire," he said. "Sit up a while. The

bedroom on the top floor is where I'm staying, but feel free to take your pick of the others."

Chase left Miriam to her…whatever was going on with her, and finished stacking the firewood and kindling in the hearth.

She'd vanished down the hallway, declining his offer to carry her suitcase or show her around.

"I assume the bedrooms are the ones with beds," she'd quipped.

Once the fire was crackling, he stayed where he was on the rug, kicked off his sneakers and reached for his wine-glass. All the tableau was missing was a sleeping golden retriever sitting by his red-and-white-patterned socks.

Mimi had been gruff and short with him at the same time she'd been kind and hesitant. He could guess she would have preferred to come stomping in here and read him his rights, but she'd never been able to be truly cruel. He wondered if that's how she thought he'd treated her back when they split. *Cruelly.*

Seemed crueler to him at the time to drag her away from her family and the lake town she loved and into a world of politics and oil—both of which she'd hated then and was clearly no fonder of now.

When he'd first spotted her on the video at the gate, he hadn't believed his own eyes. And when she'd climbed from her truck while he stood in the frigid snow watching her advance, he'd made a decision then and there.

She wasn't leaving his house without fully understanding where he'd stood all those years ago. She wasn't the only one with an axe to bury.

He'd lied to her earlier when he said there were two topics they agreed upon. There was a third area where they'd excelled. In bed. Or, on the beach. In the car. He was equally sure they'd be able to navigate that particular act without fail now, and in a variety of locations.

Underneath her need to put him in his place, her high chin and straight shoulders, was the soft, warm woman who'd rested against his side. The giving, loving woman who'd opened up an entirely new world to him. Mimi wasn't a hookup—she never had been.

And maybe that'd been the problem. They'd taken each other seriously in those stolen summer months. And when her roommate was out of town, he'd stayed the weekend, allowing himself to linger in the moments between Mimi's deep, quiet breaths before the sun had come up. He'd stumbled into a rare and precious woman, and had never found a replica.

Yet it'd all been a fantasy. And like all fantasies, destined to end.

When it came time to take her home to Dallas to meet his family, she'd shrunk against him. Dallas wasn't where Mimi belonged. She belonged somewhere surrounded by leaves and streams, not concrete and steel and glass.

By the time she'd met his parents and he'd felt the turgid chill coming off his mother, the fantasy had crumbled to dust. Not only did Mimi not belong in Dallas. She didn't belong *with him*. And he'd have seen that clearly had he met her any time other than during the lakeside summer vacation. His head hadn't been on straight and Mimi... God, Mimi. She'd been lovesick. It'd nearly killed him to do what was right for her and damn his own heart.

But he had.

He was twenty-six at the time and no more able to know who he wanted to spend forever with than what corner of politics he'd end up occupying. Hell, he'd had his sights on president of the United States at one point, an office he knew now he wouldn't hold if he were the last qualified candidate on earth.

A door closing brought him back to the present before the faint sound of a shower running filled his mind's eye with Mimi's slim frame, lithe legs and pert, round breasts. The first time she'd untied the string on her bikini top and flashed him, he'd stared slack-jawed at her pale skin, lightly freckled from the sun, and known he'd do anything to have her.

He shifted from his cross-legged seat on the rug, his thoughts looping a similar track tonight. To hold that fiery, uncertain, passionate woman against him again would be…

"Wrong," he said aloud.

But as he reminded himself of that, a certain part of him stirred from dormant sleep when he pictured her beneath him. Or on top of him.

"Hell." He pinched the bridge of his nose and blew out a breath. As impossible as it would seem in this circumstance—as great as the chances of his failure were, he wanted her like he'd wanted her the first time he caught sight of her on that crowded beach ten years ago.

He hadn't been able to resist the tantalizing and confusing combination of sensitivity and strength, wrapped in a tangle of poise and chutzpah. Now that he'd gone ten years without meeting a woman who possessed even half of Mimi Andrix's attributes, he'd likely go another ten once their stint in this mansion ended.

And he wasn't the only one who'd noticed the spark between them.

When they were sharing pie, her eyes had lingered on his mouth. He'd wanted to lean forward to sample her lips and damn the consequences, but the timing had been off.

So. He'd make sure her response was favorable before he moved forward.

But yes, he decided. He was definitely moving forward.

Eight

Miriam emerged from the bathroom after her shower, hair dry since she'd washed it yesterday, her striped pajama pants paired with a Montana State University sweatshirt over a T-shirt. She opted for no bra after a bit of hesitation, but who was she kidding? It wasn't as if corralling "the girls" into a brassiere was necessary—not for her.

In stockinged feet, she shuffled out of the bedroom she'd chosen, pleased with her pick. It boasted a queen bed and was large enough for a stuffed chair by the window. A flat-screen television was mounted over the dresser, and had a private bathroom attached. It was as close to a hotel suite as she could come.

She'd climbed under the covers and flipped through TV channels, but nothing kept her mind from wandering beyond her borrowed bedroom door. She was wide awake and hyperaware that there was a man on the other side of the house.

She assumed Chase was still awake. He'd been a night owl like her that summer, but many things had changed since then. Maybe he was no longer nocturnal.

She decided to find out.

She found him sitting on the corner of the sofa, legs crossed at the ankles, frowning down at his phone. He was still dressed in a sweater and jeans, the jaunty design of his socks causing her to smile. *Not so buttoned-up after all.* The way he was lounging in front of a fire he'd built made him appear welcoming. Comfortable.

Maybe that's why she plucked her half-full wineglass from the island and sat on the love seat across from him.

He looked up when she sat, but she kept her eyes on the fire, feeling not the least bit sleepy.

"Get settled?" he asked after a prolonged beat where neither of them spoke.

"Yes. Thank you."

He rested his elbows on his knees and tossed the phone onto a wood-and-metal coffee table that was both modern and rustic.

"Do you stay up late every night or only during snowed-in vacations?" she asked.

"Are you questioning my nocturnal habits?" He let the question hang and she fought the urge to think about sex. Specifically, sex with him.

"I have no right to judge what you do at night," she said. *Or who you do.* There was an unpleasant thought—Chase sharing a bed with another woman. Not that she had any claim over him, but the thought was still unsavory.

"Yes, whatever you do, don't question my sleepless nights filled with reading biographies or complicated state plans." His lips quirked at one corner, an even split of confidence and self-deprecation. "How about you? You don't appear to miss much beauty sleep."

"I'm not much for early to bed, early to rise," she said, refusing to acknowledge his sideways compliment.

"I'm already healthy, wealthy and wise," he quipped, finishing the saying she'd started. "Why mess with perfection?"

"Oh, so you're perfect now."

"My methods. Not me."

And humble, she thought, keeping her smile hidden. With a subtle shake of her head, she sipped her wine.

"What room did you choose?"

"The smaller one near the kitchen. With the en suite."

"The one with the stone shower?"

"That's the one." Stone walls and a glass partition separated the shower from the rest of the bathroom. No rods or shower curtain rings—just a big open square with a rainfall-style shower overhead. Bliss.

"I showered in there the day I got here."

The idea of sharing a shower with him—well not *sharing*, but kinda—was a distracting thought. She drank a little more wine.

"Seemed a waste to only use the shower upstairs."

"Your room's the largest I take it?" she happily changed the subject.

"It's the largest. Has its own sitting area. Overlooks the trees, the lake. There's a fireplace in the corner. I'll show it to you later."

She would've liked to convince herself that she'd imagined the heat in his eyes at what could be an innocuous invitation, but it was there, all right. Darkening the gray-green to smoky jade and knocking her for a hell of a loop.

"I'd planned on making a fire in there and spending the weekend laid out in the giant bed."

Yes, her cheeks were most definitely aflame at the picture his words evoked. Chase in naught but a pair of low-slung sweats, sheets barely covering his naked torso…

"Now that you're here, hiding out isn't as intriguing."

"Go ahead. I can fend for myself." She cleared her throat and the image from her head. "I know that you have the makings for grilled cheese sandwiches, and a frozen pizza. I'm sure there are eggs in your fridge."

"Right on every count but one. I don't eat eggs."

"Really?" She tried to remember if she'd seen him eating an egg when they dated. "Did you ever?"

"Not really. I mostly eat smoothies with protein powder or toast with avocado slices."

She made a face. "I assume you don't have a box of Froot Loops hiding in your cabinets?"

"Grape-Nuts."

She couldn't help joining him when he laughed.

"It's to go on top of the yogurt I bought."

"Vanilla?" she asked, hopeful.

"Plain."

"You're killing me, Mayor." And with that comment the tense mood and stilted conversation eased. It hadn't taken much to get them there.

"I can't risk getting old and fat or having a heart attack like Dad." His smile faded and so did hers.

"Your father had a heart attack?"

He confirmed with a nod. "Surgery, too. He's in good health now, but it rattled me to see him in a hospital bed."

"Enough that you cut out three-cheese omelets."

"I indulge sometimes."

"I didn't accuse you of anything." She held her hands up.

"No, but you're looking at me like I'm as bland as the yogurt I mentioned."

A smile played at the corners of his mouth but there was a dash of sadness ghosting his expression. Like he cared what she thought of him.

Impossible. He was the most independent, self-assured man she'd ever known.

"I have a surprise for you," he said, standing from the couch.

"Oh? Did you lie about the Froot Loops?"

"Sorry. No." He bypassed the love seat where she sat and opened a tall cabinet on the other side of the room. On the shelves sat folded blankets, a few decorative pillows and board games. He closed the doors and turned back to her, holding a familiar oblong box.

"Monopoly?" The box appeared brand-new, though it wasn't wrapped in from-the-factory plastic.

"I was poking around while you were in the shower and found this, Risk and Battleship." He set the game on the coffee table and, after moving his wine to the side, lifted the lid of the box. "I had no idea there were games here. The house was stocked and decorated by a design team when I bought it. Wanna play?"

"Didn't you refer to that game as the 'ender of relationships'?"

"I did. But our relationship has already ended, so what's the harm?" His gaze warmed when he added, "Or maybe it'll have the opposite effect and we'll end up sharing a bed while you're here."

A startled laugh emerged from her throat. It was part *he's insane* and a sliver of *how fun does that sound?* The latter scared her more than a little.

"More wine before we start?" he asked as if he hadn't casually mentioned them sharing a bed.

"Water." No way was she drinking more alcohol tonight given the dangerous bend of her thoughts.

He returned from the kitchen with two bottles of water, sat down and raised his eyebrows. "What do you think?"

What did she think? All sorts of interesting, steamy, forbidden thoughts rolled around in her head. Chase. Hot, thirty-six-year-old Chase. With that smooth voice and slow hands—an attribute she recalled too clearly. He knew how to take his time. He'd been able to draw her to the brink of orgasm and let her linger there until she begged for release. Even at the tender age of twenty-three, she'd known that the sex was unparalleled. And when she'd ventured into dating a year later, she learned she was right. No one that she'd dated or slept with held a candle to the man sitting across from her bathed in firelight.

What tricks had he learned since then? A delicious shiver trickled down her spine.

"Scared?" he asked, mistaking her shudder of pleasure.

Terrified. Not of him but of her lack of willpower where he was concerned.

"Don't be," he continued. "I haven't played in years. You'll probably own my ass faster than I can say Marvin Gardens."

The game! Right. Not sex. She snapped the lid off her water and drank a few guzzles.

"If you're sure you can take me," she told him. "Bring it."

An hour and a half later, it was clear that she was going to lose.

Chase had monopolies with hotels on the scariest properties—not the blue ones. Park Place and Boardwalk were the obvious choices because of their price tags, but that wasn't how you won the game. No, the way to won was to buy up the yellow, orange and magenta properties so that in between the jail square and the go-to-jail square you would be fined into bankruptcy. Even owning all of the utilities and two railroads couldn't get her out of this mess.

"You're about to forfeit," he pointed out. "I can tell by the crease right there." He leaned forward and pressed the pad of his finger into the dent between her eyebrows. She slapped his hand away.

He was sitting on the couch at the long side of the coffee table and she'd sat opposite him on a big square cushion. Her dwindling pastel-colored dollars didn't inspire hope, but as far as forfeiting…

"Never." She narrowed her eyes and he grinned.

"Very well." He set the dice on the board without rolling

his turn and purchased several more houses. Then he rolled and landed on Boardwalk, a property he already owned.

Miriam was in "jail" and rolled for the third time, trying for doubles so she didn't have to pay the precious fifty-dollar fine to leave. She didn't *want* out. Not with all those plastic houses and hotels Chase had built that were waiting to empty her bank account. If she rolled two fives, she could not only get out of jail free, but rest on Free Parking for a breather. And win the money in the middle—only forty dollars, but every little bit helped.

But fate was not smiling on the less fortunate today. She landed on Tennessee Avenue, the property where Chase had just added another house.

"Game." He remained where he was, elbows on his knees and awaited her concession.

"Game," she said through her teeth.

He started filing away his money and she did the same, which took her a lot less time than it took him since she had so very little of it. By the time she was sweeping the houses off the board, she could feel the frown between her eyes deepen.

A low chuckle punctuated the air.

"What's so funny?"

"Nothing." He licked his lips as he helped organize the cards into stacks. "You're not a gracious loser, Mimi."

"No one likes to lose, *Chase*." Some of the fire went out of her voice, though. He looked genuinely relaxed and happy and it was hard not to replicate his mood. It was obvious from the faint lines between his dark eyebrows that he typically worried more than he relaxed.

Game boxed, he stood and put it away. When he paced back, he offered a hand to help her off the cushion on the floor. She accepted, his warm fingers curling around hers and making other parts of her warm, as well. Naughty, tingly parts. Oft-ignored parts.

She tugged her hand away and he tossed the square cushion she'd been sitting on onto the chair.

"Do you have everything you need for the evening?" he asked.

A jerky nod was all she could manage in response.

He lifted his hand to her cheek and brushed the back of his fingers from her jawline to her neck. His mouth pulled flat.

"I wish things wouldn't have ended so poorly between us, Mimi."

Her heart, her damned heart, dusty from being ignored for so long, thudded with regret.

"So do I," she admitted.

He gave her shoulder a gentle squeeze, his eyes on hers, his head tilted at the right angle for a kiss. Not that she should be kissing Chase Ferguson, but if he leaned in… *oh yes*, she'd kiss him. She'd kiss the life out of him if for no other reason than to learn if her lips still fit against his like they were made to.

They did. She knew it.

Instead of bending for a kiss, he returned both hands to his pockets. The heat in his eyes banked.

"There was nothing I could do at the time except wish you well."

The words stung like a rubber band snapped against her skin. They also snapped her back to reality. There was a warm fire and wine and casual, fun banter, but there was also ten years of loss and pain that separated them. A mountain that, while scalable, wasn't worth risking her heart to climb.

"Nothing you could do?" She threw his words back at him, mentally lacing up her hiking boots to climb anyway. "You put me on a plane the same day you brought me to Dallas. You didn't even offer me a place to sleep."

"Why would I have offered to take you home with me?" His expression was genuinely sincere.

"Because—" *I loved you* "—it was the decent thing to do!"

His face remained blank, his voice calm while she'd entered the lower range of yelling. "It would've been *decent* to break up with you and then invite you back to my bed? You were upset. You needed to go home where you belonged. Holding you while you cried wouldn't have eased the transition for either of us."

She wanted to scream or slap him. Or both. Instead, she welded her back teeth together and forced a breath through her nose. This was an old argument. One that couldn't be resolved then and sure as hell wouldn't be resolved if they talked about it now.

She hadn't seen Chase sending her away as *decent*. Especially after a flight where they'd made love in the private plane's cabin and he'd told her he was glad she'd come with him to Dallas. At the time she'd believed what they had was real and lasting, and she thought he'd believed that, as well.

Until dinner with his parents ended after Eleanor had made her opinion abundantly clear. Chase had dumped Miriam right there in the driveway.

The memory stung like a cloud of angry wasps...

Nine

"*My* mother's right," Chase said from the driver's side of a sleek black Porsche. Miriam was still getting used to this much finery...and getting used to learning that his family owned an oil company. Like, one of the biggies.

"Right about what?" She stopped digging through her purse for her Chapstick and regarded him.

"Right about my career. I hadn't been thinking about it this summer." He faced her, his expression tender, his voice low and filled with regret.

She felt the hard kick of her heart against her ribs and forced a smile. Reaching for his hand, she said, "She's not right. She's wrong. You're going to be an incredible politician and no one, especially Mimi Andrix from Bigfork, Montana, is going to hold you back. The public will see us together and know what we have is real. How could anyone miss it?"

Squeezing his hand, she kept the smile on her mouth but he continued to look distraught.

"I wish that was true." He pulled his hand away and wrapped his fingers around the steering wheel. "Unfortunately, the position I'm in with my parents owning one of the biggest oil conglomerates in the state, I'm not at liberty to push back on any of this. My responsibilities to them, my *interests in politics—having a say about how the people are treated in my city—matter."*

She wanted to ask him if she also mattered, but was half afraid of the answer. It was like his mother had slapped a script in his hand. This wasn't Miriam's Chase. Her Chase had stripped her out of her dress and made love to her long and slow on a private jet hurtling them toward Texas. Her Chase had lain in that same bed and told her how beautiful her body was, before placing a kiss on each part he mentioned.

"You're scaring me," she confessed.

"We can't know so soon." His lowered eyebrows communicated regret at the words coming out of his mouth—words echoed from his mother, who'd said that exact phrase at dinner. "What happens from here on out, Mimi?"

She swallowed past the lump in her throat threatening to choke her. "What do you mean?"

"Do you move here from Montana? Leave your family? Marry me? What happens when I run for governor or mayor in the future? What happens when my opponent digs up proof you experimented with pot or a girlfriend in college? Or if we find out someone has photos of the night we skinny-dipped in the lake? Or made love on the shore?" he added darkly.

"I don't care about any of that." Her voice took on a desperate quality, but she didn't care. In no way would she entertain this line of thought. What they'd shared in her hometown wasn't tawdry or dirty. It was beautiful—the start of their forever. "I care about you."

"You'll care when the press involves your parents. Your siblings. When a smear campaign starts and—"

"You're borrowing trouble, Chase. Right now, you're finishing law school. You could end up working for Ferguson Oil the rest of your life."

"And that would be okay with you?" He drilled her

*with a look that roiled her stomach. She'd never been a
fan of the corrupt oil monopolies, but neither could she
deny that she loved Chase too much to let his family ties
keep her from him.*

*"I care about you, too," he said, and she heard the un-
spoken "but" that was about to follow. "Too much to let
you go down this road." He captured her chin between
his thumb and forefinger. Hot tears rolled from her eyes
and scalded her cheeks. "Let's slow down. Think things
through."*

*"There's nothing to think about!" Her shout was shrill
in the closed interior of the car. It was September in Texas
and plenty warm. The AC blew gently against her face,
chilling the trails her tears left behind.*

*"We didn't think at all this summer," he said, gaze once
again on the windshield. "I didn't think."*

The argument had escalated from there, Chase closing
off and her growing more emotional. Before she knew what
was happening, he was on the phone with the pilot who'd
flown them in earlier that day.

"Good night, Chase," she said now, her mind on that
fated night, her voice rigid from spent grief and too many
regrets to count.

There were so many things they should've said. So
many things they *shouldn't* have said. Once, she'd considered him her everything, and now he felt as remote as
a desert island.

But none of that mattered anymore. He'd made his decision to toss what they had aside, and she'd boarded the
plane home willingly.

Memories weighing down her limbs, she trudged
to her bedroom—toward the sweet relief of an empty
mattress, and away from Chase's hurtful words—to be
alone with her heart that still mourned the loss of what
could've been.

* * *

Chase propped his hands on his hips and dropped his head back, studying the ceiling, or perhaps seeking advice from the Almighty.

"Got anything?" he asked the beamed ceilings.

No answer.

He hadn't meant to traipse down bramble-strewn memory lane. He'd meant to tell her that now that she was here, in his house, he wanted her in his bed again. He was going to follow that up with a promise that she'd never regret saying yes.

They should at least be kissing, if not half-naked, his lips wrapped around her nipple, his fingers in her underwear.

They should be exorcising the demon that had been unleashed, not arguing about why it existed at all.

Nostrils flared in frustration, he forced himself to stop thinking. He'd done too much thinking already. He followed the path Mimi had taken to her bedroom and stopped outside the door, fist raised to knock.

Before he could rap on the wooden panel, it opened. Mimi jolted in surprise. She wasn't expecting him. He lowered his hand, keeping it balled into a fist at his side.

"Hi," he said.

"Hi." She folded her arms over her small breasts. "I forgot to grab a bottle of water. I like to keep one on the nightstand." Her eyes flitted to the side, making him wonder if she was telling the truth.

"I didn't mean to hurt you back then."

He hadn't wanted to send her home. He'd selfishly wanted to take her home with him and soothe her. Stroke her hair and tell her everything would be okay. But there'd been no way to know if *anything* would be okay. There'd been no way to know she wouldn't wind up hating him for dragging her away from her life of pine trees and shorelines and into one teeming with politicians and oil tycoons.

Keeping her at his side would have been about him, and he had forced himself to think of her—of who he'd have to ask her to become if she stayed.

She'd loved him then. He'd foolishly thought she'd continue loving him through her heartbreak. Long enough for them to see how his career would shake out. Long enough for her to decide for sure if she wanted to be a part of that life.

"I hate that I hurt you, but I had to—"

"Don't. Don't say that you had to focus on your career or your business or any other multitude of things that were more important than me at the time."

His scowl hardened and not in his own defense. He had done that. But he'd done it to protect her. *For her.* Evidently she wasn't ready to hear that.

"I can take care of myself, Chase. You don't need to worry about me now. I'm a big girl, and I'm not afraid of bad publicity."

"That's because you haven't been the target of it. You don't know what they'll say about you to get to me. I'd lose the election after the press learned I was beating the hell out of anyone who verbally attacked you."

He'd expected at least a half smile in response to that, but he didn't get one.

"I agreed to leave that day. It's not like you tied me up and dragged me into the plane."

"You only agreed to leave because I asked you to." Regret wasn't a familiar feeling, but it took residence in the center of his chest now. "I pushed you away."

Her dark eyes swept up to meet his. "It would be a hell of a lot easier to blame you for everything, but the truth is…" She licked her lips before she finished. "I was starting to wonder if I was right about us or if I'd been caught up in the fantasy. I didn't want to lose you, but I didn't want to leave Montana. In the car when you were shattering me—and make no mistake, Chase, you shattered me—"

He winced, hating hearing it but knowing it was true.

"—I was courting second thoughts." She laid her palm softly against his sweater and her warmth eased the sting of her words. "I can't let you shoulder all the blame. The lion's share maybe, but not all."

Instinctively, he cupped her hand with his own. The speed of his breaths increased, his heart rate ratcheting up along with them, a thumping they could both feel.

"This is so dumb," she said, her voice barely above a whisper.

He stepped closer, his other hand wrapping around one petite shoulder. He wasn't sure if she meant that talking about their past was dumb, or considering kissing him was dumb. Either way...

He ducked his head, pleased when she lifted hers to receive the kiss he was angling toward her plush mouth. In the split second before he closed his eyes, he watched her lids sink and felt the soft tickle of her breath against his mouth.

Their lips touched, his firm and solid against hers pliant and giving. He gentled her open and stroked the tip of her tongue with his. A sigh of longing mingled with loss coated his mouth when he moved to deepen the kiss, and that was the instant Mimi pulled away.

She lowered from her toes to her heels, eyes still closed, hand still on his sweater—now bunching the material.

"Dumb," she whispered again.

"Oh, I don't know. It wasn't so bad."

That earned him the hitch of her mouth: the smile he'd been gunning for. He swept her dark hair aside, the waves silky and oh-so-touchable.

"I've been thinking of kissing you since the day I saw you at the supermarket," he said.

Her eyebrows lifted like she was amused. "That would've been awkward."

"Timing is everything." He took a breath and spoke the words he'd wanted to say all night. "I swear, Mimi. If you come to my bed tonight, you will not regret it."

His voice was low and lethal, tight with the sexual tension that had strung his balls to his spine like a cable car.

Her expression shuttered. She yanked her hand away.

Too soon.

"Hang on. That's not—" He tried to backtrack but she cut him off.

"Let's pretend that last part didn't happen."

He braced his hands on the doorframe, effectively blocking her in as he leaned close to say, "Not what I was going to say."

She ducked under his arm and walked down the hallway toward the kitchen. He turned his head, resting his cheek on one outstretched arm to watch her go. Those round hips swishing away from him, her hair bouncing halfway down her back.

Damn.

Damn.

Ten

Outside Miriam's bedroom window, snow fell as hard and fast as ever. It was a beautiful inconvenience—a minor interruption in what was an already amazing life. She had much to be thankful for. Something she'd tried to remind herself last night while she lay awake feeling complete FOMO about missing out on Black Friday shopping with her sisters.

It wasn't the shopping itself she was mourning, but the time she'd miss spending *with them*. Dining out and then grabbing lattes for dessert. Juggling the to-go cup and a plethora of shiny shopping bags while one of them dug the keys from Wendy's purse so they could find the car.

She'd tried to reach either Kristine or Wendy on their cell phones. No luck. There were probably wrestling a discount television away from a grown man at a big box store, or maybe they'd opted for an early breakfast complete with mimosas.

After sending a group text—Buy me something of high value with a low price tag!—and tossing the phone on the bed, Miriam pulled on her jeans and layered a few long-sleeved shirts for warmth.

The house was cozy. The bed was a dream. She'd slept great once she'd finally fallen asleep.

When she'd returned to her room with the water bottle, Chase had no longer been looming at her doorway looking sexy and slightly rumpled and thoroughly kissed. He'd gone upstairs, she'd assumed. The house was large enough he could've been literally anywhere save the room she'd just come from. He hadn't said goodnight.

She'd lain in her bed and wondered if he was in his own bedroom reliving the smoldering lip-lock they'd shared in the doorway. If he still tasted her on his tongue the way she tasted him on hers. If he was considering coming back downstairs to sample her mouth again...

But he hadn't.

And now that she was awake and en route to the coffee maker, she tried to convince herself she was glad he hadn't come downstairs to finish what he'd started. Relaying those thoughts to her heart was easy. Getting them past her raging hormones and that irritating fluttering at the V of her thighs was another matter altogether.

It'd been a while since she'd had sex. It'd been even longer since she'd had really *good* sex. It made sense that the physical reactions in her body were shouting *Hell yes*! Her nipples had hardened and pressed against the T-shirt she slept in, begging for attention. She'd resisted the urge to relieve that pounding pulse between her legs herself, balling her fists in the blankets and squeezing her eyes shut. She thought about camp budgets and depleting rain forests and other unpleasant topics, but no matter how she'd tried to distract herself, memories of Chase—from last night and ten years ago—led the pack.

It was simply *him*. He had commanded her full attention since the first time she laid eyes on him. There was a pull surrounding him and whenever she was in his atmosphere she couldn't keep from being drawn in.

"As evidenced by my ending up snowed in here," she said to herself. What other than the idea of Chase Ferguson alone on Thanksgiving would have convinced her to come out in a snowstorm?

She paced to the kitchen, located the coffee and made herself a single-cup serving. After only three hours of sleep, she needed it. No sign of her housemate yet, but she could guess he hadn't slept well either.

She opted to give herself a tour of the house while sipping her coffee. She started with the main floor, most of which she'd familiarized herself with last night. The living room where they'd played Monopoly, the kitchen where Chase had heated his delivered dinner, and of course, her bedroom.

She'd had a peek at the other larger bedrooms dotting the halls when looking for her own, and took another gander now to be sure she was happy with her choice. She was. She'd chosen the smaller room because it was close to the kitchen and because it had a bathroom attached. Her idea had been to hide out until the storm blew over—the literal snowstorm and the one brewing between her and Chase. A cowardly plan. There was no escaping the blizzard just as there was no avoiding what had happened last night.

Upstairs she found a sitting area surrounded by bookshelves. A chessboard stood on a side table with two straight-backed chairs. She could imagine Chase hunched there, a wrinkle of consideration on his forehead, his fingers resting against his mouth while he thought of his next move. The room suited him, but the shelves on the walls—with a few generic leather-bound books and a random vase or decorative bowl taking up the empty space—appeared more what his decorator had deemed appropriate and less what Chase would've chosen for himself.

The library's window, pointed at the top to match the pitch of the roof and as wide as the room itself, looked over the deck at the back of the house and the snow-covered lake beyond. Natural light flooded in, but even the sun felt cold, too far away to melt the ice clouding the glass. In a pair of comfy sneakers, she stepped silently across the shining hardwood floors. A doorway beckoned her, the edge of Chase's bed in plain view, his own sneakers standing at the foot of that bed.

Light choked this space, streaming in from more floor-to-ceiling windows where the bed faced. His comforter had been thrown over the bed in a half-assed attempt at making it, two pillows stacked on one side. Jeans and a button-down shirt were draped over the bed like he'd been about to put them on but decided against it.

Where is he?

She stepped deeper into the room and ran her hand over the cream-and-dark-blue quilt, her fingers grazing the sleeve of his shirt. She could picture him here. Last night. Right now…

"Having regrets about what room you chose to sleep in last night?" a voice asked from behind her. She placed her hand over her heart in an attempt to slow its speeding rhythm.

"You startled me," she said breathlessly.

Facing him didn't help her catch her breath. He was shirtless, barefoot and water rolled in rivulets down his naked chest. He held a royal blue towel over his hips, grasped with one hand.

"You're wet," were the only words she could think to say. The only two words that eked from her suddenly parched throat. The only appropriate words she could've said out loud—and even those didn't sound appropriate. Her eyes feasted on the dark hair whirling on his chest, the trail of it leading down his flat belly and disappearing into the terry cloth around his hips.

Yeah, there were no words.

"I went for a swim. Finished it off with ten minutes in

the hot tub." He stepped into the room with her and she felt the steam coming from his damp skin. "You should try it."

He ripped off the towel to expose he was wearing absolutely nothing at all. She jerked her eyes away and tried desperately not to replay the vision of the inviting appendage hanging temptingly between his legs.

Chase strolled toward his attached bathroom, not the least bit shy as he dried his arms and chest and his bare ass. She didn't mean to stare. It just…sort of happened on its own.

He had a round, firm butt leading to thick thighs that planed up to a defined, muscular back. His shoulders were strong, his traps defined…

He continued dressing, talking to her as if putting on clothes in front of an audience was a regular occurrence.

"I checked the weather this morning." He snapped the waistband of his boxer briefs and then tugged a T-shirt over his fabulous chest. "We're expecting another six to eight inches today." She didn't mean to look down when he said that, but she did and he noticed.

With a grin, he continued, "Another four to five inches tomorrow and possibly another two to three the day after that."

Covered in jeans and a T-shirt, he wasn't any less tempting than three seconds ago. He slipped his arms through a blue button-down a shade lighter than the towel he'd discarded on the floor. And now that her brain was working again…

"When do they expect to dig us out?" she was able to ask.

"There's no talk of digging anyone out, but there's an emergency service hotline if anyone is without heat or food. Both of which we have at the moment. The problem occurs when the snow becomes too heavy for the power lines."

"But you have a generator." She didn't bother putting a

question mark on the end of that sentence—the alternative sounded too unpleasant.

"It's on the fritz." He finished buttoning his shirt. He left the top two buttons undone like she remembered. "We have fireplaces all over the house. We won't freeze."

"I can take a look at it."

His face flinched into an expression of disbelief. "I took a look at it yesterday. The gas tank's full, but it won't kick on."

"Yes, but I know how to repair a generator. Do you?" She propped one hand on her hip and sipped her coffee, letting that new detail sink in.

"Not particularly."

"I've repaired one before. And don't make a joke and ask if I brought my pink toolbox."

"Hopefully it won't come to that." He sat to pull on his socks and slipped his feet into shoes he didn't have to tie. "Again, I'm tempted to ask who the hell you've been dating. I'd never ask you if you have a pink toolbox. You hate pink."

He remembered, and that made her smile.

When he stood, he stepped closer to her, smelling woodsy and fresh rather than like chlorine. He looked as delicious wearing clothes as he did out of them. Unbelievable.

"May I?" He held out a hand for her coffee mug and she gave it to him. He took a sip, swallowed and closed his eyes to let out a soft "ahh" before handing her mug back. "I swam before I indulged. That tastes incredible."

She bet he did, too.

See? It was thoughts like that she needed to eradicate. Neither should she swoon because he'd remembered she hated pink.

"Um. Sorry to intrude," she said belatedly. "I wanted to check out the rest of the house."

"No intrusion." His voice slipped into a seductive husk

that she'd started accepting was simply his normal speaking voice. "You're always welcome in my bedroom."

"Very funny, Mr. Mayor." She forced a droll tone.

"Can't blame me for trying." He smiled, his gaze fastened to hers and for a moment she wanted to say to hell with dancing around each other. She wanted to suggest they rid themselves of any restrictive, unnecessary clothing and make love on his massive bed while the snow fell and the wind howled. They could spend the rest of the day—*the week*—buried under thick quilts and silky sheets, leaving the room for food or drink. And only then to restore their spent energy so they could twist up the bedding again. Instead, she said nothing.

"The coffee is tempting. You're even more so." He drew her chin up with a knuckle and she got lost in the greys and greens of his irises. "But if I can't have one, I'll take the other."

Eleven

"Grilled cheese isn't the same without a ripe, red tomato." Chase turned with a plate of grilled cheese sandwiches—three of them. They were toasted to golden, gooey perfection, and Miriam's mouth watered. "Especially if it's from Texas."

"You brought tomatoes from Dallas?"

Red fruit in hand, he gestured to her with it. "I wasn't sure I could trust Bigfork's produce department." He set the tomato on a cutting board and cut it into thick slices. "Couldn't risk it."

"What happened to your accent?"

"Accent?"

"Yes," she said with a dose of sarcasm, "you know, the one you were taught in the great state of Texas."

"You prefer it?"

"No," she lied. "Just curious."

He flashed her a brief smile, one that made her wiggle in the seat she'd taken at the island.

"Well, darlin', if you want me to lay it on thick for you I can do that." He gave her a wink. "Real thick."

Rapt, Miriam twirled her hair around her finger, her other elbow resting on the island's countertop. The second she noticed she was doing it she folded her hands in front of her.

She shouldn't prefer his accent. It reminded her of being young and carefree and…stupid.

Stupid is the word you're looking for.

"Voice coaches," he said in an accent-free timbre. "Years of them. It creeps in every once in a while, when I let my guard down."

Something he rarely did, she imagined. Everything Chase did seemed intentional.

Coming here. His career. Dumping her.

"No tomato on my grilled cheese sandwich. I'm a purist. Just cheese."

He'd made the sandwiches with reckless abandon; three types of cheese oozed onto the plate from the center of the diagonally cut stacks.

"You don't like tomatoes?" He put a few thick slabs in between the bread of his own sandwich.

"I do—I just don't want them on my grilled cheese."

"Suit yourself."

"Do you have any pickles?"

"Sadly no. It's tomatoes or bust. I thought you were a purist."

She picked up a triangle. "There's nothing purer than a pickle on a grilled cheese sandwich."

If the crunch of the toasted bread wasn't enough to send her into blissful abandon, the gooey, stringy cheese would've done it.

Chase lifted a half and took a bite. After he was done chewing he continued. "Damn. That is good. But no more moaning from you unless I elicit that response."

Her mouth was full so she had to finish chewing and sip her water before she responded.

"Okay. I feel like we have to talk about the kiss." She dusted her fingers onto a paper napkin.

"Okay." He continued eating, gesturing for her to go ahead.

"You can't kiss me and expect me to reciprocate."

"You *did* reciprocate."

"Going forward." She karate chopped the air in front of her. "You can't kiss me going forward."

"That's entirely up to you. But you can't stop me from trying to seduce you."

Shock unhinged her mouth. He was trying to seduce her?

"Are you trying to seduce me?"

"Do you think I trot out my famous grilled cheese for any woman? No, ma'am," he said, his accent creeping in. "Only one who is willing to tromp through Bigfork's worst snowstorm in a decade to bring me pie." He picked up the other half of his sandwich.

"I'm being serious."

"All right." In a blink, he'd dialed down the charm and upped the intensity. "Let's be serious."

He polished off that half in three big bites, took his time chewing and swiped his mouth with a napkin. Once he'd swallowed a generous amount of water, he flattened his hands on the island where he stood across from her and leveled her with a look.

Miriam was beginning to panic and had no idea where to settle her gaze. On him wasn't safe, but was by far the most appealing.

"You came here for a reason," he said. "What was it?"

"I told you. To set you straight. And, as you concluded, to make sure you ate a decent Thanksgiving dinner."

"What's under that, Mimi?" His tone was serious, his expression patient. "What is this?"

He gestured between the two of them and she could only assume that by *this* he meant the thrumming sexual attraction saturating the air. Since the kiss last night *that* had picked up where it'd left off years ago.

He offered her another half of a grilled cheese. She accepted, but didn't take a bite.

"Okay, fine," she admitted. "Yes, there's something here. But nothing we can act on."

"Why not?"

"Um, in case you don't recall, we failed miserably the first time."

"We won't make the same mistakes this time around. We're older and wiser. I have no accent now. Totally new experience."

Now, see? When he did that she wanted to argue that she wasn't interested in a second "time around" and assure him as much as herself that she didn't want to reexperience him...

But while her head was absolutely clear on that direction, her body was melting into a puddle. Chase was an experience—a fantastic one if memory served. And *fantastic* hadn't been an adjective she'd used to describe anyone who had graced her bedsheets since the man standing across from her.

"Whatever you say, Mr. Mayor." She laced her words with sarcasm and offered a laugh.

Then she took another bite—a big one—so that she wouldn't have to give him an answer.

Mimi was putting up a good front, Chase would give her that.

Reading people was a talent he'd honed. It's what made him a great politician. And since he knew how to read people, he could tell that as much as Ms. Andrix was protesting this truckload of sexual attraction, she also wanted to test the boundaries between them.

Last night her body had responded to his when he'd kissed her. She'd held on to him like he was the only thing keeping her from floating off the ground. But he had to be careful in his approach. Schmoozing her wouldn't work, and neither would plying her with wine to lower her inhibitions. Inhibitions weren't her problem—she'd been plenty bold with him before.

She was nothing like the women who'd been in and out of his life over the past several years. Mimi had never been impressed with his money or his status. If anything, those were in his *con* column. No, when it came to her, his only choice for getting to the yes they both wanted was brash, flat-out honesty. That, he could do.

"The sex would be good," he told her. "Probably great but I couldn't commit to that adjective until after." He grabbed a bag of potato chips from the pantry, giving her a moment to absorb what he'd said. When he turned back, her eyes were wide with amusement.

"Is that so?" Done eating, she sagged on the barstool and folded her arms over her chest.

"I'm not playing with you, Mimi. It's not my style. I'm letting you know where I stand. If you change your mind about having sex with me, let me know. I'll have you out of those tight jeans and into my arms before your next breath. Either you'll give me the opportunity to show you how serious I am about making you feel incredible, or you'll refuse me until it stops snowing." He looked to the window where it appeared it would never stop snowing. "Those snowflakes are the sand in our hourglass. Eventually, they'll stop falling and then our time will be up."

"I'm aware of what our time being up feels like." Her expression was not one of hurt, but resolve. It was no surprise that she'd be cautious where he was concerned, a fact he'd overlooked until just this second.

"Guess when I implied you'd been dating some real winners, I didn't factor in myself, did I?"

Some of the fire swept out of her and her mouth lifted on one side. "That was a long time ago."

"You wear your heart on your sleeve. You always have. Meanwhile, I keep mine in a cage locked in a vault at the bottom of a dormant volcano."

That brought forth a closed-mouth smile but he felt pride knowing she was fighting a grin.

"I'm sorry."

Her smile swept away. "Don't…"

"I'm sorry I hurt you and put you on a plane to Montana ten years ago. It was all so…"

"Juvenile."

"No," he argued, meaning it. "Yes, we were young, but what we had wasn't meaningless. And it wasn't juvenile." He raised an eyebrow. "Pursuing you now isn't about my being an opportunist or checking off some bizarre sex bucket list. It's about you. And me. And what we could make of our time together."

"Scratch an itch?"

"Why not?"

"So, what is this conversation? A negotiation?" She smoothed her hands along the countertop in front of her. "Where's my contract?"

"It's an offer. Plain and simple." He lifted the plate where the last half of a sandwich sat. "More?"

"I couldn't. Thanks, though." A gap of silence followed. Chase lifted the sandwich half at the same time Mimi stood and backed away from the island.

"I'm going to turn in."

"At eight o'clock?"

"Yes." Her smile was tight. "Thanks for dinner."

"Sure."

She grabbed her water bottle and walked away, and every step had him growing more and more confused. Had he completely misjudged her interest? Had he said the wrong thing—the wrong *everything*? He'd gone into this day sure of his ability to convince her. Especially after she'd hungrily eaten him up with her eyes this morning.

His instincts pushed him to go after her, but he rooted his feet to the ground. Ten years ago, he'd worn her like a second skin day and night. She'd responded to his every touch and kiss by igniting in his arms. Pretending they could pick up where they left off wouldn't work.

He uncorked a fresh bottle of wine and poured himself a glass. He wasn't giving up, but it was time to change his strategy. She needed space, but he needed her.

They'd have to meet in the middle.

His eyes went to the snow—falling and filling in the gaps where he'd shoveled the deck this afternoon. He'd take as much time as Mother Nature would give him.

"Keep 'em comin'," he said to the wintry white sky.

Twelve

Miriam awoke to a scraping sound, which she'd grown accustomed to over the many winters she'd spent in living in Montana. It was the sound of a shovel sliding over concrete and sweeping the snow aside. She stretched her arms overhead and let out a shudder from the chill in the room. It was a touch colder in here than it'd been yesterday.

Last night she'd retreated to her room to think—or *not* to think, as it turned out. She'd pulled out her iPad and watched YouTube videos about yoga and how to truss a turkey. She'd watched makeup tutorials and learned how to build a "capsule wardrobe." She'd checked her social media and used her meditation app and played a colorful puzzle game on her iPhone. None of those distractions took her mind off Chase.

Or how she'd walked away last night when what she'd wanted to do was say not just yes, but *hell yes* to his offer. He'd told her the truth about what he wanted, and she hadn't been brave enough to do the same for him.

"When did you become such a coward?" It wasn't like she could hide from him the entire time she was here.

She peeked through the curtains and saw that Chase did indeed own boots. He was wearing a pair, and hunks of snow covered his knit hat and black coat. He hefted another heavy shovel load and stopped to take a breather. How long had he been out there?

He looked cold, his face red from windburn, and the snow wasn't slowing. The area he'd cleared was already filling in with fresh flakes.

Well. She wasn't going to stay ensconced in her bedroom like a princess in a castle. She wasn't afraid of hard work. She layered a pair of yoga pants under her jeans and slipped her feet into two pairs of socks before pulling on her boots. By the time she buttoned her coat and stepped into the garage—after first *finding* the door to the garage in the massive house—she blinked in surprise at what she saw.

Not at Chase's new SUV, which he'd purchased after landing in Bigfork, but by what sat next to it. Her truck. He'd found her keys and then shoveled her out before parking her truck in a spot next to his. She skirted a puddle of melted snow, in search of a shovel to help him in his endeavors, kicking a gas can on the way. She nudged it with her boot. Empty.

He'd filled her tank.

She shut the cabinet and punched the button for the garage door, watching as it rolled up and revealed first a pair of tied boots, then snow-covered jeans and then his long wool coat. When the door sat at the top of its hinges, the rest of Chase was revealed—his breath visible from parted lips, a knit hat pulled snugly over his ears, snowflakes nestled in his thick lashes... Just the sexiest man alive.

"What are you doing?" she asked. "Shouldn't you be packing all that snow against the door to keep me here?"

He grinned, a puff of steam escaping his mouth. She joined him outside, the air blasting her face shockingly cold compared to the much warmer garage. The air iced her lungs, but she couldn't help admiring the view. She walked across the mostly cleared driveway, stopping short of the three feet of snow lining the edge to look out beyond the lake. Sturdy green pines were coated in snow, their limbs drooping from the weight. The lake was frozen—at least on the surface, and a gust of wind swirled the snow over it.

"Beautiful," she sighed.

"Gorgeous." Chase agreed, but when she looked back at him, his hand was resting on the shovel's handle, his eyes were unmistakably on her.

He broke the tender moment with, "I forgot how cold it is up here. Remind me to visit in the summer next time."

"You filled up my truck. You're clearing the driveway. Trying to get rid of me?"

"You know that's not true."

"I came out to help."

"I'm almost done."

"You should go in. The cold has a way of creeping up on you out here. You're not used to it." She slipped one glove off and touched his face. It was like the chilly air was embedded in his cheek. "You're freezing, Chase. Come inside and warm up."

Sensuality crept into her voice without her permission. She let the offer dangle while he watched her carefully.

"Will you build a fire for me?" she asked.

"Am I to believe that you, the wilderness woman, can't build a fire for yourself?"

"I can build a fire better than you can," she said, pulling her glove back on. "But I want you to do it for me. It'll help you warm up."

Without waiting for his answer, she turned and strolled through the garage, around their cars and back inside. To her everlasting satisfaction, he didn't stay outside to prove he could shovel the driveway. He followed her in.

Well, this is new.

Much as he hated to leave a task incomplete, he couldn't

resist following Mimi inside for a couple of reasons. First off, she was right, he needed to warm up. He'd been out there so long his fingers were stiff and his legs felt like popsicles.

She hung her coat and tugged off her gloves. "I suggest you slip into something warmer before making that fire."

Like you? He kept that question to himself. What do you know? He was getting wiser.

"I'm going to change." She started down the hallway before pausing to ask, "How did you find my truck keys?"

"They were in your coat pocket." He gestured to the living room. "Now they're on the coffee table."

She uttered a noncommittal "Hmm" and then disappeared to "change" even though he thought she looked fine.

Ten minutes later, he was downstairs wearing a sweatshirt and running pants, his legs still so cold that the newfound warmth was almost painful.

"Coffee or tea?" Mimi called from the kitchen.

"Both. Either. Add some antifreeze." He knelt in front of the hearth, looking over his shoulder to catch her laugh, but she was facing away from him. A pair of tight skin-hugging pants rounded her bottom. He promptly forgot about building a fire. No need now that there was one flaming to life in his pants. Damn, she looked good. Those subtle curves more pronounced thanks to the stretchy material. He watched her backside while she reached for mugs and bent for spoons.

When she hid that fine ass behind the kitchen island, he went back to his work. Which was…what again? Oh, right. Making a fire.

"Coffee," she said when he'd bent to light the twisted newspaper. He accepted the mug and watched as flames licked along the bottom of the wood.

"Not bad." She reached in and adjusted a log. He snatched her hand away.

"Don't put your hand in there. It's on fire."

"It's not going to catch unless you allow some air between those logs. Fire needs air. Your stack resembles a log cabin. It'd be lucky to see a faint draft."

"Very funny." He handed her the wrought iron fire poker. "Use this. I happen to like your fingers attached to your body."

She slid him a foxy little glare and he got out of her way. Her butt shook as she poked and prodded his handiwork. That sexy wiggle made him want to beg for mercy—or relief that could only come from her naked and lying against him.

"There you go." The fire was high and bright when she turned to face him. "I'll make a mountain man out of you yet."

"Sorry, honey. I'm a Texan first and foremost. But good luck with that." She moved to stand and he stayed her with one palm. "Stay put."

He pulled a folded blanket from the cabinet and tossed it to her. She spread it out on the rug in front of the fireplace and arranged a few pillows from the neighboring love seat on the floor.

He sat next to her and handed her a coffee mug, keeping his own in hand.

"Thawing out yet?" she asked, lifting her steaming mug to her lips.

"Finally." His eyes slid down her long legs, folded to one side. "I like those pants."

Her eyes widened, her lashes fluttering a few times.

"A lot." He punctuated that comment with a nod.

She threw her head back and laughed for a solid three seconds before sobering on a hum and sipping her coffee.

"Only you, Chase Ferguson."

"Only me what?"

"The consensus by most men is that a rail-thin brunette

with dark eyes, sticks for legs and a practically nonexistent chest does *not* a pin-up girl make. Yet you look at me like…" She shook her head, seemingly at a loss for words.

"Like what?"

Her cheeks went rosy and her throat worked when she swallowed. "Like you used to."

She ducked her head, but no way in hell was he letting her ignore what was roaring between them. Not again. Not after she'd come outside to pull him in from of the cold.

"Like I know your calves lead from delicate ankles to the crooks of the sexiest knees I've ever laid my lips on?"

She remained silent, but her top teeth scraped her bottom lip. For a change, she didn't have a salty quip or sharp-tongued argument.

"Like I know your hair feels like silk, and every time you pull your fingers through the strands I remember what it felt like brushing against my thighs?"

Her fingers tightened around her mug and those big brown eyes kept on staring.

"Like I know flecks of green hide in your dark irises like bursts of light?" He set his mug on the coffee table and took hers from her now trembling hands. "I know that because I remember exactly what it was like to be nose to nose with you, Mimi. I remember what it felt like with your breath coasting over my lips, your eyes open and drilling into mine while I sank deep inside you."

He scooted closer, hearing her hectic intake of breath and practically feeling the pulse jumping at the side of her neck.

"Don't get me started on your mouth." His voice was a lust-soaked rasp. "Your lips were made for kissing."

Before he could say more, those kissable lips crashed into his.

He caught the back of her head with one hand, bracing himself with the other to keep them from toppling over. An instinct. If he'd had one millisecond to reason, he'd have laid on his back and pulled her on top of him.

Her lips slid over his, the tentative push of her tongue testing his willingness to open his mouth to hers.

Willing and able, sweetheart.

Thirteen

No memories came crashing back to her. There was only the present, only the way Chase's fingers felt cradling the back of her head. Only the way his rough jaw scraped her sensitive skin as he angled his mouth and kissed her deeply.

His tongue tasted of coffee and something else—something basal and carnal and undefinable. It was *him*. And every womanly part of her reacted without her brain's permission.

His fingers left her head and rested on her nape, his thumb stroking her jawline as his tongue plundered her mouth. High, desperate sounds of longing infiltrated the space between them and at first she didn't recognize her own voice.

It'd been a while since someone had kissed her with such...ownership. No, not ownership. *Familiarity*.

He knew her body. He wasn't lying about that. She'd thought ten years had dampened memories of what it was like to be held by him, but now that she was in his arms it was like no time had passed.

He moved his wide palms until they wrapped around her ribs. Heating the material of her shirt and then burning right through it.

"Chase."

He didn't respond, kissing her as he slid his hands south, fumbling with the edge of her sweatshirt and the T-shirt under it.

"Chase."

"Hush," he said at the same time he found her bare skin. She caught his face between her hands and met his eyes. Smoky green eyes filled to the brim with heat. Lust for her. This gorgeous man wanted her. She was insane for pretending she didn't want him right back.

"Do you—"

"Don't talk. No talking." He didn't give her a chance to, either. He lifted her sweatshirt and stripped it over her head, mildly perplexed to find another shirt in its place. When he reached for her T-shirt, she grabbed the edge and held it down.

"I don't remember you hurrying before."

"There are too many things I want to do to you and not enough snow falling to guarantee you will stay long enough for me to do them." He canted one eyebrow and regarded her with seriousness.

She decided to shut up and kiss him instead of having this conversation. It was best they didn't think too much about what they were doing. It'd been a long time since she'd been caught up in the rush of physical attraction. It was futile to resist him. She'd sought him out this morning and it had little to do with helping him shovel snow. She didn't like him being far away—she liked him close. Really close.

Skin to skin.

He molded his hands around her breasts, still encased in her bra and let out a low growl of approval. "Missed these."

It wasn't a *missed you* but close enough. She reached behind her back to unhook her bra strap. When the cups sagged, his eyes grew dark and hungry. She was in awe now like she'd been the first time she'd been naked in front of him. Amazed that this stunning specimen was so eager to make her his.

"Take it off."

She obeyed his command, letting the straps fall and reveal her breasts. He wasted no time leaning forward to capture one nipple on his tongue, his thumb sweeping over the other as he pressed his weight against her. Sensitive nerve endings shot pleasure down her arms and southerly. She fell back onto the blanket, his lips and tongue working their magic.

"You planned this," she panted, her hands raking into his hair. "That's why you gave me the blanket."

"Couches are for making out," he let her nipple go to say. "You and I have more room down here and we're doing more than making out."

She clucked her tongue at his assumption, but then he lowered his head again and she forgot about taking him to task. Her hands buried in his thick, dark hair, she savored the tug of his lips as sparks danced between her legs.

He swept his mouth to the other breast at the same time his hands fisted the waistband of her yoga pants and tugged.

"Chase." Her moan was a frail breath, mingling with the sound of the crackling fire and her lost intentions.

He wrestled the stretchy material from her legs, socks with them, and then he began to strip himself.

Shoes went first, then his shirt. Then he shucked his pants and tore off his socks. She sat up on her elbows to watch the show. His quick, efficient movements revealing every inch of the man she was literally aching to look at.

He'd been leaner back then. He was still lean, but the muscles cording his arms and neck were heavier than she remembered. His chest was rounded—and her mouth went dry as she studied the hair swirling over his skin and marching a path down, down…

He climbed to his knees and her eyes went straight for

the promise of what was to come. His cock hung heavy, erect, and she swallowed. That hadn't changed a bit—that part of him had always been impressive. Able to render her a boneless mass in record time while she called his name on a loud, sated shout.

"You remember," he growled, on his hands and knees over her. "I can see it." His lips brushed against hers. "You want me. Admit it."

It took her a moment to detach her very dry tongue from the roof of her mouth, but when she did she managed, "Egomaniac."

A deep, rough chuckle resonated against her chest. He pressed his lips to her shoulder for a kiss that was a promise of sinful things to come.

Her if she was lucky.

And with Chase, she'd always gotten lucky.

"Lie back," he said. "I have to taste that honey."

Her knees locked together, thighs squirming at his brazen offer. When she didn't obey right away, he turned his head gave her a serious side-eye, letting her know that complying was the only option.

She obeyed and he was over her instantly, lifting her head and sweeping aside her hair to place a pillow under her head.

"Keep in mind—" he paused to kiss her "—with your thighs locked around my head, I won't be able to hear as well." He kissed her again. "So, speak up. I don't want to miss a thing."

He took his time descending, kissing her collarbone, tonguing her nipples, flattening his palm on her belly. When he slipped his fingers along her damp folds, she nearly shot off the floor.

"Sensitive. I like that," he praised.

He lifted her right leg and she looked down at him hovering there, his lips pressing her inner thigh. He looked good there. Like he *belonged* there. He'd always fit her in every way—heart and soul, body and mind.

Was it any wonder she'd followed him to Dallas? She'd have followed him to the ends of the earth if he'd asked.

Those thoughts were zapped from her head the moment his mouth hit her sweet spot. She arched, heat blooming in her stomach and stretching out to numb her every limb. Chase was bathed in firelight, the orange glow hugging the contours of his perfect body.

He went down on her, moving like a feral animal and devouring her like a second Thanksgiving feast. It was at once erotic and beautiful. Her nipples peaked and she reached for them, tenderly squeezing the buds and writhing in innate pleasure.

When Chase drew a cry of satisfaction from her lungs she didn't want him to ever stop. Her greedy body ached for another powerful release, but he didn't give her one, instead rising from the cradle of her thighs.

"So good," she said on a weak breath.

"I agree." He climbed her body, pressing his erection into the crook of her thigh. He nipped her earlobe. "You're delicious."

He nudged her again.

"Please," she begged, wrapping her ankles around him and pulling forward with all the strength she could muster. She was shameless. Absolutely shameless. Before she could get lost in the fullness of having him seated deep, her dormant brain kicked into gear. "Oh, God, Chase."

"I know, honey."

She almost laughed at the desperation in his voice. She grasped his face and forced his gaze to meet hers. "Tell me you have condoms."

The heat in his eyes banked as reality took a hard hold. Then his eyes sank closed and he muttered a devastating, "Shit."

"No." It was a weak plea to the otherwise cruel universe. How dare fate bring him to her and strand her in his house only to leave them moments shy of intense sexual satisfaction?

"Wait." His eyes flew open. "I had this house stocked before I came here. *Fully* stocked."

"Yes. I saw a bottle of Windex in the garage," she said, clinging to any scrap of hope that whoever thought to buy a bottle of Windex had also tucked a box of condoms into one of the medicine cabinets. It was a thin argument, but she'd take it. "Tell me they thought of everything."

He said nothing. She lost the warmth of his body a fraction of a second later when he stood.

"I'll help you look." She sat up.

"Don't move. I mean it." The shake in his arm when he pointed was almost comical. Almost. She wasn't laughing. She was too worried about there not being condoms in the house.

Please, God. Do me this one favor.

Before she could rationalize for or against praying for condoms, Chase stuffed his legs into his jeans and set off on a search of the house.

Fourteen

"Eureka." Chase had checked three of the four bathrooms before hitting pay dirt in the one near the downstairs bar. Good thing, too. He was freezing, which wasn't helping the situation due south.

Foil wrapper in hand, he started up the stairs before he thought better of it, turned back and grabbed the entire box. He'd need to keep these close for what he planned to do with Mimi tonight.

His feet like ice, he jogged upstairs and prayed she hadn't changed her mind. If she had, he wasn't above begging. He arrived in the living room and found her resting on her side, hand propping up her head, blanket covering her lower half. She'd waited like he told her. Triumph swelled in his chest.

Her dark hair flowed in waves over her back, a back he had full view of since she wasn't facing him. His eyes traced her smooth skin, all of him vibrating to life in an instant. He wasn't cold any longer.

"Found 'em." He tossed the box of condoms onto the coffee table, keeping one within reach. She peeked over her shoulder and smiled, a drop-dead gorgeous still-frame he wouldn't soon forget.

He hastily undid his jeans and pushed them halfway

down his legs. She rolled to her back, letting the blanket fall to the side, and revealed her small, perfect breasts. They'd tasted as good as she looked and he hadn't yet had his fill of those rosebuds.

"I was afraid you'd lose interest," she teased, a sparkle in her eye.

"That's my line," he teased back.

"I'll do the honors, Mr. Mayor." She swiped the condom packet from the table and tore it open with her teeth. His erection gave a happy bob. "But first…" She sat up on her knees, eye-to-eye with his…

Sweet mercy.

She took him in her mouth, softening her lips and opening wide to accommodate his girth. His hips tilted and thrust and she encouraged each pump by holding on to his thighs as she dove in again and again. One hand resting on the back of her head, he let out a harsh gust of air. His mind melted into a glob of indistinct thoughts for… he didn't know how long. When she finally robbed him of her mouth, he was hard as granite, his fingers tightly wound in her hair.

"God Almighty," he murmured—comically breathless.

Her eyes turned up to him, she licked her lips and took her time rolling the condom down his length.

"Where do you want me?" she purred.

He didn't hesitate. "Stand up."

She stood, her long, slim figure and subtle curves gliding along a narrow frame. He grasped her biceps and gave her a light squeeze.

"You've been working out."

"If you call working outdoors working out." She lifted her hands to his bare biceps. "Let me guess. From a gym?"

"And a personal trainer."

"Worth it. You're sexier than you used to be." She let out a soft laugh. He intended to show her exactly how much sexier he'd become by breaking her down, orgasm by orgasm, in a feat of animal, carnal lovemaking.

He cupped her nape and tilted her face, bending to kiss her lips. The kiss started tentatively but finished deep—their tongues tangling. Panted breaths burst from her lips as she rubbed her lithe, naked body against his.

His hips surged forward, his brains scrambling.

This woman.

No one unraveled him like she did.

He bent and lifted her until her legs wrapped around his hips, and then pressed her back to the nearest wall. She shrieked on contact.

"Cold!" Her nipples pebbled as goose bumps sprang to the surface of her skin. He bent and took a breast to task at the same time he positioned himself at her entrance and drove deep.

Her shriek of annoyance from the cold wall faded into a long moan of pleasure. One that he rode into the next thrust and the one after that.

Arms around his neck, she clawed at his shoulders, bucked in response to his driving need. He buried himself not only in her body but in her scent, the soft strands of her hair sticking to his five o'clock shadow. Her blunt nails leaving marks on his skin.

"Come for me, honey," he said between labored breaths.

"Chase."

"I have you. I won't let you go." By that he meant he was supporting her and wouldn't let her fall, but the second it was out of his mouth it was obvious that where they were concerned, it had another meaning.

He'd said something similar to her ten years ago before he brought her home to Dallas.

I won't let you go.

He had, though. And now he'd been given a second

chance, but he wouldn't make that promise again—he couldn't afford to break it again.

He tilted her hips and plunged into her again. She dropped her head back, her hair a messy tornado spread over the wall, her shoulders pressed flat, perky breasts begging for attention.

Attention he gave them.

It wasn't an easy move, but he managed thanks to his height. And it was that very move that sent her over, tumbling her into orgasm as she screamed his name with wild abandon.

Over and over she called, "Chase. Chase. Chase!" until his name faded into a contented sigh. Once she spent herself riding him, he allowed himself to let go of his own release, spilling inside her as his mind went blissfully blank.

Nothing mattered—not the past or the future—apart from the woman in his arms.

Miriam's limbs tingled like she'd been plugged into an outlet. Chase had her pinned to the wall, his forehead resting on her shoulder as his powerful back expanded with each ragged breath he took.

She was still impaled on him, loving the feel of him inside of her, his woodsy scent surrounding her. Loving his reaction when she'd taken him into her mouth before they'd started. His legs had shaken under her hands. The way she'd shaken when he took her against the wall.

I have you. I won't let you go.

She squeezed her eyelids closed to shut out his words. What they had was only physical—only an itch they'd chosen to scratch. Mimi and Chase were not "Mimi and Chase" of ten years ago, but adults who had agreed to sex and nothing more.

But the former her—the her who had loved him with everything in her twenty-three-year-old being—*wanted* to hold on to those words. To tuck them away because they made her feel warm and wanted.

She unhooked her legs from his waist and he pulled out, setting her feet on the ground. She sagged against the wall, her knees wobbly.

"Thanks, Mr. Mayor." She kept her tone cheeky and was pleased when her comment drew a dazzling, if tired, smile out of him.

"Does this tick a sexual fantasy box for you, Mimi?"

"Several." She counted them off on her fingers. "Wall sex. Mayor sex. Mansion sex."

His smile didn't budge.

He stole a quick kiss and he took a moment to visit the half bath. She watched his firm butt flex as he walked, reminding herself to send a note of thanks to his personal trainer. He reemerged as she was settling in front of the fire, pulling the blanket around her body.

"I failed at warming you up," he said.

"You *ignited* me. It wore off." She held out her palms, soaking in what little heat was coming from the embers.

He tossed another log onto the fire and stoked the flames before sitting with her. "Do you approve?"

"I would think that was obvious."

"I was talking about the fire, but I'll take that compliment." He opened his arms and she nestled into him, his hands warming her through the blanket and making her toastier than the fire.

"How are you this hot?"

"So many ways to answer that question." He ducked his head to kiss her, a long, heady slide of his lips along hers. "Next time, we won't rush."

Next time.

Those two words swirled around her mind for a second. He thumbed her lip and pulled it out from under her top teeth.

"There *will* be a next time. I didn't mean for it to be over so soon, but it's been a while."

"A while?" She regarded him with raised brows.

He let her go, lying back on the floor with his hands behind his head. She admired the strong line of his body, the muscles along his torso and abdomen, the way his cock, even at half-mast, hadn't lost any of its appeal.

"Define a while."

"Longer than a jiffy." He winked.

"Har har."

His eyes closed and she watched the firelight play on his long dark lashes. Was it true? Was this powerful, gorgeous man single? Was he lonely? She sure as hell had been. Even when she'd dated, she'd suffered from bouts of deep, unmoored loneliness. The senselessness of her being lonely here and Chase being lonely there resonated in her chest. What could've been…

Is better off left unexamined.

"I'm starving. Coffee didn't cut it this morning." She'd said it partially to keep from asking him if he'd been lonely, and mostly to keep from talking about "next time." Ideas of "next time" made her hungry in an entirely different part of her anatomy.

"I like that smile." He tapped the edge of her lips. "I must've done well."

Was it her or had his Texas drawl taken hold again?

"Shameless begging for compliments will not get you any. But I will make you breakfast." She moved to stand, but he caught her arm with one hand and gently pulled her down.

"Brunch. It's almost eleven."

"We don't have brunch in Bigfork. It's *breakfast* and sometimes we eat breakfast for dinner."

"I remember."

Those two words settled in the air, simple but heavy.

Proof that he knew her. Proof that he hadn't been a mirage. And what they'd just done together was proof that she hadn't imagined how good the sex used to be—dare she say it'd been better?

"You made pancakes one night." His smile was reminiscent, his gaze soft. "Slathered them in peanut butter and called it dinner."

She smiled at the memory. "You thought I was crazy."

"No." He looked at her, his smile fading some. "I was crazy about you. You could have fed me anything on those pancakes and I'd have eaten them."

"We were crazy." She shook her head. The days they hadn't spent in the lake or on the beach or outside soaking in the summer sun, he'd been in her apartment—both of them wedged onto her twin bed against one wall of her bedroom. "My roommate complained so much about the noise we made, she was relieved when I followed you back to Texas."

"I remember that, too." His smirk was one of pride. He'd always loved being complimented on his prowess.

"Well. I promise no peanut butter pancakes. And eggs are out since you don't have them." She wrinkled her nose. "How can you not like a cheesy omelet?"

His mouth turned down. "Yuck."

"You sounded like my five-year-old niece just then."

"I have one, too. My niece is—" Pride pulled his lips into a smile. "She's amazing. So small and beautiful and... just amazing."

"How old is she?"

"Eleven months and change. Her birthday's on Christmas Day. We were in the middle of a family Christmas, complete with ugly sweaters when Zach's wife, Penelope, went into labor. I'll never forget Olivia's wide eyes and tiny fingers. Worth waiting for hours in the hospital for her to arrive."

"Pretty name." Miriam returned his smile. "My sister-in-law endured seventeen hours of hard labor and I spent most of it camped out in the cafeteria or the waiting room absolutely dying to know if she'd had a boy or a girl."

"She kept it from you."

"From all of us. It was brutal. But then I held Raven for the first time and felt this overwhelming…joy."

"I bet you're a great aunt." He pushed a lock of hair from her face.

She'd bet he was a great uncle. Pride mingled with protectiveness in his eyes.

Proving further that he took his job as uncle seriously, he said, "I told everyone that Olivia's gifts had to be wrapped in birthday-themed paper and not holiday wrapping paper. It's a big deal to have a birthday on Christmas. I mean, she shares it with Jesus. It should stand out."

An effervescent giggle shook her shoulders. This was what she'd fallen for when she'd first met Chase. His reasoning. His involvement. Just…*him*.

"My sister's girlfriend's birthday is on Christmas and Wendy reminds us every year that there's absolutely no cheating on the wrapping paper."

"I've decided if it's pink and makes noise, I'm buying it for Olivia. Serves Zach right for being a pain-in-the-ass little brother for most of my life."

She could imagine Chase hauling in loads of bubble-gum-colored glitter wrapping paper and stacking it around his tiny niece.

"Raven is a terror but I love her. And now I won't see her again *until* Christmas." A dart of pain pinched her chest. "They live in Virginia."

More snow fell outside, reminding her that she wasn't going anywhere soon.

"I'm sorry."

"Don't be." She'd called last night to check in on everyone. Her mother said they had "a dusting" of snow, but nothing that would trap them indoors. Miriam then spoke with Ross's wife, Cecilia, and Raven, and finally, Kris.

Kris had whispered *hold on* and Miriam had listened to light footfalls as she ran up the stairs. A few seconds later, after she'd escaped the family, Kris let Miriam have it.

What happened! Did you sleep with him yet? Are you in love with him again?

Miriam had answered a stern *no* followed by a sterner *seriously*? She'd also asked her sister if she'd recently taken up day drinking. Before they hung up, Kristine issued one last warning.

Don't let yourself get towed in by a sexy guy in a suit, Meems...but if you do, and who could blame you, make sure you enjoy yourself. No guilt allowed.

No guilt allowed.

In this moment, in front of a cozy fire with a naked, sinfully sexy man sprawled on the floor next to her... Snowed inside a luxurious mansion with anything and everything she could want... Yeah, it was safe to say her reigning emotion wasn't guilt. She had no problem taking what she wanted—what she'd needed.

Chase was stroking her arm, silent and thinking his own thoughts—whatever those were. She had a pretty good idea what they *weren't*. He wasn't thinking of the past or the future. His concern probably didn't extend beyond him enjoying himself and making sure she enjoyed herself in the scant amount of time they had left.

"You know, I have frozen waffles," he said, taking her hand and weaving their fingers together. "And maple syrup and bacon."

"And peanut butter?" She grinned.

"I'm a bachelor. *Of course*, I have peanut butter." He stood and pulled his jeans on and Miriam watched the way he moved, thinking he might be the devil in the flesh for all the temptation he offered.

"Can I help?"

"No. I need you to stay naked and save your strength. I can think of another use for the peanut butter besides slathering it onto waffles." He snagged his shirt off the floor.

She rolled her eyes but couldn't deny that she could think of another use for it, too.

Fifteen

"How come you're not married with a few of your own kids running around?" Chase asked.

"Excuse me? Did you just make a barefoot-and-pregnant reference about me?" Her eyebrows rose in offense.

"No." The word was outlined with patience. "I asked a question. We already covered the easy stuff. Time to answer a few hardballs."

She'd stayed naked like he'd requested while they ate waffles, but they'd since slipped back into their clothes, lounging on the couch after he threw another log on the fire. They'd chatted about college and the jobs they'd held after graduation. They talked about their siblings and their parents—he and Mimi were both close to their families. He hurt for her when she mentioned missing her late father. Chase knew too well how it felt to watch a parent have a close brush with the Other Side. He wished he could make a deal with the universe to keep Rider and Eleanor Ferguson immortal. His siblings, too. Hell, *everyone*.

The worry over his father's heart attack had eaten Chase alive, and if his dad had met his maker that day rather than coming out of surgery like the trooper he was, Chase didn't know what he'd have done. He'd steered them from that topic back to work. Mimi had spoken about the community as it applied to her working for Montana Conservation Society and he had discussed what it was like being mayor of a huge city. Like he said, easy stuff. Now the gloves were off.

"Tell me about the guy you last dated." He was sitting next to her on the couch and moved to stretch out. "And come here."

She made a frustrated sound in the back of her throat but came as asked.

"Guess I don't need that blanket," she said as she settled in next to him. "You're hot enough for both of us. And *yes*, I know how that sounds."

He smiled at her petulant tone. She wedged herself between the couch and him, and he wrapped his arm around her. Her palm resting over his heart, her cheek on her hand, she pulled in a contented breath. Contented, despite her trying her damnedest to resist him—or at the very least to keep him at arm's length.

He liked her here in his arms, her breasts pressing his chest, her breath tickling the hand that stroked her arm. He was aware that the trade-off for her being here was that she wasn't with her family. He didn't care. That might make him a selfish bastard, but in his defense, he hadn't seen or talked to Mimi in years and they'd seen her mere days ago.

"Who was he?" he repeated, curious to hear about the imaginary guy he'd concocted. In his mind Mimi's most recent ex had a protruding gut and did nothing but drool in front of his PlayStation while drinking cheap beer.

"Why do you want to know so badly?"

Because he wanted to know who he was up against, but he wasn't admitting as much. So instead he said, "Humor me."

"Gerard Randall. He's an environmental specialist for Yore Corp, a corn-processing plant south of Bigfork. I met him at a conference. We dated for eight months before we both admitted it wasn't working. We cut our losses and moved on." One of her slight shoulders lifted in a shrug.

Chase felt his mouth turn down. He liked his own story better. This Gerard Randall guy sounded moderately successful—not that Mimi would ever stoop to date the guy in Chase's imagination—and their split sounded amicable. Though that news was good. He didn't want her brokenhearted, tossed aside.

Like you tossed her aside.

"What about you? How come you don't have a wife and children?"

"My career keeps me busy," he answered automatically. It was the truth, but an exaggerated one. He wasn't too busy for a relationship. He hadn't found anyone he wanted to pursue.

"That answer was canned." She lifted her face to look at him and for a moment his breath snagged in his lungs. Not at her astute observation, but at her sheer beauty.

"You're so beautiful." He stroked her cheek with the pads of his fingertips. "I always thought so, but you've become more beautiful."

"Nice try. Who was she?"

"Who?" His brow crinkled.

"I told you who I last dated. It's your turn!" She poked him in the stomach.

"The *beautiful* comment won't save me that fate?"

"Nope." She overenunciated and popped the *p*.

"Darla McMantis."

Mimi squinted one eye. "Did you make that up? That sounds made-up."

"We were working on a don't-text-and-drive initiative for high schoolers at the beginning of this year. She's on the school board and wanted a face for the campaign. Mine."

"I'll bet," Mimi interjected, sounding jealous enough to make him smile.

"After we completed the plans, she asked me out for a drink. That drink was followed by a few dinners and two professional functions where she stood in as my date. In April she broke up with me, ironically, via text message."

"Hopefully not while driving," Mimi quipped.

"To be honest, I wasn't aware we were officially dating. I didn't think we were serious enough to 'break up.'"

"But you were serious enough to sleep with her."

"Were you sleeping with Gerard?"

They watched each other in a silent standoff before Mimi looked away. "I guess it's hard to find the person you want to spend forever with."

Hard to find them, or hard to hold on to them?

She laid her head back onto her hand. A few beats passed while he listened to her breathe, feeling protective of her—responsible for her.

"If my reelection campaign takes a turn and the spotlight finds you…" With the arm already wrapped around her, he gave her a gentle squeeze. "I won't let it touch you."

"You can't promise that."

"I can promise if it does touch you, I'll do everything in my power to extract you from the conversation. You don't deserve any of this. Hell, that was the main reason…" He fell silent, opting not to finish the thought he'd started.

"That was the main reason for what?" She lifted her head, the dent between her eyebrows warning him to tell her the truth or face her wrath.

"Like back then, I'd never ask you to be a part of my world now. To sacrifice what you believe in, what you love, to stand at the side of a man who's an oil tycoon first and a politician second." He let out a dry chuckle. "That must sound like your worst nightmare."

Correction: that wasn't irritation on her face. Mimi was *pissed*.

"First off, Chase Ferguson—" she punctuated each word

by stabbing his breastbone while her eyes drilled into him "—you are a man with a heart and soul. A *good* man, your choice in women notwithstanding." A dig he let her have since she was right. Women always wanted something he wasn't willing to give, or were only there for the arm candy he provided. While he found neither of those situations objectionable, they didn't add up to a very flattering relationship record.

"Secondly," she continued, not through defending his honor, "you're a businessman and a politician. A damn good one if what I uncovered online can be believed."

"Uncovered? What did you uncover?"

Her face pinked as her gaze bounced around the room—landing everywhere but on him. He'd bet his bank account she hadn't meant to say that last part. He physically turned her chin and forced her guilty, dark eyes back on him.

"Mimi Andrix, did you *Google* me?"

"When I received that letter out of the blue—that *impersonal* letter—I was curious. I vowed not to go further than the city's website, but I clicked through a few of those search pages and…"

Her cheeks burned red.

"And?" He prompted.

She licked her lips before admitting, "I found an interesting website."

The heat of embarrassment burned Miriam's face. Admitting she'd dug up information on Chase like a besotted highschooler was humiliating.

"A website about me?" he asked, clearly bemused.

"Yes."

"What was on it?" He mashed a decorative pillow under his neck to hold his head up so he could properly interrogate her. "Were there photos?"

"*Yes*, egomaniac. And…stories."

"Stories?" One eyebrow arched high on his forehead.

"Fictional ones." She covered her eyes with one hand. "They were so bad. The worst fan fiction ever. About how she dreamed of you and her…" She moved her hand to gesture. "Together."

A rough rumble of laughter shook his chest, jostling her. She opened one eye to find him still laughing, throat bobbing, and was that…yes, she believed it was. She swiped a tear from the corner of his eye. He'd laughed himself to tears.

"That's…" He swiped his own eyes and sniffed. "I don't know what that is. Damn funny."

He was so appealing when he was this relaxed.

"At first I thought maybe she was a jilted ex-girlfriend, but then it was clear she'd never met you."

"What tipped you off?" He grinned, loving every second of this.

"She brought up having sex with you on a horse and—"

That brought forth another crack of laughter as fresh tears sprang to his eyes. She laughed with him, the hardy, happy sound as infectious as he was. He recovered quickly, rolling toward the back of the couch and wedging her between the leather and his hard, warm body.

"How do you know that isn't true?" His tone was sober, his eyes narrowed and assessing.

"Other than you don't seem the type to attempt sex on a horse," she said with a small giggle. "The day I invited you horseback riding."

His gaze swept to one side. "How come I don't remember that?"

"I asked if you wanted to go riding and you said you didn't trust a beast that large with your bodily safety. It stood out in my mind because you were from Texas. I thought all Texans were brought up riding horses."

"I remember that conversation now. Horses are smart. I

imagine they don't always like to be ridden. And once I'm up there, there's only one way to go."

"Down." She ran a fingertip along his bristled jawline. "They are smart animals."

"On that we agree. Horses are very smart and deserve our respect."

"So, we're on the same side of the fence on one more topic," she whispered against his lips. He was close enough to kiss, his delicious weight pressing her deeper into the couch's cushions. "Does that bring our grand total to three?"

"I can think of one more." He took her lips hostage, making out with her long and slow. One hand gripped her hip before sliding under her shirt to tickle her bare skin.

Her mind melted, her body doing a good job of following suit, as he made love to her mouth with his. He wasn't wrong. Sex was another topic both their bodies and minds agreed on.

They'd always been physically compatible. They'd proven it time and time again during many summer nights past and they were proving it again in the winter wonderland of his massive mansion. Earlier he'd claimed her against the wall. Now he seemed bent on *reclaiming* her.

She couldn't think of a single reason to argue.

"This is *incredible*." Miriam lounged in the hot tub, bubbling water tickling her bare breasts and liquefying her sore muscles.

Chase had done a good job of liquefying them earlier today—a few times.

He sat on the other side of the round tub—in-ground like the pool—and let out a long, gruff hum. A hum of satisfaction and relaxation. She liked being with him—yes for the sex, which was amazing but also for the moments that followed. She hadn't been apart from him for more than a handful of minutes today and she didn't care to leave his side until she officially walked out of this mansion.

Crazy? Possibly. But she could handle a brief affair with him. She was no longer a carefree twenty-three-year-old whose life had been overwhelmed by the sexy city boy from Texas. She was a grown, independent, responsible woman with people who counted on her—both professionally and personally. She was old enough and wise enough to understand that what had kept them apart years ago was alive and well. Their interests were as different as a Dallas oil field and a Montana nature preserve.

If, say, they had a shot at coupledom—an insane thought, but she allowed herself to have it—it'd mean her moving to Dallas and leaving her family and her beloved job behind *or* Chase moving to Montana where he'd…what? Run for mayor here? Take a seat on the county board? Fall back on his law degree and hang a shingle in town?

It was preposterous, the idea that Chase the famous mayor and oil tycoon would move away from his beloved state to live in the wilderness.

They were doomed.

Which made things easier. Back when they were together she hadn't known they were doomed. Or rather, she'd been the *last* to know. Knowing up front meant no castle-building on the clouds. She could enjoy what they had at face value and walk away with some really great memories.

"It is incredible." His agreement interrupted her deep thoughts and she opened her eyes to find his closed, his head resting back, arms spread out and resting on the edge of the hot tub.

She saw no need to share her thoughts with him. With anyone other than herself. And that certainty—along with knowing they were doomed—also felt really, really good.

She would let any thoughts of what happened next between them rise and swirl and disappear like steam from the hot tub. But she wouldn't deny herself the treasure of being with him while they were stranded.

Later, when Chase took her hand, she allowed him to lead her upstairs and into his bedroom.

Sixteen

The following day was nothing like the one that preceded it. Rather than dance around each other and spend most of the day naked, they bundled up and headed outside.

The snow was barely falling now, and Miriam had spotted a snowplow making slow progress through one of the neighborhoods at the base of the hill. They were still under several feet of snow, and the temperature remained stubbornly frigid, but at least the snow had stopped. People were starting to emerge from their homes, and from the vantage point of the upstairs library this morning she'd spotted a few brightly colored parkas dotting the whitewashed landscape.

"Ready?" Chase positioned the round plastic disc on a hill at the side of the house and held it steady for her to climb on.

"You first," she said, tipping her chin.

"No, thanks." He twisted the toboggan deeper into the snow.

"Chicken."

"Sticks and stones, Mimi. Get your very fine rear on this sled."

"It's a toboggan."

"Stop delaying." His dark hair ruffled in the breeze,

his ears bright red. He'd torn his hat off a few minutes ago when he'd gone searching for the toboggan, or *sled* as he called it, complaining he was hot. Only Chase Ferguson could be hot in fifteen-degree weather.

"After shoveling, you deserve to have some fun. Maybe we should go down together."

His eyes were uncooperative slits, but he surprisingly agreed. "Okay, fine. Take hold of this while I put my hat back on."

She squealed her way to the bottom of the hill, nestled against his front while he sat behind her. When they came to a landing at a cluster of trees she was glad they hadn't mowed into, she'd collected a pile of snow between her legs.

"Again?" Warm lips touched her cheek. "Or do you want to go inside and warm up?"

"Again!" She couldn't help herself. She hadn't done this in years. This was too fun not to continue.

They went again, *and again*, until her legs were jelly from climbing the hill and Chase had flat out given up. He lied and said he was making snow angels, but she could tell he was taking a beat to catch his breath. After their final climb up the hill, he leaned the toboggan against the garage and they shut out the cold, peeling off their snow-packed outfits before dashing inside to start a fire.

Once they were dressed in comfy clothes, fire lit and mugs of soup for both of them, Miriam's nose finally began to thaw.

"Told you I'd make a mountain man out of you yet."

"You're very persuasive." Chase finished his mug of soup and set it aside, scrubbing his hands down his legs and then holding his palms in front of the fire. "I miss Texas. Shoveling is for the birds."

"I'm sure if you lived here you'd be able to find someone to shovel for you." When he looked over at her, his brow a contemplative mar, she said, "I mean if you visit here again. In the winter. It doesn't always snow this much."

She pressed her lips together to stop the spillway of words.

"Speaking of, I need to find someone to do just that," he said. "The city will take care of the street, but this long driveway is too much work for one shovel."

"I have snow-removal guys on speed dial for my job. I can call one later on today."

"Or tomorrow." He locked his eyes on hers. "No sense in beating the street plow."

"Right."

They fell silent, listening to the fire snap and pop. Her time here was ending. She'd only been here a few days, but it felt longer. Like that summer past had bled into a fall she'd forgotten and a winter that lingered.

The same niggling, disturbing sensation of no time having passed occurred while she and Chase loaded the dishwasher. He rinsed her mug and took the spoon from her hand while she'd dropped in the detergent pod. He shut the device and pressed Start, and just like that, they'd perfected the dance in the kitchen without a word.

Like a couple who knew each other.

Like a couple who hadn't been apart for ten years.

In his room that night, she opted to leave her yoga pants and T-shirt on, though she did lose the sweatshirt. When she climbed beneath the covers, however, he snatched the blankets off her.

"What's this?" He gestured to her wardrobe.

"I'm cold!"

"You won't be with me next to you." He gestured to himself. "Human heater."

"By your own admission, you spent most of this year *not* sleeping next to a naked woman—" she sat up and gathered the blankets over her body "—wouldn't want to spoil you unnecessarily."

"Low blow, Andrix." He tugged off his sweatshirt and dropped his jeans and she pulled the blankets to her nose and admired his rock-hard, sculpted, beautiful body.

He tossed his clothes over a chair and she found it cute. From the outside, he appeared to be a neat freak yet he never truly made his bed and always tossed his clothes instead of folding or hanging them. It made him somehow more approachable. More relatable.

On her side, he lifted the blankets. "Scoot."

"This is my side!" she argued but scooted.

"Excuse me. This is my bed, *interloper*. Do as I say."

Once under the covers, he looped one arm around her waist and shoved the other beneath his pillow. On his side, he faced her, his eyes heavy.

They'd had afternoon sex in her room today. After they'd eaten lunch and warmed up from playing in the snow, he'd come in and grasped her hips, grinding into her from behind. She'd gladly stopped what she was doing—packing—and made love to him.

Made love.

She thought the words with an eye roll, but there wasn't a better way to phrase it.

He'd always had an intimate way about him that was impossible to deny. Temporary or not, when they were together, they were both focused on the finite. The immediate moment—the breaths they shared. The noises they made. The sensations in their bodies turning them inside out.

She hated to admit it, but she was hoping they'd have another go at it tonight.

"You're too tired," she said, but noticed her own eyelids weighing heavy.

"Too tired for what?" But he knew. He grabbed a handful of her T-shirt. "You're the one who's dressed. I took that as a lack of interest."

"Where you're concerned, Mr. Mayor, there's never been lack of interest." She'd meant the comment to tease, but her voice came out husky.

"I'm never too tired." His hand warmed her belly and coasted north until he found her bare breast. He tweaked a nipple and she squirmed. He did it again and he smiled. "I feel a second wind coming on."

Her answer was a lust-heavy exhale.

The blankets were gone in a sudden *whoosh* and his eyes went from half-lidded haze to heated gaze in a split second.

"Off." He plucked her T-shirt. "I'll wrestle with these stretchy prison bars," he said of her tight pants. He made short work of them, throwing her socks over his shoulder as she tore off her T-shirt. He lost the boxer briefs next and lay against her body, every simmering inch of hard muscle warming wherever he touched.

"Still cold?"

She shivered but shook her head. That shiver had nothing to do with cold and everything to do with the anticipation of his clever mouth. His attentive hands. His—

Chase's tongue circled her nipple and his fingers spread her legs. He dipped his middle finger into her well of desire, finding her wet and ready.

"No, I don't believe you're cold any longer." With a wicked grin, he kissed his way down her body and positioned himself between her legs. He stayed down there a long time, not coming up for air even when she begged him not to make her come again. Instead he wrung one more out of her, one that sent her fluttering pulse into overdrive. Her shouts of completion echoed off his bedroom walls and rang off the wide windows overlooking the silent, snowy lake.

She didn't know how long she lay on her side, suffering aftershocks from back-to-back powerful releases. When she finally heard his voice it was through a head stuffed with cotton.

"Sleep, beautiful girl," he whispered into her ear. "You earned it."

A soft but firm kiss hit the corner of her mouth and She meant to turn over and relay her appreciation, but instead slipped into the gauzy realm of deep sleep and dreamed of nothing at all.

Chase woke up confused about what time it was. The moon was out and reflecting on the snow, making it appear like early morning, but the sky was pitch-black, stars dotting the nighttime canvas.

He checked his phone for the time—3:00 a.m.—and then rolled over to wrap a palm around Mimi's breast.

Neither she nor her breasts were there.

He lay on his back in the semidark listening for her. She hadn't gone far. From the sound of fluttering pages coming from the room outside his, she was flipping through a book. After taking her on his tongue, he'd been sure she'd sleep through the night. He was beat from shoveling, sledding—or *tobogganing*—and honest-to-goodness fatigue had had him drifting off in a matter of minutes. Short-lived, evidently. Whatever had woken him, be it Mimi's wandering about or a dream that had already lost its potency after jarring him awake, he was too alert to fall asleep again.

Climbing out of bed, he was greeted by frigid air in the room. He grabbed his phone to check the app for his thermostat, bumping it up a few degrees. Then he checked his stocks out of habit, narrowly avoided his email and left the device on his nightstand. At the door of his bedroom, he found her where he'd imagined.

Wrapped in a thick quilt in the library and curled on the armchair facing the window over the lake. She was flipping through one of the books from the shelves. A murder mystery by the looks of it.

"Fan of Patterson?"

She looked up, briefly startled by him standing there. "Who isn't?"

"Good point."

She slid her gaze down his boxers-only attire. "Put some clothes on. It's cold."

"Share your blanket instead." He tugged a corner of it, exposing her bare legs. She had on panties and a T-shirt, but nothing else. Perfect.

"This chair isn't big enough for—Hey!" Her exclaimed argument faded into soft laughter as the hardbound book hit the floor with a *thunk*. He lifted her and set her on his lap, cradling her close and wrapping that blanket around his legs while he was at it.

"Plenty of room," he said of their shared seat. "What are you doing up?"

"Couldn't sleep." This close, he could see the feathered soft lines at the corners of her eyes, the faint smile lines around her mouth. The freckles that had been out in droves years ago were fainter but still present, likely from her work outdoors.

"I did everything in my power to put you out for an entire night. I was hoping you'd sleep in."

"Why? Were you going to deliver me an avocado-and-protein smoothie in bed?"

He captured her hand in his and wove their fingers together, admiring the way her long, elegant fingers fit against his tanner, wider ones.

"I was going to make pancakes."

"You're lying."

"Tomorrow, or today technically," he corrected, "is looking like our last day together. I assume once the driveway is cleared you'll go home."

"What will you do?" she asked instead of addressing his comment.

"I don't know." He pulled in a breath and let it out. "Stay. Leave. Depends."

She examined their linked hands and said nothing.

"Mimi." That brought her dark eyes to his. He took in her pretty, delicate features in the streaming moonlight, weighed her hand in his and absolutely did not say what he was thinking. Which was that his staying or leaving had everything to do with her.

He'd come here to get away. And yes, in a distant part of his mind he'd considered that he might run into her while he was here. He'd considered dropping in on her at work and buying her a coffee under the guise of discussing the photo and the letter sent from his office. He'd wanted to see her. See if she was all right. Find out if she hated him for what he did, or if they'd outgrown what had been between them.

He'd have died before admitting the unfinished business, but after he'd run into her at the supermarket he'd concluded that was exactly what it was. When she'd called to invite him to her family's house, he'd declined, guessing he'd be unwelcomed by her family and knowing that Mimi couldn't help being kind.

He never expected her to drive out to see him, end up trapped with him in this snowstorm. And even though he'd been determined to have her in his arms once she was stuck here with him, he never imagined it would be this easy. This satisfying. This…right. He hadn't counted on the onslaught of powerful emotions from years ago to resurface, either. Feelings for her he hadn't examined and would prefer not to, but stood before him now like an immovable wall.

He could see now how much she'd mattered to him back then. He'd concluded that the cure was time and space; distance should have erased the intensity between them. He'd assumed the bond they'd had then had been broken. It was beginning to appear as if it'd been merely…interrupted.

Hell, maybe he should tell her what was on his mind. He had no idea what was going on in her head and guessing would do him no good… Maybe he'd been wrong assuming she wouldn't fit into his world. Maybe—

"I think you should stay," she said, all but stealing his next breath.

"You do?" he asked like an imbecile.

"Yes. Bigfork is beautiful in the winter and you haven't been here for very long. Once they clear the snow, they'll cordon off part of the lake for ice skating. Especially if the weather stays this cold." She chattered another couple of seconds like a tour guide listing the many amenities that could occupy his time while he was in Bigfork.

But she failed to list herself among them.

"What about you?"

"Well, I live here." She looped her arms around his neck and placed a quick kiss on his lips. "I don't need to see the sights."

"I mean what are you doing while I'm here?"

She shrugged casually. "Working, most likely. I only took off through Monday."

He frowned. "Mimi."

"What?"

"Can I…" He was out of his element, which was frustrating. He never hesitated to ask for what he wanted. And what he wanted was the attention of the woman on his lap for a few more days. Hell, weeks. He didn't know. Just… more. He pulled in a breath and blew out a gruff invitation, "Do you want to grab dinner some night while I'm here, or not?"

"Charming." But she smiled when she said it.

"Sorry. I'm…tired."

"Well…" She offered a careless shrug like he wasn't hanging on her every syllable. "I might have a free night next week. You have my number."

It was a blowoff if he'd ever heard one. And he'd delivered a few in his day.

She kissed him, lingering at his bottom lip to give it a gentle bite. "I don't want to think about work. I want to think about…" She reached between his legs. "Right now."

He let out a grunt and she crushed his lips with a kiss while her hand kept stroking. There'd been a brief objection in his brain but damn if he could access it now. Her touching him had erased any brewing argument—sound or not. He was vaguely aware he should be stopping her to continue this discussion and put it to rest for good, but another stroke and her moaned "I want you" against his lips successfully deterred him.

He unwound the piled blanket from her body and shifted her on his lap. Her lips never left his. He had her divested of the white cotton panties in a blink. She yanked down his boxer briefs as far as his thighs and positioned herself over his heavy erection.

Sweat beaded his brow. He cupped her nape with one hand and rested his forehead on hers.

"Wait." His voice came out on a harsh breath. "Condom. Or…not…"

She froze. The whites of her eyes were bright in the moonlight streaming in behind him. She gulped and that was the moment he knew they were on the same page. Despite her flippant reaction to his asking her out, Mimi was invested. In him. At least for the moment.

He brushed her hair over her shoulder. "We can move this to the bedroom, or we can stay here and have nothing between us." It was a risk, and more than a physical one. "Tell me it's possible."

"Do you mean am I on the pill? Am I clean?" She pressed a finger to his bottom lip. "Yes to both, but…"

"Too much?" he guessed. No barrier put them back where they were ten years ago. In her cramped twin bed where nothing—not even a thin coat of rubber— had stood between them.

"I loved how you felt. Just you. Just us." And more than anything, he needed that connection now. For reasons he couldn't explain—or maybe reasons he wouldn't admit.

His heart gave a dangerous lurch forward.

"Are you… A lot has happened since then," she said.

"Not as much as you think." He pressed a soft kiss to her lips and cradled the back of her head, her hair's silken strands tickling his forearm. "The last woman I slept with without a condom was you."

He felt more than saw her pull her head back.

"For old time's sake?" she asked, her smile nervous rather than sly. It was more than that and she knew it, but in this dim, moonlit space on their last night together, he'd give her the out.

"For old time's sake," he agreed.

Straddling him, she held his gaze captive and sank down so slowly he had to weld his back teeth together to keep from coming too soon. She emitted a familiar sigh of pleasure that he echoed. She was soft and warm—everything he remembered mixed with everything he now knew. Being with her was different, but also the same.

She still absolutely *undid* him.

He tilted his hips, sinking into her and emitting a harsh exhale. He guided himself deep, noticing when she trembled against him. She was heat and silk and wet. Beauty and kindness and giving. Always so damn giving. Making this last would take a feat of superhuman willpower, but he'd make it last for her.

Her head was thrown back, her nipples pressing the thin white T-shirt. He absorbed her gasps, closing his lips over hers, marking her lust-heavy gaze in his memory. He made love to her with reverence, far from through with her, and hoped his actions conveyed what he hadn't been able to say. That there was a reason for her to say yes to dinner, to say yes to *him* while he was here.

No. *Longer*.

Their lazy thrusts gained speed and it was that feverish pace that brought her to orgasm. She tensed and clutched him deep, coming with his name on her lips. He followed, spilling inside her and branding her his.

Whether she knew it or not.

Seventeen

Chase was in the shower when the gate's call button rang. Miriam sent a glance up the staircase and dashed for the door, wondering if she should answer it. Who was up here in the middle of a blizzard?

She depressed the button labeled Speaker and hoped that was the right one. "Yes?"

"Good morning, ma'am. My partner and I are plowing driveways and I noticed yours needs clearing," came a slightly southern accent. She backed away from the box and studied the video screen. The black-and-white picture showed a man in the cab of a pickup truck, a woman in a scarf and ballcap in the seat next to him. His face was pleasant, his goatee neatly trimmed. Young. She guessed him a twentysomething. She had a soft spot for hardworking twentysomethings. "The main road's done," he said with a glance in his rearview mirror. "We can have you cleared in thirty minutes tops."

She remembered her own climb up the driveway. His must've been treacherous.

"How'd you climb the hill to the gate?"

A slightly chagrined smile decorated his handsome features. "Cleared free of charge, ma'am. We're taking the chance you'll hire us to finish."

Well. She couldn't say no to that. She'd planned on giving Chase her friend Rodney's number to call about removing the snow, but these two were already here. Who knew if Rodney was even available? She couldn't turn away budding entrepreneurs.

After a brief discussion of price, she agreed and buzzed them in. Feeling proud for handling it by herself, she called upstairs. "Snowplow guy's here!"

It was a safe guess that her voice hadn't carried all the way to his bedroom. This house was enormous. He needed one of those damn speaker boxes for each *floor*.

She made a fresh pot of coffee, intending to take some out to the two working in the driveway, but a knock at the door interrupted her task.

"That was fast," she said to herself, encountering Chase at the bottom of the stairs.

"What was fast?" His hair was damp, and he was dressed in a sweater and jeans. He looked so good she was struck dumb for a beat. "Did I hear a knock?"

"Lucky for you, I was here to answer your gate. We are being shoveled out as we speak." She climbed to her toes, taking a handful of his cable-knit sweater and kissing his firm mouth. *Mmm.* He always smelled good. "I negotiated a fair price."

She walked for the front door, Chase on her heels. "How'd he get to the gate?"

"Don't be alarmed, Mr. Mayor, I asked that, too. He cleared it in the hopes we'd say yes to his offer."

"Mimi, wait."

But she'd already yanked open the door. There she found the pair of entrepreneurs, the goateed guy holding a video camera and the blonde aiming her cell phone. The sound of electronic shutter snaps told her that the other woman was taking pictures. Questions from both of them came flying at her.

"Miriam Andrix, is it true that you and Chase Ferguson are rekindling your romance?"

"How do you plan to make it work being on opposite sides of the oil debate?"

"Mr. Mayor, are you planning on moving to Bigfork permanently or will Miriam be relocating to Dallas?"

Chase grabbed Miriam's arm, tugging her roughly behind him. To the pair spouting questions, he growled, "Get the hell off my property or I'm calling the authorities."

The snowplowers-slash-reporters…or whatever they were made one last attempt, shouting, "Chase, are you and Miriam in love? Will you be planning a wedding here in Montana?" before Chase shut the door with a slam. Snow swirled in from the porch and gathered in the entrance. He turned and melted Mimi's skin off with a laser-hot glare.

"I didn't know…" she started, but her voice trailed off.

"I know."

He pulled his phone from his pocket and opened the door, shutting himself outside. She listened at the door as more machine-gun-fire questions sliced the air, but one voice was louder than the others—Chase's. He was addressing someone on the phone, the police if Miriam had to guess, and saying that two unwanted guests had trespassed on his property. She watched out the window as the fakers scampered to the truck and backed down the driveway.

Chase came back inside, his damp hair dusted with snow that had frozen into icicles. He punched the Gate Closed button.

"What was that?" she asked. That insanity had happened right in front of her, yet she still couldn't make sense of it.

"That," he said as he pocketed his phone, "was your official welcome to my opponent's political campaign."

* * *

Phone to his ear, Chase waited impatiently through two, then three rings. Halfway through the third, Emmett picked up.

"What the hell is going on?" Chase barked into the phone.

Emmett's voice went as rigid as rebar. "What happened?"

"Two spies or journalists talked their way past Mimi and into my front yard. They snapped several pictures of us."

"Wearing what?" Emmett asked. Smartly.

"*Clothes*. We weren't doing anything." *At the time.*

"What's Mimi doing there?" Emmett's question was more to gather intel than pass judgement.

"She was dropping off pie when the weather snowed her in." And that was all the detail his friend was getting. "Care to explain why I'm fighting off paparazzi at my vacation home?"

"A blog posted early this morning. I literally read it five minutes ago. Haven't had a chance to think through the implications let alone call to alert you."

"In the same vein as the letter that arrived with the photo?"

"I don't know. It's gone."

"What do you mean it's gone?"

"The letter and the photo. I assume you didn't throw it out?"

Emmett knew him—knew he wouldn't throw away a photo of Mimi even if it was a photo where she was protesting the very industry that he upheld. "I locked it in the lap drawer of my desk."

A sniff that might mean *could've guessed* came through the phone.

"What gives with the Bigfork welcome? Opportunists?" Chase asked.

"Too soon. The only way someone could've tracked you

down was if they already knew you were there. Who knows Mimi is there?"

"Her sister." But he doubted Kris was their culprit. She and Mimi were close. "I have no idea what Kristine would gain by ratting out Mimi."

"Lucky find, probably," Em concluded. "They were after a reaction from you and got a twofer when she opened the door."

"Send me the link to the blog, will you?"

"Will do. I'll question the staff. If the leak's not on Mimi's end, it has to be on ours. Enjoy the rest of your vacation, boss." Then he was gone.

Chase expected to find Mimi wringing her hands after hearing his side of the conversation. Instead, she stood with her arms folded awaiting explanation.

"I promised I would shield you from any backlash, and that's what I intend to do," he told her. "In the meantime, this changes things. I suggest you stay put rather than—"

"This doesn't change anything. I'm not staying here. I *can't* stay here. I don't live here. I have to work."

"Mimi—"

"I can handle myself, Chase." She unfolded her arms and let them dangle at her sides, looking suddenly tired. "I've been handling myself without your help for a long time. You don't have to be a white knight."

"I'm not trying to be a white knight," he snapped. She didn't know the world of politics. They wouldn't give up until they found the dirt they were looking for. "They're going to harass you, and then harass your family."

"You said you would handle it. Handle it. I am *not* hiding and waiting for them to go away before I resume my life. What's the point in my hiding here?"

Because I want you here.

"I can protect you here," he said instead. "Provided you don't buzz in anyone else through that gate."

"I'm sorry I fell for the oldest trick in the book." Her eyes flicked to one side before meeting his. "I should've asked you first."

He wrapped his hands around her small shoulders, consoling her. "Right, the old pretend-to-be-snow-removal-guys-to-capture-photos-of-the-mayor-with-his-old-flame trick."

That brought a soft smile to her face.

"They play dirty."

"I've never minded getting dirty." She tipped her chin and pegged him with admirable ferocity. Once upon a time, she'd been his and he'd let her go, believing she couldn't handle his life.

Had he been right and she'd grown stronger because of it? Or had he been wrong and this strength had been there all along?

He knew the answer. It wasn't a pretty one.

"Sit tight for a few hours. I'll find out what's going on." His phone buzzed and he glanced at the screen to find the link to the blog post. "Do me that favor?"

She nodded her agreement and walked to the kitchen for a cup of coffee.

Chase began reading.

Emmett's gruff voice bounced off the walls of Chase's Dallas home and Stef paused in the doorway, wiggling her key from the lock. She'd come over to borrow a staple gun since Zach was out of town and she didn't have a key to his house. Chase had given her a key a long time ago. One she'd never bothered returning.

But she hadn't expected to find Emmett here. He was crowding her space an awful lot lately. She would have suspected he'd followed her here if she hadn't arrived second.

His phone conversation was brief, and she guessed he was talking to Chase about something serious given his clipped tone and the mention of Mimi. There was a name she hadn't heard in a while. She peeked into the dining room to find Emmett, his broad back covered in a white button-down shirt, his very short hair close cut in the shape of his perfect head.

He was a big, muscly, glaring guy. Stefanie preferred guys fun, easygoing and quick to smile. Lean muscle, not bulk. Kind eyes rather than Emmett's intense stony stare. She supposed those attributes made him perfect for security. And besides, it didn't matter that he wasn't her type. They hated each other. It was a silently agreed upon fact. It was sort of magical, actually, how they were each peeved merely by the other's existence.

"That sounded serious," she said, announcing herself.

He turned and glared and said nothing.

Typical.

"Anything I can help with?" She grinned, knowing his answer.

"Did you write an article about your brother having an affair with a woman who vehemently protests the oil industry?"

"No."

"Then you can't help." He slid the phone into his pocket and grabbed his coat from the back of a chair.

"What did the article say?"

He didn't so much as slow down as he blew past her. The disturbingly manly scent of his leather coat tickled her nostrils.

"Emmett? Is everything okay?" she called after him.

At the door, he paused, letting the cool November air blow in.

"It's clearly public knowledge. I can tell by your gruffer-than-usual attitude," she added.

He let out a long-suffering sigh—a reaction she'd come

to expect. She assumed it was also a sigh of surrender, but no confession followed.

"Lock up," were the only words he spoke before stepping outside.

"Emmett!" But he was done gracing her with his presence. Gruff, grouchy, impossible. What did her brother see in that guy?

She huffed before shutting the door behind him. Let Em and her brother deal with their mayoral drama. Why should she care?

She went back to searching for the staple gun, irritated that on a need-to-know basis she was the *last* to know.

Well. She had important things to do, too. Like decorate for her favorite holiday. Her brothers used to help her string the lights in her bedroom when they lived at home, but now they were too busy to help. Her apartment remained sadly unadorned. With Chase in Montana, Zach in Chicago and her father in the middle of the ocean, she'd been left no choice but to fend for herself.

"You could've asked Emmett," she said with a sarcastic chuckle as she checked another drawer in the tool chest. And wouldn't he *love* that? Coming to the aid of the lesser Ferguson… He was as full of Christmas cheer as the Mojave Desert was water.

She could hang her own damn Christmas lights.

She shut the last of the drawers, propping her fists on her hips in frustration before tipping her head and spotting the staple gun hanging on a hook on the black pegboard between two cabinets. "Gotcha."

The small victory's glory faded as she walked for the front door. Neither Chase nor Emmett trusted her and she didn't like that. What if she could help?

Behind the wheel of her white sports car, she punched a button to close the gate behind her and pointed in the direction of Chase's office. She'd served a summer internship there a few years ago, and guess who had entrusted her with the key?

Another key she'd never given up.

Whether it was curiosity or hurt feelings driving her actions, she didn't know. It didn't matter. She was a *doer*. She wasn't going to stay in the dark no matter what Emmett said. Chase was *her* brother, after all.

Eighteen

"I handled it for real this time." Miriam waggled her cell phone before relinquishing it to the kitchen island, feeling a touch of residual guilt.

She kept thinking and rethinking about the reporters at the gate earlier this morning. She should have known. Of course, there was no way she *could* have known. Chase held her blameless, but it didn't keep her from reliving the moment she'd pressed that button and wishing she hadn't.

Chase, finished grilling ham-and-cheese sandwiches, slid them onto two waiting plates. The sight of melted cheese made her mouth water. He stirred the pot of tomato soup on the stove.

"These must be your specialty," she said of the perfectly golden wedges.

"They are." He sent her a wink over his shoulder and went back to stirring the soup.

"I know Rodney personally. He will plow your driveway without snapping a single photo."

"Do you like crackers in your tomato soup?"

"I'll dip my sandwich in it instead."

"Exactly the way I like it. Another topic of agreement."

Yes. They'd found several.

"He'll be here within the hour," she said rather than

think of one *particular* act they had in common and were really freaking good at doing. "If you want me to handle that transaction, I can wait to take my shower until later."

"I have it." He ladled the soup into bowls, and lifted his eyes to hers. "Stop beating yourself up."

"I'm not beating myself up," she argued, though she kind of was.

"You're not worrying about me? Concerned that my campaign has been undone by a headstrong woman who protests the oil industry?"

Okay, a little. She couldn't help it. "*Protested*, past tense. I don't protest any longer."

"We suspected backlash could come as a result of the photograph. Emmett had a plan in place if it went live. He just hadn't expected scouts to find us here. And he hadn't counted on you being here, either."

"You wouldn't have let them through the gate, would you?"

"I've been doing this a long time, Mimi."

Which meant his answer was no, he wouldn't have.

"Do you trust Emmett?"

"With every detail of my professional—and personal— life."

That made her feel marginally better. Chase had someone else looking out for him—someone he could trust implicitly. She knew his family was loyal to him and he to them, but she also knew how nice it was to have that one person you could talk to in shorthand. Kris was that person for her.

"How do you stand it?" She dragged her spoon through her bowl of bright red soup. "Having people excited to expose your secrets like that?"

"I ignore it. It's a small price to pay to do the work I do. Besides, I don't have any skeletons in my closet." He gave her another teasing wink. "Save you."

"Ha-ha."

"It's not worth giving my time or attention. Not worth yours, either. There are a lot of people who don't have anything better to do than yell about what's going on in the world. The problem is, they yell and don't actually do anything. So while they're yelling, I aim to be the one doing. The one doing makes the most progress."

Spoon in hand, she paused to let that soak in. He sat next to her, eating his lunch, probably not thinking about the words that had exited his mouth. About how profound and meaningful they were. When she first met him, she'd been as mesmerized by the way he talked as she was by the way he looked. She'd been fascinated by his passionate and clear statements. Moved by his confidence. He was someone people loved to follow. A true leader.

His city needed him. Now that she'd shut down her selfish need for payback—or whatever the hell she'd been doing—she saw how *good* he was. Her instincts were spot-on. He was rich and powerful, but his will wouldn't be bent by the promise of becoming richer or more powerful.

"You're good for Dallas," she concluded.

He turned his head and watched her for a beat. "Thank you. I don't often care what other people think. But your opinion has always mattered. Always." He grabbed her hand and gave her fingers a gentle squeeze. "I know you mean it. Not many people say what they mean."

Wasn't that the truth? Her job required a modicum of political know-how in the environmental circle and hardly anyone said what they meant. She thought of her proclivity to speak her mind rather than be careful. And thought with a smile about how she'd make a horrible mayor's wife.

Wife?

She dropped her spoon with a clang. Where the hell had that thought come from?

"You okay?" The mayor of Dallas crunched into his sandwich, concern darkening his eyes.

"Yeah. Yes. Fine." Oh sure, she sounded totally fine. The mayor's *wife*. She hadn't had a thought like that since...

Since he'd worn nothing but her cheap bedsheets in her ratty apartment. Since he'd been standing in her kitchen making a lunch not dissimilar to this one. It might have been ham and cheese with potato chips, and they'd dined on her tiny twin bed and ate off paper plates, but this *felt* the same.

Or do you feel the same?

The sandwiches were gourmet and the plates were breakable this time around but there was a lot about Chase that hadn't changed. A lot about her that hadn't changed. Like the fact that she still wanted a family and a husband. She wanted an adventure, and a life beyond success at work. She'd imagined a man would fill that role eventually, but she hadn't been looking. And for some reason, sitting here with Chase now made her wonder if she hadn't been looking because she knew what she wanted couldn't be found *here*.

Because he'd always been in Dallas.

The days they'd spent together had snapped seamlessly against the days back when she'd first fallen in love with him. As fast as those days seemed to pass by that summer, being here with him was like being frozen in time. Like they'd been trapped inside a snow globe and given a second chance.

Her stomach flipped, her mind along with it. She couldn't act on those feelings—not a single one of them. She'd made that decision the moment she let him slip her out of her clothes. The moment she'd allowed him to make love to her, she'd promised herself she couldn't and wouldn't allow him access to her heart.

Not again.

"Excuse me." She practically ran from the kitchen to her bedroom, shoving ideas about time-freezing snow globes out of her head. This affair was completely separate from their past—not an extension of it. No matter how much it seemed that the present had fractured and allowed the past to seep in, it hadn't. Remembering moments with him was normal, and definitely not a sign that they could've been more or still could be more.

She lifted her half-full suitcase onto the bed and began packing the rest of her clothes and shoes into it. Her mind volleyed arguments that she was overreacting, but her heart was too tender to spend another moment in this house— or with this man. She rerouted her thoughts on work. Her to-do list waiting for her tomorrow morning. She needed to return to normalcy. To pop this bubble that bent reality and made it seem as though Chase and she belonged together. In reality, and outside of this snowstorm, he lived in Dallas and she lived here. He worked in politics, and she fought for funds from state heads. Once she returned to her own reasonably sized apartment, had a semblance of *normal* after three fantastic, but abnormal, days, everything would go back to the way it should be.

"Was it something I said?" Chase hovered in the doorway.

"Rodney will be here to clear the driveway soon." She unfolded a shirt and rolled it instead, shoving it into the corner of her suitcase.

"Yes, but there's no rush."

"I know." But even that sounded defensive.

He stepped deeper into the room, knocking her equilibrium for a loop. "Was the soup bad?"

She shot him a quick warning glare. She didn't want to joke around right now. She didn't want to *like him* right now. But she did. She did like him, dammit. She liked the way he took care of her, the way he kissed her and the way he'd followed her in here to make sure she was okay.

Which was exactly why she needed to leave.

"I'll finish lunch. I just… I want to get this done. Maybe grab a shower before I go."

He came closer, his breath in her ear when he gripped her hips from behind. The move reminded her of the other night, when he'd followed that move with a kiss, his fists squeezing her flesh possessively.

"I can join you if you like," he said, his voice gruff.

"No." She couldn't allow more blurred lines. "It's better if I go. Let's call that last bout on the library chair the end." She turned to face his stormy expression.

"The end?" he boomed.

"It's been fun, but we agreed that time would run out. The snow has stopped. It's time to return to reality."

"Which is what, in your opinion?" He sounded as angry as he looked.

She licked her lips and forced out a version of the truth she used to believe. A version before she'd been sealed inside a bubble with a Chase who was both like and unlike the Chase of her memory. He was realer, better, more grown-up. More stable in his life and more solid about his decisions. But she couldn't trust in what she'd learned over the past few days, could she? She had to trust in the ten years separating them and the lesson she'd learned during that time.

"Reality is you in your world and me in mine. *Separately.* It's you in your political career. It's me in my position at MCS." She shrugged, hoping to unshoulder her hectic, confusing emotions. No such luck. "It's time for me to leave. You know it. I know it."

"You don't know what I know, Mimi." He returned his hands to her hips, more intimate now that they stood chest to chest.

"Oh? And what do you think you know?" She shouldn't ask, but couldn't help herself.

"My mother was wrong. She thought you were stubborn and headstrong. She said you were blindly in love with the idea of who I would become. She saw a woman who wanted me for my wallet."

Even though his mother wasn't a part of her life, that hurt.

"I never saw you as any of those things," he continued, his tone softer. Gentler. "You were carefree. Independent. And not because you were trying to be. You just were. *Are*," he corrected.

Some of the stiffness went out of her shoulders.

"When I drove you to the airport and put you on a plane back to Bigfork it wasn't because I agreed with my mother. It was because I agreed with you—agreed that we had a future."

"You did?"

"I did." His voice was low, like admitting it hurt him as much as it hurt her to hear. "I knew you would've moved to Texas, because the stage was set for my future. And because you loved me, you would've come with me."

"I did come with you."

"Don't hide behind glibness." He took a breath. "Maybe my mother was right about you being stubborn, but that's an asset. It was to me…and it is to whomever you choose to share your life with."

She sort of hated how well he knew her. But he did know her. It was as inexplicable now as it was then. As if they were a reincarnated couple who'd already lived out this romance in another time. It was like she knew how it was supposed to end…and they weren't destined to be star-crossed lovers.

"You've grown from an incredibly intelligent, beautiful twenty-three-year-old into an incredibly intelligent, beautiful thirty-three-year-old. Every attribute you possess fits into my life."

Wait. What?

He released her hips and straightened away from her. Away rather than toward, the opposite direction his words had suggested.

"Years ago, I sent·you away not because I didn't think you were an incredible woman, and not because my mother is a puppet master. I did it to protect you. From all the things you couldn't protect yourself from. You would've done anything for me—to your own detriment. That's how much you cared."

It was as honest a statement as either of them had made since their reunion.

"I wanted you to know that before you left." He jutted a thumb toward her bedroom door. "I'm going to eat. Join me?"

"All I do is eat." Her teeth found her bottom lip. "Well, not all."

"No. Not all." He smiled from the doorway, but didn't come to her to seal his comment with a kiss. His distance felt wrong, as wrong as what he said next. "I won't bother you any more while I'm in Bigfork."

"Clean break?" she asked, lobbing his words from ten years ago back at him. She half expected an argument. Or maybe she wanted one.

"The cleanest." He dipped his chin in agreement.

With that, the conversation ended. A conversation so filled with unexplored topics she'd lost count. But one thing was clear.

Their time was up.

Nineteen

"It's Blake," Emmett said when he answered his phone.

"Blake Eastwood? The same guy who Stef—"

"Yes." Emmett cut him off like he couldn't stand to hear the end of that sentence.

On that count, Emmett and Chase agreed. Chase had always appreciated his best friend's surge of protectiveness where his sister was concerned. Blake Eastwood had better steer a wide berth around Stefanie if he wanted to live a long, healthy life with his balls still attached to his person.

"The rat is in-house. One of the campaign interns. Blake targeted her. She's young, pretty. His type."

Chase could practically hear the steam coming out of Emmett's ears.

"She broke into your desk, stole the photo and delivered it to Blake, who's backing your opponent financially," Emmett said. "I questioned her and she burst into tears and confessed that she'd slept with Blake after meeting him in a bar. She didn't know who he was and she definitely did not expect him to blackmail her."

"What a dick."

"He's not done yet. The intern told me before she quit that he said he was planning on staying on top of your new relationship until he hit pay dirt."

Now the steam was mostly coming from Chase's collar. He felt his face heat.

"We went through the rest of our staff with a fine-toothed comb. She's the only defector."

"Thanks, Emmett."

"Things are…good?" The pronounced pause was a clue that he wasn't asking about politics.

"Mimi went home an hour ago. We're no longer snowed in." He'd learned that the best answer was an answer that didn't commit to a direction. *Just the facts.*

Chase had walked her into the garage and held her truck's door for her while she climbed in. Before he could think better of it, and before she could stop him from doing it, he leaned in and kissed her goodbye. Her eyelids were still closed when he backed away and it took everything in him to honor her request for a "clean break" and not make love to her on the front seat of her truck. It was too soon for a goodbye. He'd just found her again, dammit.

"Are you staying in Bigfork?"

"Just until things settle down. Mimi doesn't believe this will disrupt her life. She's wrong."

"Uh-huh." His best friend's tone took on the rare quality of amused. "Not because you wanna stay close?"

More that than the other, but Chase didn't admit as much. He ended the conversation with, "Call me if anything changes" and received Emmett's typical sign-off.

"You got it, boss."

When Miriam had returned home yesterday, there were no waiting paparazzi on her front stoop. And when she drove to work the next morning, she hadn't been chased by a dark car with a long camera lens aimed out the window. Either Chase had overestimated her importance in his opponent's smear campaign, or he'd simply overreacted.

Either worked for her. She would prefer to avoid any more drama if possible.

Yesterday she'd driven away from his mansion, his kiss still burning her lips. If he hadn't pulled away—if he hadn't been the one to shut her truck door, she might've been tempted to leap out and pin him to the nearest wall.

That was the effect he had on her. Beyond attraction, his pull was more like gravity. She was the anvil dropped off a cliff. And like gravity wouldn't bear the brunt force of that fall, neither had Chase when she'd followed him home to Dallas ten years ago.

She'd do well remembering that.

On the way to her office inside the main MCS building, she encountered Darren, a fifteen-year-old smarty-pants who practically lived there. He'd started volunteering last summer and had quickly taken a shine to her. She could tell by the way he stuttered her name and watched his shoes whenever he talked to her.

He fidgeted, one tennis shoe scuffing the side of the other as she approached her office.

"Hey, Dare."

"Hi M-Miss Andrix." His smile flinched. "I wanted to talk to you."

"I have a few minutes." She unlocked her door and pushed it open, gesturing for him to go in. "About what?"

"You're in the news."

She dropped her purse and bag onto the desktop. He was talking about the article that'd run about her. Chase had sent her the link yesterday and she'd read it, both unimpressed by how little the author knew about her and frustrated that their relationship had been scandalized.

Flirting with disaster? the tag line had read.

If Chase could ignore it, so could she.

"It's not the news, Darren," she said, but accepted his

cell phone anyway. She frowned. The article on the screen wasn't the one she'd read.

"What is this?" she asked rhetorically. The blogger called herself The Dallas Duchess. It seemed the so-called duchess had been granted access to those sneakily snapped photos in Chase's driveway. There were three, one of Chase outside on the phone and glaring, and since he was in protective mode over Mimi, she found that glare disturbingly sexy. Another photo showed him pulling her away from the door. The lead photo captured her own wide eyes and slackened jaw—easily misconstrued as guilt—while Chase stood behind her, jaw set and eyes narrowed.

Mayor Chase Ferguson Stokes an Old Flame.

She wedged her teeth together, uncomfortable with the adjective *old* but she refused to give this the reaction that was warranted. Which, by Miriam's estimations, involved writing a lengthy letter of response to the so-called duchess with explicitly detailed instructions on how to extract her head from her backside.

Miriam handed back the phone and gave Darren an amiable smile. "Thanks for telling me."

"Don't you want to read the article, M-Miss Andrix?"

"No, thank you, Darren. I'm sure it's packed with lies. You shouldn't give them the hits on their website." She winked to let him know she wasn't upset, even though she was. What an antiquated idea to blame the woman for a man's demise.

"It says that you and Chase had a wild affair ten years ago and that you're pulling him into your clutches again." Darren cleared his throat and read from the article. "'Her sights set on Chase's billions to forward her own causes, Miriam—'" he glanced up briefly "—sorry, I mean, M-Miss Andrix 'plans on keeping our mayor on the hook until she bends him to her will. The duchess has always been a fan of the Fergusons, and in this egregious case I'm firmly

Team Chase. Miriam—'" Darren mumbled another apology for using her first name "'—if you're reading, leave our beloved mayor alone and find someone in your own hometown to manipulate.'"

"What the hell?" Losing her facade of calm, she snatched Darren's phone and scanned the article for more damning accusations. She found plenty. It went on about how Chase was "unbribable" when it came to money but Miriam wasn't above "using sexual favors to ensnare him." There was even mention of ten years ago and how she'd tried to fit into his life in Dallas but it hadn't worked out.

So. Not an article pitting Chase and Miriam against the world, but rather one in his defense, against the trollop who had "ensnared" him. This blog wasn't antiquated. It was prehistoric.

Numb, Miriam returned his phone and mumbled an apology. Darren offered to avenge her honor by leaving a firmly worded comment on the blog, which was sweet, but she declined.

"Thanks for letting me know," she repeated, this time walking him to her office door. She spared a smile through the crack before shutting him out.

Okay, so Chase *hadn't* been overreacting. She palmed her own cell phone and shakily dialed his number.

"Mimi."

"Our photos are on the Dallas Duchess's blog."

"I know."

"You know?"

"Yes. Emmett called me this morning. I didn't think word would reach you so soon."

"You can thank my secret admirer."

"Who's that?" His stiff tone made her smile.

"He's fifteen. Has asthma. Stutters my name." She liked that Chase sounded slightly jealous, even though she shouldn't. "Did you read it?"

"Yes."

"How does anyone other than our friends and families know we were together that summer?"

"Hard to say. Someone could have called your acquaintances, or your former workplace. It's not as hard to uncover paychecks and flight records as you'd think."

Apparently not.

"Did you…stay in Bigfork?" She sat in her chair in case his answer was yes. Somehow it was easier to stomach if he wasn't close by.

"I stayed." There was a pause during which her heart skipped a beat. "Try not to let the blog bother you. My team is handling it. We'll have this buried soon enough."

"Okay, thanks."

"You're welcome."

An hour later, a sharp knock at her office door preceded her boss Nancy walking in. "Miriam, we need to talk."

Nancy's iPad was in her hand and when she flashed Miriam the screen, on it was the purple-and-gold Dallas Duchess banner.

Chase hadn't lied when he'd told Miriam that his staff was handling things, but that didn't mean he wasn't involved.

As calm as he'd tried to sound to Mimi, he wasn't. He was beyond *pissed*.

At Blake fucking Eastwood for bullying the women in Chase's life. At the Dallas Duchess for stooping to such gossipy lows and making Mimi out to be the enemy.

The first phone call he'd made when he found out was to Zach's wife, Penelope, PR guru.

"I thought the duchess was a friend of yours," he grumbled after she answered.

"I saw it. It's ugly."

His niece cooed in the background and Pen shushed her.

"Sorry." In his rage over Mimi being attacked, he'd checked his manners at the door. Pen was his sister-in-law, the mother of his niece Olivia first. He had no right to bark at her like one of his staff no matter how sour his mood. "I can call at a better time."

"No, it's fine. The nanny is here. I'm just kissing Livvie goodbye before I step into my office." There was a brief conversation with her sitter and then Pen said, "I'm firing up my computer as we speak. Stay on the line." She talked while she typed, outlining a plan to swing the spotlight away from Mimi and over to him.

"Maybe I'll pay Blake a visit," he said, practically spitting his name. "Break a kneecap or two."

"No." Pen laughed. "Absolutely not."

He had to smile. Penelope handled a great many powerful clients with ease. She routinely put billionaires in their places. It was why Chase had entrusted her to untangle Stef and Blake after that mess a year ago. This wasn't the same situation, but it felt eerily similar. A woman he cared about was being manipulated by a douchebag who was chasing his own personal and political gains.

"I was kidding about the knees. Calling him and letting him know I'm onto him would be satisfying."

"He'll record it and then we'll have a bigger mess on our hands." He liked the way she'd said *we*, including herself in the equation. It's what made her remarkable at her job. Pen cared enough to jump in and get her hands dirty with her clients.

"Won't that help?" he asked. "I'll make sure to point out that Mimi's a victim of his hapless plan."

"That'd be great," Pen's voice resonated with sarcasm. "The press would *love* to spin that as you, a powerful political figure, taking advantage of her like the misogynistic chauvinist you are."

He frowned. He hadn't thought of that.

"Not to mention the Twitter explosion to follow."

"Twitter?"

"Mmm-hmm. Women accusing you of mansplaining to them how the world should work, when you're not arguing how women are too unstable to be involved in politics."

"Man-whatting?" *What the hell?* "I don't think any of those things."

"I know." Her tone was patient. "Trust me, Chase. It's going to get uglier if you defend her."

"I can't let him do this to her." He wouldn't allow her to be harassed. What if this incident put her job in jeopardy? For all he knew, her coworkers might see this as her bedding the enemy. That was the tack the duchess had taken, only in his favor.

"They're already doing it, Chase. If they found more ammunition to use against her, they'll likely sit on it and wait for the perfect moment to drop the bomb. This isn't your first term. You *know* this."

"It's a looming issue until the election," he agreed miserably.

"Is your fear that her reputation will suffer…" A pause. "Or that you won't win her back now that she's seen the cost of staying with you?"

Was he that transparent?

"I want what's best for her. I'm not it." So much silence came from the other end of the phone that he added, "Hello?"

"You don't think you're good enough for her?" Pen asked.

"I didn't exactly say that."

"What happened in that mansion? What happened between you and Mimi? How much of what the Dallas Duchess reported is true?"

"None of what she said is true. The exact opposite is true."

"Meaning?" Pen wasn't letting this go.

"She's not trying to get her hooks into me. If it was up to me, I'd keep her as close as possible. She's...not interested. In me. Long-term." And who could blame her? Mimi had already received a small dose of what it was like to be with Mayor Chase Ferguson.

"You're interested in a future with her." It wasn't a question, so he didn't answer.

"An upcoming political campaign is not the time to start a new relationship. Or rekindle an old one," he mumbled, hoping Pen's pragmatism would have her agreeing with him.

"That doesn't mean it can't be done."

Well. Hell.

"Don't look for something that's not there," he warned.

A few taps of her keyboard later, Pen said, "I'm looking at the blog and these photos are...well, they could be anything but now that we've talked I can see it."

"See what?" He tightened the grip on his phone and stared out the window at the snowy lake below.

"How protective you are of Mimi. And the tender vulnerability in her that you're trying to protect."

He opened his mouth to protest but he couldn't lie to Penelope, or himself, any longer.

"Have you told her how you feel?"

"I told her I'd never drag her into the world of politics and oil, yes."

"Chase."

"Penelope."

She sighed, conceding this round. "Sometimes... headstrong women don't do what's best because we're trying to make our hearts as firm as our minds. *Sometimes* we need to know what's going on in your heads and hearts so that we can make the right decision."

"Trust me, Pen. Where Mimi and I are concerned, the

decisions that have been made are the right ones. Take care of this and there's a bonus in it for you."

"Oh goody," she murmured, droll.

"I'll buy Olivia a pony."

Her laughter chimed, lightening the intensity between them. He could always count on the mention of Olivia to snap Pen out of work mode. An unfair tactic, sure, but necessary.

"I'm on it. And, Mr. Mayor?"

"Yes?"

"Don't make the decision for her. Either way."

He nodded even though she couldn't see him, and then heard a soft click as she signed off.

He hadn't decided anything for Mimi. *She'd* decided. She was the one who was trying to keep her distance. He was carrying out her wishes.

Wasn't he?

Twenty

Miriam was torn between eating or drinking her feelings.

She opened the freezer and eyed a pint of salted caramel ice cream, then closed it and opened the fridge to consider the bottle of prosecco sitting on the top shelf. Prosecco was for celebrating, and she sure as hell didn't feel like doing that, so ice cream it was.

Her phone flashed again—she'd turned off the ringer—and warily she peeked at the screen. "Unknown numbers" had been calling over the last couple of days. She'd ignored them thinking they were sales calls, but after the fifteenth one she'd begun to suspect they had to do with the current surge of blogs written about her and the mayor of Dallas.

Luckily, this number she recognized. Kristine.

"Kris, hi." Miriam dug a spoon out of the drawer and tossed the lid of the ice cream container into the sink. No need for a bowl tonight. She was bottoming this baby out. "What's new?"

"You mean besides multiple calls from strangers asking me about you and Chase?"

"Ugh. I'm sorry." Heavily, Miriam sat on a kitchen chair.

"You warned me. I'm telling them nothing."

"Thanks, Kris." It'd been two days since Nancy had suggested Miriam take a leave of absence. Word had traveled fast—and not just to her fifteen-year-old admirer Darren. One of the heads of MCS was uncomfortable with the news breaking about her "affair with a mayor." It was an ugly way to paint it, but technically it was true. Nancy worked out a paid leave, but to Miriam, being asked to leave still felt unfair.

"Are you okay otherwise?" Kris asked.

"Other than my phone ringing off the hook with questions about the mayor of Dallas?" She turned her head to the kitchen window. "At least there aren't reporters camped out in my apartment complex."

"It'll blow over, I'm sure. When's the election?"

"A year and a half from now," Miriam announced glumly. Then she blinked when a blur of movement caught her eye. Chase was walking up the sidewalk, head down, collar on his dark coat pulled up. "I have to go. He's here."

"He's there? Meems—"

"I'll call you later." She hung up, no time to talk about how she felt about Chase while he was rapidly approaching her doorway. She slid across her linoleum on slipper socks en route to the living room to check her reflection in the mirror above the couch.

She quickly arranged her hair and checked her teeth, but there wasn't any time to change her clothes. He'd have to see her in a pair of gray leggings and an oversize blue sweatshirt.

The knock came and her eyes sank shut. This was it. And she *really* wasn't ready to see him again.

She yanked open the door and pasted on a smile. "Chase."

"Hi." His shoulders were wedged under his ears, his face red from the walk through the cold.

"Come in." She stepped back and let him in, wondering how a billionaire would view her tiny apartment. If he'd judge her rattling refrigerator or her hand-me-down kitchen table and chairs.

"I called."

She closed the door, noting how much space Chase took up in her itty-bitty kitchen. He dominated the area with his height and his piney scent. She admired how handsome he was with a touch of pain in her chest, his eyes gray against his charcoal wool coat and dark stylishly messy hair.

God. She'd missed him. She hadn't missed him for years, and now two days of being away from him had left a hole in her chest.

If she'd had time on the phone with Kris, Miriam would have admitted she'd partaken of the forbidden fruit and slept with him, but she also would've stated that her only interest in him now revolved around handling the political situation. With him standing in front of her looking strong and like someone she'd like to hold and kiss—and strip naked—Miriam's heart lurched. He wasn't so easily categorized in person.

"Is your phone off?" He was looking around the room and spotted her pint of ice cream on the table. He canted his head. "Are you all right?"

"I'm on a leave of absence."

"I know. I tried your work first. Nancy answered her phone." His mouth lifted in a teasing tilt.

"I turned my ringer off. It rings constantly."

He pulled in a deep breath. "I'm sorry."

"It's not your fault I protested Big Oil three years ago." She didn't blame him for Blake. The man had no scruples and was trying to get his way at any cost.

"Zach married a woman in public relations. Penelope Brand, now Ferguson," Chase said. "She's handling this on her end. I came over to pass along her phone number so you could touch base and work out a plan. She's the best."

"If it was a Dallas number, I ignored it." She gave him a wan smile and accepted Penelope's business card.

"Understandable."

"Can I get you—" she said at the same time Chase spoke.

"I'm flying out today."

She blinked. "Oh."

"I can handle everything better from home base." He looked to the window and then back at her. "I didn't only come to drop off the business card."

Her breath stalled.

"I didn't want to leave without saying goodbye."

A familiar fault line in her heart shook. Made sense. That break never had healed properly. He came to say goodbye, which was sweet, except that it also meant he was leaving. It was what she wanted. Or, it was what she'd *told* herself she wanted, anyway.

"Do you have everything you need, Mimi?" His words were measured like he expected her to protest.

She gave a jerky nod. She didn't have everything she needed, but she wasn't sure how to voice the unthinkable.

His eyes warmed and he stepped closer. She put out a hand to stop his advance, but when her palm met his chest she smoothed over the thick cotton of his sweater instead. So big and strong and for a few stolen days, hers again.

"Are you sure?" He lowered his lips to her forehead and let out a harsh breath. "There's nothing I'm forgetting before I go?"

Her nose tingled, her eyes heated, but she refused to cry in front of him. And she wouldn't prolong the inevitable.

"I'm good," she lied.

"You're better than good, sweetheart." He pressed his lips to her temple. A shudder shook her spine. It was taking everything in her not to press against him and bury her nose in his neck. "If you need anything…call Penelope, okay?"

It wasn't what she wanted him to say. Wasn't he the

one who promised she could call *him* if she needed anything? Had she expected him to come here and make one
last profession?

*Like what? That now that his political career is suffer-
ing a blow, he'd like to marry you?*

"What time's your flight?" she asked, the insane thought
about marriage lingering in the forefront of her mind. She
needed him to leave—for both their sakes.

"Sooner than I'd like." He offered a tender smile. "Why?
Need help finishing your ice cream?"

She pulled her fingers down his sweater and stopped
on his belt, brushing the cool metal with her thumb. No
matter how much she reminded herself that he was no
good for her, she went back like an addict who couldn't
kick a habit.

When her eyes flicked up to his, it was to witness heat
blooming in his darkening pupils. He dipped his head
and kissed her hard, pushing her back until her ass hit the
kitchen wall. His hands caught her face as he blanketed
her with his weight, pressing the length of his body—and
the length of his hard-on—against her. She sighed into his
mouth, wanting him in spite of how stupid it would be to
give in to the throbbing longing in her veins, the merci-
less pleading of her heart. He felt too good—being near
him felt too good.

"Don't go," she whispered.

"Mimi." His lips were off hers, coasting along her cheek.
"Honey, I have to go." He let out a dry laugh but when he
pulled away she saw the lack of humor in his smile. "God,
I have to."

He pulled his hands from her body and pushed them
into his hair, leaving her sagging against the wall, her shirt
wrinkled, her panties damp. He looked at the ceiling as if
gathering his strength and then dropped his arms and met
her eyes again.

"What do you want?" he asked evenly.

Wasn't it obvious? Him. Naked. Now.

"Long-term. What do you want?" he reiterated. "A family? A career? A mansion?"

Her hormone-saturated brain slogged through possible answers.

"I need to know, Mimi."

"I want…yeah, a career. I want to teach and work with kids and make the environment better. I don't need a mansion." She gestured at her place. "This is fine. And I have a family. A wonderful family."

His returning nod was solemn. "Good. That's good."

"What do you want?" she asked in return, trying to decipher what he wasn't saying.

"I want to be the mayor of Dallas. I want more nieces, or a nephew. I like my mansion." His smile was lopsided, if not a little sad.

Tears burned behind her eyeballs but she refused to let them fall. The question was asked—a question they'd asked several times over in many different ways.

What did they want?

Chase wanted his life the way it was. Miriam wanted hers the way it was.

No matter how much they wanted each other, that barrier wasn't going anywhere.

"Have a safe flight." She cleared her throat when the words came out tight with emotion. She had to let him go. For the last time. "I guess it'll be a while before you return to Montana, huh?"

His smile faltered. "A little while."

"You'll be reelected, Chase. I'm certain of it."

"And you—" he moved a stray curl from her eye "—will be reinstated to MCS. I'll make sure of it."

"Don't do…whatever it is you're thinking of doing. It's my job. I'll handle it."

"It's my fault you're not there." Before she could argue, he stole one last kiss. It was far too brief. "Goodbye, Mimi."

"Goodbye, Chase."

He turned for the door without looking back.

And she didn't watch him go.

On the flight to Dallas, Chase watched out the window as clouds passed under the belly of the private jet. He'd taken Pen's advice and asked Mimi what she wanted. He'd given her the chance to say…well, whatever she wanted. Whatever she was brave enough to tell him.

What Mimi had told him was what he should have expected. She wanted to work at Montana Conservation Society and shape the youth of tomorrow. But more than what she *had* said was what she hadn't said.

A speech from ten years ago played in his head.

Back then she hadn't minced a single word. She'd plainly told him they were destined to be together. That they could weather any storm—be it geography or finances or the disapproval of either of their families. She'd mentioned them getting married, an idea that hadn't sounded as horrible to him as he knew it should've. She insisted she'd make a great lawyer's wife, and mentioned how handy—if she ever had to sue someone—it would be to have someone as smart and brave as him on her side.

"We can weather any storm," he mumbled to the window. And yet the literal storm they'd weathered—the blizzard that brought them back together—had been the very thing to drive them apart.

He swiped his face, tired from not sleeping. He'd sat up with a glass of wine or lain and stared at the ceiling over the last two nights, at a loss for what to offer her. The only answer he came up with in those dark, silent hours was to give her what he owed her. Her life back.

Emmett returned to the cabin holding a pair of rocks

glasses with a couple of inches of amber-colored liquid in each. "Scotch?"

"If I say no, will you drink both?" Chase asked. One o'clock was early for a nip, but what the hell. Maybe it'd numb the pain that was a permanent resident of his chest.

"Looks like you're the one who needs both." Emmett had insisted on flying out. Said they could make a plan on the flight home for the "situation" in Dallas.

Emmett lowered his big body into the seat across from Chase, eyebrows raised in question.

"It was always a long shot," Chase said, accepting a glass.

"What? You becoming mayor?" Emmett smirked.

"Mimi. She and I...it was never a sure thing."

"Sex muddies the mind," Emmett crossed one leg ankle-to-knee and leaned back. "Creates bonds where there shouldn't be any."

"How the hell do you know?" Chase sipped his scotch and relished the burn low in his throat. "You haven't bonded with any woman you've taken to bed, have you?"

"I wasn't talking about me." Emmett drank from his own glass, peering over the rim at Chase.

"Mimi and I aren't the same. Never have been. Us together..." He searched for the right words. "We hold each other back."

"You hold back." It was a statement that sounded an awful lot like the start of an argument. "*You're* careful. You heed warning signals. It makes you a great politician. They had to dig up a woman from ten years ago to find a scrape of dirt on you." Emmett shook his head. "Careful's good for your career. Not sure if it's good everywhere else."

"I'm not going to force her into something she doesn't want." Namely, him. And his messy life.

"Did you ask her what she wanted?"

"Yes." He was somewhat vindicated that he could answer honestly.

"No overlaps? No common denominator?"

Chase shook his head though he wasn't sure if that was true. Sure, their careers were in different states, but was that insurmountable? No, he realized. It wasn't. He could have negotiated…he just hadn't. There were too many reasons not to, at least that's what he'd convinced himself.

Emmett polished off his drink and stood for a refill.

"Dammit, Em. Are you my advisor or not? What are you trying to say? Out with it."

Emmett swirled the remaining ice cube in his glass before raising his face. "Do you love her as much as you loved her ten years ago?"

Grinding his back teeth together, Chase said, "No."

His friend's expression tightened.

"More." Chase drained his own glass in one gulp. "I love her more."

"And did you tell her that?"

Chase shook his head.

"Told you. Too careful."

Chase didn't know what he hated more, admitting to himself that he'd been too chickenshit to tell Mimi the truth, or admitting that his best friend was right.

He *had* been too careful.

But that didn't mean he was too late.

Twenty-One

That afternoon when Stefanie had followed Emmett to Chase's office, she'd learned plenty about what was going on with her oldest brother.

It'd taken some doing, but she'd eventually pried out of Emmett that all of this was over the girl Chase had met when they'd summer vacationed in Montana.

The rebellious age of nineteen at the time, she'd been *not at all* interested in her brother's love life. Not that she was interested in it now, but she was a grown woman and well aware that since he'd returned to Dallas, something was amiss.

When Stef showed up at the conference hall, she flashed a smile at the security guy posted at the door. Since he was one of Emmett's heavies, he knew her—no need to show her credentials. Inside, she bypassed the drooling, hunching horde of reporters, refusing to look any of them in their beady eyes.

Vultures.

As a Ferguson and a billionaire by her own rights, she'd had her fair share of having her name besmirched at any convenient occasion. She had no love for these people. Zero.

She slipped behind the stage and into an adjoining room

acting as Chase's hideaway. He looked more tired than usual, but there was a resolute set to his shoulders.

"I have no idea why you cater to those vultures when they're more than happy to tear you into pieces," she told him, folding her arms over her chest.

"Those *vultures* are responsible for my career."

She didn't agree with that, but any arguments on the matter had been trotted out in the past and had always ended with agreeing to disagree.

"Are you okay?" she asked, knowing that he'd likely keep the truth from her on that count, as well.

"Fine."

"I mean it." She put her hand on his shoulder. He looked up from his speech notes, decorated in red ink courtesy of the pen in his hand. "I can't escape the idea that Blake Eastwood's involvement is my fault."

He frowned. "None of this is your fault, Stefanie. It's important for you to understand that."

"It'd feel like a lot less my fault if I didn't know Blake." She added a silent *biblically*, because no matter how grown-up she was, she wasn't willing to discuss sex with her brother.

Chase straightened from his lean against a cheap desk the room had been outfitted with, and dropped his notes and pen onto it.

"Listen to me," he said. "That bastard would do anything to get to our family. The only mistake you made was trusting him." He palmed her cheek in a rare act of tenderness between them. "I should apologize to you. He took advantage of you, and you're worth more than being a pawn in a vendetta he has against me."

Gratitude clogging her throat, Stef nodded. Chase dropped his arm and bent to meet her gaze.

"Yes?" he asked.

"Yeah," she agreed.

"All right, then. Now get out so I can prepare a statement. And don't look any of the vultures in the eyes on your way out. It's as good as an invitation to harass you."

She smiled, feeling loved and cared for. Chase was a good brother. Both of her brothers were. But that warm fuzzy was obliterated by the appearance of Emmett Keaton, who was the *opposite* of a warm fuzzy.

A cold prickly, she thought with a chuckle.

"Excuse me, Lurch, I was just leaving." She smiled sweetly up at Emmett, who remained silent. His lips flinched into a flat line, which meant she'd gotten under his skin.

Her work was done here.

She sidled along the wall, taking her brother's advice to keep her eyes down. The members of the press were busily preparing for Chase's speech, either touching up their makeup, scrolling through their cell phones or practicing their intros.

As God as her witness, if she ever ended up in a position of power either at Ferguson Oil or as a politician— Ha!—Stef would never call a meeting to defend her actions.

She exited the room, making a beeline for the coffee bar. On her approach she spotted a familiar brunette woman frantically searching the halls while clutching her purse to her shoulder.

"Miriam Andrix?" Stef kept her voice low so as not to draw unnecessary attention, but Miriam heard her and stopped dead in her tracks.

"Remember me? Chase's sister, Stefanie Ferguson." Stef gestured to herself rather than offer a hand since Miriam was regarding her with wide, wary eyes. No doubt the poor woman had been hounded since the story broke about her and Chase.

"Stefanie." Miriam's shoulders relaxed some, her guard dropping. "Nice to see you."

"You, as well. Is… Chase expecting you?" Surely he would've mentioned it, or appeared more nervous…or anticipatory. Something.

"No. He's not." Miriam gave a quick shake of her head. *Interesting.*

Stefanie stepped closer. "Why are you in Dallas?"

"Um… Long story."

I bet.

"Lucky for you, I found you first. I know where Chase is, but a burly security guy is blocking the room. I can get you in."

Hope blossomed on Miriam's face—she really was beautiful. Elegant and lithe, with full lips and expressive dark eyes.

"Penelope told me where to find him and about the press conference." Miriam's mouth curved into a slight smile. "I came, which I'm sure is a terrible idea. Or at least it is for his career."

"Why's that?" Stef leaned in, interested. The reason behind Miriam's presence was too juicy not to pry.

"Stefanie, darling, there you are!" Eleanor Ferguson approached with quick steps. "Am I too late? Did the press conference start without me? Have you seen Penelope?"

Before Stefanie had a chance to answer any of those questions, Eleanor did a double take of Miriam. Stefanie watched as her mother's face drew down in recognition.

Miriam faced her, pulled her shoulders back and addressed her curtly. "Hello, Eleanor."

Definitely, Miriam hadn't thought this through.

By the time she'd arrived at that conclusion, she'd also arrived in Dallas thanks to a hefty sum paid for a private jet so as not to risk being delayed at the airport.

She couldn't afford to delay one more moment. Ten years had been long enough, and then she'd gone and tacked on another week or so for good measure. Every inch of her ached with words unsaid and emotions unexpressed.

Penelope had called yesterday, and since Chase had delivered her phone number personally, Miriam knew to take the call. The other woman had a plan to unravel the "bad press" surrounding them, but Miriam didn't care about her reputation. She only cared about Chase's.

"If he's anything like his brother, my husband," Penelope had told her, "then Chase is not going to take my advice. He wants to call off the hounds, but I advised him not to come to your defense with the press. I'm concerned they'll twist the story and make him the bad guy. I don't want you to worry about that, though. Don't think of me as taking sides where you and Chase are concerned. My job is to preserve *both* your careers and reputations. Everyone's winning."

Miriam liked Penelope's confidence, but she liked more what she'd said about Chase coming to Miriam's defense. Penelope shared details about the press conference and dropped the name of the conference center, though it was more conversational than intentional.

"When the news hits, and videos and Tweets start, we'll be an hour ahead of it," Pen had said. "One of the stipulations for the press members we chose was that they agreed to wait sixty minutes before sharing anything they learn in that room."

Miriam had gone to bed that night, but she hadn't fallen asleep. She'd stared at the ceiling, stealing a glance at her glowing blue alarm clock now and then. First at midnight, then 1:00 a.m., 1:30 a.m., 2:30 a.m. and finally 4:45 a.m., when she'd given up trying to sleep at all.

She couldn't sleep. She couldn't escape the idea that nothing was as it should be. Chase should be in Dallas: of that she was certain. But not without knowing the truth— a truth she hadn't shared when he stood in her kitchen a few days ago.

Sure, she'd told him a partial truth. She wanted to work with kids. She wanted to save the environment. But she let him believe that her future was wrapped up in her job and that none of it involved him.

That couldn't be further from the truth.

In her defense, she hadn't admitted as much to herself until he was thousands of feet in the air and zooming away from her and her beloved home state.

The next morning, after drinking her second cup of coffee, she made the jittery, spontaneous decision to fly to Dallas.

Ten years ago, he'd put her on a plane back to Montana. He'd let her believe that her leaving was what he wanted. Even recently when they were snowed in together, he'd defended his actions by saying it'd been the right thing to do. He believed he'd been chivalrous, that he'd been protecting her, but she didn't think he'd done what he *wanted*.

Miriam had come all this way, to interrupt the press conference in what might be her worst laid plan to date, to give her and Chase one last chance. One of them had to be brave. She didn't know what he'd say, or what the future would bring, but she knew she could find a job "saving the world" anywhere she damned well pleased. Texas was in as much need of environmental love as Montana.

And she was fairly certain that Chase asking "What do you want?" had everything to do with him catering to her wishes, and nothing to do with what *he* actually wanted.

Déjà vu all over again.

Facing his mother now, Miriam straightened her spine and vowed not to let this woman intimidate her. Ten years ago, she'd endured Eleanor's taut words and prim body language not knowing how to respond. But Miriam was stronger now.

"Is Penelope aware you're here?" Eleanor, who endeavored to take control of every situation, asked.

"I'm not here to see Penelope. I'm here to see your son, Chase."

The older woman's eyebrows climbed her smooth forehead. "I know you don't have much political know-how, but surely you're aware that your being here puts his campaign in grave jeopardy."

What Miriam was sure about was that Chase was an amazing man, an amazing politician with amazing friends on his side—one of them a plucky, capable PR maven. He'd come out of this snag just fine. He'd been certain of it, and so was she.

"He's a big boy," Miriam replied. "I'm sure he'll handle whatever fallout occurs from my walking through those doors and saying what I came here to say."

Affronted, Eleanor's jaw dropped. "Stefanie, kindly call hotel security before Miriam causes a ruckus."

"I want to hear what she has to say." Chase's sister flashed a pretty smile, and like that, Miriam became a big, *big* fan of Stefanie Ferguson.

Acting on instincts born of a thirty-three-year-old woman—and far from the headstrong twenty-three-year-old she'd been ten years ago—Miriam reached out and touched Eleanor's arm.

"I don't want this to end with me crying or hating you again. I don't want this to end with me conceding and him staying quiet to keep the peace. I'm going to tell Chase how I feel and let him decide what to do from there."

"How *do* you feel?" Eleanor's voice was coated in shock, or maybe denial. Miriam wasn't sure the woman really wanted to know, but she'd asked, so here went nothing.

"I loved him ten years ago. I wanted nothing more than to be at his side for the rest of our lives. I never thought I'd see him again. He's the one who came back to Montana— who bought the mansion above the beach where we used to trespass and skinny-dip."

Eleanor paled, but Miriam wasn't through yet.

"I was the one who showed up on his doorstep with sweet potato pie, but make no mistake, Eleanor. Chase is the one who came back."

He'd pursued her under the guise of getting her back into his bed. Under the guise, she suspected, of proving to himself that he was over her. But the conclusion she'd arrived at that sleepless night was that he'd needed that guise. It was the safest path out of Montana and back to Dallas. To his destiny, and leaving her to hers.

"I never expected to fall in love with him again," she confessed. "In a way I guess I didn't. I think I never fell out, and those dormant feelings were jarred awake when I spent Thanksgiving weekend with him. I know you don't think I'm good for Chase, but I don't care what you think. We were too careful the first time around. I'm not going to make the same mistake this time."

An excited squeal came from over her shoulder. Miriam turned to find Stefanie cupping her mouth with both hands and bouncing on the balls of her feet.

"Sorry," she parted her hands to say. "I'm sorry. This is so exciting." She raised her eyebrows and grinned at her mother.

Eleanor's expression was more downtrodden and tired then argumentative. That was certainly a surprise. Miriam remembered the older woman's words being formed of steel wool. No doubt a similar speech lingered at the base of Eleanor's throat about how Miriam and Chase were too young or would never make it, or about how Miriam would ruin his reputation. Or… maybe not? Maybe Eleanor had learned something over the last decade, as well.

Chase's mother scanned Miriam's attire, a simple black dress, high heels and long coat. Miriam gripped her Coach purse, the only nice handbag she owned, and bore the older woman's scrutiny.

"You're serious," Eleanor concluded. "You love Chase in a real and lasting way."

Miriam shook her head, but not in denial. "*Real* is the only way I know how to love him."

Twenty-Two

Without introduction, Chase stepped onto the stage in the conference room. A hush fell over the invited members of the press, and he squinted against the hot lights over the podium.

Pen had advised him on how to handle questions about Mimi. She'd reminded him again on the Post-It note attached to his speech that arrived by courier just twenty minutes ago. Red ink decorated the edges of the notes—his changes—including the X he'd drawn over Pen's Post-it note suggestion. His sister-in-law wasn't going to like what he'd say, but he'd ignored advice before to cater to his own gut call.

Today was one of those days.

"Thank you for coming out today at my office's request," he started. Cameras flashed and pens were set at the ready on notepads. "As you're aware, I've been recently accused of involvement with a woman who has ties to environmentalist groups. Groups that stand against entities like Ferguson Oil. I was involved with this woman ten years ago, over a summer spent in Bigfork, Montana. Our relationship predated my political career, and though she'd vocalized her distaste for my family's industry at the time, she didn't hold it against me."

He couldn't help smiling at the memory of when he'd broken the news. Miriam had looked politely appalled, and then resigned. She'd rolled her eyes and said something to the effect of *Good thing I love you.*

Chase folded his notes and set them aside. The rest of what he had to say wasn't going to be read from his prepared speech.

"A good friend of mine dispensed some valuable advice recently. The kind of advice you don't want to hear, but he tells you anyway."

Emmett was keeping an eye on the crowd, but Chase made out the slightest half smile on his friend's profile.

"He told me I was too careful." Chase pulled in a breath of pure will. Admitting he was wrong had never been a strength. "My friend was right. I am careful. Service has long been my role. My function. As the first-born son of the Fergusons, my destiny is to serve my family and my voters and our shared business. I can't afford to serve myself. Or…" The next vulnerable admission required a brief pause before he decided to hell with it. "Or my heart."

Gasps rose in the crowd, one notably from his mother who just entered the room. Good. She, especially, needed to hear this.

"As the slander continues from my opponent's team, I'm faced with my past and the unfair way it's being portrayed. I don't care what dirt you find on me from that summer ten years ago. I only care about how you treat Miriam Andrix."

He paused to let that sink in as his sister slipped in behind his mother. Then he focused on the crowd of reporters in the front row who eagerly scribbled onto notepads or pecked notes into their phones. Cameras with bright lights closed in to capture his face during this truth-telling debacle—something Penelope Ferguson would reprimand him for, he was sure.

He held up the papers he'd set aside. "This speech would

have me confessing that I was young and foolish years ago. That I followed my heart and not my head, and as a result became entangled with a woman who wasn't destined to become my future. I've always known who to serve, and in what order. My family. The great city of Dallas. My family's business. Breaking things off with Miriam was the right thing to do for my career and for her. I never wanted her to have to deal with scrutiny. I never wanted her under the microscope with me. It's what I signed up for, and nothing she would ever ask for. I've long been in the habit of protecting the ones I love."

Quiet whisperings rose but fell silent again when he continued.

"Miriam Andrix has a big heart and a strong will." He allowed a smile when he pictured her stubbornly standing her ground. "For as long as I've known her, she's been hell-bent on saving the world. An admirable feat since most of us downgrade to simply saving ourselves. I'm not here to admit I was a foolish youth. I'm here to make a request. When I left Bigfork, Montana, I left Miriam to her life and she let me return to mine. Leave her alone. It's past time to refocus the campaign on me and what I can do for our city."

He nodded that he was through and reporters shot out of their seats. Many waved, most called his name.

"Yes, Donna." He pointed at the older gray-haired woman in the second row.

"Mr. Mayor, welcome home. What's the first order of business?"

"You mean besides spending my first day back with you fine people?" He grinned and soft laughter rolled over the crowd. "I'll be in my office, my sights set on Dallas and winning the reelection."

Canned but charming answers were always the best choices.

He pointed at a young intern for the city paper. "Bobby."

"Uh, yes, Mr. Mayor. Will you retaliate against your opponent for trying to slander your good name?"

"We always take the high road, Bobby. You know this."

"Fiona." He pointed at a middle-aged blonde woman.

"Mr. Mayor, will you be returning to Bigfork any time soon?"

"I own a house there, so I'm sure I will return. How soon isn't something I'm comfortable sharing with you yet." He capped that answer with a smile and pointed to a white-haired man. "Tom."

"Mr. Mayor, we've heard you say in the past that the oil industry…"

And so the questions went, the focus back where it should be: on Chase's company and his position as one of the leaders of the city. Just like he'd asked, and they paid him that respect. After a few more answers, he concluded the conference.

"Now if you'll excuse me, I—"

"Mr. Mayor!" came a shout from the back of the room. The camera lights swept away from him.

Mutterings like "That's her!" and "Miriam! Miriam!" crested like a wave.

He blinked the woman into focus. *Miriam?*

The same woman who'd won his heart…twice. But who was counting?

"Yes. The brunette in the back," Chase said, enamored by her all over again.

"Are you single, Mr. Mayor?" Mimi called out.

"Pitifully so," he said into the microphone. A few of the cameras swung back to him. "As a result of a recent tragic error."

She pushed through the crowd toward him, her smile tentative. "What error was that?"

"I left the woman I was in love with in another state without telling her how I feel."

Mimi stopped moving, her eyes trained on him, her mouth parting softly.

"That *is* tragic," she finally managed.

Murmurings came from the crowd, but no one interrupted.

"If you have time," Mimi said. "I have just one more question."

Chase didn't make it a habit of being thrown off-guard, yet here he was. What was she doing here? Why had she come? But instead of asking, he simply answered her question. "I have time."

"Would you ever again consider dating a woman with a history of protesting the oil industry?"

The hope—the love—on Mimi's face echoed his own so fiercely, the next word was hard to get past his throat.

"No."

Her face fell, and the reporters around her strained closer with microphones and cameras, silent and slack-jawed with curiosity.

"I'd ask her to marry me," Chase said, a smile inching across his face, "but only if she loved me as much as I love her."

In the bright lights, he could make out tears shining on the edges of Mimi's eyelids.

"Do you love me?" he asked, swallowing thickly. Risky, this, but he was now in the risk-taking business.

"I do."

He more read her lips than heard her. His joy over those two words was so overwhelming that he leaped from the stage and rushed through the crowd. Cameras snapped; questions shot like cannons around him. He narrowed his focus on Mimi, kissing her for the world—or at least for Dallas—to see.

Three words echoed in his head as he met her mouth with eagerness.

She loves me. She loves me.

When he pulled away, she was grinning up at him, her arms around his neck.

"Mr. Mayor!" He recognized the voice of Channel 9's premier reporter who'd long been one of his supporters.

"Yes, Phil?"

"Was that a real proposal?"

Chase turned to Mimi who was in his arms, a crease of worry decorating her brow.

"Yes," he told her, his smile permanent.

"What was your answer, Miriam?" Phil asked as the crowd around them quieted.

Mimi's fingers tickled the back of Chase's neck and she tipped her chin. "I could make or break your career, Mayor."

"My career isn't what I'm concerned about. It's me who you're making or breaking."

"I'm more into making." Her smile widened.

He thought of them making out, making love, and decided she was right. She was more into making.

"Very well," she whispered in his ear. "I accept."

Caught up in her and the moment, Chase leaned in to take her lips in another kiss… But not before Fiona interrupted with, "Was that a yes or a no on the marriage proposal?"

"Should we give her the scoop?" Mimi asked against his lips.

"I'll let you do the honors."

"Yes," she turned her head to tell the crowd, and then she stood on her tiptoes and brushed her nose against his. "My answer's always been yes."

* * * * *

WILD WYOMING NIGHTS

JOANNE ROCK

To my warrior readers who've had the strength to leave unhappy relationships— may you find romance in the everyday and joy in your new journey.

One

Nerves prancing harder than the spirited stunt horse beside her, Emma Layton gripped the reins tighter. This was only her second day of shooting on location in Cheyenne, Wyoming.

She prayed there would be a third.

The gray Andalusian was specially trained for trick riding, one of a half-dozen animals delivered to the Creek Spill Ranch for filming *Winning the West*. The horse shook its long mane and stomped the ground, bristling with impatience to begin their work together. The mare was far better prepared for the day's challenges than Emma.

When she interviewed for this opening—only her fifth paying role as a stuntwoman—Emma had been so focused on nailing the job that she hadn't thought twice when asked about prior riding experience. While it was true she'd taken informal lessons as a teen on the property where her mother worked for the famous Ventura family, Emma knew she'd only been granted the job because of her connection to Antonio Ventura, the director. Not that she would see him any time soon. As a stunt performer for one of the more minor characters in the film, Emma served as part of the second unit on this location. That meant she answered to the stunt coordinator, while Antonio would direct the leads.

Both units were filming at the Creek Spill for the next two weeks, but Emma hoped and prayed the shoot would run over. She needed the work almost as much as she needed to be as far from Los Angeles as possible right now. Far, far away from her ex-boyfriend, due to be released from state prison tomorrow. This job had been a godsend, a boon that made her determined to exaggerate her limited horseback riding ability.

This morning, Emma and her assigned mare stood outside the pristine Creek Spill stables with five other body doubles and their mounts. All waited for instruction from Zoe Bettle, the stunt coordinator who also served as horse mistress for the film. Zoe, an accomplished horsewoman in her midforties with the body of an athlete, appeared to be in a standoff with a tall, impossibly handsome cowboy in a dark Stetson.

At least, he *looked* like a cowboy.

His broad shoulders filled out a fitted gray T-shirt tucked into faded jeans with creases bleached almost white where the fabric contoured to his movement and muscle. His boots had the distressed leather look that costume designers labored to replicate with sandpaper and acetone. But the weathered appearance didn't extend to the rancher's face. He had the square jaw, chiseled cheekbones and full lips a camera loved. Clearly, he was one of the lead actors—someone with enough clout to raise Zoe's hackles. Emma could tell by the set to her shoulders that she was not pleased with whatever the man had to say.

Already, Emma didn't like him. She needed her boss in a good mood today so Zoe would be forgiving of the mistakes Emma was sure to make. As it was, the woman appeared ready to fire the first stunt rider foolish enough to screw up. Emma tried to calm her nerves by stroking Mariana's soft gray muzzle.

"Fine." Zoe's last word had enough volume to reach Emma's ears. She turned toward the assembled stunt talent. "A change of plans today, ladies and gentlemen." She strode closer to them, her tall riding boots stirring up dust from the pasture. Although she was just barely five feet tall, she carried herself like an Olympic gymnast, her perfect posture and musculature outlined by tan jodhpurs and a bright red T-shirt. "Our host, Mr. McNeill, has expressed concerns about our *horsemanship*." She articulated the word with all the affront she must be feeling. "So I have assured him we will slow down our training schedule to meet the ranch's safety standards."

Their host? Emma glanced back at the rancher she'd mistaken for an actor, seeing him in a new light. If he was responsible for this sprawling ranch with its well-kept fields and neatly maintained barns, he excelled at his job. The Creek Spill was like a minitown in the middle of nowhere, from its bunkhouse full of ranch hands to its on-site cooking facilities and dedicated water tower.

"Ms. Bettle, I think you misunderstood me," the

cowboy called from where he stood near the freshly painted four-rail fence that separated the pasture from the paddock area.

The stunt coordinator ignored him. She folded her arms and glared at the talent.

"We will divide into two groups. Ms. Layton and anyone else involved in the race scene, please show Mr. McNeill how well prepared we are for the stunt." Zoe's eyes bored into Emma's, warning her not to mess up. "The rest of you, come with me. We will be working in the far pasture so as not to disturb the local horses while they 'adjust to our presence.'"

Emma's boss did not roll her eyes, but her tone suggested how much she wanted to. Two other stunt doubles—both men, both stronger riders than her—stepped forward with their mounts and headed toward the rancher. Emma started to follow them, keeping hold of the leather reins as she spoke soothingly to the mare at her side.

"Ms. Layton." Zoe stepped closer to her, voice lowered. Hints of an Eastern European accent came through. "Carson McNeill signed a unique agreement with the production company that gives him the last word on safety conditions here. Since the Creek Spill is a working ranch, we don't have the luxury of sending him on a two-week vacation while we shoot. We must make sure he's satisfied that we know what we are doing. Yes?"

Emma nodded. "I understand."

Impressing Carson McNeill was priority one if she wanted to keep this job. Her palms began sweating on the reins as she glanced at the cowboy who now controlled her fate. Why couldn't she be filming a fight scene? Or jumping off a building? Anything but horseback riding. No doubt Zoe recognized Emma was the weak link in the stunt crew.

She'd been warned.

While Zoe and the remaining cast members mounted for the ride to the far pasture, Emma urged her horse, Mariana, forward. Morning sunlight glinted off the creek in the distance behind the ranch owner. The whole property flanked the water on both sides for two miles. When she'd first arrived at the Creek Spill two days ago, Emma had been overwhelmed by the beauty of Wyoming with its endless blue sky, rugged cliffs and rolling hills dotted with wildflowers. Now the spectacular view narrowed to Carson McNeill, where he stood under the shade of a giant ash tree.

He appeared to give instructions to both men in her group, and the guys were mounted and riding away before she reached his side. Her pulse raced; she wished she didn't have to speak to him alone. She'd mostly conquered her demons where men were concerned. After the nightmare relationship with her former boyfriend ended three years ago, Emma had started training herself for this competitive profession to supplement her work as a personal trainer. Stunt work appealed to her need to be more sure of herself, and she'd fooled a lot of people into thinking she had already arrived at that goal.

Right now, she was more worried about Carson McNeill calling her out for a fraud where her riding skills were concerned. Without the men in her crew to hide behind, she would be making it easier for the rancher to see her weakness. But the idea of appearing weak steeled her spine as she walked over to him, giving her the shot of bravado she needed to pull this off.

"I'm in the race scene, Mr. McNeill." She tipped her chin up and braced her shoulders. It was her personal "ready" position. "What would you like to see from me?"

She had a degree in exercise science. She'd trained hard to be here. This man would not send her packing.

"Call me Carson." He just barely touched the brim of his Stetson, a cowboy tip of the hat.

"Emma Layton." She didn't offer her hand since she held Mariana's reins with her right one and it was slick with nervous sweat. In her left hand, she clutched the strap of her riding helmet.

Carson McNeill was even more compelling up close, where she could see past the shadows cast by his hat. His eyes were pale blue. A hint of dark hair escaped his hat, curling at the base of his neck. His gaze dipped over her briefly, inspiring a flare of unexpected heat along her skin even though she was thoroughly covered in a standard workout T-shirt with the jodhpurs and riding boots Zoe had provided.

"Nice to meet you, Emma. And I assure you, I didn't mean to start the day on the wrong side of your boss." There was a certain practiced charm about his smile. She bet he unleashed it on other women with great success.

Emma couldn't afford to be interested, despite that lick of warmth she felt along her skin. The sensation wasn't from the smile that was too automatic, but from the intelligence in those blue eyes. A shrewdness that told her there was more to the rich rancher than a handsome face and honed bod.

"Zoe knows stunts and horses as well as anyone." Emma had read everything she could find about the woman on her flight to Cheyenne, and she'd been impressed. "She's probably not used to having her judgment questioned."

"I don't question her horsemanship, only the skills of her crew members." His gaze moved from Emma to Mariana, and he reached to stroke the mare's nose. "In particular, I noticed yesterday during the workout that you appeared uneasy at times."

Her stomach dropped. She hadn't known she was being observed.

"Yesterday we were simply tasked with getting to know our mounts." Sweat broke out along the back of her shoulders, though it wasn't all that hot for August. A breeze stirred the mare's mane and made Emma's skin turn clammy. Her heart rate quickened. "I've never worked with a horse that uses so many specialty commands. She's highly trained."

"Unlike you." He reached for the bridle. "May I?"

His fingers brushed hers, the contact sparking unwanted heat despite how he'd just insulted her. Relinquishing the leather, Emma tamped down her anger, knowing she needed to smooth things over with him or Zoe would send her home.

"Mr. McNeill—"

"Carson," he reminded her, letting Mariana's lead dangle to the ground. "And you don't need to hold her so tightly. That's why she's rocking her head like that. She wants some breathing room."

"Carson." She took a deep breath and tried to calm herself. Seeing the way Mariana quieted, Emma could hardly argue with him. "Stunt work involves a wide variety of skills. While I may not be the expert horsewoman that Zoe is, I assure you, I am well qualified

to scale heights, take a fall or drive a burning car into
a building."

He folded his arms across his chest, seeming to take
her measure. "But you're not working with a car or a
building. You're working with a nine-hundred-pound
animal with a will of its own, and that brings a whole
new level of danger to the job."

"That's why the production company imports horses
like Mariana. They're used to the rigors of filming and
working with a variety of people."

"That doesn't mean you can waltz in here after a
Saturday at the local dude ranch and expect to pull off
a stunt on horseback."

Too bad she had to do just that.

"Then tell me, Carson." She looked him in the eye,
unwilling to back down. "What do I have to do to prove
to you I belong here? You name it, and I'll rise to the
challenge."

Because whatever dangers Mariana and the Creek
Spill Ranch held for Emma, they were nothing compared to the damage an angry ex could do if she went
back home now.

Emma Layton was turning out to be an enticing distraction he hadn't anticipated.

Carson stared into her deep brown eyes, her gaze unwavering as she awaited instruction. She was scrubbed
clean of makeup, her brown hair scraped back into a
ponytail and wrapped into a haphazard knot. Everything about her said she was here to work, from the determined set of her full lips to the tense shoulders she's
squared to him.

She was a half foot shorter than him, with the kind

of lean muscles that dancers possessed. She was hardly what came to mind when he envisioned a stunt actor but based on her scowl, he guessed she might breathe fire if he spoke that thought aloud. With her long elegant neck and delicate features, she looked more suited for ballet than daredevil tricks, but to each his own.

Or her own.

The fact that he found her grit and determination incredibly appealing should not be on his mind right now given how much production the Creek Spill Ranch lost every day that shooting continued on his property. Carson had his overly cautious twin brother to thank for all the added clauses in the contract with the film company that said the McNeill family had the last word on safety for the duration of the shoot. Normally, Carson was the easygoing twin and Cody took care of being the hard-ass. But Carson had needed to step in and fill his brother's shoes. Cody had a lot on his plate with his girlfriend expecting a baby. And now they were dealing with a new crisis: Cody and Carson's stepmother was in a coma.

Paige had been in intensive care after a fall while hiking in Yellowstone, putting the whole family on edge the same week the film company came to town. Making matters more complicated, just a day before the accident, Carson's youngest half sister, Scarlett, had received a blackmail note threatening to reveal some secret from Paige's past that would damage the family.

While hell broke loose all around them, Carson was left to oversee the Creek Spill, plus make sure Cody didn't overlook anything at the other major family holding, the Black Creek Ranch, while everyone took turns sitting with Paige at the ICU in Idaho. Thankfully, Paige was being transported to the Cheyenne hospital today, now that she'd shown signs of coming out of the coma.

Still, it definitely wasn't a good time to be noticing the sex appeal of Emma Layton, who stared him down as though she wished *he* was the one driving a car into a burning building. Preferably at full speed. More often than not, women found him charming. How damned ironic that the one woman to turn his head in recent memory looked like she wanted to take his head off.

"I want you to feel more at ease on horseback," he told Emma finally, reminding himself he was not the demanding, inflexible McNeill brother. "That will decrease your risk of injury considerably."

Once he felt assured of her competence, he would return to work. She was a professional, after all, and she had a stunt coordinator watching over her shoulder. The company was insured for this kind of thing and the ranch wasn't liable.

Except Carson had a conscience to answer to, and damned if it hadn't grown bigger with his ever-responsible twin out of the picture. Their own mother, an experienced rancher, had died from injuries sustained while trying to separate a bull from the cattle. Carson had been four years old at the time, and he'd been there, along with his older brother. Her death had haunted the family and changed their father forever. He knew all too well that animals could turn unpredictable.

Emma lifted her riding helmet and strapped it on her head. "I'm ready."

"I sent your two colleagues out to the arena to work on their leg positioning." He pointed out the track his younger brother, Brock, used to show and train quarter horses, a lucrative side business at the Creek Spill.

"There's a training area beyond that, next to a tack shed. Let's take your horse out there and we'll start working on your hands."

"Her name is Mariana." She pointed toward the horse as he began leading the gray mare out to the training field. "And what do you mean about my hands?"

He took the quieter shady route behind the barn, his boots finding the worn grassy path that hadn't been trampled to dirt yet. He thought he'd been prepared for the added activity of a film production on his property, but he'd underestimated how much equipment and manpower it required.

"They're too stiff." He hadn't given riding lessons since Scarlett was a girl. "You need a more elastic hold that doesn't place extra pressure on the bit. As it is, Mariana will get confused about what you want from her if she feels like you're tugging."

"I'm a fast learner." Emma slanted a look his way, peering over the horse's nose. "Just tell me what you want to see from me, I'll do it. I can't afford to lose this job."

There was more to that story. He could hear it in her voice. See it in the hint of vulnerability in those dark brown eyes. And he regretted that he couldn't give her the reassurance she clearly sought.

Opening the gate to the training area, he waited until Mariana and Emma were through before he latched it behind them. "And I can't afford for anyone to get hurt on my property. I made it very clear to the production manager when I signed the contract that a ranch is a dangerous place. I won't allow you to continue if I think you're at risk."

She huffed out a breath, regarding him with frustration she didn't bother to hide. Hands on hips, she faced him.

"Every single thing we do in my business puts us at risk. In my last job, I once had to reenact a knife fight over twenty times before it was right. The take they liked best was the one where I took a slice to the right calf that sent me to the ER. That comes with the territory and I know that going in." Her cheeks flushed with color.

He'd hit a nerve. Or else just wounded her pride.

"I'm more concerned about head trauma. If your horse throws you—"

"I'm trained to fall the right way," she reminded him.

"For a woman who is concerned about keeping her job, perhaps you should listen more and interrupt less," he suggested mildly, even though she was beginning to get under his skin.

She pursed those full lips thoughtfully. Then her shoulders eased a bit. "You're right. I'm nervous and defensive, and that isn't going to help. What should I do first?"

He had to admire how fast she shifted gears.

"Hop on your mount and I'll show you." He watched as she placed a boot in the stirrup and swung her leg over. Smoothly. Easily.

He amended his earlier assessment of her skills. She had more in her background than a weekend at a dude ranch.

Quickly, he ran down what he wanted to see from her, starting with an explanation of what her hands were telling her horse. She practiced gripping the reins farther apart so she could feel the horse's natural movement, allowing her to stay in sync with the animal. While the horse trotted around the track, Carson stepped out of the practice yard to check in with the two male riders in the arena. They looked better, but Carson wasn't releasing them yet. He called over Nate—a ranch hand who'd been working closely with Brock and the quarter horses for more than a year—and tasked him with giving the riders a few more tips.

"Me? I'm no riding instructor." The younger man scratched his head under his hat as he stared out at the arena, planting a dusty boot on the lowest fence rail. "I train horses, not people."

"But if you had to give these guys a handful of tips to make sure they survive two weeks on horseback, what would you say?" Carson glanced back to check on Emma, who had slowed to a walk.

"I'd say I'd rather work the hot brunette." Carson followed Nate's gaze, and noted the appreciative grin pulling at his mouth as he watched Emma.

His protective instincts stirred, surprising him.

"Seniority has its privileges." Though Carson didn't plan on pursuing his attraction for the prickly stunt double, he needed to keep safe for two weeks, especially after seeing that vulnerable look in her eyes.

Then again, he wasn't ready to walk away yet, either.

"You're the boss," Nate told him agreeably, turning his attention back to the stunt actors riding circles around the dirt track. "But the dude on the left rides too high in the saddle. Guess I could pull off his stirrups. Get him to work on his seat."

Carson clapped Nate on the shoulders. "Good thinking. Whatever you can do. By the end of the week, they're going to be racing and fighting on horseback, so I'd like to do whatever we can to keep them in one piece."

Leaving Nate to take over with the men, Carson returned to the practice yard, his attention fully on Emma. The thought of her racing at breakneck speed in just a few days from now made him edgy. He didn't want to tick off the stunt coordinator any more than he already had, and he had to get back to overseeing ranch operations, so he didn't have time to interfere with the filming. But he wasn't impressed with the level of safety he'd seen on set so far.

"Am I doing it wrong?" Emma called over to him as he neared her and Mariana. Her lean body swayed in the saddle. "You're scowling."

Of course he was. He wanted to drag her off her horse and see if those full lips were as soft as they looked when he kissed her. Instead, he was stuck teaching her how to stay on her horse before she broke her neck performing unwise stunts on his property. The thought of something happening to her only made him scowl more.

"Your hands are fine, but your seat is all wrong." Had it been a mistake to work with her? To get involved when he had a multimillion-dollar ranching operation to oversee?

Heat crept up his back as he stared at her, an amused smile playing around her kissable mouth.

"My seat." She forgot about her hand position and let the reins go slack as the horse halted beside him. "I didn't know I could mess that up."

He would have preferred crooning extravagant compliments in her ear about the tight curve of her ass, but that wasn't going to help her stay upright during a race scene. Tightening his hold on his control, he reached to touch her left hand, nudging it higher.

"You need to be aware of your body at all times. Right now your hands are sending a bad message."

Her eyes widened for a moment before she redirected her focus and moved her hands to the exact position he'd shown her ten minutes earlier. Away from his touch.

"Right. Like this." Her cheeks pink, she stared down at Mariana's head. "What else?"

He shouldn't touch her again. Not when the point of contact from the first time still supercharged the air between them. He hadn't gotten involved today because he wanted to hit on her, damn it. He was only trying to keep her from getting hurt.

"You're sitting too far back in the seat." His gaze veered to her hips as she edged forward. Saddle leather creaked. She used a hand on the pommel to inch along.

Killing him.

Making his throat dry as dust.

"Better?" she asked, her voice a quiet stroke to his ears.

He nodded. Then, forcing himself to finish the instruction since it was damned important, he touched the back of her thigh.

"Legs should be directly under you." He let go almost instantly, backing up a step.

Still, the feel of her—lean muscle under those body-skimming jodhpurs—imprinted itself on his brain. He would be tracing a lot more of her in his dreams later.

"Is this better?" Her voice took on a husky note that he told himself must be from the dust in the air and not because the touch affected her as much as it had him.

"Looks good," he managed. "Take a lap or two and see if you can maintain it."

She rode off in a hurry and it was all he could do not take off his hat and use it as a fan.

Damn.

He'd exchanged far more provocative talk—and touches—with willing strangers in bars that had left him cold. Why was this bristly, defensive stunt performer getting under his skin so fast?

The sooner he finished the riding lesson the better. He had a ranch to oversee, a family falling apart and a blackmailer to catch. Thoughts of Emma Layton would have to wait.

Two

Four miles into her evening run, Emma regretted the decision not to take the cast shuttle back to her lodgings at White Canyon Ranch.

She'd been in a hurry to burn off the keyed-up awareness she'd felt all day working with Carson McNeill and thought maybe she could jog away that hypersensitive energy. Now, her thighs burned with a soreness that no workout had ever given her before. As a personal trainer strictly for female clients, she had plenty of thigh workouts in her personal inventory. In the future, she'd have to start recommending a day in the saddle to women who complained about their inner thighs.

Slowing to a walk on the grassy path alongside a fenced-in field between the Creek Spill lands and the guest ranch where second unit cast and crew members were staying, Emma checked her directions on the

GPS. She'd asked one of the stable workers about the route she'd chosen, and he'd assured her the dirt road was good enough to drive on in a pickup truck. Running would be no problem. She'd thought she'd been well prepared, peeling off the jodhpurs and stuffing them in her nylon knapsack along with an extra bottle of water. She'd changed into a clean pair of cropped leggings along with the running shoes she'd packed for her evening workout. Her boots she'd left tucked in a corner of the tack room, at the suggestion of the ranch hand who'd told her about the path.

The sun was sinking low on the horizon, though, and it occurred to her that it was liable to be very dark at sunset. Not like her neighborhood in Studio City, where she could run at all hours of the night and still see because of the streetlamps. Taking a moment to stretch in the hope it would ease some of the stiffness in her muscles, Emma breathed in the scent of fresh air and wildflowers. The breeze stirred the tall grass inside the four-rail fence.

She was just about ready to start running again when the hum of an engine alerted her that a vehicle was heading her way. Her shoulders tensed. Yes, Emma had taken plenty of mixed martial arts classes, training that served her well in stunt work and helped to make her feel sure of herself in isolated places. Still, she couldn't shake some of the old fears. Her ex-boyfriend was a fellow fitness trainer who'd hit her in a public place, in front of a room full of witnesses after a kickboxing class he'd taught. He'd tried to play it off like he was giving her an extra lesson, but thankfully no one else in the class believed that. An off-duty cop had been among the attendees, leading to the battery charges that kept her ex locked up for almost three years.

She didn't want to ever need saving again, though. She tightened her ponytail and started a light jog that irritated her burning thighs.

As the sound of the engine drew closer, punching up her heartrate, she turned to see a two-seater utility vehicle with an open cargo bed in back. The compelling cowboy she'd been trying to excise from her thoughts sat behind the wheel.

Her fears dissipated fast.

Carson McNeill braked to a stop beside her. The tension inside her shifted from fright back to the attraction she'd been fighting all day. She told herself it shouldn't matter that she was red faced and sweating. But it was tough not to be aware that she looked like roadkill when he looked like he'd just had a shower, with his hair still damp and his face freshly shaved. He wore a white button-down with the sleeves rolled up and a clean pair of jeans.

She paused beside the vehicle, swiping the back of her hand over her damp forehead. "You can't possibly be here to critique my form. On my own two feet, I absolutely know what I'm doing."

He didn't even crack a smile. "My foreman told me you decided to run back to the White Canyon."

"When running alone, it's a good safety practice to let someone know where you're going." She'd taken extra precautions. "I told Zoe, too."

His jaw flexed. She'd seen that look often enough today when she'd tried his patience. Now, the furrow in his brow said he was downright aggravated.

"Speaking of safety practices, how many times did I mention that a Wyoming ranch can be dangerous? That animals can be dangerous?"

"Several." Hot, tired and sore, she was beginning to feel her own patience fray. "But since I'm off the clock for the day, I'm no longer your concern."

"If you're on McNeill lands, you're my responsibility." He swiped his Stetson off the passenger seat and tossed it in the cargo bed behind him. "Get in. I'll drive you the rest of the way."

She didn't appreciate the command, but she also didn't want to antagonize a man who still had the power to send her packing. Besides, her legs hurt and twilight would turn to full dark soon.

The vehicle didn't have a door so she swung into the passenger seat while holding on to the roll bar. Carson revved the engine once she was seated with her safety belt buckled.

"Nice ride," she remarked lightly, hoping he wasn't going to hold this latest transgression against her during this extra stressful week.

She'd had multiple texts from her roommate and her mother reminding her not to answer any calls from unknown numbers this week. They were both worried about her, with her ex getting out of prison. As if Emma wasn't worried enough on her own. But she couldn't imagine how Austin would find her here. Hollywood made no secret of lead actors' whereabouts, but anyone looking for information about stunt roles, especially smaller roles like this one, would be hard-pressed to find it. Another bright spot was that Austin would have no idea she'd gone into stunt work, even if he wanted to find her.

Beside her, Carson remained silent while the stars popped out overhead. One. Two. And then a million. The sight was breathtaking. She craned her head back to stare straight up, but she didn't need to. Pinpoints of blue and white light blanketed the sky in every direction.

"Wow." She glanced over at her silent driver, wondering if he'd grown immune to the beauty. "I've never seen stars like this."

Maybe some of her wonder seeped through his frustration, because he slowed the vehicle, then stopped altogether, the engine rumbling at idle in the creeping night. They sat on a hilltop with meadows rolling out into the distance on one side, and a shadow of rocky cliffs and trees on the other. He snapped off the headlights to give them a better view and turned off the ignition. The engine ticked for a few moments and then went silent.

"It's amazing how much the lights of a city detract from the night sky." Carson tipped his head back, too, his hands resting on his sprawled denim-covered knees.

The right one hovered close to her leg, radiating a warmth she could feel. Or maybe it was the electric current of attraction that made her skin tingle that way beneath her leggings. She had been on a few dates since breaking things off with Austin but nothing serious. She definitely hadn't experienced the sizzling awareness she got from being around Carson. What a shame for her body to finally wake up again around a man she needed to impress with her professionalism.

"It's funny," she said, needing to break the intimate thread of silence between them, "because I always think I live in a quieter area of Los Angeles." She tried not to think about his knee next to hers. His hand close to her leg. But memories of the way he'd touched her earlier— shifting her thigh on the horse—sent a fresh surge of heat through her.

"Even in Cheyenne, you can't see the stars the way you can out here. There aren't many perks to ranching, but the night sky is definitely one of them."

Straightening in her seat, she peered over at him. The breeze turned cooler.

"You don't like your work?" She was curious about him, this man who allowed a film production company onto his property but couldn't really relinquish control. "After seeing you on horseback today, I guess I just assumed you were born in a saddle."

He'd ridden beside her briefly before setting her loose to try the track on her own.

"Almost." She thought she heard a hint of a smile in his voice. Or was that wishful thinking? "But I never imagined myself overseeing cattle at my age. Ranching is fine for my twin brother, but I thought I'd be riding rodeo into my thirties."

She hadn't known about the twin brother. Or the rodeo past. Still, she could relate to what he was saying. She felt him shift beside her, turning toward her. A gust of wind blew through her hair, flicking strands against her cheek.

"I never thought I'd be recreating sword fights or high-speed chases, either. But sometimes life takes surprising turns."

"I'll bet it's an interesting story how you got here, Emma Layton." Her name on his lips felt as intimate as a caress to a woman who hadn't been touched by a man in a long, long time.

The rush of heat through her veins shouldn't have caught her off guard—she'd been feeling it all day around him. She'd run four miles to try to escape it. Even so, the magnetic force that seemed to pull her toward him was like nothing she'd ever experienced. Her shoulders shifted fractionally closer. Her knee brushed his.

She drew in a sharp breath at the contact, ripples of pleasure radiating out from the point where she touched him. She forgot what they were talking about. Couldn't think of words to say even if she remembered. There was only the moment and the man. The endless starry sky enveloping them like a dream.

Maybe that was why she found herself leaning even closer—it all felt surreal. Like a time-out from the worry and stress of her real life, where everything was suddenly simpler. Where kissing Carson McNeill seemed like the only thing that mattered.

Her hand landed on his chest. Warm. Strong. Inviting.

She splayed her fingers wider, wanting to feel more of him. Then she tipped her face up to his. She was close enough to see him well despite the darkness. His eyes locked on hers for an instant—like two stars close up.

And then his lips claimed hers.

Carson had been wrestling with the need to touch Emma all day. For hours, they'd been in close proximity, and the urge to kiss her had been there. Every. Single. Moment.

He'd resisted. Triumphed. Walked away from her at the end of the work day, satisfied that he'd done the right thing.

But as soon as he'd spotted her treating his ranch like her personal gym out on the pasture road, her glossy brown ponytail swinging while she jogged, he knew his restraint was all out for the day. She'd worn right through it with her bullheaded determination to fake her way through a horseback stunt. Hell, she'd shredded it with her grit and bravado that rivaled any bull rider's.

So now when she tipped her mouth up to his, freely offering the taste he'd battled his conscience over all day, he didn't have a prayer of turning away. Petal-soft and strawberry-scented, her lips parted on a sigh, molding to his. Yielding sweetly. She skimmed her palm over his chest, sliding lower. He wrapped his arm around her, anchoring her against him, feeling the swell of her breasts as she eased nearer.

Wind whipped around them, stirring the scent of her fruity shampoo as tendrils escaped the ponytail and tickled his cheek. Hunger for more surged, hunger he couldn't possibly satisfy. He'd never had a woman affect him like this—so swiftly or so completely. Her fingers clenched around the hem of his T-shirt, her nails gently scraping his skin and arousing a whole other heat they couldn't possibly indulge…

"Emma." He blinked his way through the sensual fog, hoping he'd regain reason as he broke the kiss.

As it was, he simply tipped his forehead to hers, waiting to catch his breath. Her eyes stayed closed a long moment. When she opened them, she edged away even more.

"Sorry," she murmured.

His eyes were adjusted enough to the dark that he could see her run her fingers over her lips. The gesture made his insides twist with need.

"I wish you weren't. Sorry, that is. I'll be damned if I am."

He debated starting up the utility vehicle and flooring the gas until he got her back to her room for the night. Behind a locked door. But his stepmother was being transferred to the local hospital tonight, and he wanted to be there for his family when she arrived in Cheyenne.

"You wouldn't say that if you knew why I'm here." Emma tightened her ponytail in a gesture he'd seen her repeat often over the course of the day.

He'd be willing to bet she didn't let her hair down often. And yeah, maybe that made him want to crow with victory that she'd seemed to forget everything else with him just now.

"What do you mean?" He forced himself to focus on her words and not the leftover heat still sparking through him. Then he started the vehicle, knowing he needed to get on the road for the hospital soon.

"I mean, I'm not an up-and-coming starlet, in town because I'm so excited to further my career." She hugged her arms around herself, sitting back farther in her seat.

"You're not trying to get ahead in your career?" He didn't follow what she was getting at. "Could have fooled me given how hard you worked today."

"Yes. Well, I want to keep my job. Desperately." She slanted a look his way as they skirted a patch of trees and neared the lights of the White Canyon Ranch. "But that's because I need to be anywhere but LA this week since my ex-boyfriend is getting out of prison tomorrow."

Carson tried to process that. He hoped like hell that the ex in question hadn't hurt her. But damn. Wouldn't that account for her level of determination not to be in California this week?

"I'm sorry to hear you were in a bad relationship," he said carefully. "And I'm glad to know why it means so much that you stay in Wyoming for the film. But that doesn't make me the least bit sorry I kissed you."

"There's relationship baggage, and then there's relationship kryptonite. I'm pretty sure a felon ex-boyfriend puts me in the latter category." She lifted her nylon knapsack off the floor and set it in her lap, as if she couldn't sprint out of the vehicle fast enough.

Carson slowed to a stop outside the deep porch of the huge log guest ranch, wanting to tread warily in this conversation, but also needing to reassure her that her past didn't change how he viewed her.

"Your ex being in jail doesn't reflect on you. Only on him."

She unfastened her seat belt with a jerky movement. She was upset and he regretted having any part in making her feel that way. He'd watched her overcome one challenge after another on her horse today, admiring her never-ending supply of resolve.

"He was in prison for hitting me." She looked at him, her gaze unwavering. "And once he's freed, he'll come looking for me. The last thing I want to do is drag an unsuspecting man into the drama."

She bolted from the car as if she hadn't just dropped a bombshell in his lap. By the time he shook off being stunned and set out to follow Emma, the screen door was already banging behind her.

Three

Emma realized she was being a coward the moment she got through the door of the White Canyon Ranch.

She'd kissed Carson and let that kiss carry her away. Then, when she acknowledged to herself how much she'd enjoyed it, she had panicked. She'd flung her past in the man's face and sprinted. If she ever wanted to move beyond the abuse, she needed to stop acting like this. Like she was ashamed and embarrassed about it.

More than that, if she was going to move forward with her life, she had to stop putting up smokescreens when a hot guy tempted her to take a chance on the opposite sex again. She had to take ownership of her feelings.

Forcing herself to stop, she pivoted on the toe of her running shoe before she hit the first step of the main staircase. She wasn't surprised to see Carson striding

through the front door and into the huge foyer with cathedral ceilings.

Her pulse stuttered, then quickened. He'd been appealing, sitting next to her in the darkened vehicle under
the stars. Here, in the light cast by the huge antler chandelier overhead, he stole her breath. His gaze locked on
her as he closed the distance between them, and those
blue eyes saw right inside her.

"Can we talk privately?" he asked, his expression
concerned, his touch tender as he wrapped a hand
lightly around her forearm.

"Sure." She nodded. "I was just thinking the same
thing." Peering around the empty foyer, she set her
knapsack in a window seat behind a floor-length curtain draped around a wooden pull back. Then she followed him back outside to the wide front porch that
wrapped two sides of the building.

Although the guest ranch was full to capacity with
cast and crew members this week, the property was
relatively quiet now. Emma recalled seeing a bulletin
on her phone that a charter bus had been scheduled to
transport interested sightseers into downtown Cheyenne tonight for dinner and entertainment.

As Carson guided her toward the railing at the far
end of the building, she decided to save him the trouble
of asking her more about her past.

"That was wrong of me to spring on you," she said,
leaning a hip into the railing while he turned to face her.

"On the contrary, I'm glad to know so I can make
sure you're safe here." His jaw flexed as he stared down
at her. "I'm just sorry you went through that."

"Thank you." She couldn't help but feel touched. His
words sounded heartfelt. "It's not something I make a

habit of sharing. But I guess I got rattled after the kiss, and felt like you should know."

"I'd like you to move to the Creek Spill, where I have top-notch security."

She noticed he didn't say anything about the kiss, which was probably just as well. Maybe he wanted to forget about that moment of heated craziness, too.

Her thoughts skipped ahead to her position in the cast and what he'd just said about her staying at the other ranch. "Do you mean I can keep this job? You don't plan on making Zoe send me back home?"

A hint of a smile pulled at one corner of his mouth. She remembered what it had felt like to kiss him and got a pleasant shiver just thinking about it. It wasn't going to be easy to forget what had happened between them.

"One thing at a time," he cautioned. Pulling his phone from his back pocket, he tapped in some commands. "I've got a family obligation tonight, but I can have someone help you pack your things and move you into a suite at the Creek Spill."

"That's so kind of you, but I don't need help—"

The warning look in his eyes stopped her protest. "Then consider it a favor for my peace of mind. From now on, you're my personal guest."

The seriousness in his voice made her wonder how personal a guest she was going to be. Plenty of the first unit cast members were staying on his property, so she assumed she would be housed with them. Still, it might make things a little awkward with Zoe and her second unit crew if she wasn't staying with them.

"I'm not sure if my director will think that's such a good idea."

Carson finished whatever he was doing on his phone

and pocketed the device. Then he put both hands on her shoulders, causing a warm heat that made her insides flutter.

"Then you can tell her the rationale, or I will, but she's going to have to agree to the arrangement." His thumbs sketched a light touch along her collarbone, and her skin heated everywhere. "I just asked one of the White Canyon staffers to meet you at your room, and transportation is on the way. The attendant will help you with your bags and see you into the vehicle. You'll be met on the other end by my housekeeper, Mrs. Tillson. She'll show you the suite where you can put your things and will have dinner ready as soon as you arrive."

She tried not to notice the way she wanted to sway toward him. No man had touched her this way in years. As for tending to her every need so thoroughly? No man had done that. Ever.

Emma reminded herself not to get used to it. As soon as filming was done, she would be back in LA, trying to carve out a life for herself while Carson McNeill would still be lord of all he surveyed in Cheyenne. She couldn't afford to get used to the sort of help he offered.

"That's more than generous." Blinking, she straightened away from his touch, needing to stand strong on her own feet. "Thank you."

He studied her for a moment longer before he gave a clipped nod. "I'd help you settle in myself but my stepmother has been in the hospital and my family is expecting me over there. I'll see you in the morning, though. Help yourself to anything you need while I'm away."

He moved toward the driveway where he'd parked his vehicle, but stopped when she didn't join him.

She was still stuck on what he'd said about helping herself. While he was away.

Did that imply he'd be…with her when he returned?

The breeze blowing off the hills made her wrap her arms around herself, as a chill set in from the sweat that had dried on her skin after her run. A chill…or a pleasurable shiver. She didn't know what she was feeling, but she knew she needed to get a handle on herself.

"What is it?" he asked, though he didn't move toward her.

"I. Um. Just wondering." Nerves skittered through her. "Where exactly will I be staying at the ranch?"

He frowned. "The bunkhouse and external buildings are filled to capacity with the ranch's employees and with the film's cast and crew. But there's plenty of room in the main house. You'll stay with me."

Carson couldn't stop thinking about Emma.

He sat beside his stepmother, who'd finally been transported to the Cheyenne hospital after a week in a medical facility nine hours away. She had been cleared for a flight on a fixed-wing medical plane at the family's expense so she could recover closer to home.

And she *was* recovering, according to her team of doctors, even if Carson couldn't see much improvement in her condition. At least she was off the ventilator now. And all three of his half sisters—Scarlett as well as Maisie and Madeline—had been in the room with her yesterday when she'd opened her eyes briefly, a sign Paige was pulling out of the coma.

That was why Carson didn't consider it disrespectful that his thoughts wandered to Emma so often in the hours that he'd been watching over his stepmother in her private room. The door was closed to shut out most of the sounds in the hallway. A nurse came in every half hour to check monitors and adjust IVs, but other than that, the room was quiet except for a gray clock ticking on the far wall. His half sisters had left to grab some dinner and change before Scarlett—the youngest of the daughters Paige had with Carson's father, Donovan—returned to relieve him.

Carson had plenty to worry about right now with overseeing the ranches, making sure the filming didn't interfere with day-to-day operations, and beginning a private investigation into his stepmother's past to see if there was any merit to the blackmailer's claim. Yet as he sat in the big gray lounger between the window and the hospital bed, what concerned him most was Emma.

He'd been floored by the idea of any man raising a hand to her. The thought still made him sick hours later. He wouldn't have been able to take his shift at the hospital tonight if she'd refused to settle into a suite at his house. Because at least now he had the satisfaction of knowing—thanks to a text from his housekeeper—that Emma was safely ensconced in his place, behind doors with a security code. She was surrounded by ranch hands who worked for him, plus a security guard he'd paid to ensure the equipment barns and horses under his care remained untouched for the duration of the filming.

Carson had already requested two more security guards to start tomorrow. One to ensure Emma's safety. Another to patrol the grounds. They needed to keep a watch for Emma's ex, but it would also help the McNeill family to monitor for any new threats from their mystery blackmailer. Emma's past gave him a good justification for the additional security since his siblings had agreed not to tell their father about the blackmail note Scarlett had received during her visit to LA the day before Paige's accident.

As for Emma—no one was getting close to her on his watch.

Except for him.

The thought didn't just whisper across his consciousness. It roared and shouted. The kiss they'd shared had seared itself into his brain, making him realize that despite his good intentions where she was concerned, staying away from her for the next two weeks was going to be impossible. It would have been tough enough for him to keep his distance while they worked together on her riding. But now? All that combustible attraction was going to be front and center, 24/7.

But she had to stay with him.

He'd kissed her. Touched her. Shared her confidence. That made him want to protect her.

The wide door to Paige's room creaked open and Scarlett backed into the room, juggling a balloon bouquet, flowers and a brightly striped duffel bag.

Carson shot out of his seat to give her a hand, darting around the rolling table with a water pitcher.

"Thanks." Scarlett threw him a grateful smile, her long dark curls still damp from the shower. "I couldn't resist loading up on things at the gift shop since we couldn't bring the flowers from the other hospital with us."

Carson set the hot-pink roses on the bedside table before tying the balloons to a handrail against the far wall. "I'll make sure she gets more in the morning."

When he finished the task, he hugged his sister, hating to see her look so worn-out. Not that he'd tell her as much. She was a beautiful woman, but she'd always considered herself less attractive than her older sisters. It was something about looking more like her mother, whereas the rest of them took after their dad. Carson knew it was baseless nonsense. But Scarlett had once filled his favorite boots with rocks and flung them into an irrigation pond after he'd told her she looked like a cartoon giraffe. He'd been twelve.

And he'd learned not to tease her.

"How are you holding up?" he asked as he pulled away, taking an extra minute to look in her eyes.

As the recipient of the blackmail note, Scarlett had borne an extra burden before their mother's fall. She'd been given the message during a confrontation with one of the actors in *Winning the West* at a Hollywood nightclub. A guy she'd dated briefly. Scarlett had gone to LA, wanting to set the record straight with the dude before he showed up in Wyoming to do the film. During their argument, a man neither of them knew had slipped her the paper. The message implied that Paige had had a different identity prior to marrying Carson's father.

Scarlett had been caught flat-footed when Paige had the accident before she could share the information. She'd told her siblings in the hospital, but regretted not speaking up sooner, during the hours when Paige had gone missing the night before.

"I'm fine." She nodded, then went to work around Paige's bed, straightening the already straight blanket, fluffing the pillow behind her mom's head. "No news from the private investigator you hired to look into Mom's past?"

"No." Carson knew Scarlett hadn't been keen on the idea, but her older sisters had been worried about the danger a blackmailer presented. "But in all fairness, the guy has only just started making inquiries."

For the first few days after Paige's fall, her health had been the number one priority and the family's time had been consumed with that.

"Dad will be angry when he finds out." Scarlett paused in her busywork, turning worried blue eyes toward her brother.

In the quiet of the room, the balloons bumped one another as they swayed from the air-conditioning blowing through a nearby vent.

"No, he won't." Carson had watched his stern father crack under the fears for his wife after her disappearance and then her fall. And even before that, Donovan McNeill had been dealing with his own father's reemergence in their lives after a long period of estrangement. The stress of the last year had changed him. "He's got enough to bear right now just worrying about her. He texted me a little while ago to tell you he'll be in around midnight."

The fact that Donovan had texted him in itself told Carson a lot about how his father had changed. Carson had opened his home to his estranged grandfather, Manhattan-based resort mogul Malcolm McNeill, when the old guy showed up in Cheyenne. Donovan hadn't spoken to Carson for weeks afterward, refusing to acknowledge the billionaire father he'd bitterly cut out of his life decades ago. But now, Donovan seemed to have moved past that, too worried about his wife to care about the old grudge.

"Okay. Thanks." Scarlett dropped into the chair closest to the bed and held her mother's hand, careful not to bump the IV line. "How's the filming going at the Creek Spill?"

Thoughts of Emma filled his head. Her scent. Her touch.

The danger she was in.

"Everyone is still settling in." He wasn't ready to say anything about Emma when they'd only just met. No matter that he'd moved her into his house. "Shooting starts tomorrow, though."

Scarlett stared at him expectantly. Had his sister already heard rumors about him spending all day with a sexy stuntwoman?

"Damn it, Carson, don't make me ask. Have you seen Logan King or not?" She leaned closer, one of her dark curls falling onto her forearm.

"Sorry." He'd been so wrapped up in thoughts of Emma, he'd forgotten about her sister's tangled connection to one of the stars of the film. "I've been busy making room for the extra stunt animals they brought for this thing. When they wanted to house animals, I didn't realize they'd be high-strung Spanish dancing horses that needed a whole damn barn to themselves."

"Spanish dancing horses?" Scarlett grinned. "You mean like Andalusians?" At his nod, she continued excitedly. "They're some of the best-trained animals in the world. I doubt they're high-strung."

His thoughts strayed to Emma again, as he remembered her working on the complex commands with Mariana. The horses knew how to fall, roll and do a series of complicated jumps.

He'd started out the day worrying about how Emma would do with the animal. Now, he was far more concerned about how she'd fare with a bastard of an ex circulating among free men again.

Before he could respond to his sister, two nurses entered the room, pushing a rolling cart between them. It amazed him how many different tests they needed to run on patients.

"I'm going to let you handle things," he murmured to his sister before kissing her on the cheek. "But I'll keep an eye out for Logan and let you know how the shooting is going tomorrow, okay?"

She nodded while the nurses moved the cart closer. "Sure thing, Carson. Thanks."

He didn't need to check his watch as he left the hospital room. He knew that Emma would be long asleep by now back at his ranch. But that didn't slow him down any.

He'd rest easier once he was at home, under the same roof with her, personally making sure she stayed safe. The fact that he would relive every second of that kiss in his dreams tonight was just an added bonus. And something he couldn't help.

Emma stood on the balcony of the suite Carson had given her long after dinnertime, staring out at the ranch under the rising moon. She knew the moon was the same size everywhere, but right here, where she could see it break over the horizon, it was a huge white spotlight turned on the Creek Spill. She wrapped her flannel shirt tighter around her to stay warm against the cool night breeze. She hadn't brought a bathrobe, so she'd put on the flannel over the pajama T-shirt she wore with an old pair of running shorts. Summer was warmer in southern California.

The balcony under her feet was made of smooth planks covered by a big woven rug in sunset colors. The wooden chairs were made of narrow logs, the knots still visible, the cushions as thick as her mattress back home. She'd switched off the lights in the room behind her so no one roaming around outdoors would see her up here.

Or at least they wouldn't see her well. She'd been drawn outdoors by that big glowing moon, but now that she was out here, she took a minute to orient herself. The main house overlooked stables and a lighted swimming pool, along with numerous barns and sheds, all landscaped and much of it fenced. The buildings she could see, however, were small compared to the stables and barns where the stunt horses were kept and where Zoe was staying with many of the other crew members. She'd read online that the Creek Spill and its neighboring ranch, the Black Creek, were a combined fifty thousand acres, an amount of land that had boggled her mind.

It made her wonder how the owner of all that property had time to watch her ride a horse today.

Carson had an army of people working for him. She understood that now after meeting his housekeeper, who had shown Emma her room. A maid had brought up her dinner, which had been prepared by a cook. Knowing there were so many people on staff in the house had helped her feel a little less awkward about sleeping in Carson's home. It wasn't as if she was alone in the house with him.

Deciding she needed to stop thinking and start sleeping, Emma was about to return to her suite when a shadow emerged near the illuminated swimming pool.

A very male shadow.

The heavy shoulders and narrow waist told her as much. But she'd spent enough time admiring that particular masculine physique today that she didn't have to guess who she was watching.

Carson McNeill had come home.

He stood at the deep end, facing the house. Facing her. She recognized his clothes from earlier; he must have just returned from his family obligation. She didn't move, not wanting him to see her.

Wanting to watch him a little longer.

But then he raised his hands and dragged his T-shirt over his head. The light from the pool glinted off the bare muscle of his arms. She couldn't see his abs in the shadows but her imagination supplied a picture of them just fine.

It was too late to shout down to him. Or at least, that was what she told herself. She seemed to have forgotten how to move, let alone speak.

His hand moved to his belt and he stepped out of his boots. Her mouth went dry when he reached for the button on his fly.

She gasped out loud when he stepped out of the denim.

That must have been what he heard. His head snapped up then, his gaze immediately finding her.

Her heart thudded so loud in her own ears she wondered if he heard that, too. Still, she couldn't seem to lift her eyes from the slim-fitting boxer shorts that hugged his hips.

"Emma?" His voice smoked through her, heating her skin from the inside. "Is that you?"

Four

There would be no slinking back to her room now.

Emma struggled to find her voice, flustered to her toes to be caught gawking.

"Carson?" She feigned surprise, as if she'd been standing at the railing staring at the moon and not the almost-naked gorgeous man in the courtyard. "I—er—didn't see you there." She cleared her throat to smooth over the cracks in her voice. "It's a little cool out for a swim, isn't it?"

She couldn't quite peel her eyes away from him. But it was dark enough he couldn't possibly tell exactly where she was looking. She hoped.

He grinned, his teeth a flash of white in the moonlight. "Spoken like a southern California girl. And no, it isn't too cold." He backed up a step, retrieving his jeans and shirt. "I thought you would have been asleep by now or I would have checked on you."

Moonlight played over his muscles as he slid the denim back up over his hips. The light in the pool cast a watery glimmer on his chest until he put his T-shirt on. Having him less naked helped her brain cells start functioning again, but she wasn't forgetting what she'd seen any time soon.

"I'm fine." She wondered what "checking on her" might have involved, though. "Mrs. Tillson made sure I had dinner and helped me get settled."

She noticed he left his boots by the pool as he jogged across the pavers to the wooden staircase at the far end of the upper deck. The deck that led to her.

Straightening, she remembered what she was wearing. A flannel shirt over an outfit she normally wore to bed. It was decidedly lacking in coverage. While Carson climbed the steps, she discreetly adjusted the waistband of the shorts, easing them a bit lower on her hips to cover the tops of her thighs before wrapping the flannel shirt around her again.

Her heart thudded hard against her chest as he strode closer, his steps light on the planked decking that lined the whole upstairs floor along the back of this section of the house.

"Are you sure there's nothing else you need?" he asked as he reached her, his gaze missing nothing.

For one heated moment, she allowed herself to consider the question. Then reason returned and she shook her head. "I'm all set. And I appreciate the hospitality. I certainly never would have expected you to—"

He waved off her thanks, leaning on the rail as he faced her. "Don't think twice about it. I will sleep better knowing you're as safe as we can make you here."

A different kind of warmth filled her at his kindness. "Thank you." She soaked in the comfort of his protection for just a moment. His caring. Then she remembered his quick exit earlier. "Is everything all right with your family? I'm sorry that your stepmother is in the hospital."

He looked out over the ranch for a moment, his jaw flexing. He nodded. "Things are better now. My stepmother has been in a coma since she fell in a hiking accident, but her doctors say she's coming out of it."

"I'm so sorry. That must have been frightening for your whole family." Her hand landed on his forearm. Squeezed. She had a tenuous relationship with her own mother, but she couldn't imagine life without her. Jane Layton was the only family Emma had since her father's suicide when she was three years old.

A cool breeze chilled her, sending a shiver up her spine.

"I just hope they'll let her come home soon. Worrying about her has really taken a toll on my father." Carson glanced over at her, frowning down at her bare legs. "You're cold. Let's find a spot to sit away from the wind for a minute and then I'll let you get to bed."

He palmed the space between her shoulder blades, steering her toward the seating area close to the French doors that led into her suite. As she dropped into one of the thick cushioned seats, he tugged a throw blanket off the love seat and laid it over her legs.

"It's okay. I'm too wound up to sleep anyway." She hadn't anticipated her ex's release from prison to churn up so many old insecurities, especially after the months she'd trained to feel strong and confident. She tucked the edges of the blanket—a soft wool blend—under her to keep the wind out.

"I ordered more private security starting tomorrow."
He lowered himself into the love seat, putting him at a
right angle to her chair.

His knee brushed hers through the blanket, and she
remembered exactly what he'd looked like when he'd
been moments from jumping in the pool earlier. Her
gaze found his in the light filtering through the French
doors, her skin humming with awareness beneath the
layer of wool.

"Thank you. But you've already done more than
enough. I feel safe here." She couldn't allow herself to
live in hiding, continually running from old fears. She'd
worked too hard to overcome them.

"Nevertheless, I don't want you to worry if you see
a guard keeping tabs on you. I'll introduce you in the
morning."

She hesitated, not sure how she felt about having
someone watch over her all day. "I have an early call."

Carson grinned. "I'm a rancher. Early is all I know."
His smile faded, his expression turning serious. "Besides, we're working together for some of the morning.
A security detail can't keep you safe in a horseback
stunt, but elevating your riding skills will go a long
way toward that goal."

"I can be at the stables by ten." She wasn't ready to
share the details of the rest of her day, which involved
demonstrating a few moves for a knife fight assigned
to two other members of the stunt cast.

Fighting, she was good at. No doubt because she'd
spent an inordinate amount of her training time on
mixed martial arts in the last few years.

He looked like he wanted to ask more. To insist she
meet with his security guard first, but he simply nodded.

"I'll introduce you to Dax at ten, then we'll get to work." He shifted on the love seat, leaning forward as if he was ready to leave. "I'll let you get your rest then." His gaze held hers, making a spark leap inside her. "Unless you're game for a night swim?"

A shiver coursed through her that didn't have the slightest thing to do with the cold.

She shook her head, unwilling to get any more tangled up with Carson McNeill. "A good professional risk taker knows where to draw the line."

His blue eyes lingered on hers for a long moment. "Maybe that was my problem as a bull rider. I never could walk away from a challenge."

Her heart thudded faster. Harder. If he'd leaned any closer, she wouldn't have been able to resist kissing him. Tasting him again.

But he rose to his feet with a terse "Good night" and strode down the deck in the opposite direction from where he'd come. She watched him for a moment, long enough to see him open the next set of French doors beyond hers.

He would be sleeping close to her then. Which would give her plenty to think about while she lay in her bed. Alone.

Scarlett McNeill was not at her brother's ranch in the hope of sighting Hollywood's hottest up-and-coming young actor the next morning. Of course she wasn't.

She had permission from the film production company to take some footage behind the scenes for a promotional video the McNeills could use afterward to tout their properties. She had a legitimate reason to hover around the site of today's shoot. The fact that

Logan King was going to be in the scene filmed on a high meadow north of the Creek Spill main house had nothing to do with it. She had recovered from her old crush on him.

Mostly.

Besides, she had already suffered the indignity of flirting with him, falling into bed with him and then having him ghost her. The last thing she needed was a reminder of how mortifying it had been to have her texts ignored for weeks. But her family came first, and this footage could help the White Canyon Ranch for years to come. The video would also give more visibility to her brother Brock's business of breeding and training quarter horses.

Still, as she checked the settings on her phone's camera app, it bugged her that she needed to be in close proximity with a man who'd treated her the way Logan had. She'd even traveled to Los Angeles a week ago to try putting the situation firmly in the past by telling Logan off in person. It should have been gratifying to give him hell on his home turf before he showed his face in Cheyenne. But he'd turned the tables on her by announcing he hadn't meant to ghost her. He'd just been on a difficult shoot in the Congo, at the mercy of the notoriously hard-nosed director Antonio Ventura, the same guy directing *Winning the West*. Ventura had demanded the young cast "bond" and taken away their cell phones for two weeks.

The excuse had sounded overly convenient at the time, but she had done an internet search when she got home and the stories she'd seen backed up what Logan said.

Then there was the mysterious message about her mother from that night.

"Scarlett." Startled out of her musings, she nearly dropped her phone in the meadow grass.

Logan King stood a few feet away in all his glory, with his chiseled jaw, dark brown hair and deep green eyes. He was dressed in period costume, like a cowpuncher from the Old West, with cotton trousers, worn leather chaps and tall boots. His white shirt was half-open and stained with dirt, his leather vest soft enough to mold to his chest.

How fitting that her gaze ended up there. Cursing herself, she shoved her phone in her back pocket and resolved to look him in the eye.

"Hello, Logan." She tipped her chin up, ignoring the urge to smooth her windblown hair from her face.

"I hope your presence here means you've decided to bury the hatchet?" He stepped closer and lowered his voice at the same time.

A conversation for her ears only.

She realized he probably knew the handful of others milling around the big camera set up on a wide rug nearby. There were two screens mounted inside a rolling cart full of electronic equipment, with a canopy over it to minimize the glare. She didn't recognize any other stars among the group, and guessed they were technical experts of some sort.

"I'm only here to film some video to promote the ranch." And possibly to mingle with the Hollywood crowd since she had every intention of leaving Cheyenne for good this fall to test out a career in acting for herself. It was a dream she'd deferred far too long to help out her family. "So no, I don't consider the hatchet buried."

"Even though I was hamstrung by a despotic director?" He glanced over one shoulder before continuing. "Wait until you meet this guy. He might have some critically acclaimed pictures to his name, but this is the last time I work with Antonio Ventura."

"He's that bad?" she asked, telling herself she was curious more for the sake of her future acting career than because she was tempted to give Logan a second chance.

But he smelled amazing as he stood beside her. Like soap and aftershave. A hint of leather. She breathed deeper, remembering how he'd dazzled her when they first met. They'd been in first class on a flight to the West Coast. She'd been taking a shopping trip for her mother's birthday. They'd flirted. Kissed. Had an incredible surprise night together. She had thought it was about more than lust, and grew certain the feeling was mutual when they messaged each other briefly afterward. Then he'd mysteriously stopped, the growing silence hurting her more each day.

What if his ghosting her had been out of his control?

"He's arrogant, demanding and unreasonable," Logan continued, bending down to snap a sprig of white yarrow from the stem. "If I hadn't already signed on for this picture, I would have never worked with him a second time."

His gaze traveled her face, lifted to her windblown curls. Then he slid the wildflowers into her barrette before tucking some of her hair behind her ear. She told herself to move away. But his touch still affected her. Made her long to bury that damn hatchet after all.

She might have done it, too, if she hadn't remembered her sister Maisie's suspicions about him. That

Logan could have been involved with the mysterious third party handing her that blackmail note.

That Logan himself could be the one who knew something about her mother's past and wasn't afraid to use it for leverage against the McNeill family.

Do you know your mother's true identity? You might be surprised to find out her real name. And to learn her marriage to your father was never legal. I will make trouble for your family if you continue your plan to let Winning the West *film on McNeill land.*

She'd memorized every word. And although she could buy into the idea that Logan might want to stop the filming of *Winning the West*, she couldn't reconcile the man who'd just slid a flower into her hair with someone plotting to take down the McNeills. He was Hollywood's golden boy.

His past was the kind of story Hollywood loved. He'd traveled to LA from the Ozarks as a teen without a penny to his name, doing odd jobs until he turned eighteen. Then he'd gotten a GED and started working as an actor. Just two months ago, at age twenty-six, he'd catapulted from small-time fame to the A-list when his breakout blockbuster released, giving him enough wealth and fame that it simply made no sense to turn to blackmail.

"Seriously, Scarlett," he told her, tipping her chin up to look him in the eye when she didn't respond to him. "I know you're angry with me, and I don't blame you. But when you come to LA and start working, please don't take any jobs with Ventura. He's a tyrant."

The fact that Logan King—a celebrity on the cover of half the magazines at the grocery store checkout right now—was not only looking out for her, but that he remembered and actually believed she could be an actress one day, broke through the last of her defenses.

She didn't believe him capable of trying to blackmail her family.

"I won't," she promised, gathering up the hair still blowing in her face and holding it in one fist. "And I would consider burying the hatchet with you if you help me with something."

"Really?" The smile that teased his mouth made her want to kiss him. "Name your price, Scarlett McNeill. I'm so there."

Her knees felt weak. Was it any wonder the man had won the hearts of every female demographic in the US? Maybe she was crazy for giving him another chance, but what if he could lead her to the blackmailer?

Two other actors arrived on the set, a makeup artist dressed in black trailing behind them, wearing a work apron full of cosmetic brushes. They must be getting ready to start the scene soon.

She kept her voice low. "I want you to help me find the man who passed me that note at the club in West Hollywood last week."

His green eyes held hers. He frowned for a moment. "He was wearing the pin-striped jacket, right?"

"You remember him?" A tremor of excitement passed through her. Maybe she should have asked Logan outright about it sooner, but she'd been so fearful that he could have something to do with it. And, of course, then her mother had gone missing and had the accident in quick succession.

"I've seen him around before." He nodded when one of the other actors called to him, acknowledging the guy by holding up a finger to indicate he needed a minute.

"I can find out his name for you. But you have to do something for me in return."

"I'm already considering burying the hatchet," she protested. "I think that's plenty."

He shook his head, shifting closer to speak in her ear. "You have to let me take you out to dinner tonight."

The tickle of his breath on her ear made her skin tingle with awareness.

"I'm busy," she told him, so damn breathlessly he had to know how much he affected her. But her mother was still in the hospital, and family came first.

"Friday, then?" he persisted, wrapping one of her curls around his finger.

She had to lick her lips before she spoke, her throat dry as dust.

"Okay," she agreed, telling herself it was for the good of the family.

Knowing that was a big fat lie.

"I'll text you, but you have to unblock my number." He backed away as his cast mates called to him a second time.

She smiled to think he knew she'd blocked him. Maybe he really hadn't ghosted her on purpose.

"Deal." She got out her phone to take some footage behind the scenes for her video as Logan walked away.

Had she made a bargain with the devil? It wouldn't be easy to ignore the heat simmering between them, but if Logan had any answers about who was threatening her family, she needed to find out everything he knew. She just hoped she didn't get burned in the process.

Five

Settling his hat on his head as he left the foreman's office the next morning, Carson went to the stables, dark mood lifting at the thought of seeing Emma. His meeting with the Creek Spill foreman had run long thanks to a dozen pieces of business that had cropped up because of the movie crew's presence. Deliveries needed to be delayed because of storage issues. Grazing field rotations had been interrupted in some places and field maintenance was on hold in others because the crew wanted to shoot in a meadow with tall grasses.

Carson had agreed to all of it ahead of time in an effort to placate Scarlett and Madeline, who'd made the best case for the promotional value of the film for the guest ranch. But Carson had also done it, in part, because his twin brother had been so stubbornly opposed to having anyone on his own property, the Black Creek Ranch. Carson had been happy to step in as the good guy and offer up the Creek Spill instead. Butting heads with his twin was second nature by now after a lifetime of not seeing eye-to-eye. Carson had to admit his brother may have had a point on this one.

Cody had been adamant about safety precautions on the ranch given the way their mother had died. Now that Carson had the safety of a movie crew and cast on his shoulders, he could see why. If he ever found time away from the Creek Spill again, he'd owe Cody the courtesy of telling him he'd been right all along.

Although, if Carson hadn't signed off on *Winning the West*, he wouldn't have Emma Layton sleeping in the bedroom next to his. He'd take that trade-off again, even knowing the headaches that would come with housing extra people, equipment and animals.

As he neared the stables on foot, his brother Brock pulled up in his 4x4 pickup with the horse trailer already hitched. He called to him through the rolled-down window.

"Carson. Do you have a minute?" Brock was dressed for a meeting, his black button-down paired with his good Stetson, as opposed to the battered hat and dusty T-shirt that he wore when he worked with the quarter horses.

Carson didn't see Emma near the stables, but the security guy, Dax, lifted a hand in greeting from where he stood near the arena railing.

"Sure thing. You have a delivery today?"

Brock nodded. Folding his arms across his chest, he stared out at the stable yard where the stunt coordinator was working on a jump with another rider.

"I asked a long-distance customer to take delivery early on a couple of horses so I could have a few days away from the movie madness." He gestured to the stable yard full of strangers, his elaborate forearm ink on display where his sleeves were rolled up. "I'll be the first to admit I wasn't expecting the carnival to come to town when we said yes to this."

"I was thinking the same thing this morning. It's just for two weeks, though." Something he needed to keep in mind where Emma was concerned. He wanted her, no question. And he couldn't afford to wait if she was heading back to LA that soon.

"I've read that movie productions are notorious for underestimating the timetable. Especially films this Ventura guy is associated with." Brock turned toward him and lowered his voice. "But more importantly, I wanted to ask if you've heard an update from the PI you hired to find the blackmailer."

"No." Carson had meant to check in with him today. "But it's been a week with no new demands. Maybe the note Scarlett received was just a shot in the dark. A one-off from someone maneuvering to keep the production in LA."

Out in the practice arena, the horse and rider fell as one. Brock swore softly, his shoulders tensing until the horse and rider both popped back on their feet.

"That's damned impressive, even if it's hell on the nerves," Brock muttered before returning his attention to his brother. "And as for the blackmail note, it seems too specific about Paige to be a shot in the dark. Someone has dirt on her and thinks we'll pay to hide it."

Carson frowned. "And if she married Dad under a false identity, it means the marriage isn't legal. At first, I wasn't too concerned since Paige and Dad have been together for over twenty years. In most states, that would be more than enough to have their union legalized as a common-law marriage—no matter her name. But I looked it up. Wyoming doesn't recognize common-law marriages."

Brock's jaw flexed. He scrubbed a hand over his eyes. "I know. And that makes me wish we brought Dad in the loop so he could put a lawyer to work on that."

"I'll call the PI today," Carson assured his brother, clapping him on the shoulder. "And I'll tell Scarlett she's got to make it a priority to ask Paige about it the next time she wakes up. She's remaining alert for longer periods of time now."

"You realize there's a good chance the person who sent Scarlett that note in the first place is someone who is here now, actively involved with the film?" Brock's expression turned to a glower as his gaze swept the stable area.

"The thought has occurred to me." Carson didn't want to think about a traitor right under their noses. "But I hired more security." He pointed toward Dax. "In fact, I have a meeting with one of the new guys now."

"I'll let you get to it then." Brock backed toward his truck, the door newly painted with the ranch's logo. "I'm going to escape the mayhem and deliver one of my best two-year-olds to a ranch on the West Coast. Take my time. Maybe come home Sunday unless I'm needed back here?"

Brock looked so damned hopeful Carson had to laugh.

"We should be fine. I'll let you know how Paige is doing and if there are new developments."

He left Brock to find Emma, surprised he hadn't already seen her around the stables since it was after ten. He'd barely slept the night before, thinking of her in the next room over, dressed in her skimpy night shorts. Her bare legs had been all he could see until he'd covered her with the throw blanket, her toned muscle and creamy skin a feast for the eyes.

That visual, coupled with the memory of her kiss, had fueled enough fantasies to make him restless. Edgy. Ready to have her all to himself for a while. He wasn't going to bank on *Winning the West* staying in Cheyenne more than two weeks. He needed to make his intentions crystal clear where she was concerned.

But first, he needed to find her.

He approached the bodyguard still standing at the arena fence. "Dax, I had hoped to introduce you to the woman who will be your primary assignment, but I don't see her. Can you check with your colleague who worked last night and ask about Emma Layton? I told him to keep an eye on her."

Dax, whose scuffed boots suggested it wasn't his first time on a ranch, nodded as he withdrew his phone from his pocket. While he tapped out a text on the screen, Carson scanned the stable yard one more time.

What if he didn't see her because her ex-boyfriend had found her first? A sickening feeling chilled his gut. He knew he'd been low on security yesterday. But he'd hired more for today—

Relief hit him fast when he saw Emma rushing his way, her glossy ponytail bobbing as she double-timed her step. She was smiling, but something about her expression struck him as off. Nervous, maybe?

Or was that just his leftover worry about her?

"Carson." She darted around one of the film crew

pushing a big cart full of electronic equipment. "I'm so sorry I'm late."

"Is everything okay?" His gaze locked on her dark brown eyes. He reached for her, still sensing something wasn't quite right. She looked agitated, her attention jumping around the practice area.

"Everything is fine," she assured him, turning to extend her hand toward the bodyguard. "You must be Dax. I'm Emma, and I'm sorry I got held up."

Dax took an extra moment to finish reading something on his phone before he shook Emma's hand. "It's nice to meet you, Emma. My colleague just texted me that you were cut up pretty bad this morning. Are you sure you're all right?"

Carson's stomach dropped. Ice filled his veins.

"You're hurt?" A hundred ugly scenarios filled his brain. "Your ex—"

"No." She shook her head. "Nothing like that. I was just working on some fighting techniques—"

"You were fighting." Some of the iciness in his blood started to thaw. Her ex hadn't been involved. But if he had a megaphone at that moment, he would have shouted to everyone within listening distance that the film was canceled and they all had to go the hell home.

"It's just a scratch on my arm—" she began, pointing to the hint of a bandage peeking out from her long-sleeve T-shirt.

"Excuse us, Dax." Carson didn't take his eyes off Emma.

Now her expression—the agitation, the nervousness—made perfect sense. He tucked her under his arm and drew her away from everyone, toward where his own truck was parked.

"Carson, I'm fine." Emma laid a hand on his chest.

Was she honestly offering comfort to *him*? Damned ironic when he wanted to wrap her in cotton and take her far away from here. Reaching his pickup, he opened the passenger-side door for her.

"You'll be even better after you take care of yourself."

She didn't make a move to get in his truck. She folded her arms and glared at him. "I have to work on my riding today. You're supposed to be helping me get better for the race scene."

"We'll practice when I'm sure you're all right."

"My word isn't enough?" She looked ready to dig her heels in.

Clearly she didn't know how serious he was about this.

"Not when I've seen you throw yourself from one dangerous situation into another. No." He leaned closer when she still didn't move. Quietly, he spelled out her options. "The alternative is that I get Antonio Ventura on the phone right now, and tell him the deal is off because safety measures aren't being met."

Her eyes narrowed. Her lips pursed.

He guessed she was debating the merits of arguing further. But maybe she could see that he had no intention of backing down, because she huffed out a sigh and stepped up onto the running board of his truck instead.

"Where are we going?" Emma asked as Carson drove right past the main house.

She'd assumed that was where he was taking her. Enforcing a day off or something. But now, as the truck wound down the long access road leading to a county highway, she had to wonder what he had in mind. He drove underneath the wooden arch where a sign hung for the Creek Spill Ranch.

"Depends." He glanced over at her. "Do you need stitches?"

"Absolutely not." She debated showing him the cut on her right arm to convince him it wasn't a big deal. Instead, she laid it on the door's armrest. "I refuse to be stuck with needles just to humor you."

He nodded. "Then we're going somewhere quiet to have lunch. Food will help you recover."

Defensiveness prickled. "I'm a physical trainer, Carson. I'm very familiar with health, nutrition and recovery days—"

"Sorry." He reached across the truck and covered her hand with his. "I know you're well trained. It's just that I'm only now starting to recover myself from when Dax said you were cut up. The first thing I thought of was that your ex somehow found you."

The admission eased some of her defensiveness.

"I hadn't thought of that." She flipped her hand over and squeezed his, her skin tingling where they touched. "I'm not used to anyone worrying about me." She tipped her head back against the leather bucket seat.

Yesterday the connection she'd felt to him had been all sizzle and steam, hot attraction coming to life after her libido had been on a long vacation. Today, in light of his moving her into his house and worrying about her ex-boyfriend, she couldn't deny feeling protected. And yes, cared for.

"Worry isn't something I'm used to doing." He surprised her with a wry grin, and then let go of her hand to put both of his on the wheel. "Hell, ask anyone in my family and they'll tell you I've never wasted a minute thinking about tomorrow."

When they reached the main county road, he didn't turn toward Cheyenne, making her wonder what he had in mind. But she was more curious about what he'd said.

"That reminds me of something you said yesterday. I got the idea your twin brother is the born rancher, and you wanted a future in rodeo."

His grin faded. "I've been the reckless twin my whole life. Cody ran the ranch. I tempted fate on the back of a bull. It was a role I was comfortable with."

She straightened in her seat, not believing her ears. "You were a bull rider? And you give me a hard time about stunt work?"

The truck slowed down for a hay wagon spitting grassy bits at their windshield.

"I give you a hard time because I recognize how demanding your work must be. I know it takes guts and maybe—excuse me for saying so—a certain amount of crazy to risk your neck day in and day out." He cast a sidelong glance her way.

Emma mulled that over as he turned off the main road.

"I'm not sure if I'm more offended that you think I'm a reckless nutjob, or if I'm more surprised that you think you are." She tried to identify where they might be going, but the road held no clues. Tall grass grew on either side of the truck. Yarrow and hyssop flowers bent in the perpetual breeze.

The pungent scent of the yarrow filtered in through Carson's half open window.

"I meant no offense." He sounded sincere as they drove under a sign for Black Creek Ranch. She recognized the name of the place. The film company had wanted to shoot here originally, but Carson's brother had denied the request. "But it takes a unique personality to put your neck on the line every day."

Unlike the Creek Spill, the Black Creek Ranch was quiet as they neared the main house. Three tractors worked in a distant field, and a couple of ranch hands whistled to three dogs that went chasing after them toward the stables. But there were no concession tents for roaming cast members. No camera crews setting up shots. No stunt riders working with horses.

"I don't consider stunt work risking my neck." She glanced over at him as he parked near a large pine gazebo with a handful of picnic tables underneath. "I think of it as a way to prove to myself, every day, that I'm tougher than what life doles out to me."

He switched off the engine and turned to face her. "I guess it shouldn't surprise me that your reasons for what you do are a whole lot better than why I kept bull riding."

She waited, the fresh air still blowing through the window, riffling Carson's dark hair. Seeing him in his gray T-shirt with the ranch logo, she couldn't help thinking about how he'd looked the night before, stripping off his clothes by the pool.

"Why did you?" she asked, wondering how she was going to stop herself from kissing him again.

She might have rebounded from the damage inflicted by her last relationship, but that didn't mean she was ready for a new one. Even though Carson couldn't be more different from her ex, she simply didn't have the emotional resources for…whatever it was Carson made her feel.

Still, her heart picked up speed as he turned his blue eyes on her. He didn't seem in any hurry to get out of the truck. Then again, it wasn't even noon yet, so she wasn't particularly hungry for lunch.

A different kind of hunger stirred, though, making her restless. Warning her that she played with fire by being alone with this man, who could make or break her fledgling stunt career.

"We all did it for a while. My brothers and me. We started the sport because our father told us it was a good way to learn respect for an animal." He dragged in a deep breath. "Looking back, I'm sure it was connected to our mother's death. She died trying to separate a bull from the cattle, and I think my dad wanted us to grow up aware of the dangers."

By throwing his boys on the back of a bucking bull? Emma's vision of his father shifted as she tried to envision the kind of man that would do that to his kids. "I'm so sorry you lost your mother."

She understood better than he knew, having lost her father at a young age. But she didn't want to lose the thread of what they were talking about. She touched his knee with the hand of her uninjured arm, the gesture of comfort bringing with it a heated awareness. Birds chirped outside the truck, the soft rustle of leaves blowing a testament to how quiet it was here.

"Thank you. We all dealt with it differently. Dad retreated into himself, not paying much attention to us for—a long time afterward." Carson's gaze dropped to where her hand still touched him. Then, gently, he picked up her palm and laid it between his. "I kept riding bulls for years after my brothers stopped because it felt like a way to even an unspoken score between my father and me. A way to prove I could take whatever he dished out."

She watched Carson lift her captive fingers to his lips. It was easier to let herself be distracted by the brush of his mouth along her knuckles than to feel the ache of empathy for a young man seeking a father's approval.

"What made you decide to stop?" she asked, breathless from the tender kiss.

Slowly, he lowered her hand to rest in his on the leather console between them.

"After one too many surgeries to repair fractures or torn muscles, my father showed up at the hospital with an ultimatum. Quit bull riding or quit the family." He shook his head, a wry expression twisting his lips. "Guess he'd been banking on all of his sons walking away long before then. And he made it clear I was being selfish to put rodeo before the ranch."

Emma wondered about the surgeries and repairs. How much pain had he endured to prove a point to a stubborn man? She gave his hand a squeeze. "Did you remind your father it was his idea in the first place?"

Carson laughed. "No, ma'am. One surgery a week was enough for me. Risking Dad's wrath didn't even cross my mind."

She knew he wasn't completely serious. But she suspected there was a grain of truth in what he said. His father cast a long shadow over his life.

"And now? Are you glad you walked away from it?" She wondered if he was happy.

A strange thing to wonder, perhaps, about a man who had so much wealth and power. But then her mother had worked in the home of the rich and famous Ventura family for many years, and she'd shared with Emma plenty of incidents that suggested power and privilege did not make them happy people.

Carson tipped his head to one side, studying her as he thought about the question. "I don't miss the thrills and the roar of a crowd nearly as much as I thought I would. Ranching may not be as exciting, but it's a whole lot more satisfying." He lifted a dark eyebrow, casting a sidelong look her way. "Although, this week has been plenty exciting, now that I think about it."

The heat in his gaze sent her pulse into overdrive, warning her she ought to open the passenger door and get some fresh air before the spark between them caught into full-fledged flame.

He still held her hand, though. Or maybe she was holding his. The touch seemed so mutual, so necessary, she couldn't be sure. Her whole body warmed just looking at him, the moment wrapping around her with sensual promise.

Words eluded her. Until a tiny, frightened piece of her psyche piped up.

"I don't think I can afford any more excitement in my life, Carson." The words felt disjointed, like a ventriloquist worked her mouth to make the statement happen. But they were wise. Smart. Even she could see that as her skin smoldered from wanting his touch. She forced herself to let go of him. To open the passenger-side door. "Not now. Maybe not ever."

Six

Carson understood that Emma needed time.

She'd made that clear two days ago, after she'd cut her arm practicing a stunt. He'd backed off then, recognizing that she was going through a lot between the stress of her ex being released from prison and her effort to improve her riding skills for the horseback scene.

Today, he stood well behind the film crew as Emma performed the race stunt flawlessly for a third time in a row. As she took direction from the stunt coordinator before running through the action for a fourth time, Carson saw a new confidence in her while she stood beside her horse. An ease that hadn't been there the first day they'd met, when she'd been scared of losing her stunt job.

He knew that the time was right to pursue her.

Emma wore period costume for the scene. She had

on a long white skirt with a matching high-necked blouse, and a wig on to give her a dark braid that spilled halfway down her back. Leather boots and a leather vest with a gun belt completed her outfit. Apparently, her character was some kind of highborn frontier wife forced to fend for herself and her children after her husband's death. The guns weren't loaded in the scene— the only thing Carson had personally asked the crew about that day since he tried to stay out of the way for the most part.

But safety on the set was still his number one concern. And with Emma's most challenging scene over after today, he thought they'd both breathe easier. There would never be a better time to take her out. To convince her to spend the rest of her time in Cheyenne pursuing the heat that hit him like a flash fire when he was around her.

Ever since that day in his truck, he'd been avoiding her whenever they weren't working on her riding skills, trying his damnedest to respect her wishes. Now? He saw no more need to give her space.

She was safe. Well-rested. The cut on her arm was healing. Security kept watch for her ex, but so far there'd been no sign of unusual activity on the ranch. Tomorrow was her day off. So tonight, he planned to take her out to celebrate her successful completion of this challenge. He wanted to talk to her. Touch her. Know more about her.

The need for her ate away at him even when he wasn't around her, and he had to think she felt the same way based on how she shivered when he touched her in passing. How he caught her gaze following him when she thought he wasn't watching.

"Looks good, doesn't it?" The feminine voice at his elbow startled him, making him realize how all-consuming his thoughts of Emma had become.

He turned to see his sister Maisie wrestling her thick dark hair into a short ponytail. This past winter she'd had a razor-sharp bob, but it had grown out. Maisie never wore makeup unless she had a reason to dress up, and then it always surprised him how his toughest sister could turn into a bombshell. Today, though, she was dressed in her usual ripped jeans, worn boots and a T-shirt for a long-ago rodeo.

"What looks good?" he asked, rubbing a hand along the back of his neck where a tension with Emma's name on it had been riding him for days.

Maisie straightened. Rolled her eyes. "The scene. Isn't that what you're watching? Or is there some unsuspecting female out there about to come under the sway of the full-blown Carson McNeill charm?"

She turned her gaze out toward the fourth take of the race scene.

"I'm just making sure everyone stays safe." It was true, damn it. "Dad and Cody will have my head if the ranch ends up in the news because someone got hurt out here."

"Save the BS lines for someone who will buy them." Maisie didn't even bother looking his way, her attention trained on the horses. "Only women can distract my brothers to that degree. Although I will admit a stuntwoman isn't exactly your regular type."

The tension in his shoulders moved to his head. "I have no regular type."

"That's not true." She turned toward him, a smug

grin on her face. "Cody only dates women he wants to marry. You only date the kind you won't."

"Ludicrous theory." He returned his focus to Emma, not wanting to miss her when she finished for the day.

"Except it's true," Maisie continued, managing to gloat in a matter-of-fact tone. "Which has given Cody the most boring dating career on record—going from one serious girlfriend to Jillian. Marriage is only a matter of time there."

Carson said nothing, although he acknowledged the truth of Maisie's words. Cody was seriously involved with Jillian Ross, the film scout who was now carrying his child.

"And you don't pursue women, but they all flock to you just the same." She folded her arms and glanced his way. "Which means, if you're actively scoping out someone and getting all prickly about it, you're breaking your pattern. And it tells me this woman is different."

"You're fishing, and you're wrong," he told her flatly. Then, needing to change topics, he brought up a far more pressing issue. "Any word on your mom? Has Scarlett asked Paige about the note yet?"

Over by the camera crew, he heard the stunt coordinator call for the cast members to run the race scene one more time.

Beside him, Maisie nodded, letting herself be distracted by the new question. "Mom's doctors might let her come home tomorrow if she continues to do well. Knowing we need to tell Dad soon about the letter, Scarlett and I sat down with her yesterday to show her the note and see what she knows about it."

"And?" He tensed, wondering why no one had phoned him. As the point person for the family's contact with the investigator, he expected to be kept in the loop. "The PI needs to know what she said if we want him to find out the truth."

"We learned nothing concrete," Maisie assured him. "Mom turned ten shades of white and called for a nurse."

Carson swore softly.

"I know. We felt terrible for pushing her, but between you and me, I'd guess there was some truth to the accusation in the note, or it wouldn't have upset her so much."

"If you bring it up again, make sure you stress to her that we love her and don't care about her past. We just need to know who might want to use the information to hurt the family." Carson might have issues with his father, and some with his twin, but he would do anything to protect his family. "I have the feeling we'll hear more from the blackmailer soon enough."

"I hate the idea that it could be someone we're hosting." Maisie hugged her arms around herself. "You remember whoever wrote that note didn't want the filming to happen here in the first place, so they must have something to do with *Winning the West*."

"Did you warn Scarlett to be careful around that actor?" Carson had put Logan King at the top of the list of people to investigate since his youngest sibling had a history with the guy.

"I did, but I don't think she listened. I saw them together yesterday."

"His past is shady." Carson knew that much from the PI. "Except for a younger sister who went into the foster system and got adopted, his family members are all in jail or dead."

He couldn't let Scarlett get hurt. He had enough reasons to regret letting the movie crew onto his property. The safety risks. The slowdown in ranch production. Ticking off Cody and his father, which—despite what they might think—hadn't been his primary objective in offering use of the ranch.

But as Carson peered back out over the meadow where Emma was riding hell-for-leather on the back of her gray mare, he acknowledged there was still one reason the he wouldn't trade the decision for anything.

When Emma finally finished the last take on her horseback riding scene, she was ready to run a victory lap.

She'd stayed on Mariana's back successfully despite the speed of the gallop and the other horses crowding her. She hadn't flipped over the mare's head any of the times the horse had to make a quick stop and turn, which was the other tricky part of the stunt.

With the thrill of triumph still in her veins, Emma slid to the ground and patted Mariana's neck as she looked over to the place where Carson had stood watching her for most of the filming.

Disappointment stung when she didn't spot him. It surprised her how much she was looking forward to sharing this moment with him. It was his success as much as hers, considering how hard he'd trained with her these last few days to keep her safe.

She told herself it didn't matter. She'd asked him for more space after that day in the truck when she'd been ready to come out of her skin from wanting him. So she could hardly hold it against him now that he'd done as she'd asked.

Handing off Mariana's reins to one of the handlers, Emma went to the wardrobe tent, where she changed out of her period garb, retrieved her phone and purse, and turned in her skirt and blouse to the costume mistress. She'd worn simple khaki shorts and a white tank underneath, so changing was fast. Before she went back outside, she decided to check her messages. There were a couple of other cast members running in and out, but Emma had a quiet corner behind a rolling rack to herself.

There were a handful of texts from her mom that she'd look over in a minute. But the one that caught her eye first was from Carson just a few minutes ago.

You rode like a pro! Celebration dinner under the stars at 7:00? I want to show you a new view.

The thrill of anticipation that shot through her was like nothing she'd ever felt for another man. The promise of passion was a lure she couldn't resist. Not with Carson. Besides, she was free from her past—she deserved to seize the moment with a man who treated her well. He applauded her strengths even as he tried to protect her. He gave her the space she asked for, even when he could have used the simmering heat between them to overrule her common sense.

Continuing to deny the attraction hadn't made her feel stronger. If anything, it made her worry she hadn't fully recovered from her past so that she could take this kind of risk. Still, her fingers trembled just a little as she typed out a response.

Yes.

She hit Send and barely had time to exhale before his response made her phone chime.

I'll meet you in the courtyard of the main house at seven.

She would be alone with him tonight. Desire smoked through her at the possibilities, yes. But she couldn't deny that the emotional risk scared her. Giving herself a minute to slow her racing heart, she tried to read her mother's long, rambly texts.

Tucking one foot under her, she scrolled through the messages, skipping past some of the drawn-out worries about Austin finding Emma again. Emma had spent enough of her own energy fearing that without allowing her mother to wind her up again.

Jane Layton had been diagnosed with bipolar disorder after Emma's father committed suicide, and her mom had been on medications ever since. She'd been in a long depression for much of Emma's childhood, but the last five years had been full of mood swings, manic episodes followed by prolonged crashes. Emma tried not to add to her mother's stress, so she needed boundaries for how much she shared about her own life.

However, she couldn't remain quiet for too long, or she'd add to her mother's anxiety. It was a constant tightrope walk to help her mother stay level.

From what Emma could glean from the long texts, her mom's latest fear was that the McNeill family was going to take advantage of Emma. Mom had read about the family online and was worried they were entitled and privileged. There was a long rant about how money did not equate with honor. Another text compared the

Venturas—the family who'd employed her mother for decades—to the McNeills, with some discussion of how rich people used others for their own ends.

Emma finally switched off the screen in the middle of reading a text, unwilling to get sucked into baseless fears. She'd been in family counseling more than once, with her mom and by herself, to learn strategies for coping with this kind of thing. And right now, when Emma had just enjoyed a professionally rewarding day, she reminded herself that it was okay if she didn't respond yet. She would enjoy tonight with Carson, savor the triumph of the race scene and then reply tomorrow. In the morning, she would craft a calming, neutral answer.

Still, as she walked back to the main house to get ready for her night out, she couldn't help feeling a sense of foreboding. Because sometimes, at the heart of her mother's outsize fears, there was something legitimate, which always made it difficult to discount them completely.

What had her so upset about the McNeills?

From what Emma had seen, they were generous to allow a film crew so much access to one of their working ranches. She hadn't met Carson's brothers or half siblings, but she'd gathered they were a tight-knit group who operated connected businesses. And as for Carson...

Her heart galloped faster at the thought of their upcoming date. Slipping into a back door of the Creek Spill's main house, Emma hurried to the stairs to reach her room. Tonight clearly wasn't about working together to keep her safe on the back of a horse. Carson's celebration seemed entirely personal.

And no matter what her mother might think of the

McNeill family, Emma trusted Carson enough to be alone with him. That was more than she could say for any man she'd met in the last three years. Was it so wrong to want to enjoy this moment of feeling like she'd made progress in her journey toward healing?

The door to her suite was open, the way she'd left it this morning. But it was clear someone had been inside. A stack of crisp white boxes rested on the brown leather sofa in the sitting area, the name of an upscale women's boutique written in block lettering on each one. The smallest of the pile was a thin, flat package, crisscrossed with bright blue ribbon.

Sticking out from the ribbon at an angle was a card with her name scrawled in bold penmanship. When she flipped it over, there was a message:

Pulling out all the stops to celebrate. If you want to set aside your boots for a few hours, I picked out some things I thought you might like.

Intrigued, Emma slid a finger under the ribbons and pulled them off. She opened the box to find a delicate platinum chain, the loops so fine they looked like lace. At the center was a pendant of diamonds in the shape of a horseshoe, the polished stones cut to refract light in every direction. Her finger trailed over the jewelry, hardly daring to believe he would give her such a gift.

She couldn't keep it, of course. But she also couldn't ignore that kind of thoughtfulness. She would wear it to dinner and enjoy the feel of it on her neck. For this brief window of time, she would celebrate the way the McNeills did—with extravagance.

A thrill shot through as she turned to see all the other gifts stacked up and waiting. Excited to see what each one held, she pulled out one beautiful thing after another. A white crepe top that looked like it would bare her midriff. A full-length black silk skirt with a daring slit up one leg. Tiny diamond hoops for her ears. Bright teal-colored high heels with straps that went around her ankles. A tiny satin drawstring bag to carry her things—black on one side and teal on the other so she could choose which to use.

There were silver combs for her hair. A designer makeup kit in a travel size.

Everything she could possibly need to feel glamorous.

It was perfect. Exciting. And the only cloud hovering over her evening was the knowledge that her mother sat alone somewhere, worried that Emma was going to be taken advantage of by the rich and powerful McNeills. What would Jane Layton say if she saw the way her daughter took her time showering and applying her makeup for a date with her host tonight? The way Emma slid into that black silk skirt and felt like the most sensual creature on earth?

No doubt, her mother would tell her to run.

But Emma had been doing that for three years straight. Tonight, she was done hiding. With the thrill of a successful stunt behind her, she hoped she had the courage to take the one risk she hadn't dared in all that time.

Carson's breath stuck in his chest when Emma stepped out of the house dressed for the evening. He'd been sitting by the pool while he waited for her, messaging the private investigator and checking in with his sister Madeline about Paige's condition.

But one look at Emma's thigh through the high slit in

the black skirt she wore had his brain scrambling like he'd just been bucked off a two-thousand-pound bull.

He gave an admiring whistle and shoved his phone in the pocket of his tux jacket.

"Well, thank you." She tucked a flyaway hair behind her ear, the diamond hoops glinting in the sinking sunlight. "You've got some good taste, Carson McNeill."

"I only chose the date and the horseshoe necklace." He edged past a lounger to meet her at the end of the pool deck. "But I agree, my taste in those things is outstanding."

Seeing her now, with strawberry-colored gloss slicked over her lips and something shimmery on her eyelids, made him realize she hadn't worn makeup any of the times they'd been together before. She didn't need it any more than she needed silk clothes and diamonds, but she carried herself differently tonight. And he liked that a whole lot.

Offering her his arm, Carson led her down the wide stone path toward the car he'd rented.

"Then who chose all these beautiful things for me?" She kicked out a foot to show off her bright blue shoe. Pink toenails peeped through the straps. "And it all fits."

"My half sister Madeline runs the guest ranch where you were staying before you moved over here. When I asked her about her favorite boutique, she quizzed me until I told her your name. She remembered you from check-in."

"I remember her, too." Emma paused in front of the limo. "What's this?"

"Our ride to the airfield." He stood back to let the driver open the door for her. "I didn't think the pickup would cut it."

"Airfield?" She bit her lip.

His gaze tracked the movement, and the desire to taste her became a tangible need.

"There aren't many options for fine dining nearby. I thought a night in Jackson Hole would be nice."

Plus, taking her away from the ranch and Cheyenne meant a night off from worrying about her ex finding her.

"A benefit of being a McNeill." Squaring her shoulders, she stepped into the limousine and slid into the plush leather seat that wrapped around the back corner of the vehicle.

Carson settled into the seat beside her while the driver shut the door and put the car in motion. He reached for the champagne in the ice bucket.

"Ready to toast your success?" He spun the bottle so she could see the label to make her decision.

"Actually, as a personal trainer, I try to walk the walk with what I tell my clients and really limit alcohol intake."

"I respect that." He tucked the champagne back into the ice. "But I can't let it stop me from making a toast." Reaching past the silver bucket to the mini fridge, he found a bottle of sparkling water and cracked it open. "It's important to celebrate milestones."

The limo pulled out onto the main road. Carson noticed that traffic was heavier than usual in the other direction. But then, it was Friday night, and there were more visitors in town than normal with the film shooting here. Everyone else was headed downtown for an evening out, making him glad they were driving toward the private airstrip instead.

"Here." Emma leaned forward to retrieve the crystal champagne flutes. She held one out for him to fill, then the other.

Her bare knee grazed his as she shifted on the seat. Her light lemongrass scent drifted toward him, making him want to get closer and find the places on her skin where the fragrance hid. When she leaned back into her seat again, he realized he'd been holding his breath.

Damn. What a powerful effect she had on him.

He clutched the base of his champagne glass, the chill of the water reaching the stem as he lifted it. He told himself to keep the focus on a friendly celebration. To give her time to enjoy herself. She deserved that.

"To you, Emma. To your grit, your daring and your skill. You impressed me all week with your commitment to improving, but I admired you most today, when I saw you ride the stunt over and over again like you'd done it a hundred times."

She laughed, shaking her head like she could wave off the praise. "You don't know how scared I was."

"I do." He'd seen how hard she worked to get better. And he thought he understood the nuances of what drove her to keep this job. It wasn't just about avoiding her ex, but triumphing over that chapter of her past. "That's what made it so special. Cheers to conquering the challenge."

Her gaze turned serious. "Cheers."

They drank at the same moment, gazes locked until Emma glanced away. She set aside her champagne flute as the vehicle turned. Through the tinted windows, he saw a handful of private planes. Two of them were on the tarmac, ready for departure.

His plane—his grandfather's Learjet that he'd welcomed the family to use while he stayed in Wyoming—and another that Carson didn't recognize.

He did recognize the woman standing near the jetway, however.

"Isn't that one of your sisters?" Emma asked, sitting forward while the limo rolled to a stop, kicking up a small cloud of dust on the gravel parking area. "And she's with Logan King." Emma's hand squeezed Carson's arm lightly. "One of the lead actors."

Carson knew damn well who Logan King was.

And even though his date was the most compelling woman he'd ever been with, it still took superhuman willpower for him not to sprint out of the limo ahead of her to ask the guy just what the hell he thought he was doing.

Seven

Of all the luck.

Scarlett had to resist the urge to chew on her freshly painted fingernail as her brother Carson stepped out of his limousine at the private airfield. Her brothers never went anywhere. What were the odds one of them would suddenly decide to take a Friday night flight at the same time Logan had invited her to Los Angeles for the dinner date she'd promised him?

Carson charged toward them now, his lovely date having to double-time her steps to keep up. The woman clutched the side slit of a stunning silk skirt with one hand while Carson bore down on them.

"Do you know that guy?" Logan asked, his arm sliding protectively around Scarlett's waist.

His touch—instinctual, automatic—was a pleasant counterpoint to a situation that was going downhill fast.

"It's my brother." She glanced up at Logan while their driver stowed their overnight bags on board the aircraft.

"Scarlett." Carson sounded just like their father when he broke out his stern voice. "Going somewhere?"

"Hello to you, too." She turned her attention to the tall, beautiful creature by his side, who must have been involved with the movie. The woman had amazing legs and the bearing of someone used to being in front of the camera. "Excuse my brother's manners. I'm Scarlett, the youngest sister, who will forever be stuck at thirteen years old in his eyes."

"Emma Layton." The woman had a strong, friendly handshake. Warm but no-nonsense at the same time. "Nice to meet you. That's a great dress."

Scarlett would have returned the compliment and gladly swapped fashion notes if her brother didn't take a menacing step forward, his gaze locked on Logan.

"Carson McNeill." He thrust his hand toward Scarlett's date.

But Logan appeared prepared. He released his hold on Scarlett to shake her brother's hand.

"Logan King." He sounded relaxed, but Scarlett could see the tension in his shoulders as the two men shook. "I invited Scarlett to dinner in LA tonight."

The muscle in Carson's jaw worked, and Scarlett guessed that she had Emma's presence to thank for his restraint as he appeared to weigh his words.

"When will you be home?" he asked, a warning note in his voice.

Scarlett drew a breath to defend herself and her life choices, but Logan answered smoothly.

"Scarlett hasn't decided when she wants to return,

but I'm hoping to talk her into staying through Sunday, so she can meet my sister." Logan turned to Emma. "I saw some footage of the race scene stunt on one of the actor's phones. Great job."

Scarlett laid a hand on Logan's chest. "Logan, would you and Emma excuse my brother and me for just a second? I know we're scheduled to take off soon and I just want to give him an update on Mom."

"Of course." Logan squeezed her hip just slightly as he said it. A touch of reassurance. But oh, did it make her remember their night together—and so much more. "I can ask Ms. Layton how she managed to stay upright on that horse."

Scarlett smiled gratefully at both of them before she clamped a hand on her brother's thick wrist and drew him to one side.

He followed her, his thunderous scowl like a raincloud ready to burst. He held his peace as she stalked away from the metal steps leading to the jet door. When they got closer to the nose of the plane, the engine rumbling loud enough to mask their conversation, he stopped and leaned toward her.

"Are you out of your mind?" he asked, his expression shifting from pure Neanderthal to brotherly concern.

Her heart softened. "I know you're worried about me, but you don't need to be. I don't buy the theory that he's the blackmailer, okay? And furthermore—" she put a hand over Carson's lips to forestall the argument he had ready to roll "—Logan remembers the guy who passed me the note in the first place, and he's going to help me find him this weekend."

When she lowered her hand, Carson retorted, "So he says."

"And *I* believe him. So you're going to have to go out on a limb and trust my judgment because I'm getting on this plane with him, not that it's any of your business."

Her brother rocked back on his heels a bit. She didn't think for a moment it meant she'd won her case. Only that he needed to regroup. In that moment, she saw beyond the argument, to the man beneath. She reached up to smooth a wrinkle on his lapel.

"You look handsome, by the way," she admitted, adjusting his bow tie even though it was already straight. Her brothers were hard men, but she knew they'd been raised by a demanding father. Her mother had been good to them, but Paige had never been able to shield them from their father the way their birth mother might have been able to. Paige had deferred to her husband on everything where Carson, Cody and Brock were concerned.

"Thanks." Carson kissed the top of her head absently. "And blackmail aside, sweetheart, I just can't help but think this guy hurt you before."

She tipped her head against her brother's chest. "There's a good chance I misread what happened." Levering away from him, she looked up into his eyes, which were reflecting the bright lights of the airstrip. "And I like him enough that trying again is a gamble I'm willing to take."

"I just wish you were having dinner here. Close to home."

Stubborn, stubborn man. She peered past him to see Logan showing Emma something on his phone. Still, she couldn't leave him to make small talk all evening. She looked her brother in the eye.

"I need this break, the distraction. Do you know the

kind of pressure I've been under at home lately, Carson? My mother's been in a coma and I've barely left her bedside. She's weak and confused, freaking out when I try to ask her about her past. Plus the stress of not telling Dad about that note is tearing me up inside." She clenched her hands in frustration. "I feel like it's all my fault he wasn't told to start with, and every day we keep it from him—"

"Hey." Carson took her hands in both of his. Held them. "It's not your fault. We decided as a family that's what was best. For now. I will be the one to tell him when I get back tomorrow."

"You would do that?" Scarlett hadn't realized until just now how much that task weighed on her. But having Carson lift it away made her feel lighter. Relief rushed through her.

"Of course. This is on me." He hugged her shoulders and turned her around, back toward the metal steps leading up to the jet. "Take the weekend to recharge, but I want to hear from you if you learn anything from this guy who passed you the note about Mom, okay?"

"I will," she promised, keeping pace with him as they headed back toward their companions. "And I hope you're extra nice to Emma tonight now that she's seen your overprotective side."

"Was I that bad?" he asked, his eyes glued to the tall brunette.

Interesting. Women always noticed Carson, but he'd never given his heart to anyone as far as she could tell. Dates came and went for her brother, whose attitude toward women had always been easy come, easy go, and Scarlett had comforted more than one of his disappointed ex-girlfriends who'd thought there was a chance with him.

That he was concerned what Emma Layton thought of him—heck, that he was taking her somewhere on a *plane*, for that matter—meant she was special.

"She had to sprint like an Olympic runner to keep up with you when you were storming over to me," Scarlett observed lightly, taking just a little sisterly pleasure in his obvious worry. "But I'm sure you'll woo her well."

He grumbled something about Emma not being "like that," but by then, Scarlett had reached Logan's side.

She was more than ready to think about the night ahead as her absurdly handsome date turned his green gaze her way. Her heartbeat stuttered, her breath catching in her lungs. She knew she needed to be very careful around him if she didn't want to get burned a second time.

Still, as he reeled her closer, sliding an arm around her waist and dropping a kiss on her temple, she knew it wasn't going to be easy to stay strong.

"I missed you," Logan whispered into her ear while Carson led Emma toward the McNeill family jet parked nearby.

Tamping down the desire to lean more fully into him, Scarlett straightened and met Logan's gaze, determined to hold him to their bargain. He'd find the man who passed her a blackmail note if she shared a meal with him.

"I believe you promised dinner?"

Midway through an exquisite meal served by the private wait staff on the deck of Carson's mountainside home just outside Jackson Hole, Emma was still trying to shake off a sense of foreboding.

The evening had been picture-perfect, starting with their timely touchdown in Jackson Hole after the short flight from Cheyenne. A driver had greeted them at the airfield, and delivered them straight to the chalet Carson kept for weekend getaways, a beautiful property with breathtaking views of the Teton Mountains. Even by moonlight, the vista from the back deck was impressive.

The huge patio had been stocked with extra outdoor heaters in deference to the dip in evening temperatures here. But Emma wasn't the least bit cold, between the warmth from the heaters and the fire burning in the outdoor fireplace. And, of course, the ever-present burn of awareness for the man seated beside her. Carson had appealed to her in denim and boots when they had worked side by side at the Creek Spill. Tonight, she saw another side of him: the worldly business mogul whose holdings stretched far beyond Wyoming. From the tuxedo he wore with casual ease, to the multiple homes and staffers, Carson McNeill was an influential man who could order the world to suit him.

He had the meal catered by the local Four Seasons, and Emma had her choice of entrees prepared in the kitchen on-site. The wait staff had greeted them formally, ushering them to the outdoor table laden with candelabra and hors d'oeuvres.

Emma's salmon had been delectable, then their waiter had recommended the pistachio mille-feuille and lavender ice cream for dessert. Emma had no clue what a mille-feuille might be, but she was game to try it, especially if it helped take away the sense of unease brewing inside her ever since they'd run into Carson's sister Scarlett and the actor Logan King.

"Are you enjoying everything, Emma?" Carson asked, leaning forward in his chair. "You seem quiet."

They sat next to each other at the round patio table draped in white linen. They'd moved aside the candelabra—each flame housed in a tiny hurricane lampshade—to clear their view of the shadowed mountains and the dark hiking paths that Carson said would be ski trails once the weather turned.

"The meal is wonderful." She appreciated the effort he'd gone to for her. "I can't imagine a more extravagant celebration for today, and I am truly grateful to you for helping me keep my job."

A breeze off the mountain threaded around her legs, tickling the silk of her skirt against her calf.

"And yet, you've been lost in thought." He seemed to have heard the unspoken reservation in her voice. He reached across the table to claim her hand, threading his fingers through hers. "Are you worried about anything?"

Her mother's texts. A niggling fear that the McNeill family might have more in common with the domineering Venturas than she'd first thought. But she knew that wasn't fair to Carson, who had been kind and thoughtful, extending his home and protection to her during a stressful time in her life.

"I've been thinking about your sister, actually," she hedged. It was partly true, at least. "Scarlett."

He shook his head. "She told me I needed to make it up to you for coming across like a Neanderthal tonight."

"She said that?" Emma couldn't help laughing.

"Not in those exact words, but close enough," he admitted. "In my defense, I've been worried about her. She had a relationship with that actor before and the guy—" Carson huffed out a breath between his teeth. "I don't know what happened, but I know she was hurt."

"So you had reservations about her taking off with him for the weekend. I can see why." Emma thought back to her conversation with Logan. "Although if I had to guess, based on the way he kept glancing over at her, I would say he genuinely likes Scarlett."

Carson didn't appear reassured. He leaned back in his chair as the waiter returned with their desserts. Hers was a culinary work of art, the pastry layers delicate and flaky looking, with whipped mascarpone and pistachio between the layers. Carson had a pavlova—a meringue cake with Chantilly cream and berries. As the waiter left them to enjoy the treats, Emma picked up her fork to try the pistachio filling.

Carson watched her, his blue eyes following the movement of the silver tines as she swirled them through an airy layer of her dessert. "May I ask what made you think of my sister?"

"Oddly enough, a text message from my mother." She put her fork back down, unsure how to convey her concerns. "My mother is a perpetual worrier, and she's been messaging me often this week—as you can imagine—wanting to be sure I'm all right."

Carson gave a half nod. "I can see why she'd be concerned for your safety. But what does that have to do with Scarlett?"

Absently, Emma adjusted the diamond horseshoe pendant where it fell on her neck, a reminder of Carson's thoughtfulness, which gave her courage to share some of her mother's personal battles.

"My mother suffers from a combination of bipolar disorder and anxiety, so her fears can be excessive. But she's scared I'll get sucked in by the McNeill world once I have a taste of the finer things." The note from her mother did seem prescient, given the over-the-top private celebration Carson was treating Emma to tonight. "I know it's because she had an affair with her wealthy employer long ago, and there was a time when she thought it meant something to him." As a young child, Emma had seen her mother fall into a deep depression and it had been terrifying.

Carson listened patiently, even though she hadn't yet made the connection to his sister that he'd asked about. Drawing a deep breath of the clear mountain air, she leaned forward in her seat.

"I guess she thinks that power and influence can seduce people who've never had either." *Like me.* "And maybe she has a point. But I keep thinking your sister Scarlett grew up in that world of wealth and privilege. Yet she's been drawn in by someone like Logan King." It was true enough, Emma thought. And now that she was knee-deep into the conversation, she had to acknowledge she'd waded in with the hope of voicing her worries for herself, too.

Was she in over her head with Carson?

He studied her for a moment before he swiveled on the seat of his chair, turning fully toward her. Covering her hand with his, he squeezed her fingers gently.

"Scarlett has always wanted to be an actress. I think that's some of the reason Logan's world fascinates her. But Emma, if I've made you uncomfortable tonight, or if you feel like I've made any kind of assumptions about where this is headed, I apologize." His gaze was steady. And, if she had to guess, sincere. "We can get back on that plane anytime and return to Cheyenne. No harm, no foul."

"No." It surprised her how much she didn't want to go home tonight. Now that she'd allowed herself to think about going through with this—being with Carson—she didn't want to back out of it. "I mean, I may be having a few jitters about tonight, but I definitely want to be here."

He lifted her hand to his lips and brushed a kiss along the knuckles. She would have never thought of knuckles as an erogenous zone, but...wow. The sizzle of awareness hit her bloodstream like a whiskey shot.

"I'm glad to hear it. And I'm sure Scarlett can take care of herself."

Emma wanted to believe him. But something Logan had said in those long minutes when they'd been alone kept coming to her mind.

"You're not worried they're trying to find a blackmailer this weekend?" she finally ventured.

Carson shouldn't have been surprised.

He'd left Emma alone with Scarlett's actor friend while he spoke to his sister. And Logan probably assumed that Emma already knew about the blackmail note. Still, he hadn't expected to discuss this with anyone outside of the family. Particularly not before his father knew about it.

Briefly, he summed up the events of the last weeks, starting with Scarlett's receipt of the note, to his mother's out-of-character road trip to Yellowstone Park to do some hiking, followed by her fall and coma.

"So Scarlett is going with Logan to find the man who delivered the letter?" Emma asked.

"Logan thought the man looked familiar." Carson didn't trust the actor after what he'd done to Scarlett, but he should have some faith in his sister's judgment. If she trusted him, that had to be good enough.

Even if Carson hated it.

"I'm sorry to ask about it. I know it's none of my business, but ever since Logan used the word blackmail, I've felt uneasy." Emma tried a bite of her dessert, and he realized he'd forgotten all about his.

He picked up his fork and tried to join her in enjoying the last course.

"With good reason. My whole family has been on edge waiting for our private investigator to come up with something." Carson didn't give any details about Paige's mysterious past, since that wasn't his story to share.

Whatever secrets his stepmother was hiding, they were hers to reveal when the time was right. He hadn't asked Scarlett if Logan knew the contents of that note, but maybe he should have.

Either way, the pressure was on to speak to his father as soon as he got back to Cheyenne.

"You were probably looking forward to getting away from those worries tonight," Emma observed. "And then I had to kick the hornet's nest to stir it all up again."

"You didn't know. My family has been a target for scandalmongers, gold diggers and business rivals in the past. That comes with success." He'd escaped some of that during his years in the rodeo, but successful bull riders were targeted in other ways.

For their fame. By hangers-on who liked the thrill of the sport.

"Still, I'm sorry." She twirled her fork through the meringue. "I've been looking forward to this. Our time together tonight."

His gaze flicked to hers. His unspoken question had somehow been answered, because he knew she was thinking about the same thing as him. His pulse shifted into high gear.

"As have I." He gave up trying to eat any dessert. It was Emma he wanted to taste.

Her lips quirked in the ghost of a nervous smile.

"I—" She set aside her fork. Her elbow bumped against the table slightly, making the candle flames jump inside their tiny hurricane shades. "You should know, I haven't been with anyone since…that whole debacle in my past."

How many years had that been? He couldn't remember, but he knew it had been a long time. He reminded himself to keep that in mind. To take care with her. Of her.

"We can go slowly." He skimmed a touch up her arm, liking the flare of reaction in her eyes as much as the feel of her skin. "You set the pace."

He felt a shiver run through her, the subtle tremble igniting a fierce need of his own.

Emma pivoted on her seat to face him, the thigh-high slit in her skirt giving him a delectable glimpse of her bare leg. "Actually, if I'm being totally honest, three years is sort of feeling like a lifetime right now."

Eight

Sensation tripped through her hot under Carson's steady gaze. Emma wasn't sure how it transpired, but the fog of half-formed fears dissipated when he touched her, his fingers falling on her bare knee where her silk skirt had fallen aside. She wanted to see his hand on her, to watch him touch her and see the magic of his caress at work. Yet she couldn't tear her gaze from his.

"Would you like to come inside with me, Emma?" he asked.

His eyes asked much, much more.

A bolt of longing speared through her. White-hot. The sparks from it set fire to any lingering fears. She wanted to climb into his lap and kiss him. Wrap herself around him.

"Yes." She forced a jerky nod, her body feeling oddly foreign under the weight of her self-restraint. "I'd like that."

Taking her hand, he drew her to her feet. Her legs tingled with awareness as the cool night breeze fluttered the silk against her skin. There was a scent of applewood in the air from the outdoor hearth.

Carson's warm hand palmed the small of her back, one finger landing on the narrow patch of bare skin between the high-waisted skirt and cropped blouse. Her breasts ached to be touched, the sensitive peaks beading in response to his touch on her back. As he guided her through the French doors and into the living area, she had a vague sense of the cathedral ceiling and a loft area above, the gleaming natural wood walls giving the whole place a dull glow in the dim light from the heavy bronze sconces.

Once he closed the door behind them and stepped briefly into the kitchen to dismiss the wait staff, Carson returned to her side. She let him lead her deeper into the house, past the huge staircase to the hallway that led to the master suite. There, he closed and locked the double doors that separated his quarters from the rest of the home. Emma could see a fire already crackling in the hearth shared on one side by the den and the other side by the bedroom. Carson never hesitated as he drew her left—toward the large bed with a padded leather headboard that rose halfway to the ceiling.

A cream-colored duvet was half pulled back, revealing layers of cream and tan blankets, sheets and a spill of pillows in every size. She only had a moment to take in their surroundings before Carson was there, eye-to-eye with her, his hands cupping her shoulders.

"Are you sure?" He tipped her chin to see her face in the firelight.

She appreciated his concern. Trusted him all the more because of it.

"Completely certain." Dragging in a breath of air tinged with a hint of wood smoke and his aftershave, she felt safe sharing what she wanted. Needed. "I wish tonight would be all about us. A chance to be in the present. Forget about the past."

Understanding lit up his eyes. He curved his palm around her cheek, cradling her face as he stepped closer, narrowing the space between them to the smallest fraction of an inch.

"You can't imagine how much I'm going to like that." His thumb stroked down her cheek.

Once. Twice.

Her lips parted as she leaned into him, sealing her body to his until the only part of them not touching were their lips. She heard his sharp intake of breath and it gratified her to think this attraction affected him as much as it did her.

He threaded his fingers through the hair at the base of her neck. Angled her head for his kiss.

When their lips finally brushed, Emma thought she would come right out of her skin.

Fire blazed over her, flames licking up her legs and roaring over her breasts and belly until she yearned to peel off all her clothes. Feel his bare skin on hers. If Carson knew it—or if he felt that, too—he didn't reveal it with his kiss. He took his time tasting, nipping, exploring. He drew her lower lip between his teeth gently.

Oh. So. Provocatively.

His hands skimmed up her back, fingers gliding over the smooth fabric of her blouse, then venturing beneath it. They stood in the middle of the room and she would have wobbled on her sky-high heels if not for Carson's strong arms around her, keeping her upright. Through the tissue-thin silk of her skirt, she felt his body heat. She couldn't help but roll her hips against his, melting at the feel of him.

She felt more than heard the hungry growl of want that started as a rumble in his chest and ended with a quiet hiss of breath between his teeth as he reared back to look at her. She saw the flare of desire in the molten blue of his eyes and it only edged her own need higher.

"We don't need to rush," he reminded her, his breathing gratifyingly harsh.

"I've waited a long time to feel this way." A lifetime, actually, but she wasn't ready to tell him that. "So I'm finding it hard to wait much more."

She'd never experienced an attraction anywhere close to this. Was it any wonder her hands were a little unsteady as she tugged one end of his bow tie free? Then she smoothed a palm over the hard planes of his chest, very ready to touch all of him.

"In that case—" he reached between them to find the knot on her wrap skirt "—I'd better give you a hand in moving things along."

With barely a flick of his finger, the fabric floated to the floor, leaving her in a tiny pair of bikini panties and very high heels from the waist down.

"It's not fair that I practically fall out of my clothes while yours require so much extra time." She arched an eyebrow at him while she unfastened the top two buttons on his shirt.

"You maneuvered me out of the tie fast enough," he

reminded her, flicking open the tiny hook on the neck of her blouse before sliding his hands under the hem.

Seductive sensations chased over her skin, distracting her from the shirt buttons as he cupped her breasts in his palms. She felt the heat of his touch through the lace of her bra, and a shiver rocked her.

"I'm going to be naked in about five more seconds, though. And then I'll be too distracted to get your clothes off." She closed her eyes to better feel all the things he was making her feel.

His thumbs teased circles around the tight peaks through the lace and she was lost. Arching into him, she wondered how much force it might require to tip him back into that huge bed behind him.

Carson kissed his way along her jaw. She clung to him, her fingers wrapping around his arms. Holding tight.

"You let me worry about it," he murmured in her ear, pausing briefly before his lips continued down her neck. Nipping, licking, driving her mad.

"Carson." She breathed his name like a plea, unsure what she wanted.

Him, obviously.

But all of him felt so good, she couldn't decide where to touch next. And all of *her* felt so damn good, she couldn't get enough of his touch. His body. His *mouth*, which drove the hunger higher with each movement of his lips.

He wrapped his arms around her then, lifted her high against his chest and deposited her in the middle of his bed. She tried to keep him there with her, but he edged back to stand at the foot of it.

With deliberate fingers, he unfastened the buttons

on his tuxedo shirt, one after the other, his blue gaze never leaving hers.

Intrigued by the hint of muscle in the gaping V of the placket, she lifted herself up on her arms to better admire him.

When he shouldered out of his jacket, the shirt went with it, giving her a view of his squared shoulders and strong arms. Inspired, she took the hem of her wrinkled blouse and lifted it over her head, letting the material fall along the side of the bed while Carson's hands moved to his belt. And his zipper.

Firelight bathed his skin in a tawny glow while leaving his face in shadow. She watched, fascinated by the movement of his abs as he stepped out of the trousers. Then she stared at the boxers beneath them. She forgot all about her own undressing, her fingers going still on the bra straps she'd been about to shrug out of.

Carson was…impressive.

All of him.

"I. Um." Her throat was dry. She'd forgotten about birth control. Still, she couldn't quite link her thoughts to her speech. She was too busy ogling.

A hint of a grin played at his lips. "That's exactly how I'm feeling right now," he told her as he joined her on the bed, stretching out beside her.

His thigh was hot next to hers, the bristle of his hair tickling her oversensitive skin.

She watched as he turned her toward him, flicking open the hooks of her bra so the lace fell aside. He kissed each peak, making her forget everything but this. Him.

The want.

"So beautiful." He said the words into her skin,

pressing them in with kisses as he worked his way up her chest.

When he reached the hollow of her throat where the diamond horseshoe pendant lay, he kissed beneath it, the stones clinking dully on his teeth.

She wrapped an arm around him, pulling herself closer to him while he covered her hip with one hand. He spanned her belly with his palm and desire pooled between her thighs. He slid the lace panties down and off. She was so very ready.

Except that she hadn't brought any protection.

"Do you have anything?" she blurted, placing a hand on his chest, needing to settle this now before she got so caught up she forgot everything else. "I mean, do you have—"

He reached behind her head on the bed and came back with a foil packet.

"I smuggled one in my jacket pocket. Just in case."

"One?" She couldn't hide the hint of dismay.

"There are more in a bathroom somewhere," he promised, tearing open the condom and rolling it into place.

"Good." Relief settled over her, allowing her to be more fully in the moment. To soak up the pleasure of being with him. "That's very good."

Their eyes locked. Emma reached to touch his jaw. She kissed him, her hips sidling closer to his. Grazing the hard length of him.

He slid an arm around her and rolled her onto her back before he settled himself between her thighs. She felt her heartbeat quicken for the space of a few beats.

And then, he eased inside her by slow degrees, taking his time and kissing her. She buried her face in his neck, breathing in the scent of him and tasting the hint of salt on his skin. Pleasure built as he thrust deeper.

Wordless, she could only hold on while he coaxed responses from her body that surprised her. Release came fast and hard, her body clenching around his in one lush spasm after another. He went very still, waiting, wringing every bit of delicious sensation from her body as he kissed her breasts, drawing her deep into his mouth.

And then, while she was still breathless, he began to thrust inside her all over again. Slowly at first. But then building momentum. This time, he touched the damp heat between her thighs, close to where their bodies joined, and she flew apart on contact. She writhed with another toe-curling release. Except this time, Carson came with her, his body tensing everywhere, sweat popping out along his shoulders where she held on to him.

Heat broke over her again and again. She heard his hoarse shout, but her heart pounded so loudly in her own ears, the sound only vibrated through her. He was careful afterward not to collapse on her; instead, he fell heavily on his side and turned her with him, holding her so close that her temple rested just above his heart. Her eyelids fluttered shut, and she settled deeper into him, her own heart finally slowing down along with her breathing.

Sleep could have claimed her if not for the slow return of reason. As happy as it made her to think she'd fully reclaimed her life now, moving on from her painful past in every way, Emma recognized that this night would change things between them. Irrevocably.

She tried to quiet those thoughts while Carson pulled

a sheet around them, tucking her close. But too soon, the questions bubbled to the surface. Would he regret what they'd shared? Was he in a hurry to rejoin his family while the McNeills tried to find their blackmailer?

He'd been vague about the details of the note, and she certainly understood why. But the fact that he hadn't shared much with her about all the tumultuous events in his world spoke volumes about her place in his life. Had she acted too rashly? It had seemed so logical an hour ago, and now as her body cooled, she wasn't as sure.

"Emma?" Carson's voice, soft and close to her ear, startled her eyes open. "Everything okay? You were frowning."

He tucked a finger into the chain on her necklace and straightened the pendant. The cool platinum slid smoothly against her skin.

"Yes. I just—" Hesitating, she weighed how much to say about what was on her mind. "I feel a bit guilty keeping you here now that I know all you have going on back home."

"I wanted to bring you here," he assured her, levering up on one elbow, his forehead furrowed. "That was my choice."

"But that was before you knew your sister was going out of town." She didn't mean to stir trouble. She also didn't want to be taken by surprise if Carson decided he wanted to leave.

And maybe a part of her recognized that what she'd shared with Carson gave him far more power to hurt her than Austin ever had.

"I don't understand." Carson tensed as he straightened. "What are you saying?"

She drew the sheet tighter to her chest, knowing it would be easier on her if she was the one who set boundaries. Who made sure her heart was safe. "I'm saying we should consider flying home tonight."

Carson didn't argue.

Not even a blind man could miss the walls Emma put up after they made love. As much as he was tempted to kiss her and entice her to stay, he knew that would simply delay the inevitable. She was having second thoughts, and he knew she'd been through a lot. He'd make a tactical retreat. For now.

That was why, shortly after midnight, Carson found himself back in Cheyenne. He walked up the flagstone path to the main doors of the Creek Spill ranch house, Emma by his side. She had fallen asleep on the short plane ride home. Or pretended to. He honestly wasn't sure. He simply understood Emma needed to retreat. And after the way their night together had rocked him, too, maybe that wasn't such a bad idea. When he'd pursued the attraction full tilt, he had anticipated the off-the-charts sensuality of their joining. But he sure as hell hadn't expected the lingering need to protect Emma. Keep her safe.

That element of his relationship with her—wanting to take care of her—complicated things. Hell, here he was, protecting her from *him*.

Pausing to disarm the security system, Carson opened the door for her. He'd given her one of his T-shirts for the ride home. She wore it with her long skirt, the neck of the shirt sliding off one of her shoulders. He wanted her even more now. Even knowing that she was pulling away. Even when he understood their time together could be limited.

But for tonight, he would let her go.

Tomorrow, he'd figure out his next move.

"I understand if you need to leave," Emma told him as she slipped off her high heels and bent to pick them up. The brief glimpse of her thigh through the slit of that long skirt threatened to shake his restraint. "If you want to be with your family. I feel totally safe here."

She was giving him the green light to leave. Another push for space? Frustration ate at him as he flipped on the elk horn chandelier over the main staircase. He had to remind himself they were both tired.

"It's late. I hadn't planned on leaving." Although he had promised his sister he'd speak to their father as soon as he returned to Cheyenne. "And I would appreciate it if this information about a blackmailer targeting the McNeills remains strictly between us."

"Of course." She halted on the first step, turning to look back at him as he pulled two bottles of water from a drawer in the refrigerator. "I would never share something like that."

He nodded, trusting her word on that. Rejoining her on the stairs, he handed her a bottle of water.

"Thank you." He would head to his parents' home on the Black Creek Ranch first thing in the morning. "Not everyone in my family is aware of what's happening yet." A scandal had the power to affect far more people than just his brothers and half sisters. There were McNeill cousins all over the world.

His phone vibrated in the pocket of his tux jacket, which he was carrying over one arm.

"I'll let you take that," Emma told him as they

reached the top of the stairs. "Thank you for a beautiful evening, Carson."

He could see her retreating and felt the sting of disappointment, though he knew he needed to give her space.

He kissed her cheek and stroked a thumb along her jaw, just enough to hear the gratifying intake of breath. See the way her pupils dilated a fraction. When he backed away, though, she hurried into her room and shut the door.

It was a fitting end to a night when he felt like he'd made one misstep after another with her. Withdrawing his phone, he checked his messages. The text from his dad caught his eye.

Paige in tears. Says she won't rest until Ventura is off McNeill property. Need help calming her down.

Carson didn't think twice.

Tossing his tuxedo jacket on a chair in the hall, he headed back down the stairs and out the door. Re-arming the security system, he jumped in his truck to see what he could do. Because Donovan McNeill never asked for help. If he admitted that he needed it now, with his own wife, something was really wrong.

And it gave Carson an uneasy feeling that his stepmother was upset about Antonio Ventura being in town. Hadn't Emma just mentioned that family tonight over dinner? She said her mother had compared the Venturas to the McNeills.

It was probably just a coincidence.

But he couldn't ignore his family when they needed him now more than ever. Carson planned to look more carefully into the *Winning the West* director to figure out why having him around would upset his stepmother so much.

Even if that meant the next step in Carson's pursuit of his stuntwoman guest would have to wait.

Nine

Alone in her suite, Emma stepped out of the steamy shower and toweled off with one of the Turkish terry cloth bath sheets. She should be exhausted from the long day and the stress leading up to the stunt, all the wondering if she would be able to pull it off.

But her evening with Carson had left her wound up. Exhilarated. She was unable to settle down even though it was well after midnight. Their time together had been surreal, so special it almost felt like it had happened to another person.

But now she wasn't sure how to face the days ahead with him when she knew that what seemed life-changing for her was just a passing pleasure for someone like Carson McNeill. That had been the point of her mother's urgent texts earlier today. A warning to Emma not to fall for a McNeill the way Jane Layton had once fallen for her employer, Emilio Ventura, father of the man now directing *Winning the West*. The affair had destroyed Jane's marriage, probably playing a role in Emma's father's suicide, although Jane had never admitted as much. Hurt stabbed through Emma at the thought of her dad, her memories of him painfully scant.

She combed the tangles from her damp hair, wishing she could sort through her muddled thoughts as easily.

She recognized how she might be following in her mother's unwise footsteps. Because while neither Carson nor Emma was married to other people, there was still the same kind of imbalance between them. Carson moved in a world of privilege and wealth that allowed him to jet around the country at a moment's notice. Emma was a maid's daughter still trying to duck a jailbird ex. What was more, she wasn't sure she'd come to terms with the fact that she'd stayed in a relationship with Austin after he'd hit her the first time. She wanted to think she would have kicked him to the curb on her own without the intervention of people at her gym the day he'd been arrested. But that decision had been taken out of her hands by the courts, so she'd never had the satisfaction of making it herself.

All this time—training harder, becoming a stuntwoman, getting physically stronger—and she still had no idea if she was tougher where it counted. Emotionally.

That fear was what had sent her running from the best night of her life. The best man she'd ever met.

Yet she had his T-shirt to remember what had transpired between them. Slipping it back on now over her naked body still warm from the shower, Emma padded to the bed and slid between the covers. Everything about her room was luxurious, from the high thread count sheets and white goose down duvet to the thick pile rugs and custom furnishings with rustic touches. Yet the thing she liked most about it was wearing Carson's shirt. The soft gray cotton held the clean scent of detergent, but underneath that, just barely, she could catch the scent of him. His aftershave. His soap and skin.

She switched off the lamp on the table beside the bed, but the skylight overhead kept the room from being totally dark. She closed her eyes, knowing she'd dream of Carson. Only to have her phone chime with a text.

My sister Scarlett asked me for your #. She has a question about the Ventura family. Do you mind if I share? I'm at my father's now. My stepmother is not well.

Emma bit her lip, hurting for Carson. He must be worried about his stepmom. She wished she could offer him some comfort. But why did Scarlett want to speak to *her*? Surely Logan King knew more about Antonio Ventura than she did. Although, when Logan had asked Emma about her riding, she had mentioned her early lessons at the Ventura family's stables. Maybe he'd shared that information with Carson's sister.

But Logan King had worked with Antonio on a film abroad. She remembered reading about it in the Hollywood tabloids. Her mother's apartment was always full of them, her conversations dotted with references to film and television personalities—especially the ones who stopped by the Ventura residence while Jane was working.

Emma had always thought it peculiar that her mother

would choose to continue in the employ of a man who'd once been her lover. A man who'd broken her heart. Emma's counselor had suggested maybe it was a way for Jane to remain close to him. To feel like she was a part of his life.

Remembering that made Emma breathe a bit easier about her night with Carson, at least. She'd moved on from Austin—completely. Being with Carson tonight had proven that.

Taking a deep breath, she texted Carson back.

Of course Scarlett can have my number. Is there anything I can do to help with your stepmother? I'm sorry to hear she's not improving.

She waited a moment, wondering how she could help. But he responded quickly.

No, but thank you. Rest up from your big day. Hours on horseback can be tiring when you're not used to it. I'll check in with you in the morning.

He was a thoughtful, good man to think of her comfort when his own family was dealing with so much. It would be easy to fall for him.

Lying back down on the bed, Emma tried not to think about that. About how incredible the night had been. Instead, she deleted all of her mother's messages, refusing to get caught up in them. She scheduled a message to go out at nine o'clock in the morning, to avoid an all-night text fest with her mother, who often had trouble sleeping. Emma wrote a few sentences about how much she loved the job and how beautiful the scenery was in

Wyoming. She ended with a quick line of assurance she'd visit when she returned home.

Done.

She wondered if she'd hear from Scarlett tonight. It gave Emma an uneasy feeling to know that Scarlett had gone to LA to look for a blackmailer and suddenly had questions about the family that had been a part of Emma's life for as long as she could remember. A shadowy part, yes. But she'd spent time in the Ventura home, occasionally helping her mother clean. Emma had taken those long-ago riding lessons at their stables, in fact.

Now, closing her eyes once again, Emma breathed deeply to catch the scent of Carson in his T-shirt. She tucked her nose into the ribbed neckline, rubbing her cheek along the seam, remembering his touch. But the sweet dreams of what they'd shared seemed out of reach with a new fear creeping closer.

What if she never experienced another night like this one? Never felt a touch to rival Carson McNeill's? Because if that was true—and she feared it could be— maybe she couldn't afford to waste the rest of her time in Cheyenne being scared of what he made her feel.

Scarlett was alone with Logan for the first time since they'd touched down in LA.

No doubt she was a little nervous about that, but that was only part of the reason she was texting her brother for the twentieth time to try to get an update on what was going on back home. Yes, she was trying to distract herself from the prospect of being in Logan's Malibu home for the night. But also, how could Carson be so stingy with details?

She sat in a bright turquoise chair in the midcentury modern living room at Logan's place on the beach, the long fireplace beside her taking the chill out of the air from the breeze blowing off the Pacific. The whole living space opened onto an outdoor patio, with what must be stunning views of the water during the daytime. But now, well after midnight, she only had the salty scent of the air and a few boats bobbing off shore to clue her in to the massive ocean crashing on the rocks below.

"Let's go sit outside," Logan urged her for the second time, his fingers grazing her arm lightly as he stood near her chair. He'd been the consummate gentleman all evening, taking her to one of the best restaurants in the city for dinner and then making good on his promise to find the guy who gave her the blackmail note.

Except the mystery man had apparently skipped town, according to Logan's bartender source at the club where it had all gone down. But they'd learned his name was Ron and he used to work as a groom for the Ventura family stables.

Or so he claimed. No one had seen him around the club in the last week, and the bartender had overheard the guy tell someone else at the bar that he was going to Belize. All of which Scarlett had texted to Carson. In return, he let her know he'd already broken the news about her mother's blackmailer to their father.

"I just want to get a few more answers from my brother." Scarlett was already texting as fast as her fingers would allow, her skin still humming pleasantly from Logan's brief touch. Would she be able to resist the attraction? Did she even want to? She hadn't thought it through, and wasn't sure she trusted her decision-making power now that the man was so temptingly close. Clearing her throat, she paused and glanced up at her host for the weekend. "Carson said he told Dad about—"

Breaking off, she remembered she hadn't told Logan the contents of the blackmail note. He'd asked, but hadn't pushed her to reveal details. And since she wasn't sure how much to trust him, she'd been vague.

"It's okay," Logan assured her, his fingers brushing along her shoulder in a gesture meant to comfort. "You don't have to share specifics. But you've put a lot of time into helping your family for the night. You deserve to relax." His green eyes locked on her, making her stomach flip. "Come outside with me for a minute. Unwind before bed."

Her heart skipped a beat.

Logan had worn a gray suit tonight for dinner, but his jacket had disappeared along with his tie. Those two open buttons on his custom-tailored dress shirt didn't show off much of him. And yet...to Scarlett's eyes, he appeared appealingly undone.

She nodded, leaving her phone on the chair so she wouldn't be tempted to keep checking for another of Carson's terse one-liners that told her nothing.

"You may be the first person in my life who has ever implied there's such a thing as 'enough' time to give to my family." Scarlett smoothed nervous fingers down her pink skirt embroidered with exotic birds. The green one-shouldered blouse she wore with it fluttered against her skin as they left the shelter of the living area and stepped out onto the stone patio.

Logan's hand palmed the small of her back lightly to guide her toward the two big seats positioned to look out over the rocks that led to the beach. Landscape lighting illuminated the path.

She dropped into one of the cushioned Adirondack chairs. How had she become the focus of this man's attention when he had his pick of the world's most beautiful women? Scarlett wouldn't even register in her own very attractive family if not for the glittery accessories and flashy clothing choices. Whatever it was he saw in her, he had the most flattering way of conveying his interest with his eyes. How they'd followed her all night.

"I spent my whole childhood scrambling to help my own family stay afloat." He settled into the chair beside hers, resting his arms on the wide wooden armrests. "Only to have things fall apart in a spectacular way." Giving her a sidelong glance, he shook his head. "Not that my criminal relations are anything like the McNeills. But I did learn the need to carve out goals that were mine alone."

She tipped her face to feel the light mist of ocean spray borne on the wind, wondering what it must be like for Logan to live in this dream home now after being on the run and sometimes homeless with his family.

"I'm going to do that. Follow my own goals, I mean." She'd crunched the numbers to prove to her father she'd more than repaid the family for financing her education through the years she'd worked as an assistant to the Black Creek Ranch foreman. "I'm giving my two-week notice at the end of the summer. Then I hope I'll be able to move in with my friend Lucie who already lives here." Lucie had relocated to LA from London last year and worked in casting.

Maybe it was too late for Scarlett to pursue her own dream of acting. But she'd never know if she didn't try.

"Good for you." Logan's hand slid closer to where hers rested on her armrest. "And you are welcome to stay here anytime if things don't work out with your friend. It can be hard to find a place."

Surprised by his offer, she turned to gauge his expression and see if he was serious. "You don't think it would be awkward for you to have an old fling sleeping upstairs when you brought home a hot date?"

"I've been angling hard for you to be my hot date as often as possible." He sat forward in his seat, swiveling toward her. "But perhaps I need to be clearer about what I want." He didn't touch her except where his pinky finger stroked along the top of hers on the armrest.

Just there.

She wasn't sure if it was that simple touch or his words that sent heat licking all over her skin.

"I—" Her voice cracked. She took another breath and reminded herself that this man had vanished from her life without a word. "You have a funny way of showing it."

"So you keep saying. And if you won't accept my apology and my assurance that it was a mistake, I'm going to ask for a do-over." He curled his pinky around hers, holding it there. "I want a chance to make things right with you. I had hoped this weekend would be a start—by helping you find that guy who passed you the note."

She stared into those green eyes for a long moment while one wave after another broke on the shore below, a soothing sound that lulled her to acquiesce. To wish that what she'd felt with him that one night together hadn't been a mistake. The heat in his gaze mirrored everything she was feeling.

"I appreciate that." She knew it was only a matter of time before Carson's PI figured out who was harassing her family, and discovering some clues to the identity of the man who'd delivered the threatening message was going to speed things along. "But I have only myself to blame if I make the same mistake twice."

The muscle in his jaw flexed. He nodded, rising to his feet.

"I understand. In that case, I'll let you get to bed. I know you must be tired." He offered her his hand and she took it, allowing him to help her to her feet.

Regret nipped at her that they hadn't been able to put the past behind them. That she'd clung to evidence of his treachery even though he'd apologized. And explained.

Was she being petty? Overindulging wounded pride?

As she walked with him into the living area, she second-guessed herself.

"Don't forget your phone." Logan leaned over the chair where she'd left it earlier and passed the device to her.

She didn't bother checking it, too worried she might be screwing up the possibility of an incredible relationship with a man who'd done everything he could to make things right between them.

He shut down a few of the lights on a post near the stairs and then hit a button to close the living area doors, locking out the sound of the waves for the night.

Scarlett bit her lip as she followed him up the stairs toward the bedrooms, her chance at salvaging this night fading.

As they reached the landing, Scarlett stepped in front of him. Placed a hand on his warm chest.

"Logan?" Nerves trembled through her. But damn it, she didn't want to lose this chance if she'd been wrong about him.

"Scarlett." There was a weary note in his tone, a wariness in his gaze. "Honey, if you're not ready for more, I think we need to retreat and regroup." Gently, he bracketed her shoulders.

And shuffled her aside.

But that was because he was being gentlemanly, right? She reminded herself she was supposed to be carving out goals of her own, damn it.

And she wanted this. Him.

"Consider the hatchet buried." She stepped in front of him again. Determined. "Also, that the do-over has been granted. And that I'm ready for more."

She felt a piece of her wounded heart heal at the way his nostrils flared and his pupils dilated a fraction, the irises becoming a narrow strip of color around the dark centers.

For a moment, however, he said nothing. He merely stared back at her, breathing hard in the narrow hallway full of bright artwork and tiny spotlights.

Then, before she could restate her case, Logan stepped toward her. His hands skimmed her waist as his lips closed on hers. He lifted her up, bringing her eye level to kiss her thoroughly, his strong arms banding her to him.

Just when she'd gone breathless, her thoughts scattering and disappearing, Logan broke the kiss. He leaned back to take her measure, her body melting into his.

"You're not going to regret it," he assured her, his

voice a hot vibration against her ear as he opened the door to a bedroom. "Not for a second. Not ever."

She ignored the warning voice inside that reminded her that was what she'd hoped the first time. Because if Scarlett ever wanted to start over—to reinvent her life and sense of purpose—she wasn't going to second-guess herself anymore.

Ten

Carson urged his mount forward through a thicket, determined to find Emma after his long night spent at his father's house. Tracking down his houseguest wasn't as simple as joining her for breakfast in the kitchen, however. His housekeeper had told him Emma went to the stables. One of the grooms had shown him the general direction she'd ridden.

But in the end, Carson had needed to text Dax to pinpoint her exact location.

Now, with afternoon approaching and the sun disappearing behind the storm clouds moving in, Carson finally saw her with his own eyes as he broke through the tree line. In the distance, a slim figure in black running shorts and a tank top sprinted up a hillside, arms pumping as her hair bounced in a topknot on her head.

The sight of her there, working with a relentlessness

apparent even from this distance, hammered home to him how driven she was.

Or, perhaps, how deeply wounded.

As much as he wanted to believe that Emma's workouts were a way for her to stay on top of her profession, a part of him wondered if it was more a need to prove her physical strength. Did old fears spur her to be stronger just in case she needed to protect herself again? Catching sight of her bodyguard off to one side of the meadow, Carson waved him off, releasing Dax from his protective duty now that Carson had found her.

A nudge to his horse's flanks set the bay mare in motion again, faster this time. The animal seemed as eager as Carson for the burst of speed after the tedious pace of searching for the past half hour. Yet Carson's need to reach Emma's side was deeper, memories from their night together never far from his mind. He'd wanted to give her space after the way she'd backed off. With their time together so damn brief, however, he found it impossible to stay away today. Especially with a thunderstorm due soon. Did she even realize it was turning darker by the minute?

By the time Carson reached the base of the hillside, Emma was running down it, her long strides fluid and athletic. She must have noticed him, but her focus remained on the path until she slowed down. Then her gaze went right to him, the expression in her brown eyes concerned.

"How is your stepmother?" Emma walked in a slow circle, stretching her legs with an occasional lunge. "Is she showing any sign of improvement?"

Carson swung down from the mare, the need to be

closer to Emma drawing him. He dropped the reins to ground tie the animal.

"Not unless you count the fact that her sedative finally kicked in around seven o'clock this morning." The time with his father and Paige had been agonizing. "I left so my dad could get some sleep while my stepmom was resting. She's got a health aide with her for the day, so I'll be getting updates."

Emma stopped in front of him, her forehead damp from her workout, her breathing still fast. A pang of empathy gripped him hard. No woman should have to run from the kind of demons that haunted her. He had to battle the urge to pull her against him and assure her he'd never let anything happen to her again.

"What about you?" she asked, her brown eyes tracking his. Her hands fluttered close to his chest, as if she wasn't sure about touching him. Then, thankfully, they landed there. "Did you get any sleep?"

A warning rumble of thunder sounded in the distance.

"Enough." He didn't want her to worry, and he had too much on his mind to close his eyes for long. He took her hands in his and lifted them to his mouth, kissing the back of one, then the other. "And it's not me who was supposed to take it easy today," he chided gently. "I can't imagine what your legs feel like after the hours in the saddle the last few days. Especially when you haven't ridden in years. No amount of exercise can really prepare you for that."

A sudden breeze whipped the wisps of hair that had slid free from her topknot.

"I was sore," she admitted. "That was half the reason I thought I'd come out here and run. To loosen up."

He wanted to get her out of the weather before the storm broke, but something about what she'd said caught his attention. He released her hands to stroke back a glossy lock of her chestnut-colored hair. "Half the reason?"

"I was also trying to gain some perspective on what happened between us yesterday. And how I felt about that."

His mare whinnied anxiously as the sky darkened, a far-off crack of lightning flickering in the mountains.

But Carson remained rooted to the spot, hating that he'd given Emma any cause for regret. "Emma, my whole life I've been the reckless one in my family. But with you, I swear I tried my best to be careful. To go slow."

"And you were careful. Absolutely." She fidgeted, freeing the knot in her hair, letting the wavy mass blow in the wind while slipping the pink band around her wrist like a bracelet. "I was the one who rushed things, so that's on me." She peered up at the sky as another clap of thunder sounded. "And it's pretty clear that *I'm* the reckless one, since I didn't even look at the weather before I jogged out here."

Carson followed her gaze. "We won't make it back to the main house before the skies open up. But my brother's place is just over that ridge." He remembered how eager Brock had been to escape the filmmaking for the weekend. Picking up the bay mare's reins, Carson swung up on her back. "You can ride with me."

He held out a hand to her, fat raindrops beginning to fall.

"Are you sure?" She chewed her lip nervously.

"Hurry," he urged, feeling the horse's agitation. He

nudged the stirrup forward with his boot. "Use the stirrup."

Emma stepped up and he shifted forward in the saddle, giving her room behind him so he could keep better control of the mare. By the time Emma was settled, her arms around his waist, the rain had let loose.

The bay needed no urging. At Carson's command, the quarter horse took off, hooves pounding, long legs stretching out into a gallop. Carson leaned forward and Emma did the same, her cheek and chest warm against his back while the downpour turned cold.

The path to Brock's place was well-worn. He'd recently completed his house after years of picking away at it in his free time. It sat right on the Black Creek, the center point between his brothers' ranches, so he had easy access to both without having to commit to either. When Brock had lobbied for this slice of land from their father, Carson never imagined his quiet, almost taciturn younger brother would build something so damn beautiful with his own two hands.

The bay would have headed for the stables if not for Carson tugging her toward the house. He wanted to drop off Emma under the cover of a deep vaulted porch first. Once she was under the shelter of the overhang, he took the bay into the stables, grateful to find a ranch hand at work. The younger man seemed pleased to escape the job of stall mucking for a little while to brush out the bay, allowing Carson to sprint back to where Emma waited. Her wet clothes clung to curves that had him aching to touch her again.

He entered the last code he remembered for the front door. It wasn't armed with a security system, but Brock had used a keyless entry. Thankfully, the lock gave and the handle turned.

"Oh, thank goodness," Emma gasped as they stepped inside, dripping water all over the mat.

"I'll get us some towels." Toeing off his boots and removing his hat, Carson padded across the tile floor through the kitchen to the laundry room. A stack of folded white towels sat in a basket on the dryer.

When he returned to the foyer, Emma had her running sneakers off. Rivulets still streamed down her bare shoulders from her wet hair, her cotton workout clothes shrink-wrapping her body in a way that made him forget all about the chill from the rain.

"Thank goodness," she said again. Her teeth were chattering as she reached for a towel. "I can't believe how cold the rain felt."

"When the weather comes down off the mountains it's like that." He tore his eyes away from her, knowing he needed to back off after what she'd said about rushing into things.

But then a good idea occurred to him as he patted his own towel over his face.

"Come with me." He took her hand, leading her into the living room.

"I'm all wet," she protested. "We're leaving footprints everywhere."

When he reached the doors to the deck, he pointed to the sunken tub tucked under another vaulted porch. Steam escaped the leather cover in every direction. His brother must have the heater on a timer.

Bless him.

"Since we're wet already, we could always warm up

in there." He pointed to the hot tub, but Emma was already darting past him to get outside.

She'd given zero consideration to what she was wearing, not caring if the shorts and tank went in the hot tub since she was drenched already.

And chilled.

So when Carson lifted half of the leather cover from the tub, which emitting a cloud of steam over her, she simply stepped down into the bubbles. She found a molded seat in one corner and dropped into it so the hot water reached her neck.

"This feels amazing." Closing her eyes, she leaned back against the neck pillow as her body thawed.

The tub was recessed under the overhang of the vaulted porch so the rain didn't reach them, but she could see out over the landscaped yard to the wide creek that rushed past the house. River stone lined the bank of the creek and it had been used generously around the house, too. The bottom half of the house was stone—or at least faced with the gray rock—while the upper portion was natural wood. It was both rustic and luxurious, with deep porches to enjoy the incredible Wyoming vistas.

She pulled in a breath, her body relaxing as she warmed up, and glanced over at Carson.

And promptly swallowed her tongue.

He, apparently, had no intention of getting into the tub with his clothes on. His jeans long gone, he stood on the deck in fitted black boxer shorts that hugged his muscular thighs. He hauled his wet T-shirt up and off, flinging it to the planked floor before he stepped down into the tub alongside her.

She didn't blink, unwilling to miss a moment of Carson McNeill. The night before had been so heated and, thanks to her, too rushed. She hadn't really gotten to enjoy seeing him like this—unfiltered and utterly masculine in the light of day.

As he sank into the seat next to her—close to her, so his body grazed hers at her elbow and knee—she felt a wave of hot desire that had nothing to do with the temperature of the tub.

Hadn't she thought to herself last night that she should take advantage of this week? This time with him that was a surreal pleasure she'd never be able to replicate?

"Are—um—we alone?" Her voice was too husky with want to sound as cool and casual as she would have liked.

No doubt he guessed what she was really wondering.

He turned blue eyes on her, an answering desire evident there.

"There's a ranch hand in the stables, but the house is very much empty." His focus dipped to her mouth and hunger for him swelled.

"Whose house is this?" She licked her lips, remembering his kiss and how it felt. How he tasted.

"My brother Brock lives here, but I texted with him this morning and he was still in Bakersfield, California, where he plans to spend the night."

"Does he have a maid?" Emma knew her mother had walked in on people in compromising situations during her years in service to the Ventura family. She wouldn't want to make things awkward for Carson by being careless. "Or domestic staff?"

Just outside the deep overhang of the porch roofline,

the rain pounded harder, torrents of water falling in sheets.

"Brock cares more about his horses than anything else, so he only hires help for them. He doesn't have anyone for the house." Carson angled toward her, his shoulders rising above the water line. "We are absolutely, one hundred percent alone."

Her belly flipped. The possibility of being with him again became real. A breath-stealing proposition.

Steam rose from his skin, framing all that taut muscle in soft focus. She ran a hand over his upper arm to feel his tantalizing strength. He sucked in a breath. A deep thrill coursed through her to know she affected him that way.

"How fortunate," she murmured, tracing a droplet of water with her finger as it slid from his shoulder down his chest.

She thought about licking the next one. Chasing a drop with her tongue.

"Is it?" He studied her, his expression guarded. "Last night, I got the idea you weren't ready to spend more time alone with me."

She smoothed her palm on his skin, flattening it against him. She wanted to press all the rest of herself to him just that same way.

"I've since reconsidered." She ventured forward, needing to close the distance between them, wanting to show him she was thoroughly invested in this. In him. "I'm living in the moment from now on. No more borrowing trouble. No more fearing what tomorrow brings."

When her lips hovered near his, she breathed him in,

anticipating what was to come. She took her time in a way she hadn't last night.

She kissed him, knowing that he was letting her make the first move because of how she'd retreated the day before. And she appreciated that. Respected the kind of man who did things that way.

At first, she was the one who gave the kiss. It was a tentative brush of exploration. A makeup kiss for the way she'd pulled back the day before.

But Carson had another kind of kiss in mind. He lifted a hand to her cheek, tilted her face and angled his jaw. Just like that, the contact went from tentative to provocative.

Sweet to sensual.

Flames streaked through her. It was as if they'd never touched before, as if it was all new. Longing and need swirled between them. Carson shifted closer, one thigh settling between hers, fanning the fire. Making her restless with want.

She wished she wasn't wearing her running shorts. That she could press against him and he could be inside her already.

Now.

But he just kissed her. Exploring her thoroughly, making her feel like she'd never been kissed until now. Until this. The sensation made her all the more desperate to make this moment with him count. To soak in the feel of him, the taste and scent and magic of what they did to one another.

Then he pulled back and she felt dazed. Unfocused.

"Come on." He took her hand, tugging her upward.

She followed blindly, water sluicing off their bodies as they stepped out into the cool, storm-laden air. He didn't lead her toward the main house, however. Instead, he headed to a small wooden shed she hadn't noticed off to one side of the deck. There were no windows on the building, and as Carson pulled open the door, steam wafted out along with dull red light.

A sauna.

She followed him inside, and he closed the door and locked it behind them. Her heartbeat went wild. He stepped toward her, casting a strong, impressive shadow in the dim room. To hell with the possibility of regrets. She needed him. Now.

Before he could take a second step, she flung herself into his arms.

Eleven

It had been less than twenty-four hours since he'd slept with Emma, but it felt like they'd been apart for a lifetime.

He tossed his jeans on a bench before he hauled her closer, lifting her up in his arms to take her mouth with his. Over and over again. The hunger for her hadn't been sated yesterday. If anything, last night had stirred a deeper longing unlike anything he'd ever felt. He speared a hand into her damp hair, losing himself in the slick mating of mouths.

The dry heat of the sauna turned steamy from their bodies and wet clothes. Clothes he needed gone. He peeled her shirt away, breaking the kiss just long enough to tug the clinging sports fabric up and off. It left her breasts bared and impossible to resist, the rosy peaks tightening under his tongue as he tasted each one.

He toed open an insulated box under one bench seat and bent to retrieve fresh towels from the storage bin, tossing them on one wide bench beside the sopping jeans he'd brought with him since there was a condom in one pocket.

Her hands were already busy gliding down his back, smoothing over his hips, reaching beneath his boxers to stroke him. He bit off an oath, teeth grinding at the need for restraint. It was worth it, though, when she glanced up at him with her wide dark eyes full of surprise at what she did to him so damned effortlessly.

He peeled off her shorts and panties and she dragged his boxers down. He fumbled for the jeans' pocket on the bench behind him, but before he'd found it, she was wrapping her calf around his, bringing all that sweet feminine warmth closer to where he wanted her. Needed her.

Dropping to sit on the bench, he found the condom as she straddled him, her legs sliding around his waist in a way that pushed him to the brink. And he wasn't even inside her yet.

Emma took the foil packet from him, tearing it open and rolling the condom into place.

Then, finally, he was thrusting deep inside her.

At last.

His forehead tipped to hers as he guided her hips, steadied her on top of him. The perfection of the moment, of her, slammed home, making him want to hold on to this for as long as he could. When he moved inside her, her moan echoed his, reminding him he wasn't alone in this. She was right there with him, feeling all the pleasure in this union that he did, going through every breathless sensation.

He didn't want to ever let her go.

The thought hit with all the force of a release, but it was hers that came first, sending her body into one lush spasm after another. Seeing her that way, unguarded and undone, made him forget everything else. He could only hold on to her hips and steady himself as she moved. When he followed her a moment later, finding a level of completion he hadn't experienced with anyone else, Carson hugged her tightly. His arms around her neck, her legs around his waist, they clung to each other like there was nothing else in the world. And they stayed like that long afterward.

But as their breathing finally slowed and awareness returned, Carson knew he was playing with fire to keep seeing Emma. To be with her this way and want more.

Closing his eyes, he allowed his head to rest on the wall behind him, thinking it would be easier if he didn't care so much. For years, he'd had easy relationships because they were safe. Neat.

No one got hurt.

His sister Maisie hadn't been all that wrong when she'd told him he only dated people he wouldn't fall for. People he wouldn't marry. Losing his mother as a kid would have been difficult enough, but watching helplessly as she was trampled by a bull had provided enough loss and heartbreak for a lifetime. Carson wasn't against relationships. Just the deep, profound ones that could level maximum damage.

Being the reckless twin had served him well in that regard, keeping people at arm's length.

Yet now, with the most desirable, fascinating woman he'd ever met raining lazy kisses along his shoulder,

Carson recognized he was in danger of getting too close. Caring too deeply.

Worse? Maybe he already did.

An hour later, Emma dressed in her freshly dried clothes in a downstairs bathroom at Brock McNeill's house.

Carson had run their things on a high heat cycle to dry quickly after their time in the sauna. He had been thoughtful, laying out deli meats, cheeses and fresh bread for sandwiches while they waited for the laundry to finish. He'd entertained her with stories about his absent brother, recalling some tales from their bull riding days before Brock had left the sport.

But something about Carson's manner seemed…off.

Not distant, really. She couldn't call him that since he'd been perfectly charming. Yet she sensed a new barrier between them that hadn't been there before. Like he'd been the one to pull away this time, only he did a much better job of disguising it than she had last night.

Or was she looking for trouble where there was none?

"Ready?" Carson asked as she emerged from the bathroom. He was already dressed, his still-damp hat in hand. "I went out to the stables to get a horse saddled for you, too."

He pointed to the huge windows at the front of the house, where she could see his bay mare next to a smaller roan. It had stopped raining outside, but the skies remained gray, the heavy clouds still low in the sky.

"Thank you." She slid her hair band off her wrist to tie her hair back. "Although I have to admit, I didn't mind riding double on our way here."

It had been downright sexy, actually.

She saw a flare of heat in his eyes at the shared memory, but then it was gone again, his expression shifting to an easy smile as he opened the front door for her.

"That makes two of us." He palmed her back, guiding her ahead of him outside so they could mount.

Something was definitely wrong.

Determined to confront him about it, to get it out in the open, she turned toward him.

Only to find Carson several steps behind her, his gaze glued to his phone. He stood frozen in place.

"Carson?" Her thoughts shifted away from her worries, knowing he had a lot on his mind right now. "Is it your stepmom? Is everything okay?"

He looked up at her slowly, his blue gaze not quite focused.

"Paige got a letter from the blackmailer today, demanding five million to be deposited to an off-shore account." He gripped his phone tight, his knuckles white.

Her stomach knotted. She couldn't even imagine what he must be feeling.

"Carson, I'm so sorry." She moved to his side to offer whatever comfort she could, but he was rigid as stone when she touched him.

"I need to be with my family." He shoved his hat on his head and pocketed his phone. "I need to get home."

"I'll go with you." She wanted to be there for him the way he'd helped her this week. She had her own bodyguard and a top-of-the-line security system protecting her from her ex-boyfriend, thanks to Carson.

She wasn't even certain that he'd heard her as he headed for his horse and put a foot in his stirrup, but she understood he must be reeling from the news.

She followed suit, moving toward the roan.

Behind her, Carson cursed.

"I'm sorry. I'm not thinking." He appeared at her side, giving her a boost onto the back of the mount, even though he must know she didn't really require a hand. His deeply engrained manners were automatic, even when he was this upset. "If you ride to my father's house with me, I'll let Dax know where you are so he can see you safely back to the Creek Spill."

"But I'm happy to stay with you. I don't have to work today—"

"Thank you, but that won't be necessary." His blue eyes were steely as he stared up at her. "Dax will make sure you get home."

Could he have made it any more plain he didn't want her comfort? Or even her company? Hurt and knowing this wasn't the time to talk about it, she simply nodded.

She would follow Carson to his father's house and wait for the security guard like he'd asked. But it was obvious the risk she'd taken in letting her guard down with him had been a major miscalculation.

Not only had she been unwise in opening herself up to potential hurt, she had also undermined all the hard work she'd done in the last few years to feel emotionally strong. Independent. Because as she nudged her horse into motion to follow Carson across the Wyoming hills, Emma knew she'd lost a piece of her heart to him today. Based on the way he'd retreated from her, he somehow knew that she was falling for him.

And despite the sizzling passion, the feeling simply wasn't returned.

Twenty minutes later, Emma regretted slowing down Carson on the ride to his parents' home. No doubt he could have raced over the rugged but familiar-to-him Wyoming terrain in half the time if he'd been alone, but he maintained a more reasonable pace for her sake. Especially when they'd had to cross streams overflowing from the recent rain, or when they'd had to pick their way down a rocky bluff because it was faster than going around.

He may have withdrawn from her emotionally, but she couldn't fault him for lack of chivalry, even when it was obvious he was worried for his family. As the simple two-story home on the property of the Black Creek Ranch came into view, she did a double take, seeing a man who looked just like Carson stepping out of a big gray pickup truck.

His twin.

When Carson's brother came toward them, Emma could see subtle differences in the way they carried themselves.

She reined in when Carson did, swinging down to the ground before he could help her.

"Carson." His twin nodded at him, his tone brusque.

There was a stiffness about their greeting that Emma suspected might be there even if this wasn't a devastating day for the family.

"Cody." Carson nodded back, his gesture mirroring his brother's. Even their hats were the same. Carson drew her forward. "Emma, this is my brother Cody. Cody, this is Emma Layton. She's a stunt performer."

"A stunt performer?" Cody held out his hand, his blue eyes kind under the brim of his Stetson. "Nice to meet you, Emma. Looks like my daredevil twin has met his match."

"It's nice to meet you, too," she murmured, unsure

about his comment since she'd never seen that side of Carson. Had it been a subtle dig? She couldn't help but feel defensive of him, no matter that Carson didn't seem to want her around for the family meeting. "And Carson has been helping me to stay safe during the riding stunts. He's been a good influence."

Cody's eyebrows lifted, his gaze darting to his brother. "Is that right?"

But Carson's attention was on the driveway where another vehicle had pulled up. "Here's Maisie." He turned back to his twin. "You know Scarlett is still in LA, Madeline's at the White Horse and can't get away, and Brock is in Bakersfield for the day. So it's just the three of us for this."

"Emma makes four," Cody pointed out.

Carson tensed beside her. Did the idea of having her there with his family upset him that much? Or did his reaction have more to do with whatever undercurrent ran between him and his twin?

"You really think Dad will talk in front of anyone who isn't family?" Carson responded tightly.

"He'd probably be glad to have someone sit with Paige," Cody explained. "I would have brought Jillian, but she's battling some fierce morning sickness."

Emma could see some of the tension seep out of Carson's shoulders. How strange to think she could already read his body language that way.

"I'm sorry she's not feeling well." Carson sounded sincere.

"Thank you. She usually perks up later in the day, but I didn't want her to tire herself out more. See you both inside." Cody touched the brim of his Stetson and gave Emma a nod before striding away and into the modest two-story house.

She understood this family meeting wasn't going to be pleasant and she hadn't meant to make things more awkward. "I can still wait out here for Dax, if you prefer."

"It's not that I'm trying to cut you out," Carson assured her, though his eyes didn't quite meet hers as he glanced over to where his sister was walking toward them. "I just wasn't certain how much my father would say in front of you. He only found out about the blackmail note himself just now."

"Well I'm very happy to sit with your stepmother while the rest of your talk if you would like me to," Emma told him, her eyes shifting toward Carson's sister, dressed in worn red cowboy boots, jeans and a dusty T-shirt with the ranch logo printed on it.

Like the other McNeills, her dark hair and bright blue eyes gave her a distinctive look that marked her as family. But there was a no-nonsense clip to her walk and her gaze was frank.

"Yes. My God, yes. Please sit with my mother." Maisie already had a hand out to shake Emma's. "I'm Maisie and thank you for volunteering for that."

Emma liked her already, appreciating the warm welcome after the awkwardness between Carson and his brother.

"Emma Layton." She squeezed Maisie's hand.

"The stunt rider. I attended some of the race scene filming yesterday, and I thought you were fantastic." Maisie flipped her bangs out of her eyes. "Plus, it was sort of refreshing watching my reckless big brother be scared for someone else's neck for a change. In the past it was always us holding our breath to see if he lived through another day." Maisie winked at Carson and looped her arm through Emma's. "Come in and I'll introduce you to Mom. If you can distract her, that would be great. She's been wound up and confused ever since she woke from her coma and I'm sure the latest news isn't helping."

Emma wasn't sure how to refuse, let alone how to get a word in edgewise with Maisie's nonstop talking. She had a hunch that the other woman was trying to ensure Carson didn't gainsay her, though, so the torrent of words was more to prevent him from interrupting than to silence Emma.

Still, she glanced back at Carson to see if he was frustrated at the way his siblings had coerced him into inviting her inside. But he followed them up the flagstone path, hands shoved in his pocket, his expression inscrutable.

Maybe he didn't want her to come in, but clearly his siblings welcomed the help on a difficult day for the family. And there was something comforting about that, when Carson was pulling away from her as fast as he could.

Because even though her relationship with Carson wasn't going to survive, Emma would never forget the way he'd helped her this week when she'd been at a personal crossroads. His patient teaching had given her the skills needed to keep her job. He'd given her a safe place to be when Austin was released from the state penitentiary.

Best of all, his tenderness and passion had given her a glimpse of what real love should look like. Their time together had proven to her that she'd healed from her past.

So even though what she had with Carson couldn't last, Emma wouldn't trade her time in Cheyenne for anything. And if she could do this small thing to help him in return for all he'd given her, then she would gladly sit with his stepmother all day long.

For all Emma knew, it might be her last chance to be close to Carson McNeill.

Carson put on a fresh pot of coffee in his father's kitchen, listening to his family argue about whether or not to call the police. The kitchen opened onto the living area, so he could still chime in if he chose. But as he filled the glass carafe with filtered water, he wasn't sure where he fell in the debate.

Then again, maybe he was just too damned distracted thinking about Emma. Remembering that hurt look in her eyes when he'd suggested she go home with Dax.

It was a hurt that he'd seen in her eyes even before then, starting when he'd pulled back after making love in the sauna. She'd seen the walls go up. Recognized the withdrawal for what it was, even if she hadn't called him on it. He hadn't ever wanted to cause her pain. But somehow, he was going to do just that.

And now, she was in Paige's bedroom, trying to distract her from the threat of extortion with talk about horses. The weather. The beauty of Wyoming. Carson had wandered past the open door enough times since Emma had gone in there that he knew she was doing a good job of keeping things light.

Keeping Paige from joining the argument in the living room.

That Emma would put his family first touched him,

even as it made him more certain he was all wrong for her. She deserved the kind of man who would put her first, too. Someone who wouldn't put her love at risk.

"Carson," his sister called from the living room, "do you think we should call the police?"

"The letter doesn't explicitly say not to," he observed, thinking out loud more than necessarily giving an answer. He went into the living room and picked up the note, which his father had already slid into a plastic bag to preserve as evidence. "It says, 'Paige's secrets will be revealed in the most public possible way, across all social media channels, three days from now at 6 p.m. Pacific time unless five million dollars is sent to an off-shore account. Routing information will arrive at 3 p.m. that day.'"

"And there was no postmark," his father added, his weathered face as worried as Carson had ever seen.

Well, as worried as he'd seen since those horrific days after his birth mother's injury. For the three days that Kara Calderon McNeill had clung to life after being run down by a bull, Donovan had been a shell of a man, his face a mask of fear.

Then, after her death, Donovan McNeill had become someone different. An intense man, fiercely devoted to the ranch and his family, willing to cut off anyone and everyone who threatened either. But he didn't show emotion. Not even when he'd walked away from his own father for good.

For Carson, seeing his father shaken again brought back unwelcome memories. And hammered home the gravity of the family's situation.

"So the letter was left by someone locally." Cody sat in the recliner, but kept his feet planted on the floor, an elbow on each knee. "I still say it's someone on the set of *Winning the West*. Someone who didn't want to film up here in the first place. That's the only explanation that makes sense for why Scarlett got a note in LA, and now we got a note in Cheyenne."

Maisie sat sideways on the love seat, boots off, feet propped on the cushion next to her. "Right. Plus the first note warned us that we shouldn't let the movie film up here. Maybe the blackmailer didn't want Paige to recognize him."

"We only have three days to figure out what we're going to do," Carson reminded them as he headed back into the kitchen. "And we've had a private investigator working on it for five days already."

"Only to come up with nothing," Cody muttered, scratching a hand through his hair.

"He got sidetracked looking into Logan King's background. So far, the actor seems clean, but since Scarlett is in LA again with him, I thought it wise to have someone make sure she stays safe."

Maisie gave a dismissive snort. "Scarlett will lose it if she finds out you're having her followed, do you know that? Lose. It."

Carson hadn't considered that. But damn it, her safety came first.

Their father folded his arms across his barrel chest. "Scarlett aside, do we really think the cops are going to do any better than a PI with the best possible references?"

The coffee maker chimed on the counter, the machine spewing steam as it burbled. Maisie shifted her feet off the love seat to stand, joining Carson in the kitchen.

"Before we go any further, we need to call Grand-dad," she announced. "This blackmailer isn't just going after Paige. He's going after the McNeills. That involves a lot more people than the ones who live in Cheyenne."

Dad swore. He hadn't spoken to his father in over twenty years. But Carson had hoped that maybe he was ready to put it behind him when Donovan had willingly stepped onto his father's private jet for the flight up to Yellowstone where Paige had been in her hiking accident. Before that, Malcolm McNeill had rented a small hobby ranch in Cheyenne around Christmastime to try to make amends with his son, and he'd kept the house since then in an effort to show he was serious about salvaging their relationship. Carson liked the guy. They all did, actually. Cody was the lone holdout besides Donovan who hadn't paid a visit to Malcolm's place.

But Cody surprised Carson by backing up Maisie. "She's right. This is bigger than us, Dad. If Mom's past has any kind of scandal that could hurt Malcolm's business, or his other grandkids' businesses, we at least owe him a heads-up."

Maisie poured two cups of coffee and brought one of them—black—to their father. "Here, Dad." She set it down on the coffee table in front of his spot on the sofa. "You really don't have any ideas what Mom might be hiding?"

Donovan shrugged. "She came to Cheyenne to start over. I knew that. Figured she had a dad who beat her or something, with the way she's always been skittish."

Carson ground his teeth. How could his father not know after being married to Paige for so long? Carson had only known Emma a short time, and already he wanted to put walls between her and anyone who wanted to hurt her.

Not just this week, he realized. But for as long as she'd let him. The thought stopped him cold.

"What about her family?" Carson pressed, taking Maisie's forgotten coffee over to her and setting it on the coffee table next to her. "The PI says that no one who shares Paige's maiden name of Samara has ever heard of her in that tiny Canadian town where she said her aunt Mary lives. You don't know anyone else from her past?"

Donovan started to shake his head when a voice from the hallway joined the conversation.

"I do." Emma stood at the edge of the room. She held a round locket in her hand, a necklace Carson recognized as Paige's. "I know the woman pictured in here. And her name isn't Mary."

Twelve

Emma couldn't stop shaking.

She watched as the necklace quivered in her grip, wondering what on earth the locket meant. Whatever it was, she couldn't shake the sense that something bad would come of it.

Carson moved to her side, ushering her into his father's living room. "Is Paige okay?" he asked quietly, his strong arms so incredibly welcome. So grounding. If only she could trust in what she felt. "Should one of us go sit with her?"

"She fell asleep a minute ago," Emma told him, realizing Carson's whole family was staring at her, sitting forward on their seats.

Had she been too quick to run out here to share her discovery with them? She'd just been so…stunned.

Her gaze flicked to the man who must be their father, a big cowboy wearing a leather vest and boots, his blue plaid shirt and jeans giving him the stamp of another era. His arms were folded across his chest as he eyed her skeptically.

Carson's twin sat near him while one of their sisters perched on a heavy coffee table, two cups of java close to her as she swiveled around to have a look at Emma.

"She showed you her locket?" Maisie asked while Carson guided Emma to the sofa.

He sank into the cushion next to her, his presence comforting. Strong. Warm. His touch settled her nerves, making her question her haste to share. She'd never liked feeling anxious—a sensation she associated with her mother, who'd spent whole years of her life being worried. With an effort, Emma took a deep breath.

"Not exactly," Emma admitted, dropping the necklace into Carson's open palm. "Paige was holding on to it when I went into her room. I asked her about it, thinking that was a good topic since Maisie said to distract her."

Maisie nodded, so Emma continued, hoping she hadn't spoken out of turn to divulge a family secret, or to reveal something Paige had kept private. But the McNeills had been through so much. They deserved to know what Emma had learned.

"Paige clutched it tighter, like the locket was meaningful. Then she told me a story about her aunt Mary, who had always struggled with addiction but was actually a sweet person. So I talked a little about my mom—" She slanted a glance toward Carson, trying to remember how much she'd disclosed about her mother. "She's good-hearted, though a bit unstable, even if addiction was never one of her demons."

Carson squeezed her shoulder, and she was tempted

to tip her head to rest it briefly on him, as if she could absorb his strength. The conversation with Paige—while brief—had been more draining than she would have anticipated, given that her mission had been to avoid conversational land mines and keep her calm.

But Carson had only gotten involved with her to keep her safe. Not to care for her. Definitely not to love her.

"I don't remember Paige ever saying Aunt Mary was an addict," Carson's twin said. "Dad, did you know that?"

Their father shook his head before he asked, "What else did she say?"

"Not much." Emma tried to remember. "Besides, I was more focused on thinking of topics that weren't related to her past in case that upset her. That's why I brought up my own mother—to maybe redirect her."

"You did well," Carson assured her softly, his palm flat against her back. Rubbing lightly. "Thank you."

She knew she shouldn't take so much comfort from his touch when he had pulled away from her after the sauna. This tenderness he showed her wouldn't last. When her part of the filming was over, Carson wouldn't be clamoring to see her again.

Reluctantly, she straightened, distancing herself ever so slightly.

"Anyway, she fell asleep after that and she dropped the necklace. I picked it up so it didn't get lost in the linens, thinking I'd set it on her dresser, but since the locket was open anyhow, I glanced at the photo inside."

She'd been stunned to recognize the face.

"Who is it?" Carson asked.

"Her name is Barbara Harris. I've seen her photo

plenty of times at the Ventura house when I helped my mother clean." Remembering that Carson's family didn't know anything about her, she explained, "My mom is a maid for Emilio Ventura, Antonio's father."

Maisie turned to her dad. "Antonio is the director of *Winning the West*," she explained. "All the Hollywood tabloids say he's a first-rate tool, but his movies make lots of money. And his father, Emilio, was a director before him. They're sort of Hollywood royalty, but neither of them sounds like a particularly nice guy."

"So who the hell is Barbara Harris to the Ventura family?" Donovan McNeill asked, his voice raised with exasperation. "And why is my wife calling this woman Aunt Mary for the last twenty-some years?"

Emma couldn't answer the latter, but she felt compelled to address the former. "I just know that Barbara acted in a lot of B movies that Emilio Ventura directed. Horror flicks and low-budget stuff. Emilio has a framed poster of a zombie film in his office and Barbara's on it."

"Maybe Barbara is a stage name and her real name is Mary," Carson suggested. "Actors don't always use their real names."

Across the room, Cody nodded. "Or Mary could be Barbara's twin," he said drily.

Emma couldn't deny the possibility, given how much Carson and Cody looked alike. But that didn't feel right. Carson had said that Scarlett wanted to ask Emma about the Venturas. There was a connection between the McNeills and the Venturas, she was certain of it.

Maisie took a sip of her coffee. "Or for all we know, Barbara could have worked as a model before she became an actress, and her face was the photo that came inside the damn locket when Mom bought it."

Her sarcasm suggested they were getting off track with all the conjecturing.

Donovan swore softly before he pounded the heel of his hand against his forehead. Once. Twice. "None of this gets us any closer to the truth. And time is ticking. Do we call the cops for help, or not?"

"First, we ask Granddad," Maisie insisted, getting to her feet.

She strode toward the front door with purpose.

"What are you doing?" Donovan asked. Through the picture window behind him Emma could now see an elegantly dressed older couple slowly make their way up the walk.

The woman had long gray hair piled into a chignon and kept in place with a jeweled comb. She held a closed umbrella in one hand and used it like a cane. Next to her, a silver-haired man in a trench coat clutched her arm tightly, though it was unclear which of them supported the other.

Something about the way they touched said they were very much in love, the tenderness so evident it made Emma's heart ache for all that she wouldn't experience with Carson. She couldn't pretend she didn't long for that kind of love.

"I texted your father to come join us," Maisie explained to Donovan McNeill before opening the door. "So your feud with him ends right now, Dad."

Carson had to hand it to his half sister. She didn't pull punches.

He'd been trying for months to convince his father

to make peace with Malcolm, to no avail. But Maisie went straight for the jugular. She pulled open the front door of their father's house to admit Malcolm and his girlfriend, Rose Hanson, wrapping each of them in a quick hug.

Cody had been the last holdout among Donovan's kids to smooth things over with their grandfather. Yet even he'd caved last week after Malcolm had offered his plane and pilot at a moment's notice when the family needed to fly to Yellowstone.

Carson reached for Emma's hand and squeezed it, telling himself he needed to protect her in case fireworks broke out between his dad and grandfather. More likely, Carson simply craved her touch on a day that had left him reeling.

It had to be tough for her, too. Talking about her mother's issues in front of his family, people she'd only just met, couldn't have been easy. But she'd done it to try to help solve a mystery that he was chasing around and around his head. His father knew that just the name Ventura upset Paige. Yet he'd remained silent about that in front of the family, not relating last night's episode when Paige hadn't wanted to go to sleep until Antonio Ventura was off McNeill land.

Did his father know more than he was admitting about Paige's past?

But right now, the bigger issue was the McNeill showdown in his father's living room. Cody and Carson rose to greet the older couple at the same time. Carson introduced Emma to them both. And then, there was nothing to do but see how Donovan reacted.

Carson held his breath during a moment of awkward silence.

Then, slowly, his father rose from his seat.

Donovan's expression revealed nothing as he approached his father.

Rose pressed tighter to Malcolm's side. It was just a hint of movement, but the gesture was so damned endearing. As if this tiny wisp of an eighty-year-old woman was prepared to protect Malcolm from any rejection by his middle-aged son.

Donovan cleared his throat.

"Thank you for coming, Dad," he said finally, belatedly holding out a hand as if to shake.

Malcolm took an awkward step forward, his arms outstretched. "Always."

The two men hugged, clapping each other on the back. Malcolm's eyes squeezed shut, but Rose didn't bother to hide a few tears, her smile wide as she nodded her approval.

"Now." Malcolm straightened, using the back of the recliner to aid his balance. "Let's put our heads together and figure out how to protect that wife of yours, shall we? No worthless blackmailer is going to rip apart the McNeills as long as I draw breath."

An hour later, after much catching up, more coffee and then a rehashing of details about the blackmailing incidents so far, Carson realized his father was leaning toward brazening the whole thing out, come what may for the family.

Donovan didn't want to negotiate, and he didn't want to bend. He wanted to just see what the blackmailer did next.

Malcolm seemed prepared for the worst, although he was making notes about whom to phone so that all of his grandsons could be prepared. Maisie was already searching for publicity firms that could help control the McNeill side of the story if it came to that. Carson thought he should probably take Emma home. He was about to offer when his phone vibrated.

He checked it since the whole room turned to stare at him. They were all on edge after the blackmail letter arrived.

"It's Scarlett," he informed them, his stomach knotting with a new worry. "I'd better take it."

Make sure she was safe.

"I messaged her about the letter," Maisie called over the screen of her laptop as Carson excused himself from the living room to answer the call.

No doubt his youngest half sister was worried about her mother. She probably wanted to come home as soon as possible.

"Scarlett." He moved deeper into the kitchen, so he could still see his family over the breakfast bar, but wouldn't distract them from their conversation. "Everything okay?"

His gaze met Emma's, her attention suddenly turning his way. She must have heard the concern in his voice even though they were in different rooms. That silent connection between them made him think about Rose Hanson pressing close to Carson's grandfather. A wordless gesture of support.

But Carson hadn't earned that kind of support from Emma. He'd sought to protect her from her stalker ex and now it appeared he'd embroiled her in a crisis of his own. Before Emma, he'd always kept relationships simple, with minimal emotional drama. But now, the whole damn world was upside down.

The thought evaporated as Scarlett drew a breath and let loose on him, her voice vibrating through the phone.

"No, in fact it's not at all *okay*," Scarlett practically shouted at him.

"Honey, what's wrong?" He tensed, prepared to fly to California personally to take apart this actor boyfriend if he'd hurt her. Again.

"What's *wrong*?" his half sister asked, as if he ought to know. She sounded frustrated. Angry, actually, more than hurt. "I'll tell you what's wrong, Carson. You hired a private eye to spy on me. Is that your idea of fun? Keeping tabs on me without telling me?"

Ah, damn.

He felt the pinch of guilt, but only for a second. He'd only been looking out for her, a protective instinct drummed into him at a young age.

"Scarlett, I was worried about Logan. I wasn't trying to spy on you. I just wanted to make sure that the guy wasn't the blackmailer."

Was it so damn wrong he needed to keep her safe?

"And you don't trust my judgement on this? Did you listen to a word I said when I saw you last night at the airfield?" Scarlett was always the sweet sister with her butterfly hairclips and bangs, her glittery shoes and whimsical outlook. But right now, she sounded furious. "Did you hop on Gramp's jet two seconds after we spoke and start texting California investigators?"

Emma started to walk his way, perhaps drawn by the tone of his voice. Before she reached the kitchen, however, she stepped out the front door, lifting her own cell to her ear.

Carson turned his attention back to his sister, feeling torn, wanting to know more about the tense expression on Emma's face. "Scarlett, it wasn't like that. I've been working with an investigator to look into the blackmail. I just asked for extra protection for you while you were in LA, since you were obviously targeted by the blackmailer the last time you were there."

And speaking of extra protection, was Dax outside to look after Emma? They weren't on the Creek Spill property here since his father's home sat on the Black Creek Ranch. Carson had messaged Dax long ago, but the guard might have left since then.

He hated to interrupt Scarlett. But she seemed okay. She only wanted to vent about Logan getting into a scrap with the guy when he'd caught him lurking around his place in Malibu. Then she threatened to move to the West Coast and not speak to Carson again.

"Honey, I'm sorry," he tried to interject gently while he moved toward the front door. "Truly, I am. But things are falling apart here, and I need to check on Emma. I can call you back—"

He realized before he finished the sentence that his volatile half sister had hung up on him. Cursing under his breath, he pocketed the phone and stepped outside. It had started to rain again, the clouds from earlier having lingered all day.

And there was no sign of Emma.

Fear chilled his gut. Just a little at first.

Remembering what her ex had done to her made his fists clench. Clearing his throat, he shouted her name. "Emma?"

He jogged out the driveway to get a better view of the

yard and still didn't see her, so he called again, "Emma, where are you? Emma!"

Only silence answered his call, turning his fear into a solid ball of ice.

Thirteen

Inside Donovan McNeill's small stable, Emma strained to hear the caller on the other end of the bad connection. The storm must have something to do with it. She'd only come in here to take the call because a few fat raindrops hit her on her way out the door. Now, the rain was falling in earnest.

"Hello?" she said again, double-checking caller ID even though she knew she didn't recognize the number.

When she'd picked up, she figured it was a client, or potential client, contacting her about the personal training services she offered. Of course, there was always the hope that it could be a casting agent booking her for another stunt job. Plenty of people did business from their cell phones and didn't list the numbers.

"How long do you think you can hide from me, Emma?"

The threatening male voice on the other end was unmistakably familiar.

Austin.

Emma told herself to hang up. But fear seemed to have invaded her limbs, making them immobile. Robbing her of speech.

Memories of her ex-boyfriend rushed through her, the shock of him punching her. The momentary confusion that came when someone you thought cared about you suddenly turned into an ugly stranger, capable of anything. An old hint of that confusion returned now, making a mockery of everything she'd done to protect herself. To feel strong.

"I know where you are, Emma," the voice crooned in a way that made her stomach heave. "And I'm coming for you."

The fear chilled her as her knees seemed to give out. With a shaking hand, she stabbed the end button on her phone, disconnecting the call. She staggered against the rough stable wall, a board snagging her tank top and scratching her shoulder.

The pain—however small—helped chase away that frozen feeling, the hurt reminding her that she had battled through so much pain and fear these last three years. She was strong. She stepped into knife fights for fun, for crying out loud. That was her job now.

Being fearless. Being tough.

She wouldn't let him hurt her again.

"Emma!"

She became aware of another voice outside the stable, calling to her through the storm. A far more welcome voice.

Carson.

Relief made her dizzy. She dragged in a breath of air scented with clean hay and horses, then cracked open the stable door to call out to Carson. The rain had slowed to a light patter.

"In here!" she shouted, willing her heart rate to return to normal as she ducked back into the stable.

She had to pull herself together to face Carson. She didn't want him to see how the call had rattled her. And while it would be easy to lose herself in his strong arms, and to forget all about being independent for a little while, she couldn't afford to do that. She had calls to make—the police, the parole board, her roommate, a lawyer? She didn't know. She needed a private space to assess her options and figure out her next move.

Swallowing down the wild flux of emotions, Emma busied herself with saddling the roan mare Carson had given her to ride from Brock's house. She needed something to do with her nervous hands and the roan was already whinnying impatiently in her stall. Emma led her out of the stall and toward the tacking area, glad for the activity when she was cracking under the pressure of too many feelings.

"Emma." Carson burst in through the stable door, his shirt wet with scattered raindrops, making the cotton cling. "Are you okay? What are you doing?"

"I'm fine," she assured him, though her voice gave her away with a tremble. "But I need to get back to the house. I—um. I have some business to take care of."

She reached for the saddle, but Carson rushed over to take it from her, settling it on the horse for her.

"Will you wait a second? What business?" He studied her face, his eyes full of concern.

But damn it, the concern wasn't because he loved

her. It was that protective streak, too engrained to ignore. And this wasn't his battle. It was hers. She busied herself with the bridle, positioning the straps as she murmured soothingly to the horse.

Or to herself.

"Emma?" Carson prodded when she didn't answer right away, his hands automatically tightening the girth, helping her with the bit. "What business? I can tell you're upset."

"I am upset," she told him, as calmly as she could when she was scared and hurting inside. But she wasn't her mother and she wouldn't fly into a panic. "My exboyfriend just phoned me, and I need to file a police report."

Carson's hands fell away from the roan. He turned to Emma, his shoulders tense. "My God, Emma. How did he get your number? Does he know where you are?"

He reached for her, but Emma couldn't let herself fall into his arms, even though everything inside her shouted at her to take the comfort he offered. She stood tall, her hand on the reins.

She really needed to leave before she dissolved into a mass of emotions in front of him. She'd already been battling heartbreak and rejection this morning after the way Carson had pulled back from her at his brother's house. It had been all she could do to hold it together in front of the McNeills. But now? Her reserves were gone after that call from Austin. She needed to get away from here, fast. Before she revealed how hard she'd fallen for a man who was more interested in being her protector than her lover.

"I don't know how he got the number," she admitted. "He said he knows where I am, but he didn't taunt me with the information, which makes me think he's bluffing. If he knew where I was, he wouldn't waste time calling me to warn me."

She backed up a step, toeing open the stable doors so she could mount up and make a tactical retreat. She just couldn't face having Carson insist on staying around her out of some protective sense of obligation.

"Emma." Carson stepped in front of her, his big body blocking her path. "You're not thinking straight. What if he's out there, waiting for you?"

She bristled at the move. "He's not. And if he is, that's my business. From now on, I protect myself. Your protective services are no longer required. I will update the police and let them take care of the matter."

The rain had stopped, and a cool breeze was blowing from the north. She needed that fresh air to clear her head. Needed the cold wind to ease the burn in her chest.

"I don't understand." Carson touched her shoulder, his hand a gentle warmth she still craved. "Whatever you're angry with me for, please don't use it as an excuse to put yourself in a dangerous situation."

"Carson, if I wasn't in a dangerous position, would you even be out here talking to me?" How had she gone from a relationship with a man who hit her to a relationship with a man who was only with her to protect her? "Thank you for helping me with my riding, but I'm not longer your responsibility."

"Yes, you are." His blue eyes narrowed. "You're still on my land. You're still at risk, only this time it's a lunatic ex-boyfriend and not a horse that's threatening you."

"So shut down the filming. Send me packing." She couldn't do this with him anymore. Wouldn't put her heart in his hands only to have him go back to being a polite stranger once she was safe again. "That would be kinder to me than making me care about you, only to pull away afterward like we had just a meaningless one-night stand. I'm not that woman, Carson. I won't be."

Putting a toe in the stirrup, she swung her leg over the roan's back and urged the twitchy mare forward.

Fast.

She squeezed the quarter horse's sides gently with her legs, propelling her more.

Carson's shout faded in the distance behind her.

Rain-washed air whooshed past Emma's face as she leaned over the roan's head, the horse's mane fluttering against her cheek. The wind dried her tears.

She'd been wrong about the cool breeze soothing the burn in her chest, though. Nothing was going to take away the suffering in her heart that had Carson's name all over it. She'd been such a fool to move in to his house. Welcome him into her bed.

But oh, hell, she couldn't regret those beautiful moments with him—in Jackson last night and again today in the sauna. She wouldn't trade that for anything.

No matter that it hurt now and always would.

She pulled the reins lightly to the right, seeing a muddy patch ahead. But the mare leaped it easily. Just when her hooves hit the ground again, however, lighting flashed in the sky.

Thunder rumbled at almost the same moment.

All at once, the horse spooked.

The mare dropped her shoulder, spinning to one side.

The movement was too fast for Emma. She couldn't do any of the maneuvers Carson had taught her. She lost her seat too quickly, flying through the air.

Coming down on her back with a sickening thud.

* * *

Carson didn't bother saddling the bay to go after Emma. He sprinted into the equipment shed and fired up his father's ATV. He didn't know where Dax was and didn't take the time to text the security guard. If Emma's maniac ex-boyfriend was out there, Carson didn't have a second to waste.

Roaring out into the woods, he hadn't gone far when the roan Emma had been riding came trotting out of the trees.

Riderless.

Carson's mind filled with a dozen scenarios and none of them were good. His gut sank.

Fear howled through him. His chest felt like it would implode as he squeezed the last bit of speed out of the ATV, pushing the thing as fast as it could go. He flew over bumps, kicking up leaves and branches as he tore through mud, following the trail the horse had left in the muddy path.

Until he spotted Emma lying on the ground, her body contorted at a strange angle.

Horror flooded him, past and present mingling as a memory of his mother's body lying prone in the cattle pen flashed in front of his eyes.

It had been his worst nightmare then, and one he couldn't accept repeating. He must have shut off the ATV, because the next thing he knew, he was running to her side. That was when he became aware of another man on the periphery of the clearing.

"Don't move her," the man shouted. "I'm calling 911."

The ex-boyfriend?

A momentary red haze passed over Carson's vision

as he turned toward the guy. But it was Dax, the security guard. He must have followed her out here, doing the job he'd been assigned. Carson blinked through the confusion, his focus returning to Emma.

"Carson?"

Her voice was whisper soft, but the word was distinct.

His heart lodged in his throat while, behind him, Dax shouted out directions to the emergency dispatch.

"I'm here." Carson kneeled on the damp ground beside her. "You're going to be fine," he assured her, needing it to be true even if her legs were twisted awkwardly beneath her. No wonder Dax didn't want her moved until EMS got here.

Carson tried not to remember the way his mother had clung to life for three interminable days when they'd careened between hope and despair. He shook off the past, needing to be here for Emma now.

Gently, he brushed a strand of brown hair out of her eyes, but it caught in her lashes.

"The thunder…" Emma's eyes opened for a moment, unfocused. "It spooked her."

He pressed his forehead to hers, willing her to be all right. He didn't see any blood outside of some surface scratches, but that didn't rule out internal injuries.

"I know, honey. It's okay. And you're going to be okay, too. Help is coming."

"The roan—" she began, her eyebrows furrowed in question.

"She's fine. She was already trotting home when I came to find you." He wanted to wrap Emma up in his arms, even though it was too late to keep her safe.

He just wanted *her*.

Needed her.

He loved this woman too damn much for anything to happen to her. Love? Why the hell hadn't he figured that out sooner, when he could have said it to her back at his father's stable? Before she rode away and...

Eyes stinging, he closed them against the pain as he kissed her forehead.

"Emma?" He wanted to tell her now. To assure her that he cared, and not just because he wanted to protect her.

But as his gaze returned to hers, her eyes were closed. Her mouth had gone slack. Thankfully, he could feel the reassuring puff of her breath on his cheek.

She'd passed out, but she was still right there with him.

Still alive.

Carson ground his teeth, willing her to stay that way.

Fourteen

Waiting was enough to drive a man insane.

Carson paced the corridor at the hospital in Cheyenne three hours later, hoping the latest doctor who was in with Emma would give the all clear for him to see her. He wasn't a relative of hers, so privacy laws meant he couldn't have immediate access to updates. Which killed him. Especially since EMS had strapped her to a board to move her, a technique that made him fear paralysis.

But about ninety minutes after the ambulance brought Emma into the medical center, her condition was listed as stable.

Not critical.

He kept reminding himself of that when he couldn't be in there with her, holding her hand. Watching over her himself. This wasn't a situation like with his mother. Emma really was going to be okay.

"You want to talk about it?" Cody asked him from a seat by the window in the waiting room, careful to keep his gaze on some point on the horizon outside and not on Carson.

Carson hadn't spoken much to his twin over the last years—they had too many fundamental differences. But Cody had been one of the first on the scene in the woods after Carson had found Emma. Cody had kept him from coming unglued when the EMS team refused to let him in the ambulance.

And yeah, it was Cody who had to know exactly why seeing Emma on the ground today had been the second most terrifying moment of his life. They'd both been there when their mother had been trampled.

"Talking. Isn't that like pouring acid on a wound?" Carson asked, not slowing his pacing as he glared at the door to Emma's room, willing the doctor to come out with a positive report.

The rest of the family had remained behind at Black Creek Ranch after the ambulance drove off with Emma, since the crisis was still unfolding with the blackmailer. Dax had driven to the hospital in his own vehicle, and remained on duty now, outside the emergency room.

Just in case.

But Carson had already called the cops to let them know about Emma's ex. She could make a more detailed complaint when she awoke. For now, Carson wanted the wheels in motion to find the guy and throw his ass back in prison for contacting her—a clear parole violation and a threatening move that had no doubt rocked her concentration in the saddle.

"Right. Maybe it is," Cody acknowledged, rising from his chair to stand in Carson's path. They stood nose-to-nose for a second before Cody grabbed Carson's shoulders. "Would you consider listening then?"

For a second, memories of similar standoffs blended together with the present one. Times Cody had held him back when Carson wanted to brawl with some kid in high school. Times Cody had tried to talk him out of hopping on the back of a bull too soon after an injury.

So many times his twin had been the responsible one, the cautious one.

Funny how knowing Emma gave Carson a window into his brother's frustration. It hurt to see people you care about put their neck on the line.

"Yes," Carson agreed, dropping to sit in one of the cheap waiting room chairs. "But only until I see Emma's door open."

Cody lowered himself into a seat across from him, his eyes taking Carson's measure.

"Okay. Then I'll come right to the point." Cody laced his fingers together, elbows on the arms of his chair. "I know what happened today had to have sucked the soul right out of you."

He didn't have the emotional resources for this. Not now. "I can't do this—"

His brother continued speaking right over him. "But she's *okay*, and it's obvious she cares about you. Don't screw things up by doing something stupid like pushing her away if you care about her, too."

For the first time in a long time, Carson looked his brother in the eye. Really looked at him.

And let out a surprise bark of laughter.

"What?" Cody frowned, leaning back in his seat.

"I was just thinking that having a conversation with you is exactly like wrestling with my conscience," Carson admitted, hating every minute spent in a hospital waiting room. Too many bad memories. "And then I remembered another time when you were doling out life wisdom when we were just little punks and I screamed at you, 'Who died and left you boss?'"

Cody rolled his eyes, but there was the barest hint of a smile on his lips. "Here we go."

"And without missing a beat, you shouted back, 'Mom did.'" Carson couldn't hold back a grin. "I believed that for a little while, you know."

"Probably because I was always so much smarter than you," Cody said, glancing up at an orderly jogging past while pushing a wheelchair down the hall.

"Not smarter. Just much less fun." Carson took a small amount of comfort from the lifelong argument, the way they'd set themselves apart from one another when they were actually—truth be told—far too much alike.

"But are you going to listen to me for once?" Cody pressed, not getting sidetracked by the old disagreement. "Admit that I might know best, and that you shouldn't push away someone you care about just because loving someone is a riskier proposition than anything else you've tackled?"

Carson wasn't ready to admit to his brother that he was already committed. If he could explain to Emma how much he cared—if she believed him—he wasn't giving her up. Emma deserved to be the first person to know that.

Besides, Carson had a question for his twin.

"Is that what happened with Jillian?" he asked. "You decided it was worth the risk even though she—"

He hesitated, knowing the mother of Cody's future child was a breast cancer survivor of two years. She'd been the location scout who had chosen McNeill lands as a good potential spot for filming *Winning the West*, a job she'd taken to see the world. She'd asked Cody to travel with her for a few months before their baby was born, and he was actively planning the trip with her. It was a big compromise for someone so focused on his business.

"—is a cancer survivor?" Cody didn't shy away from it. "Hell yes. She's worth the risk. Because the alternative is not being with her, and that's something I refuse to consider."

Carson understood all too well. He didn't want to spend any more time without Emma, either. His half sister's words floated around his brain just then, and he figured Cody would get a kick out of them.

"Maisie said you only dated women you wanted to marry, and I only dated women that I was sure I wouldn't."

Cody laughed. "Sisters have a way with words."

Carson winced. "Speaking of which, I may have screwed up with Scarlett by hiring additional security for her in LA." His gut knotted as he remembered how upset she'd been. "She was angry I hadn't told her. She threatened to pack up and move down there, and it didn't make matters any better that the call came at the same time Emma stepped out of the house and I was distracted."

"I'll get in touch with her," Cody assured him. "You concentrate on Emma."

Carson was about to thank him when the door to Emma's room opened. A short, balding doctor stepped out, holding a chart in one hand.

"Friends of Emma Layton?" the guy asked, peering over the rims of narrow eyeglasses.

Carson was on his feet. "How is she? Can I see her?"

Cody was behind him, a silent shadow. Welcome support.

"She's doing well, and she asked for you," the doc replied, glancing back down at the chart. "Assuming you're Carson?"

The fresh wave of relief nearly leveled him. It was all good news, and still, he felt like he'd been treading water for days and just got pulled into the rescue boat. Cody clapped him on the shoulder.

"I'm Carson." He tried to focus on the doctor as the guy warned him about concussion symptoms and the need to keep Emma quiet and stress-free. He was glad Cody was there to listen, too, and help him remember everything later.

"No broken bones?" Carson asked, remembering how twisted she'd looked when she fell.

"Nothing is broken. Her arm is scraped up, but her X-rays came back clear." The doctor went on to suggest her stunt work might have helped her to fall in a way that saved her.

Relief rushed through Carson. "So I can see her?"

"Of course." The doctor stepped aside. "I'll get her discharge paperwork started."

Emma could go home. Carson couldn't process anything else as he charged toward the door to her room.

He just hoped like hell that going home meant going with him.

Emma could hear Carson's voice in the hallway.

She was awake now. And conscious.

So surely she couldn't be dreaming his voice. Dreaming of him. He must have come to the hospital to see her. Judging from the tone of his voice, he was anxious to be with her, in fact.

Then again, she had to be dreaming.

Because earlier today, he'd pulled away from her after they'd made love in the sauna. All the intense heat and passion had vanished. He'd given her an easygoing smile, like they were just flirting.

He'd told her she didn't need to come with him to his father's house. That it was unnecessary.

He hadn't wanted to be with her, and she wasn't going to put herself in a situation where her heart would get broken. Not when she'd only just managed to scrape her life back together after the way Austin had messed with her head. Her self-esteem.

"Emma?" Carson's voice was closer now.

Filled with tenderness.

She forced her eyes open, willing herself to face whatever happened next. Because if she'd learned one thing about herself since the day Austin's fist smashed into her face, it was that she wasn't a quitter. And she didn't scare easily.

She'd already called the local police to report Austin, and had received a reassuring message just a few minutes ago that Austin had already been picked up in Los Angeles in an unrelated incident that the sheriff's office wasn't at liberty to disclose. Thank goodness. He'd never been in Cheyenne.

Now Carson sat beside her bed, his chair pulled up as close to the edge as it could be.

"How are you feeling?" he asked, his blue eyes searching her face.

"Better than you might think." She didn't want him to sugarcoat how he treated her in order to keep her safe.

"I appreciate you being here, Carson, but the doctor said I'll be fine." When he didn't respond right away, she tried to make her point more clearly. "You don't need to worry about me anymore. Austin is already back in police custody, and I'm returning to the White Canyon Ranch for the rest of the filming."

The words were her declaration of independence. She needed to show him she could stand on her own.

Still, they left her feeling hollow inside. She wanted more than anything to take shelter in his arms for one more day.

Or for a lifetime.

She closed her eyes for a moment, because just thinking about that made her chest constrict with anguish and she refused to let him see her cry. When she opened her eyes again, Carson's face was a mask of—she didn't know what. But his expression was unlike any other one she'd seen.

"If that's really what you want, Emma, I will do whatever I can to make the move easier for you." His words sounded wooden. As hollow as she felt inside. Then, he leaned closer and his hand grazed her arm, his expression shifting into something more real. More... urgent. "But I'd give anything for a chance to do things over today. To rewind to the sauna, and just stay there like we were."

She definitely couldn't think about that. Not with her head still aching from a fall and all her defenses crumbling. "I don't think either of us are the kind of people who would be content with just a physical relationship."

"That's not what I meant. At all." He lowered his voice. "I just know that everything went to hell when we came out of there. I didn't expect to feel so much so fast and I didn't know what to do with that—"

A nurse breezed into the room, staring at her paperwork, dark ponytail bobbing. "I hear someone's ready to go home."

Talk about timing. Emma sighed inwardly.

The woman, dressed in bright blue scrubs and a friendly smile, moved around the bed on the opposite side from Carson. She directed her attention to him. "I'm just going to pull off the monitors and go over the discharge instructions with Emma. Do you want to bring your car around while I call the orderly? We're going to take her down in a wheelchair because of the concussion."

Carson looked back to her, his eyes troubled. "Emma, is that okay with you?"

She had to return to the ranch one way or the other. And she couldn't deny she wanted to hear whatever he'd been about to say before the nurse walked in.

"Yes." At her nod, he straightened from her bedside.

"I'll see you outside then." He lingered for a moment—or was she imagining that?

She didn't imagine the tender kiss he brushed along her forehead, though, gentle as a whisper.

The nurse's eyebrows rose as Carson strode out the door. The woman—Celeste, according to her name tag—gave Emma a conspiratorial wink.

"Handsome fella you've got there," she observed, making some notes on her papers. "You let him take good care of you, honey, after the day you've had."

Emma knew it would be too easy to just forget about her reservations and do just that. But one way or another, she needed to find out if there were deeper feelings behind Carson's protective streak.

* * *

Night had fallen.

Emma tipped her throbbing head against Carson's truck seat as he drove out of the hospital parking lot. No matter what else happened tonight—if she ended up returning to her accommodations at the White Canyon Ranch—she'd need to pick up her things from Carson's house first.

They drove in silence for a few moments as Carson steered northwest out of town, toward the Creek Spill.

The rain had cleared, leaving the night sky full of stars. A twinkling canopy perfect for wishing.

But Emma knew this was the real world, and just wishing for Carson's affection wasn't going to make it happen.

"Are you warm enough?" Carson had given her the blanket he kept in the jump seat.

"I feel fine, just a little sore," she assured him. "But I'd like to return to what we were talking about before the nurse came in." Even if it hurt, she needed to know what Carson was feeling. "All afternoon, when we were with your family, I was trying not to think about how you'd pulled away from me. How you hadn't even wanted me to join you at your father's house in the first place, but Maisie kind of invited me anyway."

"It wasn't that I didn't want you there, Emma," he told her firmly, glancing her way as he rolled to a stop at a four-way intersection.

She waved off the semantics impatiently. "You wanted to give us space then, Carson. Please don't deny it because it was glaringly obvious. I know what I saw, and I know how you behaved."

"I pulled away after the sauna because I knew I was

in over my head," he told her then, not mincing words. "I felt myself sliding into deeper feelings and that's—not something that I let happen to me."

That hurt so much it left her breathless.

On the one hand, he'd neatly vindicated her argument. She now understood the situation too damned well.

She'd be spending the night at the White Canyon Ranch after all, so she could nurse her broken heart without an audience. Before she could tell him that, he continued to speak, seemingly unaware of the hurt he'd caused.

"My whole life," he said, staring out the windshield at the dark road ahead, "I've avoided meaningful relationships with women. I wasn't even very aware of it until Maisie pointed it out to me this week." He drummed his fingers on the steering wheel, a frustrated pounding. "I'm not proud of being shallow with people. I've just been focused on other things. My career. Healing from all the bull riding mishaps."

She found it difficult to reconcile the image he painted with the man she knew. But she'd had hints of that reputation. She recalled how his family thought of him as the reckless twin while his brother was the responsible one.

"I'm the last person to judge someone based on their prior relationships," she said drily.

Because even if Carson didn't love her, she still found a lot to admire about him. He was a good man. A kind and giving man. He'd spent days helping her improve her riding when he could have just as easily told Zoe that Emma was unfit for the stunt.

"I never gave much thought to what I was doing. I

was just—living. Doing my thing." His voice sounded tight. Tense. "But I know now—after seeing what happened today—I was keeping people at arm's length to avoid the kind of hurt that my mom's death caused."

She hadn't expected that. She glanced at him in the dim light of the dashboard as he turned into the long driveway that led to the Creek Spill Ranch. Carson's face was pale. Serious.

Certain.

"I know you lost your father at a young age, too, in a traumatic way." He turned to look at her now that they were on the quiet access road. "So maybe you can relate when it comes back to hurt in new and surprising ways, even years later when you thought you had it handled."

"You never handle it," she admitted. Understanding.

Her throat burned with empathy for Carson and the boy he'd been. And for the pain her accident must have caused him today. She hadn't really put that together until now.

"Never," Carson agreed. "And when I saw your horse trotting back toward my father's stable without you today, I had about fifty simultaneous realizations, all while I was scared out of my mind for you."

As much as she hated to think about what her actions had put him through, she couldn't deny a small flicker of hope at his words. Because being scared out of your mind wasn't the kind of emotion you had for people unless you cared about them.

"I'm sorry I went out on the horse. I should have never done that when I was so upset." She knew better. "I was just so afraid of falling apart in front of you."

"You don't have anything to apologize for. I hurt you today, and I regret that more than I can ever say.

But seeing you in the woods, and knowing you'd been thrown, brought back a whole other nightmare." He stopped the truck, making her realize they were in front of the main house at the Creek Spill Ranch.

She blinked back tears, regretting what he'd gone through. Wishing she hadn't gone out on horseback. Slipping off her seat belt, she turned toward him in the darkened cab.

She covered his hand with hers, squeezing.

"And it was…bad." He slid off his seat belt, too, and shifted closer. "But I realized that I'd been trying to avoid that kind of hurt my whole life. Yet when it happened, when I was confronted with the worst scenario, I decided that living in a vacuum and having shallow relationships had all been a giant waste. I hadn't avoided hurt. I'd just wasted a whole lot of time with people who didn't matter much to me."

Emma listened carefully, trying to follow what he was saying, knowing that her accident had had a strong impact on him. She could hear it in his voice. See the depth of feeling in his blue eyes.

She clutched the binding of the wool blanket tighter, wishing she figured more into his revelation but knowing she couldn't wish his love into happening.

"I understand," she said finally, her voice hoarse with unspoken emotions.

"Not yet, you don't. Because I haven't told you the most important part. I kept thinking, what if I lost you before I got to tell you how much you mean to me? Before I got a chance to tell you that I'm all-in for this." He gestured back and forth between them. "For *you*. For us being together."

That sounded…so good.

Could she trust those words? Especially on a day when she'd hit her head?

"I don't want to misunderstand." She heard the break in her voice. Knew she was showing all the emotions that she'd tried to lock down earlier today in the stable. But he seemed to be sharing his, so she wasn't going to hide hers. She licked her lips and tried again. "I worry the concussion is making me confused."

Carson took both her hands in his.

"Then I'm going to say this very simply." He leaned closer to her, his eyes locked on hers. "You are the most important person in my whole world, Emma Layton. I'm falling in love with you. Please don't leave me. Not tonight. Not ever."

Hope sparked into full flame, roaring through her with a bright glow. She leaned her forehead against his, the motion dislodging a tear to roll down her cheek.

"I don't want to leave." She edged closer to him, until he slid her carefully onto his lap. "Because, truth be told, I'm falling in love with you, too."

Sitting in his truck, wrapped in his arms, felt like the sweetest homecoming she'd ever had. She tipped her cheek to his shoulder, and he wrapped his arms around her.

"I'm so glad you're okay. And I'm so damn glad you're here with me." He said the words into her hair while he stroked her back.

The fear and tension of the day drained away. Hope and love for this man flowed over her.

"I know it's soon to feel so much—" she began.

"Is it?" Carson edged back to look at her, a smile hitching at his lips. "Maybe it's just that what we have is so much more powerful than what other people have, it's too strong to deny."

She smiled, too, happy from the inside out. Happy because he was.

"Maybe it is," she agreed, looping her arms around his neck.

"My brother told me tonight that you shouldn't push someone away just because love is a risky proposition." Carson stroked her cheek as he gazed into her eyes.

"Wise advice. And since when do we fear risk?"

He laughed. "Never. But let's take future risks together, okay? At least whenever possible?"

"No more being the reckless twin?" she asked.

"No. From now on, I'm only taking calculated risks."

"Such as?"

"Sex without a condom?"

It was her turn to laugh. "You wild man. I'm not sure I can help you with that one. It's going to be difficult enough following doctor's orders to avoid too much excitement while I heal."

Carson's expression turned serious. "No trips to the sauna for a while. I will make sure we follow directions to the letter to get you well. That much, I promise you."

She fell a little more in love with him. It was going to be so easy to fall deeper every day. Even with a concussion. And doctor's orders not to get excited.

"Will you take me home now?" she whispered, brushing kisses along his jaw.

He captured her chin in his hand, his touch tender. "I'm going to love watching over you all night long."

Her heart gave a contented sigh.

He kissed her thoroughly, threading his fingers into her hair, capturing her lips with his. Boldly claiming her, sealing their commitment to make this work. Because a future without him? Well, that wasn't one she wanted to consider.

When he edged back to look at her, she laid her hand on his chest, his heart pounding as fast and hard as hers.

"Remember when you said you wished we could rewind this day?"

"Go back to after the sauna and do it all over? I remember."

"I don't want a do-over since I don't think today turned out so badly after all." She snuggled closer, resting her cheek on his shoulder again, already looking forward to when her head was less fuzzy and she could lose herself in him.

Carson kissed her forehead before reaching behind her to lever open the passenger door. "You're the best thing that ever happened to me, Emma Layton."

She closed her eyes, feeling a wave of tiredness mingling with the happiness.

"Mmm. I second that," she told him as he carried her inside. Across the threshold. Ready for a fresh start. "You're an amazing development in my life, too."

He brought her up the stairs and paused.

"Where would you feel most comfortable?"

She glanced between her door and his. "Would you mind if I sleep in your bed?"

His feet were already heading that way.

"I'm going to do everything in my power to make you choose that every day for the rest of your life." He backed into the dim room and settled her in the middle of his mattress.

She closed her eyes, and for an instant, an image of Paige McNeill's locket flashed through her mind, bringing a wave of fresh anxiety. She needed to call her mother. To ask what she knew about the troubled actress Barbara Harris. Emma would do anything she could to help Carson find answers about his stepmother's mysterious past.

To help them locate a blackmailer.

But for tonight, she only needed to revel in the love of the best man she knew.

"Do you think kissing would be too much excitement for me?" She wanted to wrap herself around him and fall asleep that way.

Reaching for him, she pulled him down next to her.

"Just for a minute. And then you need your rest," he warned, in his most overprotective voice.

Making her smile.

"That's sixty whole seconds, you know. Don't cheat me of a single one." She pressed herself to him, looking forward to every day with Carson McNeill.

He tilted her face to his, his eyes blazing with an emotion no woman could miss.

"Never," he promised.

* * * * *

COMING SOON!

LET'S TALK
Romance

For exclusive extracts, competitions
and special offers, find us online:

f facebook.com/millsandboon

◎ @millsandboonuk

🐦 @millsandboon

Or get in touch on 0844 844 1351*

For all the latest titles coming soon, visit
millsandboon.co.uk/nextmonth